"You're H

The group was silent. L
"Who are you talking to, Victoria?"

There was a sound like someone exhaling. It was loud and filled the room, but only for a moment. An instant later, a man materialized in the dark corner. He appeared quickly, standing just over six feet tall, and wore what looked like a blue wet suit. There were solid blue eyepieces that ran from the bridge of his nose to his ears. He wore a compact blue equipment vest, tight blue gloves and boots, and a holster on his right hip that looked as though it had been vacuformed around the gun.

The man undid a strip of Velcro at his forehead, and lowered a thick faceplate. Sweat glistened on his flushed features.

He grinned. "I believe the lady was talking to me."

STEALTH WAR

Jeff Rovin

J
JOVE BOOKS, NEW YORK

STEALTH WAR

A Jove Book / published by arrangement with
the author

PRINTING HISTORY
Jove edition / January 2000

The Penguin Putnam Inc. World Wide Web site address is
http://www.penguinputnam.com

ISBN: 0-515-12724-8

A JOVE BOOK®
Jove Books are published by The Berkley Publishing Group,
a division of Penguin Putnam Inc.,
375 Hudson Street, New York, New York 10014.
JOVE and the "J" design
are trademarks belonging to Penguin Putnam Inc.

PRINTED IN THE UNITED STATES OF AMERICA

10 9 8 7 6 5 4 3 2 1

One

Dressed in a crisp blue shirt and dark blue trousers, former Central Intelligence Agency DDU operative Peter Murdock—code-named Badger by his current employers—crouched behind the forest green plastic trash can. It was the last of five barrels neatly lined on the garage side of the two-story suburban home. From here, Murdock was able to see the driveway. But he was far enough from the quiet, thickly treed side street so that no one could see him.

Murdock squatted patiently on the balls of his feet. Holding a small black leather utility pouch in one hand, the gray-haired man balanced himself by resting the ridge-side of his free hand against the barrel lid. He didn't want to put his gloves on yet—if someone did see him, they weren't part of the uniform and would be difficult to explain. The side of the hand left no identifiable prints.

Murdock waited, watched, listened, and sniffed. Not the stench coming from the barrels but the stink that hovered around him. The smell of corruption.

Like most of his Huntsmen colleagues, the taut, wiry man believed in what he was doing: cleansing the political gene pool. Disposing of one bad cell so that the body might live. But Murdock also had a philosophical problem with this town, one that had grown from his "day job" for AirTomorrow, an overnight package service. He found it offensive that people like Hoxworth or cabinet members or supreme court justices—even cabinet or supreme court *nominees*—went from being hicks or obscure academics to celebrities. How people who accused those celebrities of sexual harassment also became celebrities. People within and without the Beltway might hate their politics or despise them personally or both. People might not even *know* anything about the person's views or personality or credibility. But Washington loved and respected power and fame, and party hosts always wanted the newsmakers to attend.

Always.

Every day, Murdock delivered dozens of invitations to many celebrities. Senior Senator Hoxworth, Democrat from Mississippi and head of the Armed Services Committee, got at least three a day, though he apparently accepted very, very few. He told the press he preferred to be with his family. Whether it was the truth or a shrewd public relations move or both, the turndowns made Hoxworth seem like a devoted family man while at the same time making him a more desirable celebrity. His political power grew because he limited his social accessibility.

The entire system stunk, from the top on down. And that was where Murdock and his real employers came in.

Murdock had been recruited from the CIA fifteen years before. During the time he worked for the Huntsmen, he'd executed thirteen "perimeter penetrations" like this one, twelve of which had resulted in kills. The one that got away—number eleven, a police captain—did so because he was killed in a car crash on his way home from a card game. Murdock took a lot of ribbing from the other Huntsmen assassins about that one. They called it a tie, not a win. But Murdock didn't mind. Just as long as the sonofabitch didn't get away.

Murdock thought about Cactus, Diablo, Eagle, Fox, Granite, and Hydra. Men who were specialists, like Hickock and Graff. Others who were in reserve or else already in place, prepared to launch their own hits in an undertaking of unprecedented size and scope. Despite the healthy, competitive rivalry between the team members, Murdock wished them Godspeed. In the end, it wasn't power or ego that drove the Huntsmen. It was love of country. Love so intense that each individual was ready to die for the plan if need be. It was an axiom of true assassins that it was easier to kill others if you were prepared to kill yourself, and each of them was more than willing. That concept dated back to the very first assassins, the *hassasin,* members of an eleventh-century Islamic order who believed it was a religious obligation to kill their enemies. And if they themselves died in the process, it was all right because paradise awaited them.

Yet it was more than love of country that drove them all, Murdock thought as he waited. It was pride in the potential of this country. In what it could be—the master of the world, of the stars. *If it weren't for creatures like Senator Hoxworth and President Gordon and Vice President Catlin.*

His eyes and ears remained focused on the road as he waited patiently for seventeen-year-old Denise Hoxworth to come home from school.

Patience, he thought.

Murdock loved the word, the concept. As he'd learned during his twenty years with the CIA, if you had purpose, then patience was one of the three remaining keys to success.

Murdock had spent his entire Agency career in the DDU—the Domestic Disposal Unit. His small group covered up traces of foreign assassinations of American business and political leaders. They made sure that bomb-driven plane crashes into marshes or mountainsides were perceived as pilot error, that hotel or office fires looked like faulty wiring or careless smokers, that shootings or explosions appeared to be the acts of unhappy government employees rather than terrorists. As articulated by DDU chief Gil Catlan, the group mandate was to "keep these blips from fucking up foreign policy." It was the ultimate spin-doctoring, turning international politics and economics into an act of God.

But in covering up assassination for the DDU, Murdock figured out better ways of killing. He learned that it is also an art form. Common murder is typically an act of impulse or passion, conceived in minutes, executed in a matter of seconds, and more often than not regretted. That was why so many murderers never got away. They were impetuous and sloppy. Assassination, like the ones he now caused or helped to hide, was the result of purpose and patience. That was why assassins, from those earliest *hassasin* to the ninjas of ancient Japan to the present, were rarely caught. Real assassins—not patsies like Lee Harvey Oswald or James Earl Ray or Sirhan Sirhan, who were set up, or the amateurs who left trails a dogcatcher could follow or got up close at a political rally because they wanted to martyr themselves. Successful killing, like successful winemaking or lovemaking, could not be hurried. And when done right, the afterglow lasted for days. He was grateful to the Huntsmen for giving him a canvas to practice his art.

Preparation was another key to success. An assassin—a good one—didn't simply grab a rifle, go to a rooftop, and start shooting. They'd get you every time. *Every* time. Murdock had watched the Hoxworth house from his delivery truck. He'd done it five Fridays in a row, ever since the Huntsmen gave him his assignment. Without exception, Denise Hoxworth always came home around 4:30 to get ready for the first of her two weekend dates with Brad. Murdock knew how and when she opened the garage door. He knew how fast she pulled up. He knew that she was usually on the cellular phone and stayed on it until she was inside. He knew how long he'd have to get into the garage before the young woman got out of the car and closed the door. He knew where she went after that, because he'd listened from outside the house. Up to her room and then directly to the bathroom.

Knowing the routine was the third key to an assassin's success.

Murdock continued to peer out from behind his sunglasses at the tree-lined cul-de-sac. He did not wear sunglasses to see better outside but inside. After infiltrating a home or business or car trunk he could not afford to waste time while his eyes adjusted to the relative darkness. He had to be able to move quickly and efficiently.

He heard a car. He glanced down at his watch. It was 4:28.

As always, Denise activated the automatic garage door opener when the Volvo was still halfway down the street. But Murdock didn't move. Not yet. He'd had a good look inside the garage the week before when the door was open. There was nothing he could hide behind, no lawnmower or coiled hose or worktable. He needed the car itself.

He watched as the young woman swung the car into the paved driveway of the suburban Washington home. As soon as she rolled into the garage, he poked his head from behind the trash cans. When he heard the brakes squeak, he crept around the plastic barrels, slid his small pouch under the car, then did a quick, tight pencil roll under the tailpipe—legs straight, arms crossed tightly against his chest. Once he was beneath the rear of the car, he turned, faced the front, and scuttled forward on his belly. What little noise he made was covered by the grinding of the garage door. He stopped just inside the front fender and pulled the pouch toward him. He lay flat just as Denise turned off the ignition.

A clean garage entry like this wasn't always possible. Sometimes, when entering a home or business, he had to wait until the small hours of the night and jimmy a window or door. But then there were also burglar alarms and multiple locks and noise to contend with. "Hitchhiking" in like this. with a car and a distracted teenager, was preferable.

Sound carried well down here on the dirty concrete, and now that the door was closed and the engine was silent, he lay perfectly still. He heard the oil burner come on in the basement. He heard his own rapid heartbeat. And he heard the high school senior chatting on her cellular phone, talking to a girlfriend about how classes had sucked and her physics teacher, Mr. Dundee, was going to fail her, but at least she had her date with Brad to look forward to.

Mr. Dundee isn't going to fail you, Murdock thought with cozy cynicism. *Not after tomorrow.*

He watched as she left the car, switched on the garage light, and punched the disarm code SRDH into the alarm keypad.

Stuart, Remy, Denise Hoxworth, Murdock thought. The initials of the three family members. Forget NPSI and the Huntsmen's "Crash" program. Even a common burglar might've guessed that one, just from flipping through the Hoxworth's mail. People were so complacent. They deserved what happened to them.

When Denise went inside, Murdock wriggled from under the car. He drew a black ski mask and gloves from his pouch, pulled them on, and waited beside the inside door. The gloves were rubber not only because they provided a better grip but because they didn't leave residue of any kind on doors or banisters. Good detectives looked for splinters in wood and for fibers in splinters. The mask hadn't been necessary outside. If he'd been spotted beside the house by a neighbor or by a Hoxworth coming home early, he was just a delivery man. There was a bundle of foreign newspapers on the back stoop, sent by an amnesty group, to prove it. But he was not a delivery man anymore. He wore the mask inside not to conceal his features but to keep hair and dandruff from falling out. If the girl saw him, he would rape her and then strangle her—with her blouse so there wouldn't be bruises to indicate the size of the hand or the strength of the attacker. He carried hair samples in his pouch, which he'd scatter around the corpse to confuse the hell out of the forensics people. There would be nothing stolen and no note left behind condemning the policies of her father. The crime would be characterized as entirely sexual in nature. There would be notoriety for Brad or some other admirer before medical analysis exonerated him. A few more inadequate home security systems would be sold in the area, and the killer would go uncaught because he was a professional. Murdock himself would have to retreat to one of the safe houses the Huntsmen maintain around the country, and the mission would have to be finished another way, another time. And if for some reason he missed an alarm or a police patrol spotted him, he would crunch a capsule of nerve agent in a false tooth and take his life. Without hesitation.

But he didn't want that. Not because raping Denise wouldn't be a pleasure. It would. She was cute, and she was spoiled. He would enjoy forcing her onto her back and looking into her wide, uncomprehending eyes. Eyes that would fill with horror as he took away her sense of security, her teenage strut, and then her life. And killing her father would be much easier after that. The senator wouldn't be able to live with the grief. It would be easy to make it look like he'd put a gun barrel in his mouth. However, Murdock didn't want to spoil his record. He also didn't want to bring a failure back to the Huntsmen.

Murdock put his ear to the cool metal door and listened. Denise was still talking. She went upstairs. When he heard the toilet flush, he opened the door, stepped inside, and shut the door behind him. He hurried toward the back of the house to the stairs that led to the basement.

He knew the layout of the ground floor. In addition to receiving invitations, politicians were sent countless gifts at home—flowers, jewelry, electronics, automobiles, and cash. Gifts that lobbyists didn't want to be logged in at the office. Deliveries like that had enabled Murdock to stand in many hallways many times. When he did, he routinely made notes about the layout of the house, about security systems, and about "wild cards" like dogs, caged birds, and housekeepers. He listened for central air-conditioning in the summer and how often the heat came on in the winter; white noise was an excellent cover. He kept a laptop in his truck and made coded entries after each visit. The assassin never knew when he would be asked to visit someone for the Huntsmen, and he liked to be prepared.

Murdock had been to the Hoxworth household eight times in the past eleven days. In addition to planning his entrance during those visits, he formulated various exit strategies. If something went wrong and he had to leave in a hurry, he could make it out the back door, the front door, the pantry window, or the deck off the master bedroom. From the house to the main road was a four-minute trip at a slow run. Before the police even reached the Hoxworth home, Murdock would be inside the lavatory at the twenty-four-hour service station on Wisconsin Avenue near Walsh Street, donning the change of clothes he'd hidden behind the trash bin earlier in the day.

Denise was still upstairs, and Murdock stopped beside the basement door. He pulled a can of WD-40 from his pouch and sprayed the hinges. That wasn't for now but for later, when he couldn't afford to make any noise. He tried the door; it opened silently. After using a handkerchief to wipe away the excess oil, he went downstairs, noting which steps creaked when he walked on them. Then, selecting a shadowy corner behind the oil burner, Murdock sat with his back against the wall and waited. As far as he'd been able to determine, the only people who ever came down here were the housekeeper, who did the laundry on Monday and Thursday mornings, and the Aqua-Pura man who brought tanks of potassium to keep the water clean. He came on the first of each month, at 1:30 in the afternoon.

Murdock waited. He waited for the senator's wife to return home from the educational toy store she owned. He waited for the senator himself to return home. He waited for the Hoxworths to go through the mail, eat dinner, and watch television before Mrs. Hoxworth went to sleep. He waited for the senator to go to the kitchen before retiring and make his three hero sandwiches for the next day's camping trip. And he waited for Denise to come home from her date with Brad. She arrived shortly before 1:00 A.M., just as she had for the last few weeks. She made a few phone calls to girlfriends; he could hear her talking through the central air-conditioning vent. When she finally went to bed at 1:45, the house was still.

Murdock waited an extra half-hour in case anyone had trouble sleeping and decided to go downstairs for a snack. No one did. Rising, he touched his toes a few times to stretch. Then, sinking at the knees to lower his center of gravity—distributing his weight more evenly and making his step lighter—he went upstairs. He opened the door and listened.

There was no one afoot. Murdock glanced down the hallway toward the back of the house. The kitchen was ten yards away, to the right, just beyond a walk-in pantry. The floor in the kitchen was ceramic tile, not linoleum or hardwood, so it wouldn't creak. He took a deep breath and then exhaled slowly, soundlessly. He was relaxed and ready.

Murdock moved quickly through the darkness, gliding past the framed family photographs and pictures of Senator Hoxworth with other celebrities. Once inside the kitchen, Murdock set his pouch on the table and went to the refrigerator. He opened the door just a crack and slipped his gloved left hand inside to depress the light switch. The TV was on in the neighbor's den, and they had a relatively clear view across the low hedge into the Hoxworth kitchen. Still holding the light button down, Murdock removed the cooler containing the senator's three sandwiches. Then he shut the door and went to the counter. A triangle of yellow light from the fixture beside the back door gave him all the illumination he needed. Most security experts tell people to leave their outside lights on all night. They say it discourages criminals. They're wrong.

Murdock opened the cooler.

The senator and his long-time friend and former army buddy General Robert MacDougall went camping on the first weekend of every other month. It was a tradition that dated back at least five years. That information had come from dear Adrienne, a Huntsman ally of many years. She worked the halls of Congress as a secretary and—"as a lover of democracy," was how she put it. Men still talked much too much under the right circumstances. Senator Hoxworth left at 5:30 in the morning, picked up the general at his

Bethesda home, and drove into Virginia's Blue Ridge Mountains. For the past three months—for as long as the Huntsmen had been watching Senator Hoxworth—the senator had made his own submarine sandwiches for the weekend. He and the general never shared, the general preferring highly seasoned roast beef to lean turkey. The intruder sided with Hoxworth on that. He couldn't afford to eat salty food and then sit behind a furnace for nine hours without water.

Four cans of root beer were stacked on their side. Murdock removed them so they wouldn't fall. Then he retrieved the bottommost hero and undid the cellophane wrapper. Thanks to the generous slathering of mayonnaise and mustard, the bread would be quite soggy by the following night. Hoxworth wouldn't notice the little extra dampness. And the small-town coroner wouldn't notice the substance in Hoxworth's system. He would blame the death on a pre-existing respiratory condition. But MacDougall wouldn't buy that. And not believing it, he would inadvertently set everything else in motion.

Murdock removed the top piece of bread and lay it bottom up on the table. He opened the silent, plastic zipper of his pouch, removed a large vial, and dribbled half the colorless, nearly odorless contents along the inside of the bread. He closed the sandwich and repeated the procedure on the bottom slice. Then he rewrapped the sandwich, put it back on the bottom, replaced the cans of root beer, and returned the cooler to the refrigerator, again taking care to keep the light from coming on. The senator would probably eat that sandwich late in the day, when things were quiet. When his companion was tired. When response time was just a little slower.

When it would take just that much longer to get him medical assistance.

He looked out the kitchen window to make sure that none

of the neighbors was looking in. Then he went to the back door, punched *SRDH* into the alarm keypad, and exited the house. When the senator left for his outing, he'd think that Denise had simply forgot to put the alarm on. Maybe he would leave her a note reminding her not to forget again. Maybe, if she wasn't too distraught, she'd show it to the police and insist that she hadn't forgotten. Maybe they'd even believe her. Maybe they'd figure out that someone had been inside. Not that it would matter. Murdock would be long gone by then, his trail utterly cold.

Once outside, he pulled off his mask and walked slowly to the lamplit street. The cool night air felt good on his sweat-dampened hair. He also enjoyed the silence—that damn oil burner had been noisy—and he enjoyed *moving* again. Patience might be necessary, but it was not pleasant. He strolled along easily to the Wisconsin Avenue service station where he'd left his truck after it developed "engine trouble." Climbing in, he started it up and drove the three-and-one-half miles to the AirTomorrow warehouse just outside of Silver Spring. There, he traded his truck for a car. By 4:10 A.M. on Saturday morning, the veteran Huntsmen assassin was on his way to the mountain safe house in West Virginia.

The campsite would be watched, and the watchers would make sure that the police thought exactly what they wanted them to think.

Two

Brigadier General Robert Charles MacDougall lay in his large sleeping bag. His big hands were behind his head, and his pale blue eyes were on the crescent moon. The threat of a smile was not upon his long, leathery face; it had been one of those weeks.

No, he thought. It had been one of those years.

It was still early in the tourist season, and, except for MacDougall and his long-time friend Senator Stuart Hoxworth, the campgrounds were deserted. The fifty-eight-year-old officer and his five-years-younger companion savored the isolation. It gave them the chance to renew the things they had in common before Hoxworth's political agenda had drawn them into opposite camps.

It also gave MacDougall a chance to take stock of his life. He had spent the last three months feeling useless. Three months during which subordinates briefed him about the top secret N-Gen project because they were required to, not because he had anything to contribute. He wasn't even needed this weekend, just days before the first field tests.

MacDougall sighed. He tried not to think about N-Gen or the path that had led him there. He focused on the penny-whistle rasp of the insects. Wherever he was, nocturnal insects always brought him back to the deep, dark nights of Vietnam. Back then, whether he was on night watch or trying to sleep, MacDougall had been acutely aware of every sound—every insect, every rustling vine, every scurrying animal. "Walk-with-me-Jesus-nights," was how Private Gallant had described them, especially when the sounds stopped. Everyone woke then, alarmed by the quiet. They sat up. If there was a full moon, their olive drab T-shirts gleamed as they cradled their M-16s in sweaty palms, listening for something. You never knew whether the sudden silence was caused by something a member of the platoon had done or by Viet Cong infiltrators. The Cong were fond of using the cover of night to set up tripwires that would welcome early visitors to the jungle latrine. The champagne cork–like blasts and the awful howling of victims were also sounds MacDougall would never forget. The explosions were always low caliber, designed to maim rather than kill. A wounded man prevented the platoon from moving out. His screams—which came from deep in the throat and lasted at least ten minutes, until the morphine kicked in— unnerved his fellow soldiers. It took additional manpower to get him out, much more than a dead man. Women were often used to evac body bags. And a soldier with his feet or arms blown off made a more compelling image for the evening news than a faceless body bag. Back then, the damn Cong knew how to play the U.S. media better than the United States government did.

Yet as frightening as those times were, and as sudden as death could be—MacDougall had feared death's random-

ness and swiftness more than its finality—Vietnam had
turned a farmboy into a soldier, a soldier into a man, and a
man into a patriot. MacDougall had only one regret: that
nothing since his two tours of duty had ever made him feel
so useful, so alive. Especially what he was doing now. Goddamn *that* turn of events.

MacDougall looked over at Hoxworth. The senator was
sitting on top of his sleeping bag, working on a crossword
puzzle. Hoxworth was a fellow Vietnam veteran and one of
his oldest friends.

He's also damned misguided, MacDougall thought. The
general tended to favor the right-wing policies—which was
why, as he once put it on TV, they were called "right."

The irony was, men like Stuart Hoxworth could cut military expenditures and establish all the social programs they
wanted. Combat would never be a political crowd-pleaser,
but it remained the quickest, surest way to make ethnic,
racial, religious, and sexual bias evaporate. If a soldier were
pinned by enemy fire or lying wounded in a ditch, he didn't
care about the color of the hand that pulled him out.

No one understood that anymore. What had started with
the shouts of hippies and peacemongers during Vietnam
continued to this day as critics censured the military for
everything it was never designed to be: economical, chaste,
user-friendly, and politically correct. They were too quick to
condemn the risks, the violence. But Gallant's older brother
had been decapitated in a factory accident. Hoxworth's
sister-in-law had been raped seventy-five miles from here,
in a ballpark restroom in Washington D.C. MacDougall's
own daughter Holly Ann had been killed by a drunk driver
while she and her father were riding bicycles. MacDougall
believed—and believed it strongly—that day-to-day life
was more dangerous than combat because your guard was
down. You didn't know where the combat zones were or

who the enemies were and where they might be hiding. You didn't end each day stronger and harder. Only more compromised and exhausted.

The general sighed again.

Senator Hoxworth dropped his crossword-puzzle book on the grass. He looked over. "Now there's a sound I haven't heard in a while."

MacDougall's eyes shifted to the senator. "What sound is that, Stuart?"

"That sigh you just made. Like a truck shifting gears."

MacDougall scowled. "You're crazy."

"Am I?" Hoxworth grinned. Tucked in a new Georgetown University sweatshirt, the barrel-chested man was resting easily against a boulder. A cool night breeze stirred the senator's thinning gray hair, which was combed sideways on his head. He reached into the cooler beside the lantern. "Did you know that the platoon had a name for your sound in Nam?"

MacDougall pressed his thin lips together. They dug dimples in his cheeks. "No. I didn't realize it was a topic of discussion."

"Hell, it was more than that." Hoxworth pulled a can of root beer from the cooler and popped the top. "We called it the MacDougrowl. We kept a count—Benson, Gallant, Cole, and me. Even Father Penny was in on it."

"Bullshit."

"It's true—I swear on my daughter's life. Whenever we heard it, we knew you wanted to kill someone." He chuckled. "Usually one of our own commanders for holding us back."

"I still say it's bullshit. Nobody ran a covert operation on me. I'd have heard about it."

"Not this one," Hoxworth said. He took a swallow of soda. "It was our own private, five-man co-op. Cole kept the secret records on the back page of his medical journal. Something to do on those long jungle patrols. If we'd let you know about it, you would've stopped."

MacDougall swore again. He looked back at the moon. He made a point not to sigh.

"So talk to me," Hoxworth said. "Who's got you pissed off now?"

"No one."

"Now *that's* bullshit."

MacDougall said nothing. He didn't like to complain. Fight yes. Bitch, no.

"Come on," Hoxworth pressed. "This is one of the only places in America we can bitch off the record."

MacDougall remained silent.

"Is it the promotion?"

"Stuart, drop it," MacDougall said. "We didn't come up here so I could piss and moan."

"I must've missed that part in our charter," Hoxworth said. He took another long gulp, then set the can on a natural ledge in the boulder. He reached back into the cooler, took out one of his sandwiches, and set it on the sleeping bag. "I know. We started coming up here to reconnect. But it's fifteen years later. We're older and crankier now. We need to out-gas, as they say at NASA."

MacDougall looked over. "We? What the hell do you have to complain about?"

"Oh—"

"Oh nothing. You're two elections away from becoming President."

"I have no complaints about my political *coin,*" Hoxworth said. "But life in the public eye—that's rough. It causes things to *get* to me faster than they did back when."

"Like what?"

"Nothing that'll surprise you."

"I want to hear it."

Hoxworth snickered. "I see. I have to talk when you want to hear, but the reverse isn't true."

"That's right," MacDougall replied.

Hoxworth began unwrapping his sandwich. "Okay. I'm annoyed at having to be seen at the right dinners, the right functions, which I refuse to do except when I absolutely have to. I hate having to watch every word I say and knowing that somebody's going to be offended by whatever word I *do* say. I loathe answering nasty questions from pushy twenty-something reporters who have more attitude than brains. Or how about fighting government agencies that were created to benefit taxpayers but are designed to screw them, from Social Security to your colleagues at the Penniesgone?"

MacDougall's gut tightened. He hated Hoxworth's nickname for the Pentagon. He used it so much on CNN and the Sunday talk-show circuit—where the two of them had regularly debated military austerity—that it had probably become reflex.

"But you're not going to turn this around and put *me* on the defensive," Hoxworth went on. He picked up strands of sliced onion that had fallen from under the turkey. He lifted the bread and tucked them back in. "So what's wrong? *Is* it the new post?"

"Yeah, Stuart. It's the new post."

"Why?"

"Why?" MacDougall muttered. He looked down. Three months earlier, he'd been transferred from a downsized INSCOM, the Army Intelligence and Security Command, at Fort Belvoir, Virginia, and put in charge of the Defense Advance Research Projects Agency at the Pentagon. INSCOM had replaced fifty-two people with one uplink to the HAVEN-7 spy satellite the army shared with the air force.

MacDougall had fought hard to keep the team together and lost. Lost and been punished for fighting. Even his ally in the struggle, ultraconservative Speaker of the House Richard Wyler, had cut him loose, let him take the fall. At INSCOM, he had been involved with operatives around the world and interfaced with the CIA and intelligence agencies in forty-two other nations. At DARPA, he was locked in a basement and interfaced with under forty people, many of them civilians, who were housed in even deeper basements. Some of them were so secretive it was scary. Even the Chairman of the Joint Chiefs of Staff wasn't informed about much of the work that went on in his division. It was important work, but also lonely and impersonal.

"It's not like you were put out to pasture," Hoxworth said. "You were named chief elf in Santa's Workshop." He chuckled then leaned toward his friend and lowered his voice. "DARPA invented the Internet. It's a place not many people even *know* about, let alone get to run."

"Stuart, I know that," MacDougall said. "But what I'm doing is caretaking, not command. I'm a soldier. I miss that."

"I'm sure you do," Hoxworth said. "And maybe that'll teach you to keep your big mouth shut."

"I doubt it," MacDougall grumped.

"So do I," Hoxworth said. He squeezed the end of the sandwich so it would fit in his mouth. "But whether you want to admit it or not—whether you *like* it or not—the old ways are dying."

"No, Stuart. They're being killed."

"All right. Fine. But rightly so. Technology is replacing people everywhere."

"It shouldn't be."

"I know," Hoxworth said. "At least once a week the CIA goes to the Congressional Intelligence Oversight Committee, hat in one hand, saber in the other, threats from your pal Lionel Gordon in their teeth—"

"He's not my pal."

"Fine. Your yokemate. Your consort. Your ally."

"Speaker Wyler's a megalomaniacal bully—" Mac-Dougall said.

"Who happens to be in the same cockpit of the same plane flying in the same direction as you," Hoxworth said. "Like it or not, that links you. Which isn't why I brought this up. Once a week, the CIA comes to us and asks for more human intelligence. They warn us that we're relying too much on electronic surveillance and not enough on spies."

"They're right, Stuart. And what bugs me is you *know* they're right—"

"They're *not* right," Hoxworth countered quietly. "They're antiquated. Hell, Robert, I know the value of having a clever national infiltrate a terrorist group. He can read the faces, look into people's eyes, interpret the mood and determination of the members. But I also know what that individual costs. You need to finance him personally, which ain't cheap, along with a support team, a safe house, ghosts to keep him straight, and backups. Then, you've got to have a team in place to hand-hold the whole string of them when someone gets caught. Like that air force officer who was hanged in Evin prison outside Teheran. When was that?"

"September, 1997," MacDougall replied sullenly. The dead man was Siavash Bayani, a colonel who had sought asylum in the United States in 1984. He returned to Iran ten years later. The Iranians never said what they caught him doing, but he was hanged as a CIA spy. "Sometimes it happens," MacDougall went on. "No one ever said national security was cheap *or* easy."

"Agreed," Hoxworth said. "But when one satellite can do

the job of hundreds of spies without sacrificing national security or lives, that makes sense to me."

"It can in many cases, but not all."

"In *most* cases," Hoxworth said. "It can go places even top spies can't." The senator lowered his voice again. "It can reconstruct conversations in an office from the vibrations of the window pane. Spies can't do that. It can store seemingly irrelevant images and sounds for scrutiny at a later date. Spies can't do that either." Hoxworth took a bite of sandwich and spoke as he chewed. "We've got a new series of satellites watching our own country for extremists. Watching the roads. Watching the remote hills where people can't always be. Then there are the technological spinoffs of electronic intelligence, stuff that makes it to the private sector. Like the personal computers and portable video cameras and Teflon from the Apollo moon program. Hell, the Office of National Drug Control Policy is using gamma rays and positron emission to sniff out drugs at our borders. We developed that technology to locate Soviet warheads in hidden silos."

"You won't get any argument from me about spinoffs from ELINT," MacDougall said.

Hoxworth smiled slyly. "I know. That's why I mentioned them. You were the original technobuff."

"But why make it either/or, Stuart? We need both assets. Technology and people."

"Uh-uh." He pointed ahead with his sandwich, toward the dark outline of the distant hills. "You see those?"

MacDougall followed with his eyes. "The mountains?"

"Yeah. Mountains like those used to be a great defense against an enemy. Then the airplane got invented, and mountains didn't matter so much anymore. It's the same today. With smart bombs and the viruses we can slip into enemy command centers—like we did in Desert Storm, which caused more effective damage than all our bombing runs—we don't need as many soldiers as we once did. Or spies. That's sanity. That's progress."

MacDougall shook his head. "It's *part* of progress. We've been through this dozens of times, Stuart. People have initiative, creativity, adrenaline, teamwork, and curiosity. Those are still the cornerstone of the infrastructure. You know damn well that ELINT alone can't watch every terrorist cell, find every new biological weapons cache, hear every despot's plans to invade his neighbor. It wasn't true in Iraq, and it isn't true now."

Hoxworth took another bite of sandwich. "That's what we call 'tolerable risk,'" he said as he chewed and swallowed. "It's an accommodation I'm willing to make because I know damn well the voters won't stand for an increase in the military budget."

"The voters," MacDougall said disgustedly. "Which is my point exactly. You've lost sight of what elected officials are supposed to do."

"Which is?"

"What's *right,* not what's expedient."

"Thus spake the idealist."

"Yeah, I am," MacDougall said. "You make that sound like a bad thing—"

"God no. Only impractical. Governing, my friend, is two percent vision and ninety-eight percent compromise." The senator threw his free hand toward the horizon. "And the mood's getting testy out there. Impatient. People want quality of life. Tax cuts and more police, not soldiers or spies. I just read a Penniesgone report about gangs that are sending members to the military then taking those skills into the street. Militias are expanding and becoming more aggressive. I just received another report, this one from the FBI, saying that some of the militias had aligned themselves with Political Action—"

The senator gagged loudly. MacDougall was still looking at the mountains and looked over. In the dull light of the lantern, he saw his friend staring ahead. Hoxworth's eyes were wide and so was his mouth.

"Stuart—are you okay?" MacDougall asked.

Hoxworth's mouth opened a little wider. "B-burning," he gasped. "Can't breathe—" Hoxworth made a retching sound and dropped his sandwich.

MacDougall threw off his sleeping bag and swung toward Hoxworth. A piece of food must be stuck, MacDougall realized. He glanced at Hoxworth's duffel bag. He considered using the senator's cell phone to call 911 but dismissed the idea. They were too far from the nearest town for help to get there in time. And there wasn't much they could tell him. MacDougall had been trained in first aid, CPR, and triage; he knew the drills designed to dislodge an airway obstruction.

MacDougall slid behind Hoxworth and hoisted him to his knees.

"Try and stay calm," MacDougall said as he wrapped his arms around Hoxworth's waist. He locked his hands against the bottom of his rib cage and pressed a thumb into his abdomen with a quick upper thrust.

Hoxworth wheezed. He was squeezing his own throat.

MacDougall pushed again. The wheezing grew weaker. If there were an obstruction, it was lodged securely.

The senator began to kick and pull at MacDougall's large hands. His panic only made the situation worse, causing his throat to tense.

MacDougall released him and came around front. He grabbed his friend's shoulders and looked into his eyes.

"Stuart, you've got to relax. We'll get you out of this but only if we work together. Do you understand?"

Hoxworth nodded quickly. He calmed slightly. His eyes were tearing, and his cheeks were red.

"Good," MacDougall said.

The officer lay Hoxworth on his back. There was haste but not panic in MacDougall's actions. Years of combat had taught him to keep an even temper in a pressure situation. There was always panic or fear under the surface. But it was dampered, kept out of the way of action.

MacDougall pulled down firmly on Hoxworth's chin. "You're doing fine," he said. "I'm going to try and pry out whatever's in there." Holding his mouth open with one hand, MacDougall took the index finger of his other hand and hooked it past the senator's tongue. He felt on both sides, trying to dislodge whatever food was blocking the airway. MacDougall found nothing. But maybe his probing had caused whatever it was to shift—

He withdrew his finger. As he did, the wheezing stopped altogether. Hoxworth's eyes opened wider, and he wriggled from side to side as he tried to suck down air.

MacDougall tried again. This time, he thrust his index and middle fingers into Hoxworth's mouth and pushed deeper, toward the epiglottis. As he did, he tilted the senator's head back even further to straighten his windpipe. He extended his fingers as far down as they could go. There was still nothing.

The senator's face was beginning to turn blue, and the veins on his neck and forehead were becoming swollen. There were no more "safe" procedures to try nor time to try them. MacDougall bunched the sleeping bag under Hoxworth's shoulders to provide him with some padding. Then he knelt beside the senator and attempted EPM—emergency percussion maneuver. He drove his hands hard into Hoxworth's chest, cupping his hands to avoid shattering his ribs. That was always a danger—the bone could shatter and penetrate the lungs or heart. But at this point MacDougall intended to follow the field adage of *"punch till he pukes"* in an effort to clear the airway. If he couldn't do that, the rest didn't matter.

He slammed down twice, three times, four times. Nothing happened. It didn't make any sense. MacDougall had been with people when they were choking on food; in Vietnam and during Desert Storm he'd seen soldiers suffer cardiac arrest in the heat or come close to asphyxiation from gas poisoning, electrical accidents, and asthmatic attacks. In all of those cases, at least *some* air got through—

No. Not all the time. MacDougall suddenly flashed back to the jungle survival training he'd received before going to Vietnam. It was possible that Hoxworth had suffered a bee sting and was allergic to the venom. A swollen air passage was characteristic of anaphylactic shock.

MacDougall looked down at his friend.

"Listen, Stuart," he said slowly and clearly. "I'm going to help you breathe, but you need to relax your throat."

Hoxworth didn't seem to hear, not anymore. And there wasn't time to try and explain. Pinching Hoxworth's nose closed, MacDougall put their mouths together and blew deeply. He paused to breathe and then blew another breath into Hoxworth's mouth. Then a third.

Not even a whisper came from the senator's throat. MacDougall gave him a fourth and then a fifth round, this time holding the mouth shut and sealing his lips around Hoxworth's nose. All the while Hoxworth squirmed with increasing violence, his face becoming a rich blue along the jowls. Finally, desperate for air, the senator pushed MacDougall away and swung onto his belly. Hoxworth got up on his hands and knees and tried to pull air in or push it out—

MacDougall wasn't sure which. He watched as Hoxworth's chest heaved ineffectively as his mouth pulled into a long oval, his tongue hanging out and saliva dripping from the sides. The senator shook his head violently, lifted his right hand, and scratched roughly along the bottom of his throat.

That left only one thing more to try. Turning from Hoxworth, MacDougall bent over the cooler and fished through the contents for a knife. He had once watched a medic administer a battlefield tracheotomy. If he could find something sharp, he would try one now.

But there wasn't anything he could use. He didn't even have the car keys, which were down the hill in the van.

Suddenly, Hoxworth fell on his right buttock. His body dropped a moment later. He stopped wriggling and lay there, his face turned toward MacDougall, his eyes imploring, his lips trembling. His flesh was dark blue, as though it were bruised.

"No!" MacDougall said and jumped back to his side. He cupped his hands again and hit him hard between the shoulder blades, once every second. "Work it up, Stuart! Cough. *Push!*"

Hoxworth's lips stopped moving. His eyes continued to stare.

"Don't do this!" MacDougall yelled. He pulled him onto his back and moved down to his belly. Perspiration formed on MacDougall's brow as he straddled Hoxworth's upper legs and leaned forward. He placed one hand on top of the other just above the navel and pushed up—hard—ten times rapidly. Nothing happened. He repeated the procedure while trying to think if there were anything at all he could force down Hoxworth's throat to clear his windpipe. But they hadn't brought anything with them except food and clothes. That had been the point: the men came here to talk and walk and relax.

MacDougall leaned forward, snaked his hand under the senator's sweatshirt, and felt for a heartbeat. After a long moment, he slid away from the body and sat back on his heels. The silence of his friend, of the campsite, was the silence of death.

MacDougall reached over and closed his friend's eyes. Overwhelmed with self-reproach and frustrated by his own inadequacy, he went to Hoxworth's duffel bag, found the cellular phone, and called 911. Now that it was too late. Now that there was nothing anyone could do.

MacDougall sat beside the body of his friend and waited. He waited just as he did when combat claimed a fellow soldier or when his daughter was run down on the country road where they'd been biking. He waited for help, but he prayed for understanding. Help usually came too late. As for understanding, that never seemed to come at all. And only time made the emptiness manageable.

MacDougall grew cold as the night air chilled the perspiration on his chest, his face, and his scalp. He sat there and stared at the mountains. He thought about Stuart's passionate beliefs and about the issues they had debated over the years. MacDougall had always felt enriched by the discussions; like combat, the process made him feel alive. He'd expected that as the years went by and their points of view became more polarized the discussions would become more challenging—a battle for intellectual inches. He had been looking forward to it.

Rage welled inside as MacDougall replayed the last few minutes in his mind. There was nothing he would have done differently, nothing he *could* have done differently. The only puzzle was the last thing Stuart had said—that his throat burned. Maybe something had scratched it going down and caused it to swell. Maybe something had come up from his stomach had inflamed it.

Not that it mattered now, Robert Charles MacDougall thought as the siren wailed faintly through the trees and the distant mountaintops blurred from the hint of tears and one miserable emotional memory of Vietnam came back strong—the pain of the family who would soon be told the worst news they could hear.

Three

The ambulance had been dispatched from Warren Memorial Hospital in the small, nearby town of Front Royal. Senator Stuart Hoxworth was pronounced dead by the emergency medical team that attended him. The doctors could find nothing in Hoxworth's throat that might have blocked his airway. The tissue appeared not to be scratched and only moderately swollen. It would take an autopsy to find out what had caused him to choke.

MacDougall had left all the camping gear where it was, intending to go back for it later. Before taking Hoxworth's car and following the ambulance to town, he'd used the senator's cell phone to call Remy Hoxworth. Word of her husband's death would circulate quickly, and MacDougall didn't want the family to learn about it from a reporter, a friend, or a colleague.

Mrs. Hoxworth was asleep when he called. She was silent for a long, long while, then said that she and her daughter would call for a car and meet MacDougall at the

hospital. It was shortly after 1:00 A.M. when they arrived.
Remy was red-eyed, and her daughter Denise was still crying. MacDougall offered to make the arrangements with a
Washington funeral home to collect the body of Stuart Hoxworth. She thanked him, but said she wanted to make all the
arrangements herself.

MacDougall drove Remy and her daughter back to
Chevy Chase. Denise sat in the backseat sobbing fitfully
while Remy sat in silence beside her, her arms around her
daughter's shoulders. It wasn't until they reached Wisconsin
Avenue, just a few blocks from their home, that Remy herself broke down, crying heavily into her open hands.

MacDougall left the women in the care of Stuart's
younger brother, whom Remy had called from the hospital.
Brad Hoxworth was a Washington attorney who had his
brother's slope-shouldered walk and his rich smile. It would
be haunting to see him after today.

MacDougall took a cab home to Bethesda and immediately called his old friend Dr. Moses Cole. Cole worked for
the Armed Forces Institute of Pathology at the Walter Reed
Army Medical Center in Washington. He had been a medic
during MacDougall's first tour of Vietnam. The pathologist
was usually glad to hear from his old commanding officer,
though typically during waking hours, as he pointed out
with a groggy slur. Cole's mood changed dramatically, his
voice falling to a near-whisper, when he learned of Stuart
Hoxworth's death. Cole and Hoxworth had become very
good friends during their time together in Vietnam—the
green, conservative kid from Mississippi and the up-by-his-
bootstraps young black kid from Newark, New Jersey. Cole
took a great deal of credit for the liberalization of the Southern senator, and Hoxworth was proud that he'd never had to
pull a single string to get Cole one of the choicest medical
posts in Washington.

MacDougall told Cole that he wanted to know what killed Stuart Hoxworth. It wasn't that he didn't trust the Warren County Medical Examiner. But MacDougall was a fierce believer in the Brass Rail: if you follow the straight military line from start to finish, from objective to goal line, nothing will go wrong. He wanted one of his own—one of *their* own—to find out what happened. Cole promised he'd deliver the goods.

MacDougall showered, changed, and then drove his own car back to the Blue Ridge foothills. The chattering birds and sharp morning light made the campsite seem like another place as he gathered their sleeping bags, grip, and coolers. The sandwich Hoxworth had been eating was gone, along with those in the open cooler. MacDougall decided they must have been pulled away by animals. He left the hills quickly. He never wanted to see this place again.

It was nearly 9:00 A.M. when MacDougall swung off Bradley Boulevard onto Durbin Road. The bright skies and sunny disposition of his neighbors were at odds with his own gray mood. Mechanically, he returned the waves of the dogwalkers and lawn mowers and joggers who recognized his big, meticulously kept, blue 1976 Cutlass Supreme. Though MacDougall was a fiercely private man, familiarity was the price of community activism. Since moving here in 1988, MacDougall had been a vocal advocate of increased education budgets, harsher punishment for speeders and drunk drivers, and other public issues.

There were over a dozen calls on his answering machine from reporters who had heard the news. All of them wanted comments; all of them said they'd call back. MacDougall recorded a comment for his answering machine: "Senator Stuart Hoxworth was a dear friend whose untimely death has deprived the nation of a devoted and industrious servant, and a loving family man," he said. The press was certainly looking for something about their political differences, but they weren't going to get it. Not today. Not ever.

MacDougall had given Cole his pager number, so he turned off the ringer on the telephone and lay down on the sofa, not expecting to sleep but dozing off anyway. When the beep awoke him, the sunlight on the white wall was late-afternoon amber, and his head was lying on a pillow cool with sweat. He hurried to the kitchen and called the number, Cole's direct line at Walter Reed. As he did, his eyes fell on the photograph of Holly Ann with his late wife. It was Lucy MacDougall's favorite picture of the two of them, taken when their daughter was three. It sat framed on the counter beside the phone, just where his wife had left it. Lucy died three years after Holly Ann. The cause was cancer, which appeared in her colon and spread to her bone and brain in three months. MacDougall believed, unshakably, that she'd brought the illness on herself out of grief over their daughter's death. The power of the mind to convince, deny, or deceive was an awesome thing.

Cole snapped up the phone after the first ring. "General?"

"Yes, Moses—"

"You'd better come down here."

"What's wrong?"

"I've got something for you."

MacDougall hunched over the phone. "What?"

"Something strange. Just come down, okay?"

"All right. I'll be there in a half-hour."

Cole clicked off.

MacDougall hung up; he felt funny. Whatever Cole had found couldn't be half as strange as that call. The brigadier general left quickly.

The Walter Reed Army Medical Center is located five miles north of the White House, on 16th Street NW between Main Drive and Aspen Street. MacDougall made the trip in twenty-two minutes. Six minutes later, a nurse had led him to Dr. Cole's small, extremely cluttered office on the second floor. The short, stocky pathologist was waiting for him. He was dressed in a blood-flecked white lab coat and jeans; a surgical mask hung from his neck, and his round face was dominated by large, soft eyes.

Cole offered MacDougall his hand. "How're you doing, General?"

"All right, considering," MacDougall said. He looked at Cole as he shook the man's hand. "What've you got, Moses?"

Cole walked around him. He shut the door. "I want you to know that there's nothing you could have done to save Stuart."

"Okay," MacDougall said. He added as an afterthought, "Thanks." The news should have made·him feel better. It didn't.

Cole lifted a stack of file folders from an old leather armchair beside the desk. He dropped them on the floor. "Sit," he said as he walked behind his gunmetal desk.

MacDougall remained standing.

"General," Cole went on, "Stuart Hoxworth was poisoned."

It took a moment for the statement to register. "Poisoned how?" MacDougall asked. "Was it accidental?"

Cole sat heavily and shook his head.

MacDougall looked down. He swore quietly. "Who would want to kill Stuart?"

"Politicians make strong enemies, you know that. But the question is not just who. The question is who would want to go to this much *trouble*. Did you keep whatever Stuart was eating?"

"No," MacDougall replied. He started to speak, but his voice cracked. He cleared his throat. "The sandwich wasn't there when I went back. The drink was, but I emptied it and threw out the can. Jesus, that was stupid!"

"It doesn't matter," Cole said. "The toxin wouldn't have been in a beverage. That would have caused too much dilution. A sandwich would have been the perfect medium. Absorption by the bread, containment by the meat or spread. There'll probably be a dead raccoon or two around the campsite."

"What did the killer use?" MacDougall asked. "What kind of poison?"

"Formaldehyde."

"Embalming fluid?"

Cole nodded. "There were very high concentrations in the lining of Stuart's throat. Some formaldehyde is present in everyone's bodily tissue. Most of it comes from internal combustion engines—that's what causes our eyes and throats to burn during smog alerts. Formaldehyde is also used, as you said, as embalming fluid and it's present in deodorant, toothpaste, mouthwash, detergent soap, explosives, insecticide, you-name-it. It's an ideal preservative, and it bonds readily with other compounds. Unhealthy as hell in its natural state, and we're all exposed to it several times a day, every day."

"But not at the levels you found in Stuart."

"Nowhere near. One part-per-million level would be considered a dangerous respiratory irritant. I found seven times that amount in Stuart's throat. However—and this is significant—formaldehyde evaporates quickly, and the residue remains localized. A typical autopsy would have found a slightly elevated level but probably not enough to send up a flag."

"So whoever poisoned Stuart was probably counting on that," MacDougall said.

"Exactly. General, please sit," Cole said. "Do you want anything? Coffee? Water?"

MacDougall shook his head. It was difficult to take this in. He was angry at his own stupidity; he should have taken everything with him the first time instead of going back. He was also angry at having been used—possibly even set up.

"Tell me something. Why did you look for that as a possible cause?" MacDougall asked.

"Because I'm thorough. Isn't that why you asked me to do this?"

"Of course," MacDougall said.

Cole jerked a thumb toward his computer monitor. "I also pulled Stuart's service record. My guess is that so did whoever killed him. The files from Fort Bragg say he suffered from asthma until he was sixteen. Many people outgrow it during their late teens, in the sense that lung capacity increases so the effects are mitigated. But susceptibility to the allergens, which are the underlying cause, never really goes away, and enough of them can trigger a relapse—exposure to a heavy dose of perfume, tobacco smoke, cut grass, pollen, that sort of thing."

"Any of which would be tough for an autopsy to pinpoint," MacDougall suggested.

"Right. Stuart—like all of us—was exposed to those things day after day, and a number of them are present in his lungs in various quantities. Given standard operating procedures, the Warren County Medical Examiner would have found those, added them all up, and attributed Stuart's death to RADS—Reactive Airways Dysfunction Syndrome. Asthma brought on by a combination of allergens. It's uncommon but not unprecedented. Without the elevated formaldehyde levels, that probably would have been my conclusion as well."

"So someone killed Stuart," MacDougall said, "but they wanted it to seem like an accident. Why, Moses?"

"I don't know. Maybe he was involved with something that none of us knew about."

MacDougall made a face. "Not possible. Stuart and I told each other everything."

"No mistresses? Jealous husband?"

MacDougall shook his head.

"Then maybe there was a political rival, someone who just didn't like what he stood for." Cole pressed his lip together. "God, I hate when something like this happens."

"Assassination diminishes everyone," MacDougall said bitterly, "even the ones who it's supposed to benefit. It's the failure of ideas, of civilization."

Cole was looking away.

MacDougall's eyes narrowed. "Moses?"

"Yeah?"

"What is it?"

"I wasn't referring to assassination," Cole said. "I was talking about having to make a choice."

"A choice? I don't follow."

"General, the Warren County Sheriff's Office is going to want answers. And you know where they'll look if I turn in my report."

MacDougall's eyes narrowed slowly. "What do you mean 'if'?"

"You don't get it, do you? The investigators are going to be looking for motive and access—"

"And I had both. I get that," MacDougall said. "So?"

"So you were out in the hills alone with Stuart, and you were publicly committed to opposing viewpoints on military austerity. The police are going to put you under a microscope, and the press is going to report that fact."

"*So?* I didn't do it."

"I believe you. But you're going to get roasted, General. From top to bottom, inside and out. You think INSCOM was a hard ride? An investigation like this will finish your career."

"I won't miss it. Not where I am now."

"Then what about Remy and Denise?" Cole asked.

"Suspecting me?"

"No. Also being suspects."

"Oh, come *on*," MacDougall said.

"I just told you, I've been through this shit before. Everyone who was physically close to Stuart Hoxworth during the past twenty-four hours is going to be a suspect—"

"Except the person who actually killed him!"

"You're probably right," Cole said. "Every aspect of this thing was well planned. The trail is already cold. Nothing is gained by putting you on trial."

"By burying the truth?"

"Yes," Cole said. "The truth is a hopeless cause. We've fought those battles before, General."

MacDougall looked at the face of his old friend, at a man who had a chestful of medals commemorating his heroism. A man who had saved dozens of wounded soldiers in Vietnam by treating them under fire or pulling them to safety.

"I won't do it," MacDougall said. "I won't even *think* about a cover-up."

"It's your call," Cole said. "All I'm saying is you should take an objective look at this."

"I have. And I have a lot more faith in the system than you do," MacDougall said.

"So did I before I saw how many cases get mucked up, from the smallest small-town sheriff's office to the most elite division of the FBI. You know how many that is, General? In one out of every three criminal cases in the United States, evidence is mishandled or lost, or there are legal or procedural screwups, miscommunication, wrongful arrests, or pressure from special interests. Of the two out of three cases where there aren't mistakes, sixty percent of them go unsolved. Of the forty percent that *do* get cracked, nearly half of those are the result of perpetrator error. The person returns to the scene of the crime, does the same thing somewhere else, brags to a friend who reports him, brilliant things like that. So before we even get out of the gate, General, the odds are very, very good that this killer, a professional, is not going to be apprehended. And if that happens, the price *you* pay will be a lifetime of people wondering whether you were involved. End of promotions. End of career. Not to mention what this'll do to the Hoxworths."

MacDougall stood there in disbelief. It wasn't the state of law enforcement that shocked him. It was Cole. MacDougall stepped closer to the desk. He looked at his friend.

"Moses, you have altered other files?"

Cole regarded his former commanding officer.

"Talk to me, Moses. Have you?"

"A few," Cole said, his voice a whisper. "I've changed . . . a few."

"Why?"

"To help people."

"What people?"

"Friends, colleagues," Cole said. "People like you. People who didn't do anything criminal but would've been hurt by appearances. A married man whose fingerprints were found inside a hooker's thigh when her body was pulled from a car wreck. A female officer—a war hero—who died with heroin in her system. Her husband wanted to protect her memory for the sake of their children. In those cases and others like them, absolutely nothing would have been gained by bringing these people down."

"Nothing except the truth," MacDougall said.

"Oh, *balls*," Cole snapped. "Goddammit, General, you're talking about facts, not truth."

"You think there's a difference?"

"Yes, sir. A big one. Facts are details. They're a snapshot. They don't mean anything. Truth is a collective view of something. The *fact* is, you didn't kill Stuart Hoxworth. The *truth* is, if we let this report go out as-is people will always wonder about it."

"Not if we find the person or persons who killed him."

"You're right," Cole said. "You are absolutely right. But whoever did this wasn't only good, they're way ahead of you. Probably covered all their tracks."

"They're better than if you bury the file."

"You're right about that too," Cole said disgustedly. "But the fact *and* the truth of the matter is, your chances at best are damn-near nil."

"Maybe. But if we find the killer, we may prevent other tragedies. Isn't that worth fighting for?"

"I guess that would depend," Cole said.

"On what?"

"On whether you still have the stomach for lost causes."

"Freedom isn't a lost cause. Neither is justice."

The men were silent for a long moment. Finally, Cole said, "If you want me to release the file, I will. It's your call."

"I do want it released," MacDougall said without hesitation. "I want you to put it into the system exactly as it is."

Cole opened the file to the last page. He signed it and then took the medical examiner's seal from his desk. He slipped in the signature page and pressed down on the embosser.

"Fine. It's done," Cole said. He shut the folder.

MacDougall turned to go.

"General?"

MacDougall looked back.

"I just want to say—good luck."

"Thanks," MacDougall said.

Cole stood and offered his hand across the desk. Mac-Dougall returned and shook it. Cole held on to it.

"Also," Cole said, "I want you to know that what you think about me matters. It always has. It's just that this is a tough neighborhood. Everyone who comes in that door wants something. Either they want me to hide something I've found or find something that wasn't there. I tell most of them where to go. But where I *can* help, I do. If I stood only on blind principle I'd end up—"

"Working in a basement somewhere," MacDougall said. "I know how payback works."

"But as of right now I can still look at this fat ol' face in the mirror," Cole said. "The day I can't do that is the day I turn in my suit."

MacDougall smiled sadly as Cole released his hand. "Thanks again," MacDougall said. He turned and left, closing the door behind him.

MacDougall sat in his car for several minutes thinking about what he should do next. He would have to talk to the Warren County investigators. They'd want him to go back to the campsite with them and talk them through what had happened. They'd certainly want to search for traces of the sandwich—or the dead raccoons. MacDougall had no problem with that except, as Cole had suggested, it probably wouldn't bring them any closer to finding the killer.

But Stuart Hoxworth and Moses Cole were also very much on his mind. There was a time when neither man would yield an inch of soil to anyone they thought was dishonorable or an idea they believed was wrong. Regardless of the pressure, regardless of public opinion, regardless of the odds.

People change, MacDougall told himself. Stuart had. Maybe Moses, like Stuart, regarded MacDougall as a stubborn and ineffective relic.

Maybe they were right.

But Stuart had been wrong about one thing: people still mattered. Moses was also wrong: truth was something real, an absolute, not somebody's take on things. And people and truth were both worth protecting.

MacDougall started the car. Instead of heading home, he turned onto 16th Street. He drove south to the Potomac, the setting sun glorious on his right, and made his way through early evening traffic to the sprawling, 583-acre complex of the Pentagon.

Four

Seventy years ago, when he was eight, Bernard Schiller helped his German-born father, Thomas, and his American mother, Eva, build this small cabin.

His parents had picked a spot where the hunting and fishing were good, where the water in the river was sweet and cold, where there was wood for the fireplace, and where the air was crisp. It was also very secluded. The ledge was accessible only by one very steep path, and no one could approach without being seen. Once seen, trespassers were ordered to leave. Those who didn't were shot at. Thomas Schiller had come to America in 1917 after deserting from the German army. He arrived with nothing and had always protected what was his.

What dreams father had had, Bernard thought.

Thomas was a frowning and intense man, qualities that lived on in his son. A *Vorhandwerker* in the German army, a master technical artisan, he'd hoped to use those skills to become an architect here in America. But that changed on a warm Sunday morning in the summer of 1929.

It happened on the day they were leaving church and a gardener—who had always been prone to too much to drink and too little sense—had called Bernard's mother a sweet-cake. After dropping the boy and his mother at home, Bernard's father went back to advise the admirer that he'd been much too familiar. Thomas asked for an apology that could be carried back to the lady. When the man refused, and further suggested that Bernard looked remarkably like the local blacksmith, Thomas killed him with an axe that had been leaning against a tree. There was only one witness, his father's good friend Jackson—"Uncle" Jackson to Bernard. Jackson encouraged Thomas to take the axe and flee. They did, following the Cacapon River from Lost City to this haven.

Bernard looked around the dark cabin. His eyes rested on a window box with the irises and peonies his mother had planted and nurtured so very long ago. They had built a cabin and everything in it from strong West Virginia oak. Not a log or a chair or a plant had ever needed to be replaced. Bernard's father taught him survival skills, and his mother taught him how to read and write and do math. It was a time and place and opportunity to be both child and man at the same time.

By virtue of the second Homestead Act, the ledge on which the cabin had been built became theirs legally three years after they settled here. So did the winding lakeshore behind the cabin, where Bernard—with financial support from Boyd Robinson—had subsequently constructed other cabins. Cabins with deep, sound-proofed basements. Places where Huntsmen could relax. Plot. Train. Communicate. Hide.

Some of the Huntsmen were there now, monitoring on-line communications, collecting intel, and lending support to the men and women in the field. In those cabins and on the lake they brought the future nearer. Yet here, in this cabin, Bernard—known only as "Axe" to his people—kept the past alive. The anger.

The hate.

Like his mother's flowering plants, that too was a perennial. It was nearly forty years since the betrayal that had set him and the Huntsmen on this course, but the hate was as strong as ever. Hate that had once been hope until it got twisted and distorted. The same way his father's hopes had been corrupted by a drunken bastard of a gardener—

The elder Schillers died of pneumonia in the brutal winter of 1940. Bernard buried them on the slope in back of the log cabin. Uncle Jackson and Boyd Robinson Sr. had been the only other people there. Their graves overlooked wide, mountain-bordered Lake Miasalaro, which Eva Schiller had loved and memorialized in many of the charcoal drawings she made. At her request, Bernard had tied the drawings in a bundle and buried them with her.

After their deaths, Bernard enlisted in the army. He knew the military would be needing soldiers, and, as a matter of pride and patriotism, he wanted to be among the first to volunteer. The army found a use for the things his father had taught him. Bernard had joined to serve his nation. Because of his fluency in German, he was assigned to the fledgling Office of Strategic Services in August of 1942. There, he worked directly with its legendary director, World War I hero William Joseph "Wild Bill" Donovan. The OSS sent him on numerous missions to the Axis heartland where he quickly learned the arts of spying and assassination. Since German fifth columnists working in the United States were collecting data on American soldiers of German heritage, the OSS had taken the precaution of having Bernard Schiller "die" on a mission with the Green underground in Thebes shortly after joining Donovan's group. The young man found it both comforting and liberating to be buried beside his parents. He chose Axe as his code name, after the weapon his father had used to defend the family honor.

Following the war, the OSS was divided up and absorbed by the State and War Departments. Bernard was put behind a desk, hating it and the people who had put him there. He wanted to go after Stalin and his repressive regime. Instead, he resigned and went to live in his cabin for several months, to figure out what he wanted to do with his life. Then, in 1946, President Truman established the Central Intelligence Group. A year later the National Security Act renamed the CIG the Central Intelligence Agency. And Bernard—reborn as Bernard Hill—was asked back. He had never made a secret of his opposition to Communism, and he was sent to Eastern Europe. There, working as a housepainter, he personally recruited dozens of agents to work behind the Iron Curtain. Then as now, in peace as in war, there was no greater asset than having loyal people on-site where power is wielded and decisions are made.

Things changed for Bernard when he returned to Washington in 1958. He became instrumental in planning the disastrous *Bahia de Cochinos* operation—the Bay of Pigs invasion of April, 1961. He had helped to oversee the training of the 1,500 Cuban exiles in Guatemala and personally saw them off when they left to overthrow the oppressive Communist regime of Fidel Castro. But President John F. Kennedy refused to back the invaders with air and sea support, and they were routed. In December 1962, Bernard was part of the team that was allowed to buy back over one thousand of the captured rebels for $53 million in food and medicine. He had never felt as much shame as he did then. Shame and hate. That, compounded by the humiliating

Cuban missile crisis two months before, set in motion everything that happened next.

The white-haired man rose from behind the massive desk, which sat catty-corner from the door and across from the room's only window. He looked down at the side of the desk as he walked around it. At night, when he was a child, he used to sit on the floor and watch as his father carved the tableaux in the legs and sides of the desk. He would listen as his father told him stories about the men. The orange light of the fireplace made the figures seem to move—historical individuals like Daniel Boone and the "Swamp Fox" Francis Marion, fictional characters like Pecos Bill and Johnny Appleseed. As dark and intimidating as that big desk was, there had never been a storybook as expressive or alive.

Bernard put his hands on the small of his back and arched his shoulders back. He used to sit with his legs bent at the knees, his feet pointing back. Had he really been that flexible once?

His dark brown eyes rose to the sun-faded desktop. Four things were there. One was a framed, browning photograph of his parents. Beside it was a portable computer. Beside that was a TAC-SAT secure phone. Unlike the bulky TAC-SAT systems used by military communications specialists in the field—which relied on backpack batteries and an attached antenna—Bernard's device worked off a two-way satellite uplink. It was linked remotely to a dish the size of a campaign button and hooked to the side of the window box. The phone itself was slightly larger than a cellular unit with a scrambler the size of a microcassette attached to the earpiece. The scrambler generated an electrical field six inches beyond the phone. Eavesdroppers beyond that range would only hear static.

The fourth item on the desk was a loaded P7. Three years before, he and his associates had purchased over one hundred Heckler and Koch pistols from members of the Greek gendarmerie, the Khorofylaki. Bernard had made some very good friends in Greece during the war. Those men, and their sons, had remained loyal to him. Most people stayed loyal to Bernard. They did so either from devotion, fear, or greed. Those who chose to have no further dealings with him were careful enough to remain silent about his activities, even on their deathbeds. As his group had demonstrated on a number of occasions, they did not hesitate to punish the widow or daughter for the confessions of the father.

Bernard had only used a gun once out here. That was seven years before, when a hiker stopped by, who turned out not only to be a hiker but a reporter. She had encountered a man fishing at the lake—a man who, she could swear, looked exactly like someone who was wanted for murder by the FBI. She asked if she could use Bernard's phone to call the Bureau.

The woman was right. The man was Ben Benson, a Huntsman who had killed the head of a liberal senator's dirty tricks operation and hadn't gotten away clean. Benson was ordered to rape and then shoot the reporter, after which Axe had Benson turn the weapon on himself. Even if his assassins weren't ready to die when the moment came, most had mothers and sisters, and they knew what Axe would do to them.

Bernard glanced at the clock on the computer. Thinking of the reporter and the telephone reminded him that it had been almost four hours since the Janitor had called—the man who was responsible for cleaning up after a mission. This job had been a simple one. To collect the sandwiches and sandwich portions Senator Hoxworth had not lived to enjoy, then make it look as though they'd been dragged away by animals. The Janitor had been watching Hoxworth and MacDougall from a ridge above the campsite. As soon as MacDougall and the ambulance left, he went down to gather the evidence. A right and left raccoon claw created the impression that a scavenger had come by, while a whisk broom enabled the Janitor to cover his tracks. The death would probably be attributed to natural causes. Even if the medical examiner found the formaldehyde, Murdock would have left no trail, no clues. Besides, there'd be a patsy—the army officer who had been with Senator Hoxworth. That was the way it had been for the past thirty-six years. The Huntsmen never took the credit or blame for anything.

Thirty-six years. That's how long it had been since the day he met up here with his colleagues and with Uncle Jackson. That day was still vivid, still immediate. Especially Uncle Jackson's contagious passion for what they were about to do. For over forty years before that, his uncle's Huntsmen had used threats, financial pressure, or nonlethal violence to nudge the government into responsible courses of action. Then, on the day Bernard joined the group, they reached the harrowing but exhilarating decision to use more than a push or a shove to cause change.

The day they decided to use murder.

They had to. That wobbly boy in the White House had left them no choice. He'd betrayed the trusting Cuban patriots and given Communism a foothold off our shores.

Could the aftermath of what the Huntsmen had done have been more effective? Yes, Bernard had to admit. Vietnam had ended as a crushing disappointment. And there had been personal losses—poor guilt-stricken Timothy taking his own life that dark day in Texas. But the Huntsmen had learned from their failures as well as their successes. And they were on the verge of putting all of that learning, the years of planting and nurturing, into a single, spectacular strike.

Bernard looked to his right, above the fireplace. The axe that his father had used to build this place—and murder the "lout," as Uncle Jackson had called him—hung above it. To this day, that weapon remained the most simple thing of beauty Bernard had ever encountered.

He looked at his watch. It was time to go to the computer cabin and see what had come through on the Crash system. Crash was used to monitor on-line communications between other members of the Congressional Armed Services Committee. Crash was designed by National Privacy Systems, Incorporated, the same company that had been hired to design and install safeguards for the electronic communications systems in Congress. A fellow Huntsman was the founder of NPSI. Crash was the only program capable of breaking through the Secure Hypertext Transport Protocol system, which had been installed to protect congressional transmissions. Microcavity resonators, each 0.1 micrometer wide—the size of a dust particle—had been installed under every key of each keyboard. When the fingertips of the typists blocked the light, the altered wavelength affected a chain of photons. These sent a piggyback pulse into the phone line; there, the encryption code signal broke away and went directly to the Huntsmen mailbox. Bernard would check to see whether anyone connected the death of Senator Hoxworth with his extreme stand on military budget cuts. If they didn't, he would see to it that a word whispered in a public place or discreet, anonymous e-mail messages made the connection for them.

Bernard looked away from the axe and headed toward the cabin door.

The honor of the United States of America meant no less to him than his mother's honor had meant to his father. That honor was in grave jeopardy due to weak government and fools like the ridiculous French Prime Minister Lionel Jospin. Jospin had spit on the Iran-Libya Sanctions Act passed by Congress years before. The congressional act condemned those countries that did more than $40 million worth of business with nations that sponsored terrorism. Applauding a $2 billion dollar oil deal with Iran in 1997, Jospin boasted, "Nobody accepts that the United States can pass a law on a global scale. American laws apply in the United States. They do not apply in France."

No, Bernard thought. *But it was permissible for American boys to bleed on French beaches, to retake the country after the French military caved in to the Nazis during World War II.*

Fortunately, steps were being taken to remedy the weakness of the United States government and to prove M. Jospin and others like him wrong. Three of them, in fact—one of which had already been successfully completed. The operation code-named 415 wouldn't just restore American honor and credibility around the world. It would make sure that American laws *did* apply in France—and everywhere else. It would position the United States to become what it should always have been. Not a country that other nations mocked or challenged.

A blast . . . a video . . . and the United States would become a nation they feared.

Five

There are many astonishing things about the Pentagon, though three things in particular stand out.

First, there's the size of the building. That's obvious even from the outside. The main structure of five concentric buildings covers twenty-nine acres, and the more than six-and-a-half million square feet of floor space houses over twenty-three thousand employees, both military and civilian.

Secondly, the entire complex was finished in a remarkably short time span. Erected on what was nothing more than reedy, bug-infested swampland and dumping grounds, the Pentagon was completed in January 1943, just sixteen months after construction was begun. The entire undertaking cost $83 million dollars. It was a time of war and a time of intense and selfless national pride. The job needed to be done, and it got done.

Finally, despite the size of the complex, it takes just seven minutes to walk between any two points of the original Pentagon—that part of the complex that is located above-ground.

During the middle 1950s, it became clear that the Soviet Union had the capability to deliver a nuclear strike against Washington. Thus, construction was quietly begun on a series of four sublevels. These "holds," as they were designated, were designed to be bomb-and-radiation proof; when the holds were completed in 1960, all of the most important files, the war room, and the research divisions of the Department of Defense were moved underground. In the 1980s, Hold-4—the lowest level—became the heart of the Pentagon's sophisticated computer network. It was then that the holds acquired a new nickname: The Dungeons. Because data was so easy to obtain, it was no longer necessary for employees to go up to the archives or the map rooms, to the White House or Congress.

Though it still takes no more than seven minutes to reach the elevators that access the underground section of the building, moving through the retinal-scan checkpoint in the northwestern or southeastern corridors, as well as the descent itself, add up to two minutes of travel time. Civilian employees joke about the extended commute. Military personnel don't joke at all. There is nothing flamboyant, visible, or field-oriented about the holds. Career soldiers are sent here because they are brilliant tacticians, historians, statisticians, accountants, bureaucrats, or what the DOD has unofficially classified as PITA—Pains in the Ass—who need to be moved out of the limelight.

The small Advance Research Projects Agency complex is located on Hold-3, one floor from the bottom. Of the nineteen military persons on the team of thirty-nine, only one of them was known as a PITA: Brigadier General Robert Charles MacDougall.

While weekends at the Pentagon were fairly quiet, activity at DARPA tended to continue at a steady pace regardless of the day. The civilian scientists had deadlines and field tests to conduct, and they couldn't let go until everything was ready and "TFF": theoretically fully functional. The military staff had to revise schedules and budgets constantly based on what the scientists told them—and then inform the scientists that more money and more time weren't available. It made for a close, tense, occasionally confrontational synergy.

DARPA was mandated primarily to work on upgrades in existing military hardware and software. The current "front burner" project was improving the Starburst, a new fighter-borne antisatellite missile. The rocket had already been used to destroy a sophisticated Chinese military satellite. The air force wanted the next generation of Starbursts to be deliverable in a cost-efficient multiple-warhead mode. Each fighter-launched cluster of six missiles would orbit the earth; each rocket could be fired at will from the ground.

The one exception to the DARPA charter was the Next Generation team. Formed in 1994 to meet the increasing demand for cutting-edge technology designed for the individual soldier, the seven civilians of N-Gen now reported to Commander Amos Evans, a thirty-eight-year-old former navy SEAL.

The job of the N-Gen team was to design, bring to prototype stage, and then field test new and innovative surveillance and strike-force equipment. Their budget was entirely black op, skimmed from the funds earmarked for other divisions. The future-shaping technology they developed made N-Gen the kind of program that had to be watched, pondered, researched, and constantly refined, but only within the team. Every person who worked there had a "psi" clearance, from the twenty-third letter of the Greek alphabet. Only the men and women who held the keys to the nuclear stockpile had the higher "omega" clearance or a more thorough background check. If Evans had a life outside the Pentagon, he wouldn't have the time or freedom to live it.

Except for short daily briefings, MacDougall and Evans had spent relatively little time together. From Evans's dossier, MacDougall knew that the commander was a master tactician who had led dozens of military and reconnaissance missions into hostile territory and had also spent a great deal of time as a solo op, penetrating foreign groups in order to conduct OSTE—on-site threat evaluation. But their lack of a personal relationship was uncomfortable for MacDougall, who was accustomed to being hands-on involved with personnel working under him. But the N-Gen team was closing in on the field test stage for a revolutionary new project when MacDougall arrived. It was not the best time to get to know anyone there, and MacDougall had decided to give the team and their leader whatever space they needed.

MacDougall's small corner office was located at the end of a corridor with bright white floor tiles, walls, ceiling, and lights. A Pentagon psychologist had spent time studying personnel in post-vernal equinox Antarctica and decided that the brightness of the sublevels helped to neutralize the depression that was sometimes brought on by a perpetual lack of sunlight. MacDougall still went outside to the center court for lunch whenever he could.

The sublevels were all U-shaped rather than pentagonal, due to pre-existing basements that had been built in other areas of the complex. This particular corridor contained executive offices for DARPA and other military research and development groups. At the end the hallway turned to the left where there were washrooms and a small cafeteria. Another left turn accessed the laboratories.

MacDougall was acknowledged with a courteous nod or reserved smile by the handful of civilians he encountered.

He was saluted by the military and by the ever-present security personnel. The Pentagon is in a perpetual state of THREATCON Normal, a high-security state in which checkpoints and electronic surveillance are used to control and monitor access throughout the above-ground and below-ground complexes. At even the hint of a security breach, the building shifts to THREATCON Alpha. MacDougall had seen that only once since he'd been here, when a telephoned bomb threat brought out squads of black-clad guards, bomb-sniffing dogs, and evacuation teams.

MacDougall stopped outside his office. He pressed his palm and fingertips against a dark, glossy, chest-high panel to the right of the door. The scanner flashed red, took a moment to read his prints, and then went dark. The door latch clicked. If access had been denied, a central security station would have been notified and armed guards would have moved in on the location. MacDougall turned the knob, entered, and shut the door behind him. He threw a switch that turned on the small desk lamp.

MacDougall's office was a dramatic contrast to the corridor. There was dark wood paneling and no overhead fluorescent lighting. In addition to the desk lamp, there were two standing lamps in either corner. Between them was a leather sofa. Thickly padded, green armchairs were set at angles in front of the mahogany desk. The walls were dominated by picture frames and window boxes containing mementos of MacDougall's career: photographs with his troops, including a photo with Stuart Hoxworth, Moses Cole, Father Penny, and Clark Gallant; weapons taken from Viet Cong snipers; and twisted pieces of Iraqi tanks and planes destroyed during Desert Storm. On the desk were a secure phone, computer, monitor, printer, and a framed candid of his wife and daughter taken at the Grand Canyon—their last vacation together. There was also a large, clear vase that contained dirt—sand and soil from places as diverse as Gettysburg, the Ardennes, and Inchon. Sites where American soldiers had shed their blood for the cause of freedom.

MacDougall eased into the black leather chair and typed his name and password into the computer. The Pentagon did not permit passwords like the names of children, spouses, or pets to be used—codes that were easy to uncover with a bit of detective work. So MacDougall had used Danny, the name he and his wife would have called Holly Ann if she'd been a boy.

MacDougall accessed the Pentagon database. Recently completed, the fifteen-year project had put every one of the four hundred thousand books and 1.7 million periodicals in the Pentagon library in digital storage. Psi-level personnel also had wide-ranging access to the CIA and FBI databases. MacDougall had that clearance and added those files to the mix.

He typed *formaldehyde* and hit "search." The computer quickly found over 1,500 references. MacDougall linked the word with *assassination*. The computer isolated forty-one instances where the words appeared together. MacDougall added a third word: *food*. The computer catalogued twenty references, and MacDougall ordered them up chronologically, asking the computer to limit them to the years following World War II.

There were seventeen references. He read through them all. Eleven of the cases were from foreign sources attributing deaths—from a North Korean general in 1951 to a Russian dissident in 1978—to formaldehyde. Three of the files were from the CIA in the 1970s; the names of the operatives and victims were blacked out. The other cases involved a mob hit against a Los Angeles judge; a husband who poisoned his wife; and a college student who committed suicide. Good medical examiners had found the evidence, and the killers were caught and sentenced. Cole's name was on one of the CIA autopsies from 1979 when he was assistant ME. The circumstances surrounding the operatives death were not revealed.

None of them seemed to offer a clue as to who would have killed Stuart Hoxworth. MacDougall asked the computer to list and group any words of CABaLs—Circumstance and Background Links—the cases had in common. Within seconds the computer offered the following:

DEATHS OF FOREIGN CITIZEN: TWELVE FILES
REFERENCES TO THE CIA: NINE FILES
PREVIOUS ASSASSINATION ATTEMPTS AGAINST
   DECEASED: SIX FILES
ANTI-AMERICAN ACTIVITIES: SIX FILES
KILLERS STILL AT LARGE: FIVE FILES

MacDougall studied the list. Assuming that the death of Stuart Hoxworth was tied to his politics, he asked the computer for a CABaL-check of American victims who had advocated pacifism or cutbacks of military personnel, R&D, or expenditures.

There were two names: the judge killed by the mob and the college student. MacDougall brought up their files.

The judge, John Howland, had been planning to run for Congress in 1986. MacDougall felt a jolt when he read that the judge died after eating a formaldehyde-tainted apple in his chambers during a mob trial. The killer was found quickly—and was stabbed to death in prison. The college student, Richard Sands, was president of the Anti-ROTC League in Southern California in 1990. He, too, was considering a political career. He killed himself in a science lab one night and left a suicide note blaming a failed love affair. The girl was not named.

MacDougall dropped all but those two cases. He filed them as *HOX-A* and asked the computer if there were any surveillance records of the two men. Both had FBI files. He asked for the dates when the FBI surveillance stopped. In both cases, it was forty-eight hours after the men died. That was the usual length of time it took for death information to be noticed, processed, and a file shut. If FBI personnel had been involved, chances are good the information would have been known and the records closed sooner.

Of course, he thought, *a careful killer would have kept the files open to lead to exactly that conclusion.*

So all any of this told him was that other people had been killed the same way as Stuart Hoxworth and that two of them were also antimilitary activists.

MacDougall sat back. His chair squeaked and startled him. He took a long, calming breath and turned his attention back to the screen.

Okay, he thought. The FBI and the CIA didn't benefit from killing pacifists. To the contrary. Less money for defense meant more money for other agencies. Besides, neither group would have taken on hits for the military. It was tough enough getting the agency and the DOD to cooperate on matters of national security, let alone doing favors for one another.

Who would have done this, then? MacDougall asked himself.

Given the CIA MO regarding formaldehyde, the obvious answer—in fact, the only answer he could think of—was a former CIA operative working outside the agency. Working for someone who had an interest in the military—possibly a geopolitical or financial interest. The CIA was required to keep files of all its personnel who had "gone public," as they called it. MacDougall asked for a list of those people from the time of the first formaldehyde hit to the last. There were over nine hundred names.

Jesus, he thought. He saved them all as *HOX-B* and moved on. He was going to have to come at this from a different angle.

MacDougall wrote a new file, *HOX-C,* and downloaded all available data on the political life of Stuart Hoxworth. He asked the computer to go through all the files and see who would have been hurt by any *specific* antimilitary activities of the persons in *HOX-A* and *HOX-C.* One name came up in the case of Howland, Sands, and Hoxworth: BR Defense Systems.

MacDougall asked the computer for the Concise Subject Overview file on BR. That was a summary that was written for any files of over fifteen hundred kilobytes.

The CSO read:

- BR Defense Systems of Thousand Oaks, CA, employs 270 full-time people, averages eight consultants annually. CEO, Boyd Robinson, Jr. (1941—).
- Founded by Boyd Robinson, Sr. (1899–1965) in 1922 as Robinson Explosives.
- Awarded major contract by U.S. Air Force in 1941 for four thousand thousand-pound, armor-piercing bombs for use by the Flying Fortress.
- Changed name to BR Weapons in 1942.
- Major contract to produce four-thousand-pound bombs for the AU-1 during the Korean War.
- Tried to buy Vought aircraft plant in Dallas, Texas, in 1952. Offer rejected.

- Since 1956, involved in the production of warheads for Intercontinental Ballistic Missiles, Submarine Launched Cruise Missiles, Multiple Alternative–Targeted Reentry Vehicles, and other rocket-systems.
- Became BR Defense Systems, 1980. Military plus privately funded R&D.

MacDougall kept reading through the CSO, looking for an association between Judge Howland, Richard Sands, and BR Defense Systems. He was beginning to feel paranoid and a little foolish when he found the connection: a protest rally at the factory, which Sands led and Howland refused to enjoin in 1986.

A protest rally, he thought. That couldn't have been reason enough to kill someone.

Could it?

MacDougall brought up a biography of Boyd Robinson, Jr. Maybe there was a link between the arms manufacturer and the CIA or FBI.

There were heavy donations to right-wing reactionaries and political action committees, close ties to pro-military lobbyists—some of whom, MacDougall knew, had had meetings with Stuart Hoxworth over the years—and also a reference to a deleted FBI report. It was dated September 1987, and labeled *The Huntsmen.* It was removed, according to the first of two footnotes, because it was no longer needed. MacDougall knew that the heading itself could not be deleted because a sequential file number would have to have been removed as well, and that would have sent up alarms throughout the system.

MacDougall asked the computer to search for the Huntsmen. There were no other references. At least, none that had survived the purge.

He turned his attention to a second footnote. It was a request for access to the Huntsmen file under the Freedom of Information Act.

"Jesus," MacDougall said softly when he read the name on the application. The request had come from Richard Sands.

MacDougall sat back and stared at the screen for a long moment. He walked himself through the events. A man protests militarism. He asks for a government file. He dies. Shortly thereafter, the file is erased. The end.

The odds of that being a coincidence were impossibly high. MacDougall pushed the chair back from his desk and paced the office for several minutes. There had to be a way to find out more about the Huntsmen. He sat back down and drummed the desk for several minutes more. And then it occurred to him. A possible way in.

Sometimes typists screwed up. Especially if a name or a title was new. He asked the computer to search for *Hunts Men*.

A few seconds later MacDougall raised his fist in triumph. There was one entry on file—a starting point, at least. Hopefully, it was the same group he was looking for.

The item was a short article from a Long Island, New York, newspaper in 1963. And it was in the system—surprisingly—as part of the government research compiled during the Warren Commission investigation into the assassination of President John F. Kennedy. The entry was from the sealed files, which were finally opened to the public in 1993.

MacDougall read the short piece:

GROUP OPPOSED TO
JFK NAME CHANGE

Valley Stream, New York Dec. 2—A
group of seven picketers gathered in the
parking lot outside the Gimbels Department Store in the Green Acres Shopping
Center off Sunrise Highway on Wednesday morning. The six men and one
woman were there to protest plans to
change the name of nearby Idlewild International Airport to John F. Kennedy International Airport.

"It's a disgrace," said group leader
William Mann. "Kennedy betrayed his
country and his own military background
with his peacenik policies against the
Reds."

Mann said that the group to which he
belongs, the Hunts Men, would oppose
any and all such attempts to honor the
fallen President.

Shoppers booed the group, and police
finally arrived and ordered the Hunts Men
to leave.

Encouraged, MacDougall saved the remaining items in a
sixth file. He ran a computer check on William Mann. The
name appeared only once, at the head of another deleted FBI
file. It was erased, according to a footnote, because William
Mann had died in a car crash in Fullerton, California, in
1979. MacDougall looked up the obituary; Mann had run a
light and smashed into a dump truck. Nothing suspicious-
looking there, unless someone made him do it.

MacDougall went back to the newspaper article and re-read it. Why would the Huntsmen go to the shopping center instead of the airport?

"Answer: because at a shopping center they'd be dealing with local police instead of airport security," he thought aloud. Not as rough. Most anarchists were cowards. Also, the newspaper coverage would be different in the suburbs. It wouldn't get lost the way it would in New York. A larger piece might be seen by like-minded fanatics—a smart re-cruiting move.

What about the makeup of the group: six men, one woman? Or the reference to the Reds? Or the reporter nam-ing the group and their location—

Naming the group. MacDougall looked at the reference to the Hunts Men. He was annoyed he hadn't thought of this sooner. He typed in the name *Hunt* and asked the computer to see if there was a link between anyone with that name and anyone in the other files he'd created.

He had his answer in less than a minute. The connection was a man named Jackson Hunt. According to records from the Library of Congress—not a place MacDougall would have thought to look for information—Jackson Hunt was quite a fellow. He was born in Lost City, West Virginia and died there in 1968 at the age of eighty-two. Hunt was a for-mer coal miner who had fought in World War I and special-ized in demolitions; he lost his left leg in 1917 during an exchange of artillery fire at Château-Thierry. After recuper-ating in England, Hunt returned to Lost City and wrote a se-ries of twenty-three very successful, flag-waving boys' adventure novels set in Europe during the war. George M. Cohan actually came to Lost City to discuss turning one of the novels into a Broadway musical. The novel was *German Doughboy,* about a young German deserter who was wounded and found by an American soldier. With the American's help and encouragement, the German returned to his nation as a spy for the United States. The novel was allegedly based on the real-life exploits of Hunt's friend and Lost City neighbor, Thomas Schiller.

All of that was interesting, MacDougall thought. But what was really significant was a cross-reference at the end of the biography to a 1922 *Wall Street Journal* article. MacDougall checked it out. The report named Hunt as a major investor in Boyd Robinson, Sr's. explosives company. The elder Robinson had also been a part of the first wave of young men who went to fight in Europe with General Pershing's American Expeditionary Force. Perhaps he had known Hunt in France.

So it's very possible that the Huntsmen were formed by Boyd Robinson, Sr., and named in Jackson Hunt's honor, MacDougall thought.

It's also possible they were bold enough to have publicly assailed the memory of John Fitzgerald Kennedy within two weeks of his assassination. Could the group also have been audacious enough to be a part of it? The Warren Commission thought there could be a connection. The clipping was in their file. The FBI also thought they were dangerous enough to have on file. That is, until someone had had the data removed.

But the Huntsmen could still be radicals without having been involved in the deaths of Sands, Howland, and Stuart Hoxworth. *Why* kill those men? To make certain that BR and other military suppliers remained rich and fat? That was possible, but somehow it didn't seem to be enough. The newspapers were full of companies that were experiencing downturns. They merged or sold off interests or bought companies to diversify. They didn't kill people.

Or did they?

MacDougall dragged his hand across his face. He was

tired, spent. He had assembled some intriguing pieces but was still missing a direct link between any of them.

"Maybe this is all bullshit," he said. But he didn't really believe that. And he couldn't afford to, either. Not if he was going to find out who was behind this. He went through the files again.

The trail from Robinson to the Huntsmen to Stuart Hoxworth was there, laid out like a mathematical proof. And if the CIA weren't a direct part of the chain, they were a potential sideline presence.

But how? And why?

Confused and overloaded, MacDougall took a minute to visit the BR Defense Systems website. There was a spectacular, animated presentation of declassified new weapons systems as well as a white paper on Procurement and History Trends, news of Army Base Realignment and Closure—along with the names and e-mail addresses of government representatives to whom complaints should be sent, including Stuart Hoxworth—and news from the Army Ordnance, Missile and Munitions Center and School/59th Ordnance Brigade. It was all proactive but otherwise seemingly innocent. .

Obviously, MacDougall wasn't going to get any more information through normal channels. He would have to investigate the Huntsmen and Stuart Hoxworth's death some other way.

He looked at the computer clock. It was nearly midnight. What he needed—what he really needed—was to talk to someone he could trust. Bounce all of this off a clearer mind.

"Where are you, Stuart?" he muttered. He could use a devil's advocate about now. But there was someone else.

Though he knew that Commander Evans would be busy

preparing for his six A.M. trip to Langley, he e-mailed him at his office.

> Would like to see you if convenient.
>
> MacDougall.

Two minutes later, after e-mailing Stuart Hoxworth's secretary Adrienne to send him the militia/PAC FBI report, MacDougall received a reply from Evans.

> Will be there in ten minutes, sir.
>
> Evans.

Six

Monday, 12:01 A.M.
Washington, D.C.

Commander Amos Evans knew that Brigadier General MacDougall was probably going through hell, and he felt guilty making him wait, even for a few minutes. Hell was a place Evans knew his way around.

But before he could leave his office, Evans had to finish amending the DARPA roster and make sure the test equipment was adjusted for the size and build of the personnel. Then he had to sign off on an update regarding the performance of the digital data globules in subzero temperatures. The science team couldn't go home until he did that, and they'd already been here thirty-seven hours straight.

The DDG aspect of the program was headed by Dr. Clark Fraser who, alone among the chief scientists, wrote in language that Evans could easily understand. The digital data globules were a vital component of the upcoming SFU field tests, and Fraser reported that the team had surpassed the parameters established in earlier tests. Evans was proud of the group and he e-mailed them to that effect. He copied the material to Brigadier General MacDougall.

He also wanted to leave Dr. Victoria Hudson a wake-up e-mail giving her the test updates. He would do that when he got back to the office. He was looking forward to seeing her again. Her knowledge was a joy; she loved what she did. Because she was married, he did not allow himself to look past her mind—though there were times when she looked at him in a way that seemed to invite more. But he refused to allow himself to act on that. God, too, was looking at him.

Commander Evans left his office and moved quickly down the bright corridor. Evans was looking forward to the opportunity of finally putting years of work on the line. The SFU drills were the first field tests for the Stealth Field Uniforms, a top secret project that had occupied the bulk of N-Gen's time for the past four years. Arrangements had been made to take the suits to Langley AFB in Virginia for the open-ended trials. Evans would be going down later in the morning for a Tuesday start. Troops from different branches of the military had been seconded under the Unified Services Act. They would also be arriving later that day, though none had been told what to expect. Outside the N-Gen group, only Captain Robin McIver, the base liaison at Langley, knew why the unit was going there. The entire operation had been designed to maximize security.

Though he stood just over six feet tall, the way Commander Evans stood made him seem several inches taller. His back and shoulders formed a perfect "T." He held his head up, and he breathed through his nose; there was a short, curved scar on the left side of his forehead where a piece of shrapnel had once grazed him. Unless he was speaking, his mouth was always shut, a habit that had come from years of physical conditioning. In hand-to-hand combat, soldiers had been known to bite off their own tongues or lips because their mouths were open. Open mouths also encouraged grunting. Not only did that signal your position to the enemy, it reinforced the idea that a march, climb, or struggle was strenuous. That gave your opponent a psychological boost and had the opposite effect on any of your own troops within earshot.

But as formal and imposing as his posture was, there was nothing tense about the former navy SEAL. His arms, well-developed from years of conditioning, swung loosely at his sides. His walk was confident, and his long legs moved with an extraordinary sense of rhythm. And despite the straightness of his back, his knees were always bent just slightly. That kept his center of gravity a little lower than that of other men, his body ready to move, to act. His dark eyes were also alert and hard. It was an annealing that came from "war, peacekeeping, and bureaucracy," as his friend and former DARPA commanding officer General Orlando Vargas once described the three battlefields of the American combat soldier.

Like many Pentagon personnel, the commander did not mind being down in the Dungeon. What he minded—bitterly—were the reasons they sent him here. Evans had enlisted in the navy when he was eighteen and had spent his entire career in the field. The SEALS allowed him to fulfill the goals he had enlisted for: to defend his country, experience other cultures, and attempt to come to terms with being both a devout Catholic and someone who had to kill without hesitation. He was still working on that last.

Then came Desert Storm, and the event that knocked him out of the field and eventually landed him here. The military had declared his actions abroad as "overzealous." Evans insisted that they were necessary. Because the navy might at some point need his skills, his knowledge, they put him here. Though Evans now felt privileged to be involved with this extraordinary project—he had made it his own, enhanced it with his own vision—he had spent more than a year examining his soul and chipping away at the bitterness of being hidden here. He was looking forward to Langley, to getting out in the field again.

Though the commander's small office was located on the other side of the long "U" it took less than a minute to reach the office of Brigadier General MacDougall. Evans tugged the hem of his uniform jacket, removing the creases before knocking. MacDougall buzzed him in, and Evans entered. He shut the door behind him and saluted crisply.

MacDougall rose slowly and returned the salute. "Have a seat," he said and gestured toward the nearest armchair.

Evans removed his hat and thanked him. MacDougall watched the officer as he crossed the room. Evans didn't sit until MacDougall did. When both men were seated, MacDougall said, "Sorry for the late call."

"It's all right, sir," Evans replied.

"How are things shaping up for tomorrow?"

"Very well, sir. I was just reviewing the amended roster for the SFU field team."

"There's been a change?"

"A late addition, sir," Evans said. "The Langley medic will be available for emergencies, but I felt we should have a doctor instead of a scientist as a test subject. Just in case the suits produce any physical irregularities that the external monitor doesn't catch."

"Then Dr. Carter won't be going."

"No, sir. We've got a marine medic named Taylor. I've got Chris Sheehy retailoring the uniform now."

" 'Retailoring' doesn't seem to be the right word for that suit," MacDougall observed. "What about the latest test results?"

"Also good news. The DDGs are performing better than

anticipated. I e-mailed the summary to you before I came over." He grinned. "Written by Dr. Fraser, so it's in relatively colloquial English."

"Excellent," MacDougall said. "I'll read it as soon as we're finished here."

Evans filed twice-daily progress summaries in DARPA's central computer. MacDougall was required to read and sign off on each of them after which they were entered into the master file. Only the N-Gen command and research team had access to that file, and there was a two-password access and printout system to prevent theft. The only outside access to the system was from the science room in the DARPA field facility at Langley.

"So the only problem I see anywhere—and it's *my* problem, Commander, not yours—is that I feel like I haven't contributed anything to the N-Gen project except to sign my name to your work."

"General, you came into a fully operational team."

"Thanks to you and General Vargas."

"Sir, other officers have come into situations like this and made changes just to put their fingerprints on an operation. You didn't. We've all respected and appreciated that."

"I wish I could say it warms my heart to be celebrated for things I didn't do rather than things I did."

Evans smiled. "Everyone here also knows about the things you did, sir. How you stood up to the top brass in INSCOM. That took courage. We respect that here, too."

MacDougall thanked him. "Speaking of the team, is everyone psyched about the SFU drills?"

"The tech team is very excited," Evans said. "They wish they could go down with me."

"I don't blame them. But a few dozen scientists showing up at a remote corner of Langley might be a little conspicuous."

"They understand, sir," Evans assured him. "And they trust Dr. Hudson to give a full evaluation."

MacDougall folded his large hands on the desk. "Commander—what I was saying a minute ago about being disinvolved. One of the bad things about that is I haven't gotten to know you very well. That's something I dislike about DARPA. You serve with men in the field, you get to know them. Here"—he shook his head—"your DARPA dossier doesn't say very much about you. Mostly dates, commendations, medals, personal stats. So I took the liberty of pulling your service record. You're an exceptional man, Commander. Secret missions in Turkey, Burma, Cuba, Afghanistan, Lebanon, and two dozen-plus other countries."

"Those jobs came with the uniform, sir," Evans said.

"The file also says you were reassigned to DARPA after a mission in Iraq."

"Yes, sir."

"In from the field and out to pasture," he said.

"It was rough for a while," Evans admitted, "but I'm okay now."

"I'm glad to hear it. What happened?"

"I caused a quiet international uproar. My team was collecting on-site intel and learned that SCUD warheads were being stored in Al'Aziziya, fifty miles southeast of Baghdad," Evans said. "Four of us went in at night and found them in a school crawl space. We rigged a small charge. When the warheads blew, they took a good chunk of the town with them. There were civilian casualties."

"You knew that would happen?"

"We suspected it might. The warheads were behind bars. We weren't able to count them. Our primary concern was to make sure they weren't used against American soldiers or our allies."

"Tough call. I understand," MacDougall said.

"So did the Chief of Naval Personnel and his staff, sir. Nevertheless, I was relieved of my duties."

"I understand that, too. I've been there."

"I know, sir."

"I also recall from General Vargas's personnel report that you're a very religious man."

"Yes, sir."

"There's no conflict in that? War and religion?"

"None."

"How so?"

Evans seemed uncomfortable. "It's difficult to talk about this and not sound preachy—"

"I asked. Please."

"Sir, God has conferred on us all the right—the obligation—to take life wherever necessary for just purposes. 'See that the man who is innocent and just is not done to death, and do not acquit the guilty.' Exodus 23:7." Evans regarded his superior for a moment. "May I ask, sir, why you're interested in this?" He had a very good idea what was coming. He'd read the on-line news report earlier that evening.

"I have a moral dilemma of my own," MacDougall said. "And Commander—we may be stashing the rule book in a footlocker before tonight's through. Let's start with you not calling me 'sir' while we're alone."

"All right," Evans said softly.

MacDougall took a slow breath. "Have you heard what happened to Senator Stuart Hoxworth?"

"I have."

"And do you know how the senator died?"

"No. The item I read said that the cause of Senator Hoxworth's death was being investigated—"

"But you know that I was with him."

"Yes." Evans watched as MacDougall turned toward the computer and opened a series of files. The brigadier general was obviously tired and overwrought. But Evans knew that he had been a careful and respected intelligence officer at INSCOM.

"The senator's death and my being there has created a situation that is going to affect my ability to work with the N-Gen team over the next few days," MacDougall said. He shook his head. "Listen to me. 'A *situation*.' I've been using military euphemisms way too long. This is more than that, Commander Evans—Amos. Let me begin by telling you that Stuart Hoxworth was assassinated."

Evans eyes hardened. "How?"

"Liquid formaldehyde was placed in a sandwich and it caused the senator's throat to swell shut."

Evans just stared at him. "Do you have any idea who was responsible?"

"You know, I really wish I did," MacDougall said. "I've been working on the computer for the last couple of hours to see if any individual or group has that modus operandi," MacDougall said. "Unfortunately, they do. Liquid formaldehyde is an old CIA toxicant. It dissipates quickly and produces misleading symptoms. Formaldehyde also appears to have been used on at least two occasions by a group known as the Huntsmen. Ever hear of them?"

Evans shook his head. He was still stunned. Assassination was a repugnant form of government.

"I hadn't heard of them, either," MacDougall went on. "As far as I can tell, they evolved from some kind of right-wing cabal dating back to World War I. They're pro-military with a possible record of assassinations. The current membership seems to include at least one powerful member of the military-industrial complex: Boyd Robinson, Jr., of BR Defense Systems."

"I know them," Evans said quietly. "Boyd Robinson is very wealthy and, from what I've read in the papers, extremely influential in conservative causes. His company is one of the few military-industrial firms that funds research and development on their own and then brings the finished systems to the government. If I'm not mistaken, army field research is testing some of the company's new omnidirectional flaming mines."

"They are," MacDougall said. "The army's also bought BR's white phosphorous mortars for the signal divisions. And you're right about Robinson. He's very conservative and extremely outspoken. I was looking through his file. There are speeches and a letter Robinson wrote to *Newsweek* two years ago. He was complaining about the United Nations Human Rights Commission 'daring' to look into the use of the death penalty in the United States. He called the investigation, 'disgusting, punitive, and hypocritical' and suggested that the United States was the standard by which other nations—and I quote—'should and would' be judged."

"A grandstander," Evans observed.

"Maybe," MacDougall said. "But what if he's more than that? What if he and his 'cabal' are judges and executioners, and Stuart Hoxworth was one of their victims."

Evans was silent for a moment. Why did the first idea MacDougall ran up the flagpole have to test his confidence in the man? "That's an enormous leap," he said.

"Maybe not," MacDougall said. "I've made a series of files that I'd like to walk through with you. And just so this information stays between us, I'm keeping them on a diskette here instead of on the hard drive or in the DARPA system."

Evans nodded.

"According to the BR file," MacDougall said, "Boyd Robinson bought the Lehmann Aircraft Company in Houston back in January. He purchased Midway Boatworks in

Hawaii a month later. In boom times, these would be a logical expansion of his core weapons business. But both companies are losing money, and, with military cutbacks in the pipeline, they stand to lose a lot more. Why would Robinson buy them now?"

"For the same reason a lot of people play the stock market when prices plummet," Evans said.

"They're looking for bargains, and they expect an upturn," MacDougall said. "But there are two problems with Robinson 'playing the market.' First, it doesn't look as though BR Defense Systems had profits high enough to warrant that kind of speculation. Second, there's no reason to expect a military upturn. The world is facing mostly brushfires these days. Separatist movements, border disputes, third-world coups. Nothing militarily significant from our point of view."

"A Saddam Hussein could always change that," Evans said.

" 'Could,' yes. But that's a dangerous word, especially for a company running up as much debt as BR is. I also checked the 1099s they filed with the IRS. BR has hired over two-dozen consultants during the last eighteen months—triple the norm. I ran a check just before you arrived. The names are all in NASA's bluebook. They're specialists in fiber optics and microengines."

"I'm still not seeing anything suspicious," Evans said. "It seems reasonable that BR would have new projects in development, ones they hope will make them money."

"Yes, but *how*? Where will that money come from? With the exception of Israel, Egypt, and South Korea buying our weapons, most foreign business is going to munitions makers in Russia, China, and France."

"The orders will come from the U.S. military," Evans

said. "If Robinson's got something new, we're still his biggest client—"

"But cutting back extensively," MacDougall insisted. "Or at least, we were until yesterday night."

"Until Senator Hoxworth was assassinated," Evans said. "And you believe that will all turn around now."

"It's possible."

"I still think that's a huge leap," Evans said. "You've got suspected CIA assassins—"

"*Former* CIA assassins," MacDougall pointed out. "Commander, the navy is smart enough to reassign people like yourself, personnel skilled at espionage and counterterrorism. That isn't a standing policy in the CIA. A lot of former operatives go public and go bad."

"So you think that BR is in league with persons unknown in order to influence American military policy through assassination."

"Why not? That was one of the theories that came out of the Kennedy assassination."

"One that was never proven," Evans pointed out.

"That doesn't make it wrong," MacDougall replied. "Literally as he died Stuart was telling me about an FBI report regarding militias that are affiliating themselves with PACs. I've requested the report from Stuart's secretary. Think about it: special interests threatening or actually employing violence to advance their causes. It's like mafiosi attempting to recruit police and judicial officials but on a national scale."

"With the Huntsmen as enforcers for BR?"

"For BR and other munitions manufacturers, though obviously I'm not sure of that. I word-searched every file the DOD has access to. There was a reference to the Huntsmen in the FBI database, but it was only a heading. The file had been purged. The only Huntsman reference I was able to find apparently was spared because of a variant spelling."

"That could be simple housecleaning, not inside access to our files," Evans said.

"Granted. But a man who requested that file also died of formaldehyde poisoning."

That got Evans's attention.

MacDougall shook his head slowly. "Commander, this whole thing isn't easy for me and not just because of Stuart. I want to believe that the system *works*. That leaders, parties, and institutions can't be bullied. But that confidence has been rattled, and not just by the assassination. It's the chilling effect that one act of that caliber can have. This morning I met with a member of my platoon from Vietnam, Moses Cole. He's now the Army's ME at Walter Reed. He wanted me to let him falsify the report on Stuart's death. He wanted to change the cause of death."

"Change it to what?"

"To an accidentally induced asthma attack."

"The army ME wanted to *lie* about the senator's death?"

"Lie and bury the matter. No mention of the deadly levels of formaldehyde." MacDougall shook his head. "Moses was afraid. He couldn't even look at me."

"I hate to keep playing devil's advocate," Evans said, "but the ME could have been looking out *for* you."

"I know that," MacDougall said, "and I want to believe that. But after what I've seen and heard, what I've read, it's difficult," MacDougall shook his head slowly. "I thank you for your devil's advocacy. That's the main reason I asked you to come by. But I tell you, Commander, before today I regarded conspiracies as things whipped up by desperate journalists and delusional moviemakers. Now, I'm not so sure. I'm wondering if the big picture, with all the pieces in place, represents something I thought was an anathema to American thinking. A well-organized, well-financed

group working to control our government through terrorism."

The word hung in the air, all too familiar yet no less ugly
for it.

"I'm going to continue looking into this," MacDougall
went on. "When you get to Langley, I want you to file your
reports as usual. But if I don't sign off on them right away,
you'll understand why."

"Of course," Evans said. "And if you need anything
while I'm down there—"

"Thanks, but I want you to concentrate on the trials,"
MacDougall said. "Though I may ask your Dr. Hudson for
some hacking advice if she's up for a little rule breaking."

"She might very well be," Evans said.

MacDougall popped a diskette from his computer and
passed it across the desk. "Here's a copy of the files I've put
together on this thing. Just in case a custodian accidentally-
on-purpose spills cleaning fluid into my hard drive."

Evans put the diskette in his shirt pocket.

MacDougall rose and Evans stood smartly. The commander saluted, and the brigadier general saluted back, after
which he offered his hand across the desk. He shook Evans's
hand warmly.

"So. Thanks for all your help," MacDougall said. "Do
you have any spiritual advice for me?"

"From the Bible? No. But from Mark Twain—yes."

"Mark Twain? What did he say?"

"Do what's right. You'll please some people and amaze
everyone else."

MacDougall smiled slightly. "Thanks, Amos. And good
luck at Langley."

"Good luck to you, too, sir," Evans said. Then he turned
and left.

When he reached his office, Evans shut the door and

knelt beside his desk. He folded his hands tightly on the desktop and prayed that MacDougall would find the persons responsible for Senator Hoxworth's death. He also prayed that MacDougall would never regret choosing the road to justice rather than the simpler road to compliance.

Seven

Monday, 12:07 A.M.
Germantown, Pennsylvania

It never failed.

Whenever Major Hank Taylor managed to get leave and visit his mother—who still sent him a home-baked cake on his birthday and knit him a new sweater every winter, even when he was stationed in the desert—something happened to call him away. Once, it was Saddam Hussein figuring that it was okay to invade Kuwait. Then it was to fly to San Diego to search for a fellow marine, Lawrence Booker, who decided to drop acid and go AWOL—"A D," as the military police call it. Armed and Dangerous. They found him off the coast of Vista two days later, floating facedown in the Pacific.

Now there was this, whatever "this" was.

During his special-request Hamburger Helper dinner on the day he returned home, Taylor had received a call from the office of Colonel Bialer at Camp Pendelton in Oceanside, California. The colonel told him to sit tight for a call from the DOD; they had an important assignment for him.

Taylor asked the colonel if the DOD could please find some other token African-American Marine Corps medic for the job. The colonel assured Taylor that he had been specially requested because of his record, not his race. Taylor knew that, but he couldn't resist pulling the growling, uptight Alabama-born officer's chain. On top of which he was pissed because his leave was going to be cut short.

Taylor sat tight with his mother in her cozy Park Drive Manor apartment, chatting about friends and family and watching a Laurel and Hardy tape he'd brought her. A little before nine o'clock someone from the office of the deputy secretary of defense phoned and told him to take the ten A.M. Metroliner from Thirtieth Street Station in Philly to Union Station in Washington the next morning. Someone would be at the train to meet him. The "funcman"—which was what "real" soldiers called the humorless, desk-bound functionaries—didn't apologize for the inconvenience. They never did. He also didn't tell him what the assignment was about. He said only that the Pentagon hadn't thought they'd need a medic for certain tests but had changed their mind.

Taylor broke the news to his mother. She took it well: of *course* the marines needed him back, she said. He was the best. He was the best fighter, the best doctor, the best everything.

Taylor loved his mother.

They changed their mind, Taylor grumbled to himself as he sat in the tiny kitchen and watched his mother bake cookies. That was what was pulling Taylor away from his mother a whole twenty-two hours after he arrived. At least he'd gotten to see her, hold her, see that she was healthy and happy. And also to smell her hands. For the past thirty years, his mother had worked at the building's beauty salon. To this day, the smell of shampoo and conditioner on those small, slender hands was one of three smells that brought back his childhood in an instant. The other two were the smell of Hamburger Helper, and the smell of incense at the *dojo* where he'd studied martial arts.

As Taylor leaned the wicker chair back toward the window (and was warned, gently but firmly, to sit up straight or he'd fall and break his neck), he only wished that one of these years he'd get to look up the few friends he still had in the neighborhood. Or just walk around the town where he'd grown up. About the only thing he had managed to do—because he always did it first, just in case the marine corps decided it couldn't function without him—was to visit *Sensei* Frank Ruiz, his former martial-arts instructor. Learning how to control and destroy the human body was actually what had gotten him interested in medicine when he was a young teenager. *Could* an elbow be repaired if you snapped it? Could a person *really* die if you drove their nose up into their head? *Why* did it hurt so much if you bent someone's wrist toward the inside of their elbow?

The eighty-eight-year-old Master Ruiz still had a small *dojo* on West Harvey, and Taylor had visited earlier in the day while his mother was at work. The smell of incense was the same as he walked up the creaking stairs. So was *Sensei*. The spindly, nearly blind man could still kick Taylor's own second-level black-belt butt, as he happily demonstrated for an afternoon white-belt class. But what had always impressed Taylor more than *Sensei's* enormous skill was how gentle the man was. Military officers tended to bark to get things done. "*Yell it to sell it*" was their motto. Funcmen usually spoke with arrogance or annoyance. Not *Sensei*. He commanded students and strangers with politeness, a soft voice, and his presence. Taylor hoped that in another sixty years he'd have mastered that kind of dignity.

When the cookies were done and the cold milk had been poured, they had a long, slow talk about how they were doing. Hank said he was still having the time of his life and loved the new group he was in, the STARs. His mother said she still enjoyed talking to people as she did their hair, keeping up with their children and grandchildren, and even great-grandchildren. She had also set up a singing club here at the building. She was introducing the Jewish and Italian women to gospel, and they were teaching her songs like "Dreidel, Dreidel, Dreidel" and "Amore." She admitted that she got tired more than she used to and that the neighborhood was a little more dangerous than it used to be—tenants liked to get in and stay in after dark—but she looked and sounded happy.

After his mother went to bed, Taylor walked from the kitchen to the small living room. He shook his head as he glanced at the framed photographs of himself at NYU Medical School and at military bases in various parts of the world. The pictures lined the wall and the bookcase shelves and the coffee table, a narcissist's dream. Then he walked over to the windows. He looked out and smiled.

The *dojo* had been his after-school home when he was growing up. And on those evenings when his mother worked at her second job, cleaning the PSFS bank four blocks away, Taylor had spent many nights with the St. Martins down the hall. But his touchstone was this one-room, sixth-floor apartment with its hilltop view of roads and other apartment buildings and distant trees. Once in a rare while, the magnificent Goodyear blimp flew across the horizon, and Taylor would stare at it for hours. Located at the intersection of busy Lincoln Drive and Harvey street, the Park Drive Manor was an oasis set amidst creeping poverty. The twin towers had a big backyard, a swimming pool, and a lot of retired couples who had been very kind to his single mother and him. Taylor had never known his father, a trucker who left before he was born, but his beautiful, sainted mother had worked hard to make this place warm and happy. "Our sweet little nest," as she used to call it. Except for the vaguely embarrassing Hank Taylor shrine, it was unchanged over the years. He felt fortunate to have had it then, and to have it still. But each time he saw his mother she looked so much older and seemed to have less energy. He really needed to spend more time here—

They changed their freaking minds, Taylor thought again as he turned from the window and opened the old sofa bed. It groaned loudly. He knew how it felt. He was supposed to have a week here, not a day. Though maybe, he thought suddenly, he might get lucky. Maybe he could finish whatever he had to do in a day or two and come back. Heather St. Martin was flying in from Cleveland for her mother's birthday on Thursday. His mother said she was divorced; he'd love to see her again. Maybe they could play doctor just like they used to, and not just for old time's sake. She never believed him when he said he wanted to grow up to be a physician. Maybe she'd believe him now. Maybe he could show her some things—

Stripping to his boxers, Taylor opened the window and then eased down onto the thin, saggy mattress he'd slept on as a child. He shifted to the side so the exposed springs wouldn't poke him in the backside. Then he lay there listening to the sound of his mother snoring, to the cars on the road, to the doors slamming heavily on apartments down the hall, to a couple spatting next door—still the Dryfooses, he wondered?

He also heard something unfamiliar. Seriously subwoofered jazz coming from the parking lot along with low male voices. It used to be that when people came home at night they were laughing about a party or a movie, complaining about traffic, or arguing about the way *he* had driven and that if she didn't like it then next time *she* could drive.

Taylor was surprised that he didn't hear any other cars coming or going. He listened for several minutes, trying to make out what was being said. Then he went over and looked out.

There were three young men sitting in a car in the parking lot. They were smoking cigarettes and listening to the radio and it looked like they were just hanging. This was new.

Taylor went to the intercom and buzzed the security desk. Art Tracy answered. The one-armed World War II navy vet had been there since Taylor was a kid. In fact, Mr. T had once saved a sapling on which the boy was intently practicing roundhouse kicks.

The elderly man was delighted to hear from him. "How *are* you, Henry?" he asked. "The day crew told me you were back—hey, we're all real proud of ya. Your mom shows us every new photo you send her."

"I'm sure she does," Taylor said. "What about you, Mr. T.? You still chasing kids out of the trees and skateboarders off the ramps?"

"Got to," he said. "Feel bad 'cause they got nowhere else to play. Just like when you were a kid."

"I understand," Taylor replied. "Say, Mr. T.—there are some guys sitting in a car under the window. Old black Cadillac. You know them?"

"Oh, I know them all right," he said miserably. "The flies."

"The who?"

"The flies," he repeated. "That's what I call 'em. I don't know their real names. But you swat 'em away, and they come right back. I used to call the police whenever they showed up. But the flies see the squad cars comin' from up where they're parked, which is why they come here. And the police don't stay around long if the flies aren't here. So as soon as they go away, the flies come back, and we end up stuck with 'em. Stuck with them and their loud music and the other cars that come up to see them."

"What other cars?" Taylor asked.

"I think they sell drugs," Tracy said gravely. "I've watched from the roof. But there's nothin' I can do. Coupla times I went over to them, asked them politely to go somewhere else. They just laugh. They've got guns. And anyway, Henry—they don't bother the tenants except with their music. So we've all kinda learned to look the other way."

"I understand," Taylor said. "Listen, Mr. Tracy. I'd like you to do me a favor."

"Sure. Anything."

"I'd like you to wait ten minutes and then call the police."

"The police?" Tracy asked. "What for? What's going to happen in ten minutes?"

Hank replied, "They're probably going to make some arrests."

Taylor hung up the phone, then walked quietly back to the living room. His mother was still snoring. She could still sleep through anything, bless her.

Pulling on his jeans, USAF sweatshirt, and Nikes, and making sure he had his keys, Taylor quietly opened the door. Then, he walked swiftly to the stairwell down the hall.

Despite what he did for a living and despite his martial-arts training, Hank Taylor was a pacifist. But he wasn't a peacemonger, either. If he had to fight, he fought to win.

Yet it was knowing that he *could* kill a person with a small, stealthy blow, and it was knowing that sometimes the damage couldn't be repaired that had made Taylor regard violence as a last option. After his friend Lawrence freaked out, Taylor had attended lectures at Pendleton on recognizing and managing stress among subordinates. That was an adjunct to courses in Psy-Ops—Psychological Operations—which was available to officers. There, Dr. Fitzpatrick had drilled into him and the other officers the idea that physical conflict was inevitable only when an individual—whether it was a kid in the street or the leader of a nation—had been left with no room to maneuver and save face.

As Taylor crossed the deserted parking lot toward the Cadillac, he hoped these people fit the profile. If not, he was ready. He was still "loose" from the workout at the *dojo* and also from his daily, fifteen-minute exercise with the rope. The rope was a two-foot length of clothesline knotted into a circle. First thing in the morning, he would slip his hands into the rope, up to the wrists, then move his arms in opposite directions. He'd twine them all around his body. After a few seconds, his forearms would be tangled together. Then he'd begin moving his arms around again, attempting to free them. But the purpose of the rope wasn't just to stay loose. It was to force every joint in his body to move. Defensively, *Sensei* likened movement to trying to place quarters on a moving basketball. If you were constantly moving, an enemy's blows would roll off whatever they touched. Offensively, moving also gave you the opportunity to land countless blows—to place a foot on an opponent's instep or against a knee, to drive toes into the belly, to propel an elbow up into a jaw or sideways into the ribs, to slam a head butt into a face behind or in front of you, or to smash a backfist, front-fist, or hammer-fist into a temple, nose, chin, solar plexus, or testicles.

Taylor was about twenty yards away, close enough to see the glowing tips of the lighted cigarettes. There were three men in the car—two in the front, one in the back. They were listening to Django Reinhardt, the legendary guitar player, and they were watching him as he neared. They had to be wondering whether he was a buyer, the law, or just a tenant.

Taylor approached the open window of the driver's side. "Hey there," he said affably. "I wonder if I could ask you gentlemen a favor."

They didn't offer a response.

"I wonder if you'd mind turning the music down a bit," he said. "We've got some folks trying to sleep upstairs."

The driver was slumped back against the head rest. He tossed his cigarette out the window. "You forgot to say please," he said.

Taylor smiled. "You know, you're right. I'm sorry. My mother taught me better manners than that. Would you *please* turn the music down?"

The driver lit another cigarette. He inhaled deeply. "Too late," he said. "You blew it." The driver looked ahead as the other two men laughed.

Taylor got down on his right knee beside the car. "Look," he said. "I know you gentlemen don't *have* to do Smilin' Jack Shit for me, as we say in the marine corps—"

"Say, man, you a marine?" asked the man in the passenger's seat.

"Yes, I am."

"Then sail the fuck outta here before yo' ass get sunk."

The man in the backseat snorted. The driver continued to stare ahead, his face impassive.

"Unfortunately, I can't do that," Taylor said, smiling. "See, I personally happen to love Django but not at—"

The driver poked the barrel of a .45 over the edge of the window. "Can you do it now, asshole?"

A rush of energy flashed through Taylor when he saw the gun. The flood did not show, did not cause him to act any differently. But every sense, every muscle, every nerve was alert. Still squatting, he raised his hands face-high. He did that so his hands were level with the gun. Then his expression shaded to concern. That was designed to let the driver feel as if he were in charge.

"I, uh—I guess you gentlemen really don't want to talk about this," Taylor remarked.

The man in the passenger's seat leaned over and snickered, "What the fuck tipped you off, genius—"

While the other man was still talking, Taylor's left hand shot across his body to the right, toward the gun. At the same time, he jerked his head back, toward the front of the car, in case the gun discharged. It didn't. Grabbing the gun and the driver's hand together, he squeezed tight and yanked them through the window. As the driver's arm emerged to the elbow, Taylor also snatched it from below. He pulled the arm away from the car, simultaneously swinging his back toward the door. The twist generated momentum. The rest of the driver's arm and shoulder, along with his head, came through the window. It happened so fast that the driver didn't have time to react—until now. He screamed and dropped the gun.

Taylor heard the other men swear and knew they were probably pulling weapons.

The maneuver had positioned the back of Taylor's left elbow directly in front of the driver's face. Taylor snapped the elbow back twice in quick succession into the driver's eyes. He heard the zygomatic bone crack; it would be a while before the man would be able to open either eye. Taylor pushed him backward, into the man in the passenger's seat.

Still squatting, Taylor stepped toward the rear of the car. He stopped beside the back door just as the man there opened it. Taylor stood. As he rose, he slammed the door shut with his left thigh and snapped a left jab through the open window. The man's nose shattered and he flew backward.

Taylor turned and snatched the driver's .45 from the asphalt. He trained it on the man in the passenger's seat. He had his own .38 out, but he also had the driver kicking in pain and squirming up against him.

"Drop the gun out the window," Taylor said.

The man hesitated. Taylor drew back the hammer. The man turned and did as he was told.

"Now lower the radio," Taylor said.

"What?"

"Lower the radio."

The man scrambled over the driver to twist the dial. Taylor thanked him. Then, as the headlights of a car turned up the long, winding driveway, Taylor used the .45 to shoot out the driver's side front and rear tires. The car slumped toward him as the echoes of the shots and burst tires rolled across the parking lot.

Taylor began backing away. Behind him, lights were being turned on in apartment windows.

"If you try to run," Taylor warned the man, "shot number three will be for you. Got that?"

The man nodded.

Stepping into the darkness beside the building, Taylor waited to make sure that the car swinging into the lot was the police and not someone looking to buy drugs. It was a squad car. Slipping the gun in the waistband of his pants—on the side, where he could cover it with his arm—and very quietly opening the door, Taylor ducked back inside. *Sensei* had taught him one thing more: if you ever had to fight, do your business and get out. People who stuck around had to deal with the police or vengeful friends of the beat-up.

As Taylor walked back toward the stairwell, he encountered Mr. T. running down the first-floor hallway.

"Henry, what's all the commotion?" the security guard asked urgently. "What'd you do?"

"I took myself a little walk," Taylor smiled. "Just like I used to do with Heather." He winked. "Mum's the word, okay?"

"Huh? Oh—sure. Yeah. I got ya," Mr. T. said knowingly and continued past him.

Taylor went back to the apartment. His mother was still asleep, and he smiled as he watched the red and blue police lights flashing off the walls. Taylor didn't go to the window; he didn't want anyone to see him. The punks would describe him, Mr. T. would say he had no idea who they were talking about, and by the time detectives came to investigate in the morning Taylor would be long gone.

He lay down and closed his eyes. And in the sweet silence of the night, he thought happily of Heather and his first, chaste kiss down by the moonlit swimming pool . . .

Eight

As she sat down at a small outdoor table at the Joe's On
Us coffee bar on the corner of Christopher Street and
Bleecker, waiting for Asshole to show up, Dr. Victoria Hudson stayed calm by thinking about reality. Things she could
touch, smell, or taste. Not cyberspace—and not relationships.

After teaching four straight semesters plus summer
classes in cyberoptics for grad students and cybersecurity
for adult education, the thirty-two-year-old was happy to
be leaving New York University. She would miss the good
things about New York—the culture, the architecture, the
we-made-this fingerprints of human beings everywhere
she turned, from under the ground to over the clouds. But
she wouldn't miss the bullshit. The no-way-was-it music
crap that subwoofered from boom boxes and cars and open
apartment windows. The loud, jingling coins in the coffee
cups of the homeless or the simply lazy who saw profit in
the feel-good charity of others. The dog whose owners

thought they also owned the streets and that it was just fine if they made you step over leashes that unspooled for three or four yards or dogs who stopped to urinate on trees, buildings, or in the middle of the sidewalk.

Victoria especially wouldn't miss the students. Modern American youth with their vacant looks and baseball caps and baggy pants and pierced noses and tongues and nipples. *Nipples.* Other than possible do-it-yourself defibrilation, she didn't get that at all. These kids had no desire to do much of anything except smoke, drink, and "chill"—a word that gave her chills because the kids were inert enough. Then there were the foreign students who looked sharp and thought even sharper and who—in her mind's eye—looked at Americans the way dogs looked at uncooked steak: as something they expected to devour very soon. And the way things were going, the foreign kids just might do it.

But most of all Victoria was happy to be leaving her soon-to-be-former husband, Stephen. His long, black, tar-sticky shadow darkened everything else in her life. The lawyer who loved to talk about himself and his cases but never listened. The squash enthusiast who didn't want to help her learn the game for reasons he never made clear—and when she learned the game on her own wouldn't play with her. The prick who fucked around because he claimed she didn't give him what he wanted—two women and him. When she asked if they should first try two men and her, he told her it wasn't the same and that she was disgusting.

So much for love at first sight, especially in the dim light of a goddam singles bar. What the *hell* was she thinking? That marrying Stephen would bring love to her life? Security? A friend in a cold and shitty world?

Her college roommate Liz had told her to buy a springer spaniel instead. She was right.

Victoria knew Asshole would be late this morning because however amicable she hoped their parting could be, Stephen was and always would be a game player. He only lived a block away. She had taken care of the joint tax return, which needed to be signed and filed before she left; he knew that. He also knew that the car was coming to take her to the airport at nine. Which was why he'd probably wait until eight-fifty-five to show up, just to put the screws on.

Victoria dumped a pair of Sweet 'N Lows into her black house blend and stirred. She took a sip, then reached into her leather briefcase and took out the personnel file of the people who were going to Langley. She had intended to read it on the plane but needed something to take her mind off Stephen.

She began flipping through the pages. She'd snuck these files from the N-Gen computer late the night before, when Evans had e-mailed her the latest test results. After her disastrous marriage and her bitter conflict with Lanning & Mulholland Systems, Inc., she liked to know as much as possible about the people she was getting into bed with. All she'd had to do to get this file was go to the DOD DefenseLINK home page and customize an IBS—itsy, bitsy, spider—to leave the web and nest in the Pentagon computer system. It was similar to what that eighteen-year-old Israeli hacker "the Analyzer" had done the year before. The only difference between Victoria and the Analyzer—apart from the fact that he got caught—was that her e-mail address was in Evans's file. As a result, the security system overlooked any "incoming" data from her. When Evans sent her the data, that roused the spider, which followed the connection backward into Evans's computer. Once there, it downloaded whatever was in the N-Gen file and then self-destructed.

Since the N-Gen personnel had to be seconded from their various commands, those files were not encrypted. Unfortunately, that was all she got. Everything else about this project was off-line. Which meant that despite Victoria's four previous trips to the Pentagon she still had no idea exactly what she'd been working on. The late General Vargas had first contacted Victoria after reading her paper on SCS—Sargassum Computer Simulation, the use of computers to move molecules along microscopic copper grooves and mimic the abilities of the sargassum, a fish with sophisticated color-adaptive characteristics. So she assumed that the military had hired her to help design a new kind of camouflage for tanks or other vehicles. Since she and the rest of the team were going to Langley, the project probably involved aircraft—perhaps planes with an underbelly that showed a ground-based observer blue sky and clouds as it soared overhead.

Then again, maybe it didn't, she told herself. You never knew with the military.

Except for Commander Evans, the names in the file were all new to her. And though the four people held different ranks and came from different services, they all had one thing in common: they were all men.

What a nonsurprise, she thought. Though she often reminded herself, only partly in jest, that men needed every advantage they could get, the inequality made her want to scream. She wished she could be I'll-show-you determined instead of pissed off. Unfortunately, it just didn't work that way for her.

But Victoria was feeling sour enough without dwelling on that. She turned her attention to the typed sheets.

Colonel Matthew Lewis, age thirty-nine, was with the U.S. Army Delta Force, the 1st Special Forces Operational Detachment. He was a specialist at knife fighting, tactical force infiltration, and "flashes." From the context—reference was made to a half-dozen attacks behind enemy lines in Desert Storm—Dr. Hudson surmised that a "flash" was the latest neologism for a lightning-strike.

Major Hank Taylor of the U.S. Marine Medical Corps was a twenty-nine-year-old doctor. He was a late addition, requisitioned only the day before. Taylor was schooled in Psy-Ops and was also a black belt in Zujitsu, some form of martial arts. He wasn't married. Dr. Hudson looked back at the entry for Lewis and noticed that he wasn't married either. Neither was Evans, who apparently had no interests outside of the military and God. The next man, Master Chief Petty Officer Rodrigo Diaz, was divorced. So was the one after that, Captain Peter Holly.

Coincidence?

Diaz was one of the first members of a new breed of fighter: the coast guard SHARCs, the Sea, Harbor, and River Command unit. The group was responsible for seagoing electronic reconnaissance on and under the water. The thirty-nine-year-old Diaz was one of the designers of the SHARCs new MOATS: Mined Oceanic Array Tactical Systems. According to the file, the submersible automatic weapons could be controlled from a single vessel. They saved money and human resources by enabling just a few cutters to protect literally hundreds of miles of coastline.

Thirty-two-year-old Captain Peter Holly was also a member of a newly commissioned group, the U.S. Air Force STARs: Stealth Team, Attack-Ready. The STARs were trained in all the latest stealth aircraft technology. Dr. Hudson also knew that a division of the STARs was responsible for overseeing a system that had been completed a year before: the controversial DONS, the DOmestic Network Satellites. She had attended a seminar about privacy issues in the computer age, and the mysterious DONS were a hot-button topic. Reportedly put into orbit in 1998 by the space shuttle, the DONS—whose existence the Pentagon quietly denied—

were used to spy on America, not on foreign governments. Captain Taylor's file didn't say whether or not he was involved with the satellite network, which reportedly was tracked from STAR headquarters at Holloman Air Force Base, New Mexico. However, it did indicate that he had top security clearance. That meant he certainly had access to that resource. Holly was no slouch in the air, either. He'd flown twenty-three missions during Desert Shield/Storm and, upon his return to the United States, flew many of the test flights of the new Comanche Stealth helicopters.

She looked briefly at Evans's file. There was nothing new in it, nothing about his personal life. She wasn't surprised. Just disappointed.

She put the pages back in her leather briefcase, hidden amidst the folders of research and diskettes.

Okay, Victoria thought. Whatever the bias inherent in the system, these men were top of the line. And working with the best in any field brought out the best in her.

Victoria finished her coffee and went back inside for a refill and a chocolate muffin. Why the hell not? She sat back down and looked out at quaint Bleecker Street—at the school crossing guard, at the windows of antique stores and specialty food shops and restaurants that wouldn't open for hours, at the traffic headed toward Seventh Avenue. She loved it all, but she knew she didn't belong at the university. She was happiest in a quiet laboratory and would like nothing better than to go back to one. She had done that for several years at Lanning & Mulholland straight out of MIT. But Dr. Andrew Steele—an appropriate name—took credit for her work thanks to a cyberspace sleight of hand that downloaded her research and then locked her out of it. He was awarded several patents in his name, as his contract with the company allowed. Dr. Hudson tried to live with that for about a week before leaving the Boston-based company. A lawsuit against Lanning & Mulholland won her a small cash settlement—which went to her attorneys, along with most of her severance pay—and permission to publish the last of her research under her own name. In between teaching herself how to hack with the best of them so she'd never be locked out of anything that belonged to her again, Dr. Hudson wrote two papers based on that work, their publication bringing her to the attention of both NYU and the DOD. Though she'd informed General Vargas that she'd love a full-time position at the Pentagon—and had repeated that desire to Commander Evans—they weren't able to give her one. Budget cuts, they said. She would try again on this trip. Unfortunately, she had a feeling that the new director of DARPA, Brigadier General Robert MacDougall, would have more to worry about than the tests and her contribution to them. According to an above-the-fold front-page article in today's *New York Times,* MacDougall was "part of an investigation" into the poisoning of Senator Stuart Hoxworth. Whether that meant he was merely a witness, a suspect, or both, chances were good his mind would be elsewhere.

Victoria finished the muffin, finished her coffee, enjoyed the warm morning, and finally looked at her analog watch. It was a hair past 8:30. Her husband was nearly a fucking *hour* late.

She'd give him another five minutes while she continued to enjoy the real world. It was as easy to lose touch with reality in cyberspace as it was in relationships because everything you saw or heard seemed real. A hacked and inflated bank balance. A screen name in a chat room. A forged academic record. Stolen research. People saw it on a screen and believed it, and it became real.

A gaslighting lie from your fucking husband. *No, hon, I'm not fucking my trainer at the gym.*

The five minutes was up. Collecting her trash, she rose

from the table and walked back toward her Greenwich Street apartment. She threw out the mangled coffee cup and picked up the carry-on she'd left with her doorman. He wished her a bon voyage as she headed out to the waiting car. She thanked him. Ari was a real gentlemen.

Fuck Stephen, she thought. She wasn't going to give him the satisfaction of being there when he showed up at the last minute, her knight in tarnished armor bearing his mighty pen and cherished signature. They'd file their last joint return late and pay a penalty and to hell with him and it and their marriage. It would be a fitting finale to a disastrous life together.

She didn't bother looking over at the coffee bar as her car moved past. She felt good about that. And for the first time in months, she felt good about herself.

Nine

**Monday, 7:40 A.M.
Fort Bragg, North Carolina**

When he was growing up as an army brat, Colonel Matthew Lewis used to curl up in bed with one of the fat hardcover volumes from his father's large collection of military history books. Even before he could read, Lewis was fascinated by the detailed etchings and color plates showing the uniforms from different eras. He wasn't fond of the Asian costumes—they looked drab and clumsy—he liked the handsome uniforms the British wore during the American Revolution, and he thought the Spanish conquistadores looked pretty impressive. But the Greek and Roman uniforms were his favorites. They were colorful, proud, and manly. The weapons were also exciting: the daggers and Roman *pila*—lead-loaded javelins for piercing armor—the clubs and arrows, the pickaxes, tridents, and swords.

Even as a very young boy, Lewis knew he would have been at home back then. Especially in Ancient Sparta, circa 500 B.C. Back then, if an officer was displeased with the performance of his men, he would line them up, draw his

sword, and walk down the phalanx. Looking the soldiers in
the eye he would kill every fifth, seventh, or tenth man. The
number of murders was determined in part by how griev-
ously the men had offended him; as a practical matter, it also
depended upon how many soldiers the officer needed for his
next campaign. The remaining warriors went into battle prepared to redeem their honor and also to survive, as long as
survival didn't conflict with the other more important goal.

Lewis's troops under the command of the burly Sergeant
George Leningen could use some of that thinning of the
ranks right now. As the men finished the room-cleaning drill
with dummy terrorists and hostages, Colonel Lewis shouted
down from the hillock where he'd been watching the exercise.

"Sergeant Leningen!"

"Sir?"

"Sergeant, I want you to line those ladies up *now*!"

"Yes sir!" the team sergeant shouted back.

Sergeant Leningen gave the command, and the heavily
armed "ladies" fell in. Three hundred yards away, Colonel
Lewis angrily slung his binoculars on the branch of a pine
tree and jogged toward the practice house. He watched
through narrowed eyes as the seven commandos in black
Nomex assault suits, boots, and gloves moved quickly from
the roofless killing house to the open field. Each member of
the senior unit lined up an arm's length from the man on his
right. He stood with his feet shoulder-width and his arms
stiff at his side; none of the men removed his sweltering
black Kevlar helmet or flashproof balaclava and goggles.
Once each man had placed his feet on the grass and drawn
his shoulders back, he didn't move except to breathe. All of
them breathed the same way: from the belly, in order to take
in more oxygen after the exercise.

As he looked at the soldiers, Lewis nursed the anger he

felt over their performance. He was not a man who took pride when his troops did well. There was no point in that; more battles were lost by weakness than were won by strength. His only concern was with the areas where they needed to improve. In this case, they needed a lesson in teamwork. A humiliating lesson that none of them would forget. When Lewis was finished, the team would curse him that night and the next day and the next. But they would survive in the teeth of battle, and that was all that mattered to him.

Ironically, there was a time when lone-wolf cowboys like the seven men in the killing house below would have been welcomed and even encouraged. Maybe back in 1977, when Delta Force was first established as a small surgical strike counterterrorist unit. But things changed after eight RH-53D Sea Stallion helicopters plus special operations aircraft went into Iran in April 1980. The mission was aborted when three helicopters suffered mechanical difficulties and failed to reach the staging area. As the other vehicles attempted to exfiltrate the *Desert 1* landing site, the main rotor of one helicopter slashed through the cockpit of an EC-130 tanker causing both aircraft to explode. In the painful post mortem that spilled from the Carter presidency into the Reagan administration, Delta Force—which faced congressionally mandated extinction after the Middle East debacle—not only survived, but was given more money, more men, more materiel, and more intensive training to make sure that that kind of disaster didn't happen again. The emphasis after that was on every part of the team functioning as a whole.

Scowling, Lewis reached the young men. He stood shorter than most of his commandos, a hair under five-foot-nine. But his cable-thick muscles pushed hard against his camouflage fatigues, and when he stopped moving he looked as though he could withstand the impact of a racing semi. Lewis stood in front of Iglehart, the man standing to the left of Sergeant Leningen. He stayed there for a moment, silent and glaring.

Then he moved.

Lewis dropped his body to half its height and twisted sideways. That presented a low and relatively narrow target. At the same time, he whipped his right hand out and snatched a nine-inch knife from the sheath strapped to the man's left thigh. As he drew his hand back, he moved it in a fluid figure eight, the knife covering him as he stood erect. The colonel only took a small step back, still close enough to see his reflection in the soldier's dirty goggles. The small, dark reflection was one of unchecked fury.

"*Are you an FNG?*" Lewis screamed. "Fucking New Guy" was an epithet that commanders and experienced soldiers applied to green trainees. The men in this unit had been in training for nearly six months and were considered nearly battle-ready.

"No, *sir!*" Iglehart replied, obviously shaken.

"No sir *what*?"

"No, Colonel Lewis, *sir!* I am not an FNG, *sir!*"

"Then why'd you let me take your fucking *knife,* Iglehart?"

"Sir! You're not the enemy, *sir!*"

"You're *wrong,* commando!" Lewis raged. The fire in the colonel's eyes and voice was real, and it served two purposes. It let the commando know that Lewis was serious, and it allowed the officer to build and focus his own energy. Lewis continued, stepping back slowly. "I *am* the enemy, Iglehart, and I'm going to cut your balls off! Did you hear me?"

"Yes *sir!*"

"Delta doesn't hesitate or show mercy!"

"No *sir!*"

"Then why are you still *standing* there, creampuff? Are you going to take me *out*?"

The commando wore a Beretta 9 mm pistol with an extended magazine on his right hip. The ammunition was live. He continued to hesitate.

Disgusted, the colonel stopped roughly ten feet from the commando. "*Shoot* me, dammit!" he yelled. "Shoot me *now*!"

The soldier hesitated a moment longer. Then he drew the Beretta.

The instant the soldier's hand moved, Lewis jumped into a diving forward roll. He came out of the somersault standing directly in front of the commando. As he stood, he drove the knife up toward the commando's throat stopping it chest high. He also drove his knee into the soldier's belly. That not only weakened the commando's grip on the gun, but it bent him over; if Lewis hadn't stopped the knife from rising it would have penetrated the soldier's windpipe. At the same time, the colonel had shot his left forearm up. It caught the soldier's forearm as the gun was being drawn. Lewis swept his forearm out, like a windshield wiper, at the same time sliding his hand toward the soldier's wrist. The colonel's open hand locked tightly around the barrel of the Beretta; the knee to the belly had weakened the commando's grip so that Lewis was able to snatch the gun away with a firm tug. He aimed it at the head of the team sergeant.

The entire maneuver had taken slightly more than one second.

Lewis raised the pin-sharp point of the blade to the man's throat. "If you're going to be a lone wolf, young lady, you'd better be the *best* goddamn lone wolf you can."

"Yes . . . sir!" the commando moaned.

Lewis stepped back and glared down the line. "And if you're going to be a *team,* you also damn well better be the best team you can. There should have been *seven* Berettas turned on me when I attacked this commando, not one. *Do you understand?*"

"Yes, sir!" the men shouted.

Colonel Lewis flipped the knife and gun over so that the hilt and butt were facing out. He handed them back to Iglehart. "I believe these weapons belong to you, miss."

"Yes, sir. Thank you, sir." The commando took them back and put them back where they belonged.

Lewis yelled, "Sergeant Leningen!"

"Sir!"

"These men were not a team today," Lewis said. "They were a pack. A rabble. They were not *thinking*. When Trooper Michaelson opened the front door, he was blocking the A2 of Trooper Peel behind him. When Trooper Masur opened the door to the closet he looked in. *Why?* Trooper Bundonis was already looking in that direction. When Bundonis dropped to shoot the terrorist who was hiding in the closet, Trooper Masur should have turned to protect his back. And no one bothered to check the hostage before moving past her." He stared at Masur. "You were the first one to reach her. Did you check her?"

"No sir!"

"I put a loaded pistol under her ass before the exercise, Masur. If she'd been a terrorist in disguise the team might have taken casualties. That's two fat strikes against you—unacceptable!"

"Yes sir!"

"Sergeant Leningen!"

"Sir!"

"I want these men to take a break. I want them to take a two-day break to train, bunk, and mess with the FNGs. I want them to clean the FNG dinner plates after every mess and the latrines after every shit. And when they come back here, I want them to clear this house like commandos or they will go back to boot camp for reorientation. Am I understood?"

"Yes sir!" the men barked.

Colonel Lewis looked at his watch. "You're lucky ladies. I've got time. Before we leave we're going to make sure we can all do the Sixty. Anyone who can't will be sent home to mommy. Is that *clear*?"

"Yes, sir!"

The Sixty was a series of tests in which a Delta candidate had to score at minimum of sixty points or face dismissal. In succession, the tests—which scored ten points each—were a forty-yard inverted crawl which had to be completed in twenty-five seconds; thirty-seven sit-ups in a minute; thirty-three push-ups in a minute; a two-mile run in sixteen minutes and thirty seconds; a hundred-meter swim through a lake while wearing boots, helmet, and uniform; and a twenty-four second run/dodge/jump course.

Colonel Lewis joined the men for the trial. He knew he could make it through the Sixty; that wasn't the reason for going along. He wanted to give the men a chance to beat him. If they succeeded, that would help them regain some of their confidence. If they lost, they'd attack the two days of training with renewed determination. The Sixty also gave Lewis something to push for. Having called the men on the carpet, he needed to beat them or lose face.

Though Lewis won each drill, Sergeant Leningen threatened to overtake him on all but the swim. It was the best performance the noncom had ever recorded, which didn't surprise the colonel. The attack on the team had been an attack against Leningen's leadership.

Lewis sent the men to the main barracks. Then he went to his quarters to shower. The colonel was glad he'd been there to witness the team's shortcomings. Sending them back to review the basics was always a valuable exercise.

And running the gauntlet had been good for Lewis. He didn't know what kind of test he'd be participating in at Langley. All he'd been told was that it would be a small team and that the project was a "Hiptoss"—HPTS, Highest Priority Top Secret. However, the fact that his orders had come directly from the office of the deputy Secretary of Defense and not from the Department of the Army meant that the enterprise was probably multiservice. He'd have to be at the top of his game.

As he boarded the helicopter a half-hour later, Lewis felt taut and alert. He also felt the way he did whenever his father was transferred to a new base. That there were always things for the boy to learn and also to prove. If he was lucky, Langley would give him the opportunity to do both.

Ten

Monday, 10:54 A.M.
Above Baltimore, Maryland

Master Chief Petty Officer Rodrigo Diaz and Captain Peter Holly sat side by side against the canvas-covered fuselage of the chilly, bucking Lockheed C-141B StarLifter. Diaz was asleep and snoring, and Holly was reading the latest issue of *Air & Space*. Unlike his companion, the air force flier had gotten a good night's sleep, having been off the duty roster for three days following a very intensive two-week period with the new Comanche. Ironically, the Comanche had been flown to Langley for further tests two days before. Holly felt jealous, thinking of someone else trying on his wings.

He missed the flat, black chopper. When he climbed into the deep bucket seat he became an angel, with the chopper as both his wings and his fiery sword. He went as high or low, as fast or slow, as far over land or sea as he wanted. He could rock and roll or waltz. He could rise above the clouds and enjoy sunshine on an overcast day. He could hover beneath the moon and see in the dark and survey pockets of human industry spread across the lord's great earth.

When it was necessary, he could move his finger, and a building or tank or bunker vanished in a swirl of fire and smoke.

By comparison, riding this StarLifter was what his dad used to call *gallumphing* on horseback. Forcing a workhorse to go somewhere when it didn't want to.

Like a workhorse, the StarLifter wasn't built for comfort. Few military aircraft were, from the biggest cargo plane to the smallest, most compact, fighter jet. But riding this particular aircraft was like riding a square-wheeled cart across a cobblestone street. Stripped-down and fuel-efficient, it was designed to carry over 150 troops, along with various heavy weapons, over four thousand miles. Some Star-Lifters—like this one, which had been converted from an even less efficient C-141A—had been configured to carry Minuteman intercontinental ballistic missiles in specially made compartments. Holly had always found it amusing that the missiles got more padding than troops did. But as one of his veteran flight instructors once put it, "*TLC takes more TLC*": the larger the charge, the more tender the loving care it required. If you mishandle a gun, it could misfire and kill someone. If you mishandle a nuclear bomb, you could lose a good-sized city.

But even this bumpy, butt-killer of a ride pleased Holly. He loved flying in anything, anywhere, anytime. He had loved it ever since he was a kid, and the only flying he did was when he read *Enemy Ace* comic books his stepfather brought home from his store. He even wrote to the artist, Joe Kubert, who sent him an original drawing of the Fokker pilot. He had it on his wall for years. Later, he played flight games on the ColecoVision video game system hooked to a nineteen-inch Trinitron back home in Dallas. The comic books had taught him to read, and the games also had served him well: when he joined the air force eleven years earlier, the eighteen-year-old recorded the strongest "kill" score ever in the ten-year-old Link-7 chopper simulator—a 95/.87/100. The cockpit mock-up threw images of targets on a computer-generated windshield. The first number was the percentage of planes correctly identified as friend or foe; the second number was the time it took for the pilot to make the call *and* lock-on with his weapons. The third figure was the percentage of enemy craft he brought down. On those rare occasions when he still went to church, Holly asked God to bless his family, his country, and whichever computer programmer had invented the outer space shoot-'em-up *Zaxxon*.

Apart from himself and Diaz, there weren't many troops in this particular StarLifter, which had come out of Holloman Air Force Base in Alamogordo, New Mexico. The troops were accompanying the dozens of crates, which were also going to Langley. From listening to the airmen before takeoff, he knew that the crates contained the field-tested prototype of the new HAIR: High-Altitude Intruder Raser. A traditional HAIL, or High-Altitude Intruder Laser, sent a laser beam at a target. Once that beam was locked-on, a missile was launched and followed it to the target. A raser was more efficient and far more lethal. Instead of amplified light, it consisted of highly-focused sound waves. It also listened for disturbances instead of watching for them, making the net more fool-proof: instead of moving in a straight line, sound waves moved like ripples in a pond making them easier to intercept and track to a source. Once identified, an enemy aircraft entering restricted air space would not see or hear the HAIR coming. There would be no time to withdraw or perform evasive maneuvers. When the beam locked on, the amplification was turned up, and the aircraft came apart in seconds. The plan, Holly gathered, was to install the HAIR at the White House and then remove the surface-to-air missiles that were buried under the rose garden. The eight radar-guided SAMs were state-of-the-art when they'd been installed. But there were holes in the security net, as the pilot of a Piper Cub proved when he landed his plane on the White House grounds during the Reagan presidency. Once the SAMs were replaced by HAIR, not even a bird would be able to fly through without being seen.

Then there was MCPO Diaz. He had arrived at the base a half-hour before departure, and Holly knew nothing about the man, other than the how-do-you-dos they'd exchanged. Diaz was a member of an elite new Coast Guard unit that specialized in technological security. He apologized for being Diogenes in his tub—whatever *that* meant—but said that after testing new equipment in the South Pacific and criss-crossing the International Date Line for two weeks, then flying from Tonga to Fiji to Hawaii to Southern California, he was so jet-lagged he couldn't even remember the names of his children, let alone dig into a conversation. Before they took off from Holloman, Diaz had fallen asleep with his chin on his chest. Four hours later, he hadn't budged.

Holly put down the copy of *Air & Space,* folded a piece of Wrigley's Spearmint into his mouth, and looked at Diaz.

The MCPO was a smallish, barrel-chested, sun-bronzed man. He was balding on top, graying on the sides, and looked about forty. There was a pale spot on his left hand where a wedding band had been.

Just then, the plane hit a pocket of turbulence, and Diaz awoke with a cry. The SHARC looked ahead for a moment, wide-eyed, then turned to his left where Holly was sitting.

"Wow," Diaz said.

"Y'okay?" Holly drawled. He had to shout to be heard over the four screaming turbofan engines.

"Yeah," Diaz said. "Man, that gets your attention."

"You think that was bad?"

"Actually, yeah."

Holly shook his head.

"It was just a little thermal bounce. Hot air rising, slamming into a pocket of cold air, the two gettin' a little active. Now a lightning strike that kills your electrical power and punches a hole in your wing—*that* gets your attention."

"I'm sure," Diaz said. "I'll stick to the sea, thanks. Even ten-foot swells don't go from zero-to-sixty like that." He looked out the window.

"Checkin' for thunderclouds?" Holly joked.

"No. Any idea where we are?"

Holly glanced past him. "Yeah. We're just passin' over Baltimore. That's Fort McHenry by the water there. Where Francis Scott Key wrote 'The Star Spangled Banner.'"

"You've been this way before."

"Dozens of times. Did a lot of my early training out at Langley."

"Are you heading there now?"

Holly nodded. "You?"

Diaz nodded. "Any idea why?"

"Nope," Holly said. "Now would you tell me something?"

"Sure."

"Who the heck is Diogenes in his tub?"

Diaz smiled. "He's the seaman who wasn't."

"The seaman who wasn't what?"

"A seaman. He was a fourth century B.C. Greek philosopher, the founder of the Cynic school. He taught that a simple life is a virtuous life, and he attempted to make that point by living in a tub. Unfortunately, his fellow Greeks thought he was just plain crazy."

"Uh-huh," Holly said. "I'm not sure I disagree."

"He was definitely an eccentric," Diaz said.

"So is Greek philosophy a hobby of yours?"

"No," Diaz said. "I do a lot of reading when I'm at sea, but not Greek philosophy."

"What, then?"

"The great authors. Dickens. Melville. The stuff that makes you richer but which you'd never read unless you had weeks to do it."

"So how'd you come to know about Diogenes in his tub?"

Diaz smiled. "When I was a young boy I *loved* the ocean. My parents both came from fishing families in Guaymas, Mexico, on the Gulf of California, and I was raised in San Diego. My father operated a tug boat there. I couldn't wait for the weekends so I could go out with him. My mother used to read me anything that had a hint of the sea in it, and for as long as I can remember my favorite nursery rhyme was 'Three Men in a Tub.' You know it?"

"Rub-a-dub-dub?"

"That's the one. When I first heard it I thought it was about people like my father. Tug, tub—it was a natural mistake."

"Uh-huh," Holly drawled. He had a feeling Diogenes wasn't the only one who was a little off.

"I wanted to learn more about floating 'tubs,' so one day at school I asked my sister to read me the entry in the encyclopedia. In the middle of this long essay about cast-iron vessels and double-shell enamel, they had a small piece about Diogenes. I thought he was a sailor just like my father so I took a book from the library about him. Naturally, I was quite disappointed to find out that Diogenes didn't go anywhere in his tub. He just sat in Athens and complained."

"I see," Holly said.

"But I didn't let that discourage me. I still loved the sea. The smells, the tides, the rhythms, the vastness, the winds, the hidden life, and its struggles. It all speaks to me. In fact, the only thing I love more than the ocean are my three sons and the United States of America."

"Hear, hear," Holly said.

"I'm sure the sky holds the same kind of appeal to you."

"Truthfully? The sky itself holds zero appeal to me," Holly admitted.

"Then why—"

"Did I join the Air Force? Because I love big hunks of machinery and the feeling I get when I become part of them. It changes me into something exciting, something better."

"And 'Change begets change. Nothing propagates so fast,' " Diaz said. "That's Dickens, *Martin Chuzzlewit*. When it comes to technology, the military changes faster than the rest of the fast-changing world. It *is* exciting to be riding that wave."

"Yeah," Holly said. This guy was a piece of work.

The plane had begun its descent, and the late morning sun blazed through the cabin. Holly squinted at the glow; he was accustomed to seeing bright light through the dark visor of his helmet.

MCPO Diaz seemed like a good guy, and he was right. The world *was* changing fast. That was also something his father used to say. It was changing too much, too quickly.

As the big plane plip-plopped onto the runway, Holly thought back to a conversation he used to have with his father. It was always the same. Whenever the elder Holly returned from a late-night meeting at his gun club, he would come in and kiss his boy goodnight. Sometimes, Holly was awake and would ask his father how the meeting went.

"It went *fahn*," the oil man would say softly in his heavy drawl.

"Did you shoot?" the boy would ask sleepily.

"No," his father would always reply with a smile. "We talked."

"About what?"

"Oh—about all the things we have to do," he'd say, stroking the boy's head. "Things that we can't let change."

"Like what?"

The elder Holly would never answer. He would kiss his son on the forehead, then tell him to sleep tight and not to worry about a thing.

Holly never did find out what the group couldn't let change. A few years later, when he was ten, he met some of the gun club men at his father's funeral. His mother wouldn't talk to them, but a few of the men came over to offer their condolences anyway. They all shook Holly's hand and bent close to his ear and said that his father was a great man.

To this day, his mother refused to talk about those people or the reasons for her husband's death. She married a department store manager in Fort Worth who was a terrific guy and was very kind to his mother. She was happy, and her son was content to let things be.

The plane taxied very slowly to a stop, and Holly rose. His bones popped as he touched his toes. Then he picked up his magazine, grabbed his duffel bag, and gave Diaz a nudge; the strange little seaman had fallen asleep again.

Change was a good thing, he decided as they made their way around the crates. It kept people challenged and prevented them from becoming complacent. But it could also be frightening, which was why it was portioned out to the public rather than given to them whole.

But that's the public, he thought with a little smile. There *were* hotdogs who could handle it, who craved it.

Holly made a point of thanking the pilots for the lift before exiting the StarLifter. As he and Diaz walked out onto the hot tarmac toward a waiting jeep, Holly wondered what his father would have thought about his own work, about changes in weapons and aircraft and military tactics. Holly wanted to believe they would have pleased rather than disturbed him.

He hoped so, anyway. Because whatever *was* going on down here, he was really looking forward to it.

Eleven

The funeral for Senator Stuart Hoxworth was arranged for Tuesday at noon. Remy had requested that it be held in the small church in Chevy Chase where they worshipped. She felt her husband would have wanted to be memorialized there. She also hoped that it would help to keep the crowds down.

Brigadier General MacDougall had no intention of leaving the Dungeon until then. He had a change of clothes in the closet, and there was a shower down the hall. He had no desire to deal with friends and relatives who were concerned about newspaper reports. He didn't want to talk to the press. And he didn't want to see faxes and e-mail from cranks or distraught constituents of the popular politician. Besides, there was a great deal of work to be done. He needed to find out more about the Huntsmen.

He spent the morning going through on-line newspaper and magazine files, government reports, declassified CIA files from the 1960s—anything that might mention the group. There was nothing.

Shortly after noon, at the request of two young Warren County investigators, MacDougall went to a conference room on the main floor to meet with them. Their questions were thorough, and his answers were straightforward. He told them exactly what had happened from the time Hoxworth picked him up to the time the paramedics arrived.

It was nearly one-thirty when the investigators left. Exhausted from the sleepless night, MacDougall went back to his office and took a nap. When he woke nearly four hours later, he grabbed a sandwich and a Coke in the cafeteria, and then returned to his office. It was the first food he'd had since Hoxworth's death, and he felt uneasy as he bit into the sandwich. The things we took for granted, like the security of the food we buy.

He ate the roast beef slowly as he reviewed the thick files he'd made the night before. It was frustrating. There were fat, tangled knots of information, probably a thousand solid leads, and it would take him weeks to check them out. That was no good.

No, he thought. *The best, most direct key to learning more about the Huntsmen is probably hidden somewhere in the BR Weapons Systems computers.* Though MacDougall didn't have the technical know-how to hack his way in, he could certainly find someone who did. Possibly Dr. Hudson. Commander Evans had said she was a computer genius. A "tech-head," as they called the scientists around here. God, how he didn't belong in this place, in this building, in this city. How had such a promising and rewarding military career come to this?

The lashing of self-pity pissed MacDougall off. His friend was dead. That was the priority. He returned his attention to the matter of BR.

The question he had to answer was what would a computer break-in get him? Obtaining files illegally was useless in court. Having names with no smoking guns would also get him nothing. He needed to draw the Huntsmen out where they could be seen and snared. Maybe if he went directly to Boyd Robinson, Jr., and told him that he knew more than he actually did. That might send a scare through the system—

MacDougall noticed then that he had three pieces of e-mail. They had come in when he was resting. The first was the militia/PAC FBI report he'd requested from Hoxworth's secretary. The second was an update from Commander Evans at Langley.

There was also a message from Moses Cole. MacDougall felt a chill as he opened and read it.

General—

Urgent that we meet. Will be tied up most of Monday. Can you be at my home at seven p.m.? Will check my e-mail before I leave for the day.

Moses

MacDougall looked at the computer clock. There was just enough time to get out to Alexandria, Virginia, where Cole and his family lived in a home on the Potomac. MacDougall e-mailed Moses that he'd be there. Then, he finished his sandwich, took his can of Coke, and headed for the elevator.

Twelve

When he reached Union Station in Washington, Major Hank Taylor was met by a young air force lieutenant. The skinny officer collected him and then waited for another passenger, Dr. Victoria Hudson, who was shuttling in from New York. When she arrived, they choppered south to Langley.

Taylor sat in the backseat with the tall, handsome brunette and introduced himself. The woman was not in uniform, and he asked what her association was with the military. She said she was a consultant but offered nothing more. Though she seemed pleasant enough, she also seemed preoccupied. Taylor didn't press her. The woman also seemed a little skittish to be airborne. He'd been in so many choppers over the years he forgot how unsettling they could be.

They were met on the savagely hot field by Sergeant Rick Boots. The noncommissioned officer saluted Captain Taylor and opened the door of the jeep for Dr. Hudson. Then he helped her with her one suitcase. Taylor hated the heat, but he liked the man's manners.

As they settled thigh to thigh in the back of the cramped vehicle, Taylor looked at the woman sideways from behind his sunglasses. He still had Heather on the brain and was enjoying being close to this lady. Her long hair falling over her light brown jacket, the hint of rouge on her high cheekbone, the mist of her perfume—it was nice.

He looked away as they started out. The wind blew hot and humid as the driver shifted into gear. As they drove, their host gave them a short history of the base.

"Langley is the home of the 1st Fighter Wing," he said. The wind was drumming past, and he had to turn his head partway around to be heard. "The base is named after Samuel Pierpont Langley, an astrophysicist who began studying heavier-than-air flight in 1886. He was the first man to field-test principles he dubbed 'aerodynamics.' In 1917, eleven years after his death, the Aviation Experimental Station and Proving Ground here in Hampton was renamed Langley Field in his honor. Today, Langley Air Force Base covers three thousand acres and is home to twelve thousand service personnel and their families."

This was probably the speech Sergeant Boots gave to everyone who came here, but that was okay with Taylor. Langley was one of those names you heard from time to time without knowing who he was, so he enjoyed it. And he didn't really expect Boots to tell him why they were here—if he even knew.

To Taylor's surprise, they reached the end of the tarmac and turned toward another landing strip. This one led away from the administration area.

"Sergeant Boots?" Taylor asked.

"Yes, sir?"

"Where are we going?"

"Up ahead!" he yelled over his shoulder. "There's a small network of old bomb shelters built in the early 1950s. The entrance in Morgan hangar has been sealed off and a new entrance was constructed out here."

"Why?"

"I honestly couldn't tell you," Boots replied. "Captain McIver's been running this place for about three years now. She's the only one knows what goes on there."

"Have you taken other people out today?"

"Four others, sir," Sergeant Boots replied. "All military except for Dr. Hudson."

Taylor thanked him and sat back. This had the earmarks of what the military called a studio op. They got the idea from a motion picture studio in the 1930s. In order to create a secure environment for his operations, a mobster bought a motion picture studio. Not only was the lot already guarded, but the props and cans of films coming and going were a perfect cover to ship drugs, money, and personnel. The staff was usually oblivious, and the law was reluctant to go in; the studios kept the local economy healthy. The government liked that idea and began using military bases as a site for nonmilitary, multiservice, or occasionally private sector hi-tech activities.

The ride ended five minutes later at the edge of a scrubless field. The sergeant left the jeep running and got out. He placed Dr. Hudson's suitcase beside the jeep and helped her out. Taylor climbed from the jeep. He carried his own grip.

"It's been a pleasure, sir," Sergeant Boots said, saluting the marine.

Taylor returned the salute. He looked around. "You're saying this is it? This is where we're supposed to be?"

"Yes, sir," the noncom smiled. "Captain McIver will be along in just a moment."

The sergeant shook Dr. Hudson's hand, hopped back into the jeep, and drove away.

Dr. Hudson looked back toward the base. So did Taylor. The buildings rippled in the heat rising from the tarmac.

"This is a little too *North by Northwest* for me," the woman said. "You ever see anything like it?"

"No," Taylor admitted. He pulled a handkerchief from his pants pocket and dabbed sweat from his forehead and upper lip. Perspiration trickled down the middle of his back.

Just then, dirt crunched behind them. They turned together and looked into the field.

A woman was coming toward them. She was about fifteen feet away and walking with a swagger that was all in the shoulders. She had short, dirty-blond hair and wore wire-rimmed glasses and a smirk. When she was just a few paces away, Taylor could smell the cigarette smoke that clung to her camouflage fatigues.

"Captain Taylor, Dr. Hudson," she said in a smoker's husky voice. "I'm Robin McIver, DARPA liaison with base commander General Brad Jackson. Welcome to Langley."

"Thanks," Taylor said.

McIver extended her hand, firmly shaking Taylor's hand first and then Dr. Hudson's. McIver's blue eyes held Hudson's for a moment before she turned back toward the field.

"Follow me, lady and gentleman," McIver said.

Taylor grabbed Dr. Hudson's suitcase, and they started after the woman.

"You'll find it's hotter than hell down here this time of year and nowhere near as lively," McIver said. "Fortunately, it's going to be a busy couple of days so you'll be spared the excitement of playing computer solitaire or watching *Red Dawn* or *Roadhouse*. I think the air force got in on some kind of Patrick Swayze closeout."

"I understand that several other group members have already arrived," Taylor said.

"All the others are here, waiting patiently in our small, air-conditioned fallout homes."

Taylor didn't bother asking why they'd been brought here. If she'd wanted to tell him, she would have.

They continued in silence for more than five hundred yards. The sun was relentless, the wind was hot, and Taylor would have killed for a ginger ale. Suddenly, they stopped beside a metal disc that was slightly larger than a manhole and set just below ground level. It was already covered with wind-blown dirt. Captain McIver pulled a small remote-control-sized unit from a loop on her belt. She held it in front of her and entered a code on the keypad. A moment later, there was a low hum beneath the disc, and one end began to rise.

Dr. Hudson was standing next to Taylor. She leaned toward him. "I take that back. This isn't *North by Northwest*. It's *Dr. No*."

A secret entrance to an underground facility on this isolated field—it *was* almost surreal. Taylor took a step toward the lid. Cool air blew from deep inside, and the officer smiled as it washed over him. The lid itself was about five inches thick and appeared to be constructed of rubber. That made sense. Rubber would muffle sounds from within and take the extremes of heat and cold without much expansion or contraction. As it rose higher, Taylor could see beneath it a concrete staircase that slopped steeply into the darkness.

The lid locked soundly in an upright position, and McIver motioned for Taylor to go down. He did, followed by Dr. Hudson. There was a keypad on the bottom of the lid; as soon as McIver was on the staircase, she used it to shut the door. When the lid began to close, she threw a switch on the wall of the tunnel. A light came on below them.

At the bottom of the stairs were a few feet of a very narrow concrete corridor leading away from the steps. It ended in a door that resembled the entrance to a walk-in freezer except there was no handle. McIver shouldered around them and input a code on her remote. The door clicked; she pushed it open and entered. Taylor and Dr. Hudson followed her in.

Taylor had been expecting some kind of hi-tech haven behind the closed door. That wasn't what he got.

The room was, as advertised, a small, traditional bomb shelter. It had bare concrete walls, a single naked light bulb, whose glow fell short of the room's four corners, and two functional pieces of furniture: a rickety-looking prison-style cot and a gunmetal desk with a microwave and several bottles of water in the middle. A pair of folded bridge tables and a stack of chairs were against the wall beside the desk. There was no phone. An air-conditioning vent hummed in the ceiling, and a plain wooden door was fixed in the opposite wall. There were also three other people in the room, all in uniform. A coast guard MCPO was lying on a cot to the right, an army colonel was leaning against the wall to the left of the interior door, and an air force captain was perched on the end of the desk to the left. All three men stood quickly, as though they'd been expecting someone else.

McIver introduced them around. Taylor treated himself to a bottle of water.

"Are we all here now, Captain?" a hard-looking man asked McIver.

"We are all here, Colonel Lewis," McIver said. She closed the outside door behind her and walked toward the wooden door.

"Then someone's going to tell us why we're here?"

"Soon," she replied.

"Excuse me, Captain McIver," Dr. Hudson said.

McIver stopped and looked at the scientist.

"I'm supposed to be meeting Commander Evans. Is he here?"

"He's here." She looked at the rest of the group. "If you'll just relax, the commander will be with you shortly." She looked back at Dr. Hudson, smiled tightly, looked down, then opened the inner door and left.

The men relaxed again.

"Well that was more of nothing," Diaz said, lying back down on the cot.

Lewis began pacing. "This is getting on my goddamn nerves."

Taylor walked to the wooden door. He turned the knob. It was locked.

"Been there, done that," Lewis complained. "The outside door is locked, too. They don't want us going anywhere."

"I've been thinking," Diaz said. "Maybe this is part of a test."

"What do you mean?" Holly asked.

"Some of us have been here for hours. Maybe that's the point. Maybe nothing's going to happen. Maybe this is a Psy-Ops study."

"You mean we all just sit here while they watch us and see how we interact in isolation," Lewis said.

"Yeah." Diaz looked around. "I'll bet there's a hidden camera somewhere." The MCPO got up and began wandering around the room, studying the walls.

Lewis's eyes shifted to Dr. Hudson. "Ma'am?"

"Yes, Colonel?"

"I don't like having zero intel. I hate to put you on the spot, but you seem to know just a tad more than the rest of us."

"I'm sorry, I don't—"

"But you do. Would you mind telling us who Commander Evans is?"

She smiled, slightly embarrassed. "You're right. I do know that. My apologies. Amos Evans is the head of a division within the Pentagon's Advance Research Projects Agency."

Lewis was still looking at Dr. Hudson. "Might I ask another question ma'am?"

"Sure. As long as you call me Victoria."

"What kind of doctor are you, Victoria?"

"A micromolecular electronic engineer," she said.

"Which means?"

"When I'm not teaching, I try to figure out how to move molecules along microscopic grooves. If we can do that fast enough, and inexpensively enough, molecular chips will replace the current generation of silicon chips in computers."

"I'll take your word for that," Lewis said. His eyes snapped to Taylor. "Major, do you have any specialties?"

"Apart from medicine?" He shrugged. "Martial arts."

"You hold an advanced belt?"

"Second-degree black belt," he said.

Lewis nodded. "So everyone here is at the top of the class in something. My specialty is tactical land strikes. Diaz's expertise is in fleet tactics and oceanic electronic surveillance. Holly flies some of our most advanced aircraft."

"I still don't see what that tells us," Holly said. "Throw five folks together, and each of them's bound to be good at something."

"That's true," said a deep voice from beside the desk, near the outer door. "Only in this case it happens to be relevant."

Everyone looked over. No one spoke. Taylor squinted into the darkness. He saw no one.

"Oh my god!" Victoria said suddenly. "Oh my god, my god—!"

"What?" Taylor said.

Diaz began walking slowly toward the corner, looking up and then down for a concealed speaker.

"Mr. Diaz, *stop*!" Victoria said.

"What?"

"Just stay where you are." She looked past him, toward the shadows. "My god, Commander. You're here, aren't you? That's what you've done with the digital data globules."

Lewis walked toward her. "Victoria, who's done *what*?"

There was a sound like someone exhaling. It was loud and filled the room, but only for a moment. An instant later, a man materialized in the dark corner. He appeared quickly, materializing from the breastbone to the arms, as though a curtain had been drawn swiftly to either side. He stood just over six feet tall and was dressed from head to toe in what resembled a blue wet suit. There were large, solid blue eye-pieces that ran from the bridge of the nose nearly to the ear. He wore a compact blue equipment vest on his chest, tight blue gloves and boots, and a holster on his right hip. The flap of the holster looked as thought it had been vacuformed around the gun and covered it completely.

The man took a few steps toward the center of the bomb shelter. As he walked stiffly toward the group, he undid what sounded like a Velcro strip along his forehead. He carefully lowered a thick faceplate, which resembled nothing so much as a formfitting mousepad. The mask was also attached at the chin, and he let it hang there as he stopped in front of the group. Sweat glistened on his cheeks and forehead, and his skin was flushed.

"To answer your question, Colonel Lewis," said Commander Amos Evans, "what we've done is to perfect proto-types of the SFU—the Stealth Field Uniform. Suits which render a soldier virtually invisible to the eye and to all forms of thermal detection."

"This isn't possible," Lewis said.

"Oh yes it is." Victoria stepped forward. She was wearing the biggest smile Taylor had ever seen. "Congratulations, Commander. I'd shake your hand, but I don't want to leave oil deposits."

"Thanks," Evans said. He allowed himself a small, boyish grin. Then he looked back at the others, the smile fading. "To answer your other questions, about why you're all here, over the next few days it will be up to you to see how the SFUs hold up during simulated combat conditions."

"But this is *amazing*," said Lewis, his expression no longer dour. "Commander, how long have you been in this room?"

"Only a few minutes," he said. "I came in when Captain McIver left, through the same door."

"You walked right past all of us?" Lewis said.

"That's right. On a straight diagonal line through the center of the room. I thought this would be the best way to show you why we're all here. A little theatrical, I'll admit—"

"But effective. Damned effective," Lewis said. "Jesus, you were *invisible*, sir."

"Not entirely invisible," Evans said. "The mouth has some porous spots so you can breathe, but we'll get into that during the field tests. Right now I'd like you all to take some time to settle in."

"Settle in?" Lewis said. "I don't know about anyone else, but I've got about a zillion questions."

"Ditto," said Holly.

"At least this explains all the secrecy," Diaz said. "These uniforms will change everything. The way the military is manned and structured, the way wars are fought, the way intelligence is gathered."

" 'Change begets change,' " Holly muttered with a grin.

"We're still a long way off from remaking the armed forces or even fielding this gear," Evans said. "Throughout the development process, we've been very much aware that if this technology ever found its way into enemy hands no secret would be safe, no building or room inaccessible. That will make widespread deployment extremely risky. It's also the reason no one outside my immediate team at the Pentagon knew about the suits."

Diaz nodded.

"I don't even want to *think* about what each of those babies must've cost," Holly said.

"In terms of dollars, they're roughly two hundred million dollars each. In terms of our private lives—well, most of us who have been involved with this Next Generation undertaking have put our lives on hold for the past four years. But with God's help, the end result will be worth it."

Unlike the others, Taylor wasn't entirely focused on the conversation. Like Colonel Lewis, he was still trying to process what he'd just seen. The achievement was humbling, and the implications *were* staggering. The emotions were equally extreme. He was proud of his country, and he was eager to be a part of this, but he was also scared.

Invisible soldiers. Dr. Hudson was wrong. This wasn't *Dr. No.* It was *The Twilight Zone*—a daring, disorienting leap into the future.

Commander Evans reached into a vest pocket and withdrew a remote-control device like the one Captain McIver had used. He input a code, and the inner door opened. As the small team gathered up their belongings and followed him into the hallway beyond, there was only one thing Taylor knew with certainty. That his mother was going to be extremely disappointed. She'd be expecting a photograph from the base her son had visited, the place that had taken him away from her. Unfortunately, he'd never be able to explain to her that what looked like a landscape photograph of an open field was her son making history. . . .

Thirteen

General MacDougall never believed that there was a "rea-
son" things happened or that good inevitably came from disaster. That was the province of chronic optimists like his late
wife and Commander Evans. The general didn't know much
about Evans's faith; only that it was unshakable and he
didn't share it. He had experienced too much suffering and
witnessed too much treachery to believe in anything but
himself.

MacDougall drove slowly along Princess Street toward
the river. Cole's home was at the corner of Princess and
Union Street, and he pulled his Cutlass to the curb just after
the turn. He shut the engine and sat for a moment.

Despite MacDougall's pessimism, the e-mail from Moses
Cole had raised his spirits at the end of a miserable few
days. If Cole had returned to the fold, if he'd rediscovered
the mettle he once possessed, then some good *would* have
come from this tragedy. MacDougall opened the car door

and got out. He wished he'd had time to change. Coming here in uniform made this seem formal.

He locked the car and walked along the lawn to the front door. The smell drifting over from the roses in Lydia Cole's garden was rich and soothing. He used the knocker and waited. Cole came to the door. He had a dishcloth slung over his shoulder and a dark frown on his face.

"Hi," he said. "Come in."

MacDougall entered. He took off his hat. The house smelled of pizza. There was a beer on the living room coffee table and a game show on TV. "Bacheloring it tonight?"

"Yeah," Cole said. He shut the door. "Lydia took the kids to the movies. I'm just finishing up in the kitchen. Want anything?"

"No thanks."

"Then c'mon. Keep me company. Let's talk."

MacDougall followed him through the living room into the dining room. They turned right, into the kitchen.

MacDougall stopped as he entered. A short, swarthy man in a denim jacket was standing beside the refrigerator just three feet away. he held a .38 caliber revolver in his gloved hand. The gun was raised and extended arm's length.

Cole kept walking. He turned left, toward the sink. Then he leaned on the edge of the stainless steel basin. He didn't turn around. His head drooped slowly.

MacDougall experienced a moment of awesome sadness as he looked at the back of his former company medic. Then, crashing through the pain was the sickening realization that Cole had gone to the sink for a reason. He hadn't only betrayed him, he'd helped set the murder up so that MacDougall would turn in that direction. So the lie could be compounded. But before he could look back at the killer, Robert Charles MacDougall felt a punch in the right temple. He was dead before the sound of the gun reached him.

The assassin stepped over to the corpse and removed the casing. He placed a blank in the barrel and fired it right beside MacDougall's head. There were now powder burns on the flesh around the wound. Still wearing his gloves, the killer took out the blank, placed the original casing back in the gun, and lay the weapon in MacDougall's right hand. Earlier in the day, when the neighbors weren't home and no one could hear, he had fired a bullet into the soffit. When investigators arrived, they'd believe what Cole told them: that MacDougall had been distraught, and the gun had accidentally discharged once before he took his life.

Without saying a word, the killer hurried into the dining room and opened the sliding glass door.

"Wait!" Cole shouted after him.

The man looked back.

"My girls—"

"The water glasses on their nightstands are filled with hydrochloric acid," Cactus said dispassionately. "Empty them carefully. And remember—I can come back." He stepped outside and disappeared in the darkness.

Cole raced upstairs and saw the glasses his daughters drank from every night. He carefully carried them to the cellar and set them on the floor. He'd deal with them later. Returning to the kitchen, he turned toward the phone which hung just inside the doorway. Emotionally overwrought, he leaned against the wall, his arms shaking, tears spilling down his cheek. He glanced down at the body of his former commanding officer.

General MacDougall's legs were splayed wide, and his left arm was twisted underneath him. The large, raw wound was facing up. Blood ran down the bridge of his nose and eyelids and collected in a widening pool under his face.

Moses Cole shook his head slowly. "Damn them and damn *you*, General!" he sobbed.

Cole didn't even know who the killer was or who he might be working for. The man had come to his office late in the afternoon. He said that he'd been in Cole's home and showed him a photograph he'd removed from the family photo album. He told Cole that if he didn't cooperate his daughters would die—and there was nothing he could do to prevent it. Cole was forced to e-mail General MacDougall; if that message were ever found, Cole was to tell investigators that he had requested the meeting to urge MacDougall to give himself up.

Cole shook his head bitterly. "I tried to warn you, General. Didn't I tell you not to make me choose? But god-fucking-*damn* you. You had to do what was right, not what was smart."

Still blinking out tears, Cole sighed deeply before turning back to the telephone and calling the police.

Fourteen

After removing the SFU, changing back into his uniform, and e-mailing General MacDougall to let him know that everyone had arrived and been "suitably impressed," Evans showed the team to their quarters. These were located in the first two shelters on either side of a long corridor beyond the first shelter, which Evans called the rec room. Each shelter was slightly lower than the central corridor and accessed by a short staircase. They all had plain, white, wooden doors, and dark green industrial carpet. For Lewis, the rooms were a frightening reminder of a time when high-ranking officers felt they might need a radiation-proof command center from which to conduct nuclear war.

The next-to-last pair of shelters were a bathroom and shower facility on the left and a science room on the right. The walls of the science room were lined with equipment for monitoring the SFUs. The last room on the left had been equipped with heating and cooling systems to test the performances of new systems in temperature extremes. The last room on the right was a storeroom with a door, bolted top and bottom in the center. This used to be the access room from the base. In addition to food, medical supplies, videotapes, and other necessities, there were five large, stainless steel chests standing side by side in the middle of the room. Evans told the team that each of the chests contained one SFU.

"You're serious, sir," Holly said with a big, radiant smile. "We're really going to get to try those out."

"That's why we're here," Evans said.

Holly let out a small but enthusiastic "Woo-*hoo*!"

"We expect that because of your diverse backgrounds, each of you will discover different strengths and weaknesses in the SFUs," Evans said. "The way you move, the fine motor skills you need, the senses you rely on most, how the suit affects your balance in the air or on the water or in inclement environments—these are things we need to know in order to evaluate how the uniforms might perform in a combat or infiltration situation."

"That means we'll be moving out of the shelters at some point," Lewis said.

"Right away, in fact," Evans said. "We're going to start outside, move through basic daylight and nighttime maneuvers to break the suits in. There's rain due midweek, so we'll get to see whether the waterproofing works the way we planned."

"It'd be hell if the suits leaked," Taylor said. "You'd drown before anyone could see where you were."

Evans informed the team that Taylor would be rooming with Holly and Diaz with Lewis. Evans had his own room, which he shared with the communications equipment, while Dr. Hudson would be bunking with Captain McIver. The team members were given time to settle in and were told to meet back in the rec room at 2030 for dinner and a review of the data and schedules they'd find in folders in their rooms.

Colonel Lewis was still awestruck as he sat on his cot and unpacked his duffel bag. There were two cots with foot-lockers on either side of the door and a nightstand at the head of each cot. A manila folder marked *Eyes Only* sat on each of the nightstands.

"I gotta tell ya," Lewis said. "I used to read a lot of military history books when I was a kid. I loved armor the most. English, Spanish, German, Japanese—all of it. I used to design my own. Crossbowproof. Fireproof. Boiling-oilproof. Armored diving suits. But I never thought, never *imagined* anything like this would ever be possible. Invisible soldiers."

"Not quite invisible," Diaz said. He had picked up the folder on his nightstand and was studying it.

"What do you mean?"

"They've given us a kind of Stealth Suits for Dummies overview here," he said. "I guess it's supposed to be a rough field manual on the care and repair of an SFU. It says, 'Each suit is made up of twenty-six separate panels. The fabric in each panel is woven of light-reflective material synthesized from proteins contained in silk from the ampullate gland of araneid spiders. These panels are comprised of three layers, which makes the suit three times as thick as conventional cotton garments.'"

"That faceplate did look kind of thick and hot," Lewis said.

"Yeah." Diaz continued reading aloud. " 'The topmost of the three layers is a loose weave. The silk's reflective properties at this layer act as receptors, which I'll explain in a minute. The remaining two layers are implanted with bio-engineered chromatophores, color cells that are based on the chemical processes of the sargassum, a fish with sophisticated color-adaptive characteristics. These cells change color and are what give the suit its chameleonlike capacities.'"

"You left me back at the spider glands," Lewis said.

"Wait, this is fascinating—about Dr. Hudson's contribution. 'The digital data globules are liquid microprocessors that relay the color information from one panel to another. They flow *through* the threads that hold the panels together. These transparent stitching fibers are hollowed to 1/30th of an inch and are undetectable to an observer further than eleven inches away.' Brilliant."

Diaz continued to read—about the audio dampers, which kept incoming messages from being heard by anyone outside the suit, and subvocal receptors, which picked up the softest whisper. For the most part, however, Lewis had no idea what the MCPO was talking about and tuned him out. He began placing his things in the footlocker and thinking about what they'd been brought here to do. There weren't a lot of things that choked Lewis up, but being selected to test something this significant was one of them.

"This is amazing," Diaz said. "Just amazing. The environment around the soldier is recorded by the outermost layer of the suit. That data is relayed by the hollow fibers to the second and third layers of fabric on the *opposite* side of the suit. The color cells in those layers change and replicate the appropriate colors and textures."

"So the technology re-creates on the front of the suit whatever is behind the soldier," Lewis said.

"And vice versa," Diaz said. He continued reading. "'This function is called SLD—*strategic light dispersion.* Without it, an observer looking directly at an operative wearing the uniform would still see the soldier in the solid-colored uniform. This technology enables the SFU to continually change its color and texture based on the operative's environment. The delay in this color and texture alteration is 0.3 seconds. Standing still, the wearer is completely invisible from every angle and perspective, even in bright daylight. Walking slowly, the wearer is virtually invisible in a twilight or darkened room situation. The uniform also contains dampers, which keep down the sound of the wearer's respiration and heartbeat and weighted pads in the fingertips for increased sensitivity when handling objects.' "

Diaz put the folder down and began unpacking his grip.

"Man, when you think of the government you think of this big, leaky, do-nothing machine. Then they pull off something like this, and you're just blown away. I've been involved with high-end technology all of my adult life, and I never would have *dreamed* of something like this. And this is just the first generation suit. Imagine where it—where *we*—will be in twenty or thirty years."

Lewis couldn't imagine that. He was still having trouble processing the right here and now.

The group reassembled shortly before 2030. Captain McIver informed them that Commander Evans had to check e-mail from Washington. He had no idea how long he'd be on and told her to begin dinner without him. They walked back to the supply room—Evans's door was shut, and it seemed very quiet beyond—and selected sandwiches and bottles of water or soda from the shelves. There were trays of ice in a small freezer.

Back in the rec room, the team opened the bridge tables and chairs, set them side by side, and gathered round. Conversation consisted of the traditional MiS-SAT: Mixed Services show-and-tell. Captain McIver had to be coaxed to talk about her career. When she finally opened up, she struck Lewis as a real fire-eater. Born in Fort Lauderdale, Florida, the forty-three-year-old described herself as "unrepentently non-PC." She was honored to be the granddaughter of a whale boat captain and said she proudly displayed one of his harpoons in her office in the logistics department. She rolled her own cigarettes, even if she couldn't smoke them where she liked, had served two tours of duty in Vietnam, and she'd nearly gotten court-martialed for beating up a male protester outside a Selective Service office in Washington, D.C.

It was Taylor who asked about Commander Evans. Captain McIver told what she knew about his record with the SEALs—which included his retirement, though she didn't know the reasons for it. Dr. Hudson contributed the fact that it was Rear Admiral Chris Sheehy who recommended Evans to General Orlando Vargas, the first director of the Pentagon's Advance Research Projects Agency.

"He seems like a straight shooter," Holly said.

"He is," McIver agreed, "though he can be a little taciturn."

"There's nothing wrong with a man who listens more than he talks," Victoria said.

Holly was about to say something, but Diaz held up his hand. It took the flier a second, but then he smiled and went back to his sandwich. Taylor and Lewis both grinned and kept eating.

McIver smirked. "Cute. Real cute."

Victoria Hudson got it a second later. She flushed brightly at the neck and cheeks. Save for the sounds of chewing, the table was silent. Victoria looked down and did not look up.

A moment later, the door behind them opened and Commander Evans stepped into the room. He looked drawn as he shut the door behind him.

"It's my sad duty to report that the head of our group, Brigadier General Robert MacDougall, died earlier this evening."

Captain McIver rose slowly. "Commander, I'm sorry. What happened?"

"According to the e-mail Deputy Under Secretary of Defense Holmes sent to my office at the Pentagon, the general died of a self-inflicted gunshot wound to the head about an hour ago."

Holly started. Sitting across from him, only Diaz seemed to notice.

Evans looked around the table. "Captain McIver, Dr. Hudson, I'd like to see you in my quarters. The rest of you will study the SFU manuals and then turn in. Wakeup will be at 0500 hours."

The men acknowledged the order, after which Evans turned and left the room. Dr. Hudson and Captain McIver followed. The men who remained in the rec room looked at each other in silence—except for Holly. He was looking down.

"Captain, you okay?" Diaz asked him.

Holly nodded.

"You sure?"

"Yeah. It's nothing, thanks. I'll be fine."

"This whole thing is weird," Taylor said as he took a last bite of tuna fish sandwich. "First, Senator Hoxworth and now General MacDougall."

"What happened to Hoxworth?" Diaz asked.

"He's dead," Taylor said.

"How? I've been out of touch—"

"It happened Saturday night. General MacDougall was camping with Hoxworth. The senator was poisoned."

"Accidentally?"

"The paper said it was under investigation."

"The report I read said that General MacDougall hadn't been ruled out as a suspect," Lewis said.

"Man," Diaz said. "I can't believe it."

"I couldn't believe they were camping together," Taylor remarked. "The way they went at each other on TV, you'd've thought the two of them couldn't stand each other."

"According to the newspaper report I read, they served together in Vietnam," Lewis said.

" 'Brothers from Saigon to eternity,' " Diaz said. "That's what Vice Admiral Coldwater once called Vietnam vets in a speech at the Coast Guard Academy."

"It's true," Lewis said. "But you're right about this being weird, Major. I've known hundreds of military men in my career, and only two of them ever offed themselves. One of them was a recruit who came from a military family and was ashamed because he couldn't hack boot camp. The other was an officer who got caught with a thirteen-year-old girl. We do not have a high suicide rate, and when it happens, it's almost always over some point of honor."

"I wonder if that means the general *was* responsible and didn't expect to be caught," Diaz said.

"Mr. Diaz, have you ever heard of a soldier who tried to poison another one?" Lewis asked.

"No—"

"I haven't either. I've heard of guys who tried to stab, beat up, shoot at, run over with a car, blow up, push out a window, drown, set on fire, and strangle other guys. Fighting men have done some angry, drunk, passionate *fighting* things. But never that. Premeditated gutless murder is not a military thing."

Holly rose suddenly. "Gentlemen, I'm afraid there isn't much I can contribute to this conversation. I'm also tired. So I'm going to do what the commander suggested—read my file and go to bed."

"That's probably a good idea," Taylor said. "We're going to have some long, hot days ahead."

The others agreed. After clearing off the tables and putting them away, the men went to their rooms and read through the folders.

Captain Holly did one thing more when he was finished. He prayed. For a man he did not know and for one he had. One who had died the same way as General MacDougall. One he still missed very, very much.

His father.

Fifteen

Commander Evans was tense and silent as he shut the door. Victoria and Captain McIver remained standing as he walked to the computer. The unit sat on a metal desk next to a fax machine, telephone, and radio console for point-to-point communication. A second computer sat on a stand beside the desk. It was hooked to a satellite uplink at the base communications center. There were also a cot, footlocker, and custom-made metal locker in the shelter. The locker door was open, and inside the deep, wide cabinet was the SFU Evans had worn earlier. The suit looked oddly intimidating on its oversized hanger—stiff and full, almost as though someone were still inside. Even the headpiece stood up by itself.

Evans established a link to General MacDougall's computer. Then he looked up at Victoria and McIver. There was rage in his dark eyes though he kept it in check.

"The day before I came out to Langley, the general called me into his office and told me about a militant group he'd been investigating," Evans said. "The Huntsmen. Ever hear of them, Captain?"

McIver said she hadn't.

"Neither had I," Evans said. "But he believed they were responsible for acts of terrorism and murder dating back to World War I and escalating over the past thirty-plus years. He believed they might have been responsible for the death of Stuart Hoxworth. The general also believed that the medical examiner who performed the autopsy on Senator Hoxworth may have been intimidated by them. General MacDougall died at the home of that medical examiner."

"Do you know anything about that man?" McIver asked.

"The medical examiner?" Evans shook his head. He pointed to a diskette on his desk. "But everything the general found out about the group is on that diskette. He gave it to me because he was worried that something might happen to his computer files."

"Or him," McIver said.

"Or him," Evans agreed. He glared at the screen. "I didn't want to believe in a conspiracy of assassination. I thought maybe the general was distressed or tired. But the problem is, he wasn't suicidal. I've known men on the brink. I've known men who were depressed and suffering from post-traumatic stress disorder. The general had none of the symptoms—none of the emotional numbness, flashbacks, violent outbursts, sensitivity to sudden noises. He seemed relatively calm and determined to find out more about these Huntsmen."

"Obviously, they were equally determined to stop him," McIver said.

"Obviously," Evans agreed, "only they're not going to get away with it."

"How will you stop them?"

"I'm not sure," Evans admitted. "But I'll find a way."

"And how *far* will you go to stop them?"

"I hope I can do it legally."

"And if you can't?"

"I said they're not going to get away with this. Let's leave it at that. Right now, all that concerns me is finding out who these people are and proving that they're responsible for killing Senator Hoxworth and General MacDougall. I have no idea what will happen after that. But since I can't order either of you to assist me, what I need to know is—"

"I'm in," McIver said. "Absolutely, I'm in."

Evans looked at Victoria. She nodded without hesitation.

He turned back to the computer. "Thank you both. General MacDougall accessed a number of databases to get information about the group and their activities as well as possible connections to the military-industrial arena. The most sensitive material is on the diskette. The links to the databases are on his hard drive. I want to retrieve and download those files. And I want to do one more thing." He input http://www.dtic.mil/defenselink/locator/ to access the military mega-homepage. Established in 1994, the website is operated by the Defense Technical Information Center and contains links to other armed services and intelligence groups. "When I was still in the field," Evans continued, "I heard about a new series of satellites in development. They were code-named HOMEs—Hemispheric Overflight Multi-image Eyes. Reportedly, they were going to be managed by the National Reconnaissance Office on behalf of the FBI and the domestic counterintelligence division of the CIA. The purpose of the HOMEs series was to photograph vehicular and air traffic coming and going from major American cities. Those images would be downloaded and stored at the NRO."

"We wanted to spy on ourselves?" Victoria asked.

Evans nodded. "The project was given the go-ahead after

the World Trade Center bombing in 1993. It gave us the ability to backtrack from likely sites of terrorist activity, read license plate numbers, see who came and went."

Victoria wasn't entirely comfortable with that concept—there were privacy issues involved—but they were beside the point at the moment. "What exactly are you looking for?"

"I want to find out if you can enter the HOMEs photo file, see who might have gone to the Hoxworth house before the camping trip or been at the home of the medical examiner when the general was killed," Evans said.

"Sir, why don't we just requisition the data from the CIA's office of Science and Technology?" McIver asked.

"Because we don't know which departments may have been compromised by the Huntsmen. That was one of General MacDougall's biggest concerns."

"So we don't want to let them know we're coming," Victoria said.

"Right. We can't risk going in through the CIA website, because those hits are routinely monitored. This site isn't."

"Then let's see if we can backdoor our way into the HOMEs file," Victoria said.

Evans rose. The scientist took his seat.

"This could take a while," she added.

"That's all right," Evans said. "Will it bother you if I wait?"

"No," she said, though that wasn't entirely true. There was something about Commander Evans that had always distracted her. His quiet, loner nature. His charisma. She'd wondered if he'd noticed that she was no longer wearing her wedding band.

McIver shifted from foot to foot then looked at her watch. "I'm going to check in with Lieutenant Rhodes, see how things went today in logistics. I'll be in my quarters if you need me."

Evans thanked her. She shut the door as she left. The commander walked to the back of the small shelter.

"Were you very close to the general?" Victoria asked as she ran a diagnostic to make sure the computer had the power and accessories she needed.

"I barely got to know him."

"Did he have a family?"

"No. His daughter was killed in an accident, and his wife died not long after." Evans sighed and shook his head slowly. "General MacDougall was only with us for three months, and I was wrapped up in N-Gen the entire time. Our conversation just before I came here was the longest one we ever had. I really felt good about him. I think I would have liked the man."

Victoria surveyed the specs as they filled the screen. The computer had both the power and tools she needed. The scientist exited the diagnostics program and plugged in a diskette she had brought, her "brute force" program. This was a customized file that included common names, dates, titles of movies, books, and songs, names of cats, cars, celebrities, and also nicknames like "Rit" and "Sweetiepie." It also included an English dictionary from which she had removed words that would probably not appear in someone's password, like "dispensation" and "gravel." She ran the program. It tried tens of thousands of words a second, and in various combinations. Within moments she began typing. She successfully moved from the DOD homepage to comlink, which the air force used to download images from spy planes. She saved the encryption pattern used to decipher the downloaded pictures and asked the computer to find similar patterns. She didn't need to decode it, just to find another sequence like it. After fifteen minutes, the computer gave her several options—including the Dove, a spy satellite located in a geostationary orbit over Iran.

"Excellent," she said.

"What've you got?"

"A signal that will take us to whatever database the NRO uses to save images from space," Victoria began typing. "I'll piggyback a patented Victoria Hudson tick up to the Dove and from there go through a back door into the NRO database."

"A tick?"

"I use spiders to roam the web and nest in places where I may need them. I use ticks to hitch rides on nonweb signals. Once the tick gets where it's going, it drops off the host signal, collects data, then returns the way it came."

"You make it sound easy."

"It is easy unless you have to crack complex codes or program around roadblocks," she told him. "Right now, we aren't trying to do any of that, just open a few doors, hitch a ride."

Except for the sound of the computer fan, the room was silent.

"How long do you think this will take?" Evans asked.

"To get into the NRO computers? Anywhere from a half-hour to an hour. To get back, maybe another ten or fifteen minutes. Once we have the password to the photo files, if we're lucky it'll only take a few hours to decode it. If we're not lucky, it could take days."

"Days," Evans said. He sounded drained.

"Listen," Victoria said. "I don't need you here for this. You've got a lot on your mind, and you have to be up early to start the SFU tests—"

"You also have to be up early to monitor the results."

"But not *as* early," she pointed out. "And I'll be sitting on my butt in an air-conditioned room instead of wearing a hot, bulky suit that weighs about what—sixty pounds?"

"Sixty-seven," Evans said.

"There you go. If Captain McIver doesn't mind, why don't you take my bunk tonight? I'll let you know when I have something."

Evans looked from Victoria to the monitor. His eyes were calmer than before, but she could see he didn't want to let go.

"Commander, you won't be any good to the SFU team or to this investigation if you don't get rest. I know you're used to commanding, but let me do this. I'll be fine."

Evans looked back at her. "It isn't a matter of trusting you to do a job. It's what Captain McIver said—how far do we go and why? When does appropriate punishment, our responsibility to protect the common good, become sinful excess?"

"You mean revenge," she said.

He nodded. "I've been wrestling with that question since the general first told me about the Huntsmen. Saint Paul said that it's the job of the state to serve God. To serve him with the sword, if necessary. But the definition of necessary isn't always clear."

"Unfortunately, you're talking to the wrong one," she said. "I'm what my mother used to call a 'two-timing Episcopalian.' I make a stab at being devout twice a year on Christmas and Easter. And my mind wanders even then."

Evans looked at her and smiled. "You're not the wrong one to talk to, though this probably is the wrong time. Come and get me when you have anything—anything at all."

She said she would, after which Evans thanked her and left. The thick door closed heavily. The temperature seemed to drop back to normal. There was something about this man that *got* to her.

Victoria watched the monitor as a tick icon flashed in the center of the screen.

She wished she knew if Evans felt anything when they were together. Her impending divorce wasn't in her personnel file, so Commander Evans wouldn't know about it. On the other hand, the divorce might not make a difference. During the hours they'd spent together over the past two years, all Evans ever wanted to talk about was how her part of the N-Gen technology worked. He was obsessed with understanding things.

Almost like a catechism, she thought. Questions and answers, an orderly and single-minded progression. There was something endearing about that and also something very, very frustrating. Between work and religion, Victoria wondered if Evans even had time for anything else.

She decided not to think about that now. Trying to understand Amos Evans would only frustrate her further. Besides, there was another mystery she wanted to look into.

Her eyes drifted from the monitor to the diskette Evans had left behind.

Victoria had never met Brigadier General MacDougall. She'd never seen him on TV; her husband was the political gabshow junkie. But she was interested in using the websites and databases MacDougall had accessed as a springboard into further investigation. She was hungry for the challenge, and she also wanted to try and answer Evans's questions about the general's death.

Suddenly, the tick vanished.

She was into the NRO photo database.

Sixteen

Monday, 9:48 P.M.
Washington, D.C.

The offices of the Central Intelligence Agency are divided
into two large buildings—named, with forthrightness, the
Original Headquarters Building and the New Headquarters Building. They are separated by a large, landscaped
courtyard complete with a broad lawn, fish pond, and
trees. The public is not permitted to visit the offices,
though occasionally the agency allows outside musicians
to come into the courtyard to entertain employees and
their families.

Alan Greenberg worked for the Internet Surveillance
Unit in the New Headquarters Building. The CIA's mission
is to collect information related to foreign intelligence and
counterintelligence; by direction of the President through
Executive Order 12333, the agency is forbidden to collect
information about United States citizens.

But there's a loophole in the directive.

In order to help maintain its own security, the CIA is permitted to monitor and audit hits to its website and to related

websites in the United States Intelligence Community via
http://www.odci.gov/cia/other_links/wheel/contents.html.
This includes the FBI armed forces intelligence, the Department of State, and the National Reconnaissance Office. The
job of the Internet Surveillance Unit is to help deter hackers
and to prevent unauthorized modification of information
presented at the websites.

Sipping strong black coffee, ISU Assistant Director
Greenberg sat in his small, windowless, third-floor office. In
front of him, flush against the back wall, was a long, narrow,
laboratory table–style desk with two-tiers consisting of a
total of thirteen computer monitors. The screens showed the
various intelligence websites along with an ever-changing
number of hits in a blue square in the upper right-hand corner. Names and phone numbers flashed in the square, downloaded and saved by the computer.

Greenberg was alerted to the NRO hack by a persistent
beep that came from the third monitor from the left, upper
tier. The bald, thirty-three-year-old remained calm. Hacks
into the system were relatively common, usually three or
four a week. More often than not, it was a tech-head looking
for a thrill. They would find a way to use the website to slip
into portions of the intelligence web reserved for classified
traffic.

As was the case with this hack, the name and telephone
number of the surfer had been blocked at the source.

No problem, thought Greenberg. The intrusion triggered
what the ISU called an ERP—an End Run Program—a sophisticated "lawman" that broke through most blockades to
catch the intruder. Greenberg watched the corner-square of
the monitor, which had gone from blue to flashing red. He
wouldn't shut the hacker out until the ERP gave him a name,
phone number, and address. Depending where they were,

within one to twelve hours they would get a visit from a real lawman.

Suddenly, Greenberg sat up very straight and got very serious. The signal was coming from space.

Greenberg picked up the phone.

Seventeen

Monday, 11:10 P.M.
Allegheny Mountains, West Virginia

The call from Internet Surveillance Unit Director Cynthia Longwood at the CIA was not one that Axe wanted to get. Especially now, when Operation 415 was ready to launch.

Longwood had been informed by Alan Greenberg, her nighttime man, that someone had hacked the NRO HOMEs system. The intruder was asking for satellite views of the roads leading to and from Chevy Chase on the day Axe had visited the Hoxworth home. Those images couldn't have been excised without raising flags, but no one had expected that to be necessary. Longwood controlled access to the files. Or at least, she was supposed to.

It might be a coincidence. Longwood said, but it did seem an odd place to go. Axe agreed with his long-time CIA confederate.

The signal had come from an air force satellite. That meant it had originated at a military facility, probably air force: dedicated lines had been used to get the hacker into space. Longwood said that tracking it would be possible, though only if they left the link open on the NRO's end.

That presented a problem. If Longwood ordered Greenberg to shut the HOMEs database down until the intruder could be purged, they'd never know who might be looking into the Hoxworth assassination. If they allowed access to continue, they might be able to find out who made the request—but the hacker might also get the information they were after.

Axe decided quickly on a two-pronged attack. He told Longwood to locate the hacker even if it meant surrendering data. For while they might get the information they were after, he'd see to it that it did them absolutely no good.

As soon as Axe hung up, he went to the intercom on the back wall of the cabin, called the staging shed in back, and told his field operations director to come see him at once.

Eighteen

Evans slept well. Not because his mind was at rest; he slept well because he had to.

Since joining the navy, there was always something buzzing around his brain. The details of a mission. The safety of those serving under him. The lives of captives his SEALs had to rescue or prisoners his team had to take. The honor of the unit, of the nation.

Now as then, he slept by reading scripture in his mind. Wherever he was, in a field or a plane or a bed, he would lie down, breathe slowly through his nose, and see the page, the verse, the lines. They would occupy his brain and comfort his soul, and he would fall asleep. He'd done this since he was a fifteen-year-old growing up in the streets of Miami. That was when Father John confronted him in a parking lot on NW 11th Street. It was Saturday morning, just after 2:00 A.M., when the elderly priest boldly walked up to the two-fisted, switchblade-packing kid after he'd picked up a back-pack full of money from a bookie in a parked car. The

white-haired clergyman told Evans how his mother was
worried about him. He also told him about how mobster
Benny Hurwitz might seem to be a powerful man and how
being an errand boy could be exciting and rewarding, especially to a kid who lived with his single mother and twin sister in a one-bedroom apartment. But Father John said there
were more powerful figures and more rewarding quests if
Evans would come to church and learn about them.

There was no lecture. Just the facts as Father John saw
them in an encounter that lasted less than two minutes. But
it got the boy's attention. It wasn't just what Father John had
to say but how he said it. He spoke confidently. And he was
unarmed, except for his faith in God.

Evans stole a suit and tie and went to church the following Sunday. The visit changed his life. There was something
about the modest cathedral on NW 4th Avenue that allowed
him to relax. He felt safe here, not just from punks who
worked for rival mobsters or the alcoholic father who used
to punch him in the arms and chest with his high school ring
but also *inside* his body. As though he could let out his fears
and anxieties and not feel weak.

There was also something very compelling about the way
Father John commanded the church. Years later, at the old
man's funeral, Evans said that he was like an officer ad-
dressing his troops. Father John spoke with authority, and as
he said quoting *Proverbs* on one occasion—speaking directly to the young man, it seemed—"When the righteous
are in authority, the people rejoice. But when the wicked
rule, the people moan."

Evans began going to church every Sunday. He stopped
working for Benny Hurwitz—who was murdered less than
six months later, shot in a beach cabana—and turned to his
neglected school studies. He went to work at a local fast-
food restaurant and did odd jobs around the church on week-

ends. For the first time in his life, he was motivated by something stronger than the need to prove himself: the need to better himself. He also learned the rudiments of espionage by finding ways to eavesdrop on people in the confessional. It was quite an education, learning what some people considered sinful and what sins others had actually committed. What was most impressive was the immutability of Father John's faith. He was able to forgive those who were truly penitent, regardless of what they'd done.

Nearly a year after their first meeting in the parking lot, Father John was responsible for introducing Evans to the second-most-influential man in his young life, a former parishioner who was home on leave—Lieutenant Harry Quint, USN. Quint told Evans about the navy, and they wrote to one another over the next year. One week after graduating from high school, the young man enlisted; swearing allegiance to God and country was the most moving experiences of Evans's young life. That dual devotion sustained him after the incident in Iraq, and the word of God remained a great comfort to him whether his eyes were open or closed.

Evans awoke shortly before the alarm went off. Captain McIver was still asleep, and, dressing quickly, Evans went to his room. The outrage he'd felt the day before had hardened and set. Victoria had called it right: he wanted revenge, but not just for Senator Hoxworth and General MacDougall. He'd risked his life for his country on mission after mission. The Huntsmen had abused the liberties he'd fought for, broken the laws of God and the nation.

He wanted them.

He knocked on the door. Victoria told him to enter. She was still seated by the computer terminal. The cot was made, the blanket unwrinkled. An empty coffee cup sat beside the keyboard.

"How did I know you'd still be at it?" Evans said.

"Because I'm like a dog with a bone," Victoria said. "I even managed to have a look through the files on the diskette. I've got to admit, though, I'm kind of surprised."

"About what?"

"By this time I'd've thought they would have picked up an intruder and shut me out," Victoria said.

"Could they be trying to trace you?"

"That's highly probable," she admitted. "But they'd only get as far as the satellite downlink to Langley, and then they'd be shut out by on-line security here at the base. It'd take a couple hours for them to hack that, by which time I'll be out of there."

Evans glanced at the monitor. She was looking at a greenish-black screen with tiny smears of light here and there. Night-vision images, he knew. And not terribly enlightening, it seemed.

"What have you got there?" he asked.

"Nothing but a small, frustrating tease," she said.

Victoria saved the latest image and opened a previous file. It was a sharply angled overhead view of a large suburban home. The picture was approximately six inches high by ten inches long. It showed a car pulling into the driveway and the garage door opening. The digital clock at the bottom of the frame said *Friday, 4:02:33 P.M.*

"I've been pulling these photos from a file which includes overflights of Chevy Chase, Maryland," she said. "The NRO watches the area because of the high percentage of senators, supreme court judges, and cabinet members clustered in a relatively small area. This is the Hoxworth home. The car belongs to Senator Hoxworth's daughter, Denise. I hacked the Department of Motor Vehicles and checked the license plate."

She clicked on a frame that said 4:03:01. The car was entering the garage. There was something directly behind the car.

"This is as large and sharp as I can make it," Victoria said. "I also checked to see if there was anything in police or FBI files about Denise Hoxworth being questioned. If she was, if she noticed anything unusual when she came home, that information isn't available anywhere I've looked."

Evans leaned over Victoria's shoulder, closer to the monitor. He concentrated on the image. It was difficult to see because of the tree cover, but it looked like a dark blue mass, stretched from left to right, with large, pixel-squared edges all around. It could have been nothing more than a large trash bag caught on the undercarriage of the car.

"Can I see the previous image again?" Evans asked.

Victoria went back to it. Evans looked at the picture. Except for the front of the car, the driveway was empty. The side of the house was in shadow. There was no indication of where the object might have come from.

"And there's nothing in between those two pictures?" Evans asked.

"No." Victoria said. "The satellite takes twenty-eight seconds to download each image, so that's all we have for this sequence. The garage door's already closed in the next picture."

"Too bad."

She returned to the image with the blue object. Evans forced his eyes to go blurry. He was accustomed to looking at satellite photographs from his days with the SEALs. Unless you were reading letters or numbers, fuzzing the picture, blending the pixels together, was the best way to identify shapes. Unfortunately, the leaves still made it impossible to identify.

"What about the color blue?" Evans asked. "Does it show up anywhere prior to this?"

"I'm going to run a color search, but not until I download as many images as possible from that night—"

"In case they find you and shut you down."

"Exactly. I'm up to about 9:30 P.M. Friday."

Evans nodded. "If you find anything, let me know immediately. I'll be out in the field with the team. You can page me by pushing star one on the phone."

Victoria said she would. "Are you sure you'll be able to concentrate out there?"

"I can't contribute much in here, and I still have a job to do," Evans said.

"You seem a little calmer than last night."

"Just keeping a leash on it," he said. "Victoria, I want to thank you again for everything you're doing. I know this is more than you expected to have on your plate down here—"

"No," she said. "I came here to be challenged, and I am. I should be thanking you for that."

She looked up at him. Maybe it was because she was tired and her guard was lowered, or maybe he was just looking for it. But Evans saw something that he had never seen in any of their previous meetings. Something that wasn't, *"Let me explain"* or *"We can use DNA to construct wire less than one hundred nanometers in diameter . . ."* Something very open.

She smiled and went back to work. Evans left a moment later.

When he returned to the corridor, the others were already awake. Diaz had drawn coffee detail, and while it brewed, the others were taking quick wake-up showers. While he waited his turn in the corridor, Taylor did a *kata*, a ritualistic exercise. He went through a variety of martial arts blocks, strikes, lunges, kicks, and turns, which were beautiful in their grace and frightening in their refinement. Every joint seemed to move with firm purpose, down to the tips of the medic's fingers.

Evans went back to his room. Since he'd be working the monitors while Victoria was on the computer, he wouldn't be wearing his SFU. As he pulled on the rest of his uniform, his mind chewed over the images Victoria had hacked. And the more he thought about it the more convinced he became that the object in the photograph was a person. Someone running, ducking, or rolling after the car, using it to gain entry into the house. He'd penetrated closed sites himself over the years. One of his mentors, Rear Admiral Jason Penny, had made an art form of modern military on-site surveillance when he went into Teheran in December 1979 to photograph Revolutionary Guard checkpoints prior to the failed attempt to rescue the hostages being held at the former U.S. embassy. You always tried to go in at night. But if that wasn't possible, if doors or gates were closed—or in this case, if people were going to be home—you went in whenever you could. You also tried to enter when other people were going in. That enabled you to avoid alarms or traps and also blend in with the people who belonged there. Penny had learned that from Dan Haley, an art thief he grew up with. Instead of trying to break into a museum, Haley always entered with the crowds and hunkered down.

The team met in the rec room. After eating, they went to the storage room to uncrate the SFUs. The suits hung upright in the trunks, one uniform in each trunk. As Captain McIver watched closely, each man put on thin, white undergloves and then carefully unzipped the bottom half from the top.

There was only one chair in the room. McIver told Taylor to have a seat as the other men stood around, holding the pants section high enough to keep them off the floor. Evans had told them to make certain that nothing but the soles of the boots touched down.

"Dirt from the floors—like dirt in the field—will not be invisible when you switch into stealth mode," he told them. "Dirt, precipitation, even oil from your hands will be visible."

"Hence the gloves," Diaz said.

"Hence the gloves," Evans said.

"It feels like those lead-lined vests patients wear when they get X rayed," Taylor said. The captain held the boots off the floor and he began slipping his legs in. "The texture is a little more rubberized, though—"

"Yeah," Diaz agreed. He was fingering the waist of his own uniform. "Like a fat mousepad."

Evans told them that thinning the material out would be one of the focuses for the next generation of stealth uniforms.

The pants squeaked like new leather as Taylor slipped his legs in.

"That's going to be a problem," Diaz noted.

"Only for about twenty or thirty seconds," Evans said. "There's a petroleum compound baked into the outer layer. It liquifies at body temperature, lubricating the suit and keeping it from making noise."

"Clever," Diaz said.

"No, it's friggin' brilliant," Lewis said. "Everything about it—just brilliant."

After Taylor had the pants on, he got up, and McIver told Lewis to have a seat. Meanwhile, Evans helped the medic pull the top section on over his head.

Each uniform was extremely tight. As Holly observed when it was his turn to suit up, putting it on was like breaking in a new pair of very tight boots—all over his body. Evans agreed and warned the men that in addition to being chafed and hot, they would all have very sore muscles the following day.

It was just past seven-thirty before the four men were dressed. They stood looking at one another as Captain McIver made sure that all the zippers had been closed.

"Do you realize we're making history here?" Lewis said. "Not just American history, *human* history."

Evans said a soft "Amen." The soldier's awe for the moment touched him.

When everything checked out, the team went into the corridor. The first test was going to be a simple walk in the field, a chance to break the suits in a little before they started the stress and temperature tests downstairs.

They exited the shelters and shut the door behind them.

Nineteen

Will Bannon knew Langley well.

The fifty-one-year-old Irish-Hawaiian had begun his air force career as a reconnaissance officer during the Vietnam War. Bannon worked on the ground instead of in the air, since that was the only way some of the deeply buried North Vietnamese arms caches and tunnels could be infiltrated and destroyed. Because he looked more Asian than Occidental, he was able to enter villages inaccessible to most U.S. operatives. Once there, he would identify likely sites. Then he'd pick locks, oil and remove hinges, check for booby traps, plant explosives, do whatever was necessary to complete his mission. Occasionally, he would plant beacons for choppers and planes to attack the sites. It was dangerous, thrilling work, the most exciting time of his life.

After the war, Bannon joined Air Force Intelligence and served as assistant direction from 1988–1994. He resigned his post when the military, like the rest of the country, became responsive to the needs of every special interest group save for one: its backbone, the devoted career soldier.

Throughout the post-Vietnam years, the excitement of working in the field remained very immediate to Lieutenant Colonel Bannon. It was in his mind, in his muscles, in his senses. He could still feel in his shoulders what it was like to hunch into a dirt tunnel. He could still smell the damp earth. The only thing he couldn't feel was the intensity of living from one moment to the next, never knowing if his next heartbeat would be his last.

After his retirement, the officer was approached by a gentleman who knew of his service record and his political sentiments. He offered him a job, as the seventh member of his own very secret team—one of three who were still in the military. A member of a unit that conducted reconnaissance and, when necessary, acted on the intelligence it acquired. Acted definitely and for the good of the nation.

Bannon arranged to stay on with Air Force Intelligence as a consultant, to allow him access to data and to keep his contacts fresh, while at the same time becoming an operative known as Hydra for a group called the Huntsmen.

It was shortly after midnight when the NRO pinpointed the source of the hack as being located at Langley Air Force Base. By 2:00 A.M., Bannon was at his office on the base, and by 2:50 he had ascertained by checking uplink access logs that the hacker was based in a complex of bomb shelters located in a field beyond one of the runways. Bannon had known about the abandoned shelters and was angry that they might have been transformed into some form of communications or intelligence center without his having known about it. By 4:15, he had been joined by his Huntsmen colleague John Graff, a National Security Agency liaison stationed at the White House where he'd been backing up the prime operation. The duty roster showed that Captain Robin

McIver was out in the shelters. The roster also indicated that a Sergeant Rick Boots had made four trips to the shelters that day. No other information was available.

That was bad news. No other information meant a secret project. That could be anything from testing new security systems to designing new software for computers. But why were they based in the shelters? The Air Force Communications and Intelligence offices would have been secure enough for those kinds of projects.

Not that it mattered. The NRO contact didn't know whether the hackers had been looking specifically for surveillance pictures that included the Hoxworth home, but the Huntsmen couldn't afford to take the chance. The hackers might see Badger entering the garage. They might see him in his truck hours before. They might check AirTomorrow employment records and find out who he is. The images couldn't be eliminated, but the hackers could.

According to records, the shelters were accessible by a door dug in the field. Not only didn't Bannon have the access code, but he never liked going through the front door on any mission. Especially when he didn't know how many people were on the other side. According to computerized blueprints, the shelters had originally been built to be entered by an underground corridor that ran from a grease pit in the Morgan hangar, which abutted the airstrip. The hangar was largely unused since the latest round of air force cutbacks in 1992; that particular corridor had been closed off but never filled.

Packing a flashlight, gloves, and a pair of Berettas, Bannon and Graff went to have a look at the entranceway. A short metal ladder led to the large rectangular pit. In the center was a square iron door in the floor, slightly over two feet on each side. The door had been welded shut. Bannon found an acetylene torch on the tool shelf and ignited it. He also found a crowbar. He hoped that was all he'd need. He went back to the pit.

It wouldn't be necessary to cut through the entire weld, which would take two or three hours. All Bannon needed to do was heat one corner of the sealed door. Depending on how thick the metal was—and a tap with the crowbar rang like a half-inch to Bannon's experienced ears—if he fired the door unevenly it would buckle and snap. Possibly along the weld, possibly along a weak spot in the metal. Once there was a break, they could use the crowbar to pry up the panel enough so that they could slip down.

Bannon put the torch to the metal. It would have been easier if he'd had something cold to place on the opposite side of the door. In Vietnam, he'd carried small pouches of dry ice. As it was, it took slightly more than twenty-five minutes before the iron square burst outward along a jagged line through the center, like a hot dog on a griddle. Bannon got a brick to use for leverage, after which he and Graff used the crowbar to wrench up one side of the door and then the other. Graff shined the flashlight inside. A ladder led straight down about ten feet to a concrete tunnel. It looked like a storm drain; a person would have to squat to go through. As the fumes of the torch dissipated, Bannon could smell the air inside the tunnel. It was musty and very dry. Like the shelters it was nonporous, to keep radioactive groundwater from seeping in.

Before climbing down, Bannon went back to the tool chest and collected a selection of four screwdrivers of different sizes. He also brought along the acetylene torch, matches, and the crowbar, just in case.

According to the blueprints, there was another metal door at the other end of the tunnel, this one upright. They wouldn't be able to pop this one as they had the other: there might be people on the other side. If there were a weld, they would have to unseal it as quietly as possible. And hope there was nothing combustible on the other side.

The two Huntsmen proceeded very slowly, Bannon in front. He checked the circular walls and ceiling for alarms or motion detectors. There weren't any. Perhaps they'd find an alarm on the door at the other end of the corridor, though by then it would be too late.

They reached the door after covering roughly a quarter of a mile. When they did, Bannon smiled. The door was round, like the door on a bank vault, and made of iron. But there was no weld. The fact that the door was there at all suggested that the air force hadn't bothered to seal the entrance with brick or cinder blocks. Perhaps they hadn't wanted to eat up any of the space inside. Or maybe they just weren't expecting company.

Bannon shined the flashlight all over the edges of the round door. The door fit perfectly, forming a very close seal. He lit a match and held it close to the left side of the door. The flame flickered slightly toward the tunnel; there was air circulating inside the shelter, and some of it was leaking through the door. That meant the seal wasn't welded. He tried the knob; it turned freely. Obviously, whoever had closed this tunnel off felt there was no reason to lock the door.

Bannon held one of the screwdrivers by the tip and used the back to tap around the perimeter of the door. It sounded about an inch thick. Fortunately the sound was hollow save for three points: one on the left side, one at the top center, and one at the bottom. The one on the left sounded slightly more solid than the other two. That would be the hinge.

The top and bottom sounds were probably dead bolts, sunk from the other side of the door into the brick frame. Given the size and weight of the door, about two inches of each bolt would be buried in the brick and with an L-shaped bend and a hook at the bottom to keep them from slipping out. Those would be difficult if not impossible to chisel free. Bannon moved to the left side of the door. He rapped carefully along the center.

Because of the shape of the door there would only be one hinge. It would be a large one, but that didn't matter. It was located in the center and was approximately five inches tall. He handed Graff one of the screwdrivers. Then he indicated a spot and told him to begin chipping away at it. Bannon used another screwdriver to chip at a point half an inch higher. If he could expose the top of the hinge, then he could use the screwdriver to pry the peg up. Anchored only by the two deadbolts, the door would swing—not much, because of the frame, but enough so that the men could squeeze through.

It was seven-twelve in the morning when they were finally able to wedge the tip of the screwdriver under the head of the hinge bolt. It came free after twenty-two minutes of pushing and jimmying. Unfortunately, no one came to investigate the sounds. It would have helped enormously if someone had opened the door from the inside.

Because of the tight frame, the unhinged door didn't move much when pushed. It opened just enough for Bannon to peer through. The shelter was a storeroom with no one inside. He stuck the end of the crowbar through and pulled hard. Brick cracked along the right side. He handed the bar to Graff. The brick frame fell away in small shards.

After fifteen minutes more, the door swiveled open enough for them to slip through. They left everything behind except for the Berettas.

Twenty

As the computer downloaded more images, Victoria shut her eyes. She had to. They demanded it.

She'd wasted nearly an hour searching the downloaded NRO photo files for the same color blue in that one photo, but the computer didn't find any matches. Only after she spent the time did she realize that of course it wouldn't find a match: the sunlight at different times of day would have changed the tone of the blue, made it cooler, warmer, darker, brighter, whatever. Even a slight variation would make it difficult to spot.

She returned to the nighttime pictures. The images were dark and eye-straining and they finally forced her to rest her eyes. The hum of the computer fan was soothing. The cool air blowing from the vent above was wonderful. She was exhausted. She didn't want to move.

And there was one more thing. There was something about that brief exchange with Commander Evans that had played little games with her insides, helping to relax her.

She'd been embarrassed when he'd first walked in, not because he was in a T-shirt—but because she suspected that he'd done it without thinking. That *he'd* be embarrassed.

Maybe he was. Maybe not. But the next time they'd looked at each other, all she saw were his eyes. And he didn't seem flustered at all. She wasn't. After he left, she thought about those eyes, his arms, his chest. She shouldn't be doing this to herself—imagining, hoping—but she was too tired to fight it. And it had been so long since a man had looked at her without wanting something, whether it was copy for the college manual or her husband waiting to get a rise out of her because of something he'd said or done—

A loud scraping sound opened her eyes. It was like metal against metal, and she listened for a moment. It came again, then again. It sounded as though it came from down the hallway on the right. It couldn't be one of the team members because everyone was outside. And it definitely wasn't rats in the wall. She'd heard those in the Village, too.

She got up from the metal chair, walked to the door, and stuck her head into the hallway. She listened. It was quiet now, though she thought she caught a hint of stale, dry air coming from the right. She was about to go back into the room when she heard what sounded like footsteps.

Maybe she was tired and not in her right mind, or maybe she was tired and *was* thinking clearly. Or maybe she'd just been too immersed in paranoid research over the past few hours to be objective. But the storeroom was where Commander Evans had said the entrance to the old access tunnel was. And maybe, just maybe, she was still on-line and hacking because someone had allowed her to stay on-line and hacking. So they could trace her, as Evans had suggested. If they'd gotten someone into Langley, into the dedicated computer system, finding the signal would not be difficult.

The door of the storeroom opened slowly. It stopped.

There were more sounds from behind it. Someone *was* there.

Victoria backed into Evans's shelter and quickly, quietly shut the door. She was hyper-awake now, her heart punching fast and hard, her breath coming in short, thin gulps.

Okay, she asked herself. *What would intruders do?* They'd check the rooms as they went along, looking for the computer and the hacker. That would give her maybe two minutes until they reached this room.

If she paged Evans, he'd come down unarmed and suspecting nothing. She didn't want that. Besides, depending upon how far in the field he was he might not even get here in time.

She saved the latest data on a diskette and went to shut off the computer. She thought that she might be able to get to the front entrance and sneak out while the intruder was in another room.

Suddenly, she saw a reflection in the dark computer monitor.

Something that made her change her mind.

Twenty-one

Bannon and Graff both walked through the narrow corri-
dor, Graff checking the rooms on the left, Bannon the shelters on the right. They moved quickly and made no effort to
keep quiet. Anyone who ran from them would be hunted
down. Anyone who came forward would tell them what they
wanted to know or be shot. In the dark, any security cameras
that might spot them would see dark shapes, nothing more.
The killers would aim for a non-vital spot like the shin or
arm at first, to get them to talk; then they'd aim for the heart
or the head to keep them from talking. It was that simple. All
they wanted was to find out who was hacking the NRO and
why, kill them, destroy the data, and get out.

The first rooms they encountered were dark. Then Bannon reached a shelter where the computer monitor was on.
He entered and stayed well back from the monitor so the
light would not illuminate his features. He looked at the
screen.

There was a daytime photo of a house. The image also

showed a car pulling into the driveway and something blurry and blue behind the car. Bannon removed his glove and placed the back of his hand on the leather seat of the chair. The seat was still warm.

He ran out to find Graff; he didn't want to shout in case there were an audio component to the security system. Graff was in the rec room.

"Someone was just using the computer," Bannon said.

"Well, they're not here now," Graff told him. "The place is clean. They must've ducked out."

"Find them," Bannon ordered.

Graff acknowledged and continued moving through the complex. Bannon went back to the computer and sat in the chair, still keeping his distance. He checked the time of the image. It was 4:03:01 P.M. Badger had gone inside the Hoxworth house late in the afternoon. The blue shape behind the car could have been him in his AirTomorrow uniform.

Bannon swore. Did someone have time to figure that out? Had they downloaded the data to another site—?

He checked the disk drive; it was empty. Whoever had been working here probably didn't have time to send the information anywhere. They must have heard the men come in, popped the disk, and fled. Glancing at the monitor, though, he did notice one thing. The sound recorder function was minimized. He looked under the monitor and saw the microphone lying on the base. Someone was obviously hoping to catch some conversation, maybe a voice pattern. He yanked the microphone from its cable and threw it aside.

Graff came running down the stairs a moment later. "They're gone," he said. "Whoever was here must've left by the front door. You need a code to open the damn thing."

"Shit." Bannon picked up his gun and rose. That was the risk you took coming in loud. More often than not people came to investigate; sometimes they hid; and once in a while they ran. Bannon hated playing the odds and losing. "All right—they're still in the middle of a goddam field. I'll go back through the tunnel and cut them off, take them back to the hangar. You start a fire in here, waste the fucking place, and then follow me."

Graff nodded and went back up the stairs. Bannon picked up the flashlight and followed him. They'd left the acetylene torch in the tunnel, and Graff ran ahead to retrieve it.

Bannon was already thinking of what he'd do with whoever he had to kill up there. Leave the body or bodies in the hangar pit, he decided. Arson at a secret installation at a military base, a murdered operative—the air force would turn that one over to Internal Security, which was fine with him. IS was heavy with second-stringers and guys coasting to retirement. The real go-getters were out in support of operational forces or collecting intelligence on the weapons and aerospace systems of potential adversaries.

The IS would follow the playbook on this and take a month or two doing it. The Beretta was one of Axe's buys through a Greek arms dealer so the bullet wouldn't tell the investigators anything useful. They'd run background checks on anyone who had been in or had access to the shelters; try to track the activities of anyone who these people may have been watching or been in communication with; and search for similar break-and-enter tactics. That was when Bannon would make sure he became involved with the investigation. He had trained a number of "tunnel moles" after Vietnam. He would help look for likely suspects. Point the IS in some helpful directions. As for his own whereabouts, in case anyone asked, there was a security camera that would verify he'd been withdrawing money from a base ATM when this tunnel was being broken into. The camera would have recorded his college ring, his hat, his blazer. It would not show that one of Axe's people had been wearing them, though.

Bannon followed Graff as he quickly crossed the dark storeroom. Graff slipped around several large, open trunks and headed back toward the tunnel. As he stopped to slide through the partly open iron door, Graff's feet suddenly flew out from under him. They shot sideways, into the room. His mouth slammed into the edge of the iron door, and there was a loud crack as his lower jaw dislocated. Graff moaned and rolled off the circular door, crashing into one of the trunks. He lost his gun and came to rest on his back. He struggled dazedly to his side and shook his head.

Bannon had immediately hunched and swung his Beretta and flashlight toward the tunnel. Someone must have struck his companion from inside and then ducked back. But how did they get inside? There hadn't been enough time for someone to leave that seat by the computer, get outside to the field, and double back. And he didn't see how anyone could have snuck past them down here. He edged forward. His wide beam played across what looked like a column of radiant heat, but it was only there for a moment. He inched ahead and shined the light into the tunnel. No one was there.

Suddenly, a loud voice from close behind Bannon said, "Put your weapon on the floor."

They'd been compromised. Bannon didn't know how, nor did it matter. Graff was too dazed to act. Without hesitation, the assassin put a bullet into the man's head so he wouldn't be taken. Then he spun and fired at the voice. The Beretta chugged loudly as three bullets struck the wall on the other side of the corridor. Almost in that same moment, Bannon felt something grab his wrist and wrench it straight up. Two shots discharged toward the ceiling and pain poured up his arm as the violent tug dislocated it at the shoulder. The next instant the Huntsman operative was flopped onto his back, hard. The breath was punched out of him, but he kicked and tried to get up until he felt his elbow snap the wrong way. He shrieked as his forearm went numb. His entire right arm was suddenly dead weight.

Someone took the Beretta from his hand before he could drop it. Bannon grabbed with his left hand, thought he felt something. But when he squinted up no one was there.

A moment later, Bannon felt crushing pressure all along his jawline and under both ears. He gagged high in his throat. The choke was what special forces personnel were taught to use to do to keep captured enemy operatives from swallowing pills filled with cyanide or some other fast-acting poison that had been placed inside hollow teeth.

The dark room became two pools of swirling red mud. Bannon's legs continued to kick but only for a few seconds. The pressure increased under his ears until his head rang like a fireball.

Bannon had failed. He wasn't going to be able to get away, so he focused all his energies on one last effort that must not fail. Axe was too smart to rely on a chemical that had to be ingested. That was why he'd had the deadly VX nerve agent placed in the mouths of his operatives. Once the tooth was flipped open with the tongue and the operative bit down on the exposed capsule, there was no need to swallow. The 15 mg of direct-contact poison was absorbed into the skin and death resulted in less than a minute.

As he convulsed from the irreversible shut-down to his central nervous system, Bannon flashed to images of old colleagues he would be seeing soon—and the new ones, who would have to press on without him. They had all been prepared to die for this operation, and Bannon's last thoughts were to feel strangely honored that he and Graff had been the first. . . .

Twenty-two

Commander Evans shouldered into the stockroom mo-ments after the others had gone in. He was followed by Captain McIver. Neither of them had weapons. McIver turned on the light. Colonel Lewis, who had led the incursion through the tunnel, was visible and kneeling next to one of the intruders, the man who had been shot in the head. Blood was running from the head wound toward a drain in the center of the shelter. Major Taylor had also shut down the stealth option of his suit and was kneeling beside the other man.

A moment later, MCPO Diaz and Captain Holly materialized between them. Diaz retrieved the guns. Holly squatted beside Lewis; neither man could crouch very low because of the uniforms. The suits were scuffed and scratched from where they'd been forced through the buckled iron plate in the hangar and the partly opened tunnel door down here.

Holly brushed off some of the brick dust. "They attract dirt like a new car, but I'm glad these sumbitches work."

"Amen to that," Diaz said.

Evans stepped among the men. "Is everyone all right?"

"Yeah. Except this guy," Lewis said.

"Check them both. I want answers."

Lewis had already removed one of his heavy stealth gloves. He flexed his fingers several times, then began looking through the man's pockets. He found a laminated green card in the pocket of his shirt and handed it to McIver.

"What've you got?" Evans asked.

"It's a base pass, green for Tuesday," she said. "Looks authentic."

"All access," Evans muttered.

Colonel Lewis carefully and methodically searched the dead man, starting with the lining of his coat and moving to the sleeves. As he did, Evans turned to Major Taylor.

"What've you got?"

"This guy's gone, too, though it wasn't anything I did to him," Taylor said. He put his fingertips on the man's chin and pulled down. "Damn. I thought I had that covered."

"What?" Evans asked.

"One of his teeth is broken off. He swallowed a toxicant. I blocked his throat when I took him down, but it looks like he had one that was absorbed through the skin."

"They were willing to die rather than be interrogated," McIver said. "Who the hell are they, and what did they want. The suits?"

"And if it was, how did they know about them?" Taylor asked. "I thought this operation was hush-hush."

"It wasn't the suits they were after," Evans said.

Lewis looked at him. "What then?"

Evans said, "Major Taylor—is there any ID on your man?"

Taylor pulled a billfold from inside the dead man's air force jacket. He opened it. "Lieutenant Colonel Will Bannon," he said. "Think he's the real deal?"

"Lieutenant Colonel?" Lewis said. "Hold on. I'll let you know in a second."

Evans and the others watched as the colonel went over and loosened the dead man's necktie.

"Yup. He's career." Lewis said.

"How can you tell?" Taylor asked.

"His shirt and tie are both worn out. These guys use the same threads for a very long time."

"Nice forensics," the medic said. "But I'd still have the base medic check his fingerprints and do retinal scans, just to make sure."

"We will." Evans said. He looked around. "Where's Victoria?"

"Over here," came a voice from the doorway. The young woman's face appeared as she lifted the faceplate. Damp hair was hanging in front of her eyes, and her cheeks were flushed. She was breathing heavily. A moment later, the rest of the suit appeared.

Evans maneuvered around the others toward Victoria. He stepped in front of her, blocking her view of the dead men. McIver hurried over to lend the doctor a shoulder.

"Heavy, isn't it?" McIver asked her.

"Very," Victoria said, leaning on her for a moment.

"Are you okay?" Evans asked.

"I'm fine," she said, "though it's a helluva way to find out just how fast a person can get into one of these."

"You did great," Evans said sincerely. "Are we still on-line?"

"Still on-line and downloading." Victoria looked past Evans at the dead men. "So we've got ourselves some ticks."

"Pardon?"

"They came in through the back door, too," she said. "Do you have any idea who they are?"

"One's air force," Evans said. "The other we're not sure."

Colonel Lewis rose. "Excuse me, Doctor. You just said they came through the back door, *too*. Were you expecting them?"

Victoria shook her head. "We assumed our computers were being watched, and we thought someone might try to shut them down—"

"So you weren't completely surprised to see them."

"That's enough, Colonel," McIver said.

Lewis glared at her, turned to Evans. "Permission to speak freely?"

Evans's jaw tightened. "Go ahead, Colonel. Finish what you started."

"Sir, you obviously knew more about this than we did."

"Very little."

"But something."

"Yes. 'Something.' You've been in situations where a commanding officer has had privileged information. We weren't expecting this to escalate."

"My point, sir, is that if we'd thought about this last night we might have anticipated an attack and roped these two in. Found out more about them."

"Might have," Diaz said.

"Dead on, Mr. Diaz," said McIver. She turned to Lewis. "We could've watched and waited and diverted resources, and maybe nothing would've happened. That's how terrorists get you, Colonel Lewis. They make you afraid to move—"

"With all respect, bein' prepared ain't the same as bein' afraid," Holly suggested.

"Damn straight," said Lewis.

"This isn't helping us," Evans said sharply. He looked at

his watch. "I want us to finish up here and then meet in the rec room at 1100 hours. Colonel Lewis, Major Taylor, Captain Holly, Mr. Diaz—it was never my intention to withhold information. I'll bring you up to speed and we'll go at this as a team." He looked at Lewis. "Any questions?"

Lewis said nothing. No one else spoke.

"Fine. Then let's finish searching the bodies and get these traitors out of here."

The team went to work, and Evans stepped closer to Victoria.

"Will you feel up to the meeting?" Evans asked.

She nodded.

"How about some help getting out of that suit?" Evans said.

"I think I can manage," she said. "I'm sorry," she added quietly. "What I said about the intruders. I should've thought—"

"You did fine," he said. "Don't worry about it."

Evans turned back toward the bodies, and Victoria lumbered up the stairs. Sweat collected behind her knees and dribbled down her legs as she made her way down the hallway. Even though she had just helped to save the stealth operation, she felt guilty about what had transpired between Commander Evans and Colonel Lewis. In that respect, the military was like the industrial science world: everyone heard everything you said. And everything you said had repercussions.

But there *had* been personal rewards in the events of the past half-hour. From the time she saw the suit reflected in the dark computer monitor to the moment she heard Evans ask if everyone was all right, Victoria had never felt closer to either life or death. She had drawn every breath, taken in every sound and sight, felt and heard every heartbeat with a keen sense of gratitude for feeling them . . . and a very real fear of losing them.

And yet—

Change and challenge were what she'd come here hoping to find, and she had. In a big, quick, gratifying megadose. She'd had to think and act fast. Suspecting that this break-in might have been because of her hack, she immediately brought up a computer image she felt would grab and hold the intruder's attention, draw his eyes from where she'd be standing—in the deep shadows beside the locker. Simply by speaking aloud as soon as she had the suit on, she had activated the subvocal communications sensors in the throat. Lewis had been listening, and whatever edge he had, whatever arrogance, he did take charge at once. He told her to stay put instead of running, which was what she'd already chosen to do. Deciding that a front-door approach would make too much noise and fill the complex with sunlight, he said that he and the rest of the team would come through the tunnel entrance. What she had set in motion had *worked*. In a strange way, that gave her more satisfaction than her contribution to the N-Gen suit. That was something she'd been trained to do. This was an improvisation in an area where she had had no experience.

Victoria entered Evans's room and began to remove the uniform. After she was finished, she would shut down the computer. Though she hadn't downloaded all the images, she thought it would be a good idea to make whoever was watching think they'd been cut off. She would find another way to get back into the NRO data file.

She hung the uniform in the locker, then found a towel on the top shelf and used it to wipe her face. She sat down at the keyboard, removed the afternoon photo, then checked on the download process. Ironically, they were still on-line. Whoever sent those men didn't know what had happened so they

were keeping the trap baited. The images were up to 9:39:28
P.M. The pictures were so dark that she doubted they'd get
anything useful from them anyway.

Suddenly, Evans swung through the door followed by
Captain McIver.

"Are we still on-line?" he asked.

"Yes. What's wrong?"

"I want you to get me as many pictures as you can of the
entire Washington area. Keep at it until they cut you off."

Victoria turned back to the monitor. She accessed the
master map with its grid of the entire region. "How tight a
view?" she asked.

"Big. From Langley to the Beltway—work backwards
from 7:00 A.M. this morning and dump as many files as you
can."

Victoria started typing in the coordinates when the computer suddenly began to clatter. A moment later, the image
jumped to the satellite uplink menu with a blue and white
error banner flashing across the bottom of the screen. It told
them that the site was for red-level access only. A moment
after that, the menu vanished.

"Shit," Victoria said. "They threw us out."

"Can you get back in?"

She typed in a code. The computer was silent. The screen
was dark. She tried again. Nothing.

"Damn," McIver said.

"What just happened?" Victoria asked. "What was so important?"

Evans said. "We might've had a chance to turn the tables
on these bastards."

Twenty-three

Evans stared at the computer screen. The blackness seemed to be taunting him.

"Is there some other way into the system?" he asked.

"Not through the uplink," Victoria told him.

"You mean they'll keep all the Intelligence services in the dark just to keep us out?" McIver asked.

"The NRO will probably keep the system off-line for every outside group," she said. "They'll send over whatever geography or images are needed."

Evans looked away from the screen.

"If we hadn't stood around discussing this, we might've had them," McIver grumbled.

"The delay didn't do this to us," Victoria said. "It was shifting from one database to another. The NRO probably let us stay in the Chevy Chase file because they knew we wouldn't get anything from it. They just didn't want to give us any more than that. Why did you want the new overview, Commander?"

"The man with the visitor's badge had car keys in his pocket," Evans said. "I'm willing to bet that his security clearance data—prints, references, etc.—are going to end up missing, just like the database references to the Huntsmen. But if we can find the vehicle those keys fit, we might have been able to search the aerial overviews, spot the car, and follow it backward."

"Get right in those bastards' faces before they can re-group and come at us again," McIver said angrily.

"Sorry," Victoria said. "Even assuming that there's an-other way in, it would take hours to find it, with no guaran-tee that we wouldn't be shut right out again."

"Understood," Evans said.

"What about news choppers or police aviation units?" McIver asked. "They might have tapes of the highways."

"Possibly," Evans agreed. "But getting the tapes and re-viewing them, hoping for a glimpse of the vehicle, will take way too much time, and it probably won't give us a lot of intel."

"No, but something the captain just said gives me an idea," Victoria told him. "If you can locate Graff's car, I don't necessarily need the NRO to track it."

"Explain," Evans said.

"With the license number or registration, I can hack into either the Washington police computer system or the Social Security Administration. Find out who really owns the car, maybe where he works."

"No, don't look there," Evans said. "See if you can get into checkpoints at other bases or federal parking lots. Look for a pattern, someplace he visited regularly."

"I don't understand," McIver said. "What if the car IDs are fakes?"

"There still has to be a record of those fakes somewhere," Evans said. "We may not find out who he really is, but we can find out where he's been. See if there are others like him—other Huntsmen."

"True," McIver said. "I like it."

"It'll be a lot quicker and easier than trying to get back into the NRO," Victoria added. "Even if there's a dummy corporation or out-of-state registry, there's probably a data trail we can follow."

"Let's do it," Evans said.

"I'll start writing some software we may need," Victoria said.

Evans thanked her and left with Captain McIver, who gave her a hard thumbs-up.

"She's good," McIver said.

"Very."

"I'll get that base pass matched to a vehicle," McIver told him. "They keep those records at the main gate. In the meantime, sir, do you plan on keeping the team here?"

"I do."

"Who will you be reporting to?"

"We'll continue to record data as though we were going to submit it to General MacDougall's office," Evans said. "But we'll keep our distance from DARPA until the DOD names his replacement and I'm comfortable that he or she isn't in league with the enemy."

"How will you determine that?"

"We'll talk about that at the briefing," Evans told her. "You were right, Captain. I have no intention of taking a passive role in stopping these people."

McIver smiled.

"The one advantage we have is that the Huntsmen know us only as hackers who are interested in the Hoxworth house." Evans said. "They don't know who we are or why we did it or how much we know. And those men weren't carrying radios, so they couldn't have reported anything they found here. If the Huntsmen try to hack DOD files and find out who's based in this complex, they'll come up empty. The scientists have their individual research in dedicated systems, but the integrated files are all in my possession, on diskette, here with me. And now that the general is gone, no one at the Pentagon knows that the N-Gen team is even here—"

"So we're a stealth team in every sense of the word."

"Yes, and I mean to take advantage of that. How quiet can we keep this thing?"

"At the base? Not very," she said. "There'll be an investigation, next-of-kin notification for the air force casualty, FBI involvement because of the outsider. By tomorrow at this time, even the commissary cook will know all about what happened down here."

"Can you buy me time?"

"I can ask General Jackson to keep the identities of the men and the nature of their deaths local, top brass only. If I'm lucky, he'll give us twenty-four hours. After that, he's going to want to look into this himself, make sure there's no risk to the base."

"Try for the blackout. I don't want the air force turning over any rocks and scaring the Huntsmen away."

"Understood." They were just passing McIver's room, and she stopped. Evans continued on. "Commander?"

Evans looked back.

"I want you to know I'm sorry." McIver said.

"For what?"

"For fucking up."

"You didn't."

"I absolutely did. Security was my job."

"Like I told Colonel Lewis, we didn't know we were at war," Evans said.

"Still, I was unprepared. I never even imagined we'd

need an early warning system in a tunnel welded and locked up the way that one was. I'll have a security camera installed in the hangar and also at the door and a monitor put in my room. We won't be back-ended again."

Evans thanked the captain and continued on to the store-room while McIver went into her room to use what was jok-ingly referred to as "the bat phone," the direct line to General Jackson's office. She was the only one authorized to liaise with the base commander.

Contacting the general, she requested a repair crew, a BBU—body bag unit—and a moratorium. She couldn't explain why, since the line wasn't secure, but promised a full in-person report at 1300. He agreed to keep the mat-ter on hold until then, after which McIver turned her at-tention to the pass. She called the front gate and found out where the car corresponding to badge 10-1763 was parked. Then, getting the dead man's keys from the store-room, she went to the parking area outside the Air Force Intelligence complex.

The vehicle was a new Range Rover, thickly mud-splattered on all sides from what looked like more than a few trips on dirt roads. She set off an alarm when she opened the glove compartment; she let it beep. The registration was in the name of John Graff with an address at the Watergate Hotel. That was different from the ID on the dead man's body.

McIver brought the registration back to the shelter and gave it to Evans. Then she remained in the storeroom to oversee the other members of the team. They had all re-moved their SFUs and were moving the two bodies to the Morgan hangar where the four-person BBU was already waiting.

Evans went back to his room where he'd left Victoria.

He'd told McIver the truth. He didn't blame her for any

of this. He blamed himself. It was bad enough they'd been vulnerable down here; it may have been McIver's job, but ultimately it was Evans's responsibility. He also wasn't happy the way he'd let Colonel Lewis rough him up back there. But Lewis was a decorated leader. Coming down on him for insubordination would have stifled the man's initiative, and Evans didn't want that. Not with the Huntsmen literally at the gate.

When Evans gave Victoria the registration card, she went to the Social Security Administration website and sent a spider to leave the system and enter the files. It took just fifteen minutes for her to find out that the card was real.

"Obviously, the man didn't expect us to get to his car," Victoria said.

"It also means he probably has high security clearance," Evans said.

"How can you tell?"

"The kind of detailed background check government organizations run on you these days, you can't afford to go fake. They'll find a hole in it. Most moles turn once they're inside."

The Social Security database showed that Graff was employed by the National Security Agency. The NSA was accessible on-line through the CIA, so she went back to the CIA website.

While Victoria got into the NSA system and hacked their employment records, she asked Evans what the NSA did. He explained that their primary job was to collect SIGINT, Signals Intelligence, the intercepting and analyzing of foreign electromagnetic signals—telephone and fax, radar, and telemetry involving weapons systems and satellites. Part of that job included breaking the ciphers and electronic countermeasures used to encode the signals. He said that the NSA is also responsible for INFOSEC, Information Systems

Security, which designs methods of protecting classified information that is passed along U.S. government electronic signals systems.

Within twenty minutes, Victoria was able to access the NSA employment files. Ten minutes later, she'd retrieved the data on Graff.

Graff's title was Assistant Director of OPSEC, Operations Security. Evans explained that OPSEC is responsible for training other government agencies in matters concerning SIGINT and INFOSEC. Graff had level-four security clearance. Only the heads of top agencies like the CIA and the Joint Chiefs of Staff had level-five clearance.

"For a terrorist group, he was a helluva get," Evans said.

"You mean because he can float around?"

"Exactly. Being an AD of OPSEC would have given Graff on-site access to dozens of other government offices." Evans straightened and thought for a moment. "There's got to be some kind of duty or assignment roster. Can you see if anything like that is on file?"

Victoria moved back to the main NSA file. There were several NSA sites with a padlock icon, meaning that they were closed to all but authorized personnel. She tried one. A moment later she got a gray screen, blank save for the word *Forbidden* in small black letters.

"We'll see about that," she said. She booted a decryption program she'd written to find passwords within a system. "What kind of file would those assignments be under?"

"There's homework and fieldwork—so try field."

She typed *field* and asked the program to find a password to unlock the files. Less than a minute later, she had it.

"Sally," she said. "Cute."

Victoria input the code and sat back. The file came up in

less than a minute. She asked for Graff's most recent assignments.

Evans felt the room tilt. For the past two months, there had only been one assignment.

Graff had spent most of his time at the White House.

Twenty-four

Tuesday, 10:01 A.M.
Washington, D.C.

In 1948, during the administration of Harry Truman, the White House underwent a major renovation. The White House, the engineers said, was crumbling. The Trumans moved across Pennsylvania Avenue to Blair House, and the interior of the mansion was gutted. Paneling and ceilings were removed, steel framework was erected in place of the deteriorated wood beams, and new foundations were poured.

Engineers also dug a basement. A deep one, multileveled and fallout-proof, with heavily reinforced ceilings and walls designed to withstand a low-megaton nuclear attack on Washington. Though the Soviets didn't have the atom bomb in 1948, by the time the President and First Lady moved back to the White House in 1952, they did. Within several years, nuclear weapons became powerful enough so that a near-ground-zero hit would destroy the tunnels. By then, however, the sublevels had begun to play a significant role in other security issues, including the prevention of electronic surveillance, greater control of access to sensitive materials, and a control center for a radar net and a half-dozen short-range surface-to-air missiles, which are located on the White House grounds and protect the Executive Mansion from airborne attack. The SAM system is outfitted with lightweight Stinger-POST RMP missiles—Passive Optical Seeker Technique, Reprogrammable Microprocessor—which are five feet long and two-and-three-quarter inches in diameter.

Protecting and operating these sublevels fell to the National Security Agency, which President Truman founded in 1952 to plan, coordinate, and direct security functions in support of United States government activities. Control of communications and ID verification was the responsibility of the Navy's White House Communications Agency. With the Red Scare at its height, Truman felt that security of the facility was too important to entrust to one agency, which could be compromised by a single mole.

There are four levels to the White House basement, accessible by elevators located in the East Wing and the Executive Wing. Together, they more than double the area of the Executive Mansion. The lowest of the four levels is located nearly two hundred feet below ground.

The uppermost sublevel consists of heavily reinforced circular tunnels that lead to the Capitol Building and to the Old Executive Office Building, which is located across West Executive Avenue. Battery-powered, six-passenger trams move continuously from these three sites. The next level, called the Main Sublevel, consists of the War Room to the east, a medical room fully equipped for surgery, and the First Family safe room, which consists of three bedrooms, a bathroom, an office, and a ready room. The third level is comprised of staff quarters, a situation room for nonmilitary briefings, a data library, and technical support facilities for the War Room, Situation Room, and the SAMs. The lowest level has a mess hall, galley, and recreation areas. To protect the sublevels from accidents or sabotage, fire doors could be lowered outside individual rooms by using control panels located on the outside and inside.

On one night of every week, usually from eight to eleven P.M. on Monday or Tuesday, the President leaves the Oval Office and takes the elevator from the East Wing to the third sublevel Situation Room. Here, he holds what have come to be known as the Underground Briefings.

The Situation Room is a brightly lit, wood-paneled conference room consisting of a long mahogany table with computers at each of the dozen stations. The walls are decorated with framed photographs of presidents from Dwight Eisenhower to the present incumbent, all of them meeting here with advisors. Inside the walls are chips that generate variable frequency electronic waves to prevent anyone from eavesdropping or recording what is said. Here, the President receives briefings on three or four subjects of an extremely sensitive nature. Being away from the press, staff, partisan duties, and visiting heads of state gives the President and his closest advisors an opportunity to review data without distractions or interruption.

Typically, the President and Vice President attend these meetings, along with any cabinet member or high-ranking official whose department or agency might be affected by the discussions.

The first of the three Underground Briefings on the agenda was about the deaths of Stuart Hoxworth and Robert MacDougall. President John Gordon, Vice President Lionel Catlin, and Senate Majority Whip Mark O'Hara of California would be meeting with Julius Benson, Assistant Attorney General of the Office of Legislative Affairs; young Deputy Assistant Attorney General Clark Hickock; and

Under Secretary of Defense for Personnel and Readiness Thomas Fitzpatrick.

Hickock was looking forward to the meeting. He had wanted to meet the President for quite some time. The other two men were also looking forward to the meeting because it promised to avert a short, bloody turf war. Crimes against members of the Congress of the United States fell under the jurisdiction of the Justice Department, with the appropriate FBI field office investigating and reporting directly to Hickock. Within minutes of being notified of Senator Hoxworth's death by the Warren County Sheriff's Office, the FBI field office in Richmond, Virginia, had moved to take over the investigation. However, because of Brigadier General MacDougall's rank and his security level within the DOD, plus the fact that he hadn't been accused of any crime, the Pentagon insisted that the FBI not question him until the DOD had conducted its own investigation. And they would not do that until the medical examiner had filed his report and the Warren County Sheriff's Office had completed its initial interviews. They would not give the FBI access to one of their officers without just cause.

By the time the FBI got the case on Monday evening, Robert MacDougall was dead.

The Hoxworth briefing with the President was scheduled to last a half-hour. The FBI had interviewed Moses Cole, the DOD had seized MacDougall's computer, and there seemed to be no loose ends. At the Justice Department, Hickock had already heard that the DOD had found a diskette in MacDougall's office that had a collection of data on formaldehyde deaths. The time coding indicated that MacDougall had created the file after returning from the autopsy. The assumption was that the general was desperate to find a patsy after Cole surprised him by finding the chemical in Hoxworth's system. Failing that, he'd gone to Cole to beg for his help in covering up the murder.

All of that was good, Hickock felt. The matter could be wrapped up quickly. And then the young Huntsman could take care of the job that was his real reason for coming to the White House.

Twenty-five

It had been a very short hour.

Time always moved quickly when there was a crisis, and Evans was beginning to realize they were just skimming the surface of this one. The depth of it was deeply troubling.

After learning about Graff's White House connection, Victoria had gone to the White House homepage at http://www2.whitehouse.gov/WH/Welcome.html. Then, using her ingenious ticks and spiders, she was able to hack her way into the computer at the East Appointment Gate of the White House. She bookmarked the spot in case she needed to get back. The Gate computer gave her access to a list of people who had come to visit Graff when he worked there. Evans was hoping there would be a name or names they could look up.

There was, but only one. It was an officer who worked for the Justice Department, Deputy Assistant Attorney General Clark Hickock had been to see Graff three times during the past two weeks. Victoria input http://www.usdoj.gov and looked up Hickock's biography at the Justice Department's homepage. It had been a civilian ride all the way for Hickock, from clerking for the distinguished San Francisco Judge John Howland to becoming an assistant federal district attorney in Los Angeles to serving as district attorney in Washington, D.C., to being offered a position with the Justice Department.

Though she was exhausted, Victoria recognized the name John Howland. According to the files on General Mac-Dougall's diskette, he was the judge who died of formaldehyde poisoning.

Evans asked her to search the government database for any other mention of John Howland. There were references to cases in which he'd been involved but virtually no personal information. They went back to the Justice Department homepage and got the name of the associate attorney general. They ran a search on her name and came up with news cites of charity functions she'd attended, lobbying groups that had visited her office, and even magazine mailing lists that had her name on them—much more than they had found for Hickock.

"Either Hickock leads a very boring life, or someone's been purging his files," Victoria said.

"Probably both."

"But why? How could information about a magazine subscription be used against him?"

"Very easily," Evans said. "A magazine label indicates how long your subscription runs and when it expires. Show up at a charity function, and you'll probably be photographed; maybe you look like you just had a haircut. Put enough things like that together and you can start to track a person's movements. You were in town to subscribe to a magazine subscription. You might have said something to your barber about where you'd been the week before. The CIA and FBI look into things like that when they run background checks. You'd be surprised at how full a portrait you can sketch of someone's life."

"Amazing."

"The beauty of a purge like this, from the subject's perspective, is that even if you suspect them of being up to something there's no way to prove it—"

"Because they haven't left any kind of trail."

"Right. If we hadn't uncovered the Graff connection, we wouldn't have suspected Hickock of being anything other than a dutiful Deputy Assistant Attorney General."

Victoria tried to hack Hickock's e-mail, but she couldn't get in. She was able to get into his secretary's file, however, which contained a saved message from the White House confirming an appointment with the president for Tuesday—this evening.

Evans knew about those evening meetings. They were held in the underground Situation Room beginning around 8:00 P.M. and usually running until 11:00. He had been to one of them with General Vargas when DARPA had been asked to brief the President, Vice President, and Secretary of Defense about the "GI Bug" program. That was the first project Evans had worked on, the successful creation of beetle-like robot insects made of titanium and piezoelectric ceramics, which were going to be used to scout battlefields ahead of soldiers.

"Two Huntsmen working together at the White House can't be a coincidence, can it?" Victoria asked.

"I don't see how. I also don't like the timing. I don't like it at all."

"Why?" While they spoke, she continued to search for files on Graff and Hickock.

"After the shooting of Robert Kennedy, President Johnson appointed a group of Justice Department officials to do a quiet, independent investigation into the assassination,"

Evans said. "General Vargas was a military courier at the time, and he shuttled a lot of very sensitive paperwork back and forth. The final report was delivered in one of these meetings. Vargas didn't attend, but he told me that it became White House policy for the President and Vice President to be briefed about 'non-natural' deaths of senior federal officials—senators, congressional representatives, ambassadors, cabinet members."

"That would seem obvious. Like the Warren Commission."

"But the Warren Commission's findings were questioned in and out of government," Evans said, "and there are still doubts about whether the whole story is in there. An independent, unpublicized committee would be in a better position to get the facts."

"And knowing that, the Huntsmen might have infiltrated the committee."

"Correct," Evans said.

Victoria was silent. She was unable to find out anything else about Graff or Hickock. Evans thanked her, and then the young woman went to the rec room to get herself coffee before the briefing, leaving Evans alone.

Alone.

There had been times in the Middle East, in Somalia, in Cuba, in Colombia when he went in alone to reconnoiter, meet with intelligence sources, check on a potential safe house, or protect oil pipelines from Iranian terrorists. Even when he was on a mission with one of his SEAL teams, surrounded by personnel that comprised what they called "the safe zone," there was a powerful sense of isolation. Everything outside of them was a potential threat. Evans had never had a problem with that. The SEALs went into a hostile and foreign place to establish a beachhead, to generate short or long-term change. But he never imagined he would feel that way in the United States. That there was a threat directed at them and possibly at duly elected members of the government.

Part of him wanted to ignore the possibility. If he reported the intruders to base security, he could return to the field tests, pretend that there might be a larger, more dangerous problem. He wasn't a commando any longer. He had given that life up.

But honor and patriotism wouldn't let him do that. To the contrary. He began to experience a familiar sensation, what the SEALs used to call a "Rowbuck." A Red, White, and Blue Kicker. A stimulus that blew away fear, personal concerns, and at times even moral inhibitions. Whatever it was—an enemy threat, a death, respect for a commanding officer—it focused your attention on your fellow soldiers and your nation. It was what made a soldier charge a machine gun nest or attempt to hold a position against superior odds. It was what drove Evans to destroy those Scuds in Iraq, despite the potential risk to local civilians.

"Retired soldiers are also civilians," the SEALs chaplain, Father Calvin, had said at his hearing.

And there was something else at work. Evans's faith taught that grace was the ultimate goal, and the path to it was neither arbitrary or necessarily safe. As Father John used to put it, *"Sometimes, it's necessary to box people's ears."* He was ready to take on that responsibility.

Driven by Rowbuck, Evans began to realize that there might be a way to do this and risk only his own neck. That was the jump start he needed. A plan began forming quickly, just as they used to when he was in the field. His heart beat faster, his brain raced from point to point, and a tactical overview came together almost like a religious vision. He knew he could pull off his end. Whether the rest of it would work depended on Victoria.

When Victoria returned with her coffee, Evans asked her to get back into the White House computer. While she did, he explained what he needed her to do. Victoria said she thought she could do it, but cautioned him against it. Not because she didn't think it was right, but because it sounded incredibly risky.

"This is smoke and mirrors," she said. *"Mission: Impossible."*

He said he knew, but he only needed it to survive scrutiny for one night. Then he quoted Father John to her and asked her to join the briefing when she was finished.

As Commander Evans entered the rec room, fired up by his plan, he had a flashback to what he used to feel when he faced his SEAL teams: their palpable sense of expectation. The room was quiet, and all the faces were upturned and eager. If Lewis was still bent out of shape, it didn't show. Like the others, he was above all a professional.

Hopeful as he was about his plan, Evans wished he had something more to give these people. In the past, whenever he briefed a team, he presented them with what special ops called GAS: a *goal,* clear-cut; an *adversary* they knew something about; and both overall and specific *strategies* for dealing with the enemy. At the moment, he had none of those. His strategy consisted of an idea that might not make it past the conceptual stage and, if it did, stood a good chance of going wrong. For an enemy, he had a faceless opponent, vague suspicions of a conspiracy. And there was no defined target.

Evans pulled over a chair, swung his leg over the back, and sat among them. He asked McIver for an update on the dead men. She said that they'd been taken to the base morgue and that General Jackson would notify her if he found out anything else about them. The commander thanked her, then proceeded to tell the rest of the team everything he knew about the Huntsmen; what he, Victoria, and Captain McIver had been doing hacking the NRO; and what he thought the two intruders had come to do.

"If the Huntsmen weren't after the SFUs," Diaz said, "what do we think they'll do next?"

"Run, if they're smart," Holly said.

Taylor grinned and gave him a thumbs up.

"I doubt they'll try another strike like the last one," Evans said. "In case they do, Captain McIver is organizing security with the base commander, and we'll have to set up our own watch down here. Colonel Lewis, I'd like you to work out a roster for the next twenty-four hours."

"Personnel?"

"The four of you and Captain McIver," he said. "Captain Holly, Mr. Diaz, you've got repair detail. See what you can do about securing the vault door we've got out back. Major Taylor, as soon as possible you and I are going to get back outside and work with the SFU. I want you to do some of those exercises I saw you doing in the hall this morning. Get a read on the flexibility of the suits."

"With pleasure, sir."

"But I don't intend to depend solely on defensive tactics. Dr. Hudson and I have worked out a possible next move, which she's attempting to—"

"Definite next move if you still want it," Victoria said as she entered the rec room.

Evans looked at her. "You got me in?"

"You're on the first shift," she said, "the eight to eight-thirty P.M. list. The notification is at the gate and with Executive Secretary Nick Grillo. There were twenty-seven other names on the calendar for today, so I'm guessing Mr. Grillo won't notice that I added yours. To be on the safe side, I copied his e-mail confirmation to Hickock and sent one like it to him and to you, just in case anyone hacks your computer at DARPA."

"Excellent," Evans said. "What about the Human Resources file?"

"That was easy. Your password got me right in. I amended your Defense Department records so that you're now Director of DARPA Internal Affairs," Victoria went on. "I also gave you a fifteen percent raise."

"Thanks." He grinned.

"An e-mail memo from General MacDougall approved your reassignment from N-Gen coincident with his arrival," Victoria said.

"Fine. If anyone checks the file, verifying that will keep them busy long enough to get me through tonight."

"They'll also find today's computer log at DARPA," Victoria told him, "which shows that you spent the morning reading through General MacDougall's e-mail correspondence with Senator Hoxworth. You'll be bringing those files with you."

"Which don't exist."

"Not yet," she said. "They will by the time you leave, so you'll have something to show at the meeting."

"Very good work," Evans said. "And thanks."

"Excuse me, Commander," McIver said, "but what's this all about? Where are you going?"

Evans replied, "I'm going to a White House meeting with the President and someone who may be our key to finding the Huntsmen."

Twenty-six

Axe was quiet, but it was the silence of a stalking wolf. He disliked setbacks, and he disliked surprises. And he had just suffered both.

Dressed in a black sweatshirt and sweatpants, the white-haired man stood in the small lakeside cabin and watched as his slight, graying, chain-smoking communications chief, Mack McQueen, worked at his station. There was a wall of oak shelves stacked with computer, radio, and telecommunications equipment, all of it state of the art. Some of it had been built by McQueen; some of it had been bought from Russian dealers who had taken it from a decommissioned listening post on the Chukchi Peninsula near the Bering Strait. The Russian equipment had been bolstered by technology bought or appropriated from American firms that had been working on com systems for the aborted Strategic Defense Initiative program during the Reagan years.

That was when McQueen had also been decommissioned, losing his job as a communications security expert with the National Aeronautics and Space Administration. He spent time working for a threat analysis group composed of former CIA men. After a year, one of those men—who was also a Huntsman—put Axe together with McQueen.

It was 1:53 A.M. when he first got the call from Will Bannon that he was at a pay phone and about to enter the base. Since then, McQueen had been using his system to monitor most of the electronic communications going to and from the headquarters of Langley commander General Brad Jackson. It would have been too dangerous for Bannon and Graff to communicate with them directly, since Langley was alive with wirefree traffic and a crossed signal would have been disastrous. Bannon would call McQueen directly from the same pay phone outside the base. In the meantime, no communications to General Jackson's office would mean that the two Huntsmen had reached the hackers, taken them out, and gotten away without a problem.

At nearly half-past nine that morning, McQueen intercepted a point-to-point radio message from the office of General Brad Jackson, Langley Air Force Base commander, to Colonel James Warren, Commander of Air Force Office of Special Investigations. The OSI was instructed to have a body bag unit collect two "casualties" in the Morgan hangar, bring them to the morgue, and wait for further instructions. There was no elaboration.

Upon hearing the communication, McQueen notified Axe, who had been in one of the training bunkers. He'd been working with Diablo and Granite, who were in charge of a team that was preparing to travel to Europe for the third part of the operation. The Huntsman leader hurried over. McQueen took off his headset and put the radio on audio. While they listened, he turned on the digital recorder and played the original message for Axe.

"Two men are dead," Axe said in a low, thick monotone. "There should be an automatic code yellow security alert."

"Certainly, there should be more radio traffic about the deaths," McQueen said. "What we're *not* hearing is the equivalent of a combat zone blackout."

"They must be concerned about security breaches," Axe said. "Bannon was air force. If one man turned against them, there might be others. Until they figure it out, communications will be face-to-face or handwritten and then destroyed. Just like in the old days."

"Then why did the general make that initial call?" McQueen asked. "It was in the 800 megahertz range, easy to pick up."

"Regulations," Axe said. "The equivalent of an all points bulletin. The first broadcast before radio silence is used to put everyone on alert."

As they spoke, McQueen had been simultaneously scanning and recording radio, fax, e-mail, and cellular phone communications between the general's office and other base command centers. If any coded messages were received, they'd be run through a decryption unit that had been part of the Russian set-up. There was nothing else about the incident involving the Huntsmen operatives.

Axe spent most of that time pacing the one-room cabin, walking from the wall of equipment to a cot on the opposite side of the room. He never asked if McQueen was sure he had the right frequencies, passwords, or channels. Axe would never have brought McQueen onboard if he didn't have complete faith in him.

They waited nearly an hour. There was no further conversation regarding the dead men.

Axe announced that he was going back to the bunker. He left with his arms folded, his shoulders back, his head sunk in thought. The Huntsmen hadn't lost any personnel for as long as McQueen had been there, and Axe was upset—though at least Bannon and Graff weren't an integral part of the 415 operation. Axe also had to be concerned about why the air force was looking at a satellite database showing Stuart Hoxworth's house. The officer who'd taken the fall for the senator's death was army.

The one consolation—and Axe had to be feeling this as well—was that there didn't seem to be a way the Huntsmen would suffer exposure from this. It was just a few hours before the first part of the operation got under way. The air force would know who the dead men were, but not why they were after the hackers. Valerie Longwood had checked the NRO images as they were going out to the Langley hackers, and there was nothing of value in them. The Huntsmen and their plan would not be compromised.

Until then, McQueen knew that Axe would focus all his energies on the execution of the plan. After that, nothing would stop the Huntsmen leader from his next project.

The execution of the hackers.

Twenty-seven

Tuesday, 5:10 P.M.
Langley Air Force Base, Virginia

Captain McIver came to see Commander Evans while he finished putting on a clean uniform for the White House meeting. As he knotted his tie, she informed him that she had bought him his twenty-four hour delay though General Jackson had not been happy to give it.

"Or 'bestow it,'" she complained. "He runs this place like the Pope runs the Vatican."

Evans smiled for the first time that day. Standing in the open doorway, McIver blushed.

"Sorry, sir," she said. "I meant no disrespect to His Holiness. What I meant was that General Jackson doesn't like to bend the rules. Not even a single letter of them."

"I know what you meant," Evans said.

"I had to assure the general that there was no threat to the base, its personnel, or its facilities."

"We were the target," Evans said confidently.

"Pursuant to which," the captain said quickly, "repairs to the iron plate in the hangar will be completed by 1800 hours.

A motion detector and alarm were rigged inside, and a surveillance camera will be installed in the pit by tomorrow noon. There are also alarms attached to both doors. Mr. Diaz and Captain Holly report that they've secured the door in the back, and Colonel Lewis has worked out a watch roster for the next twenty-four hours. He and I agree that base personnel should not be involved, since we don't know who might also have been in league with Bannon."

"Agreed," Evans said as he went to the locker and removed his hat from the top compartment. He felt refreshed by the quick shower he'd just taken. He had spent the afternoon in the field with Major Taylor and was gratified by the performance of both the soldier and the SFU. But the Huntsmen were a dark, preoccupying problem, more disturbing and elusive than any enemy he'd ever faced.

"Your transportation to Bolling AFB is all set," McIver went on. "You'll chopper up at 1730, have some dinner if you want, and then a car will run you out to the White House. It'll wait and bring you back to Bolling."

"Thank you."

"My pleasure. Sir, I only caught his sweaty self as he headed for his room, but how did Major Taylor do out there?"

"Exceptionally well."

"I guess he must've been wired after what happened down here."

"Major Taylor was definitely pumped," Evans said, "but it was more than that. I started by having him go through his martial arts moves in the nonstealth mode in order to define the boundaries of where he'd be moving. I've worked with dozens of special ops people over the years, and I've never seen anyone who was so physically and mentally centered, so graceful."

"How did the suit perform?"

"I watched through the ALDR eyepiece and everything went pretty much as we expected in a bright-light situation," Evans said. "Because of the suit's thermal levels we're a little vulnerable in the infrared, but we knew that would happen."

The ALDR was the All-Light Digital Recorder. About the size and dimensions of a home video camera, it recorded images in visible, ultraviolet, and infrared light and saved them digitally for maximum clarity. A digital video disk player built into Evans's computer allowed the images to be played back and analyzed.

"You gave Dr. Hudson the DVD?"

"Yes, but I want her to get some sleep after she finishes my diskette for the meeting. What I really wanted to get from this afternoon was the physiological overview. Major Taylor is giving himself a physical now, checking dehydration levels, chafing, circulation in his extremities. He said his fingers actually got cold when he wore the SFU, due to the tightness of the suit."

"Circulation problems," McIver said. "I wonder if we can use something like the pressure nets our pilots wear. A garment to massage the torso and limbs to keep the blood flowing."

"We tried that at one point," Evans said, "but in combination with the SFU it was too cumbersome. Major Taylor suggested there may be vascular dilators we can use."

Victoria knocked on the jamb.

"We can talk about this when you get back," Captain McIver said. "Have a safe trip, Commander."

Evans thanked her; she saluted and left.

Victoria looked exhausted as she handed Evans a diskette and his laptop. "Here it is," she said. "A collection of e-mail correspondence between Senator Hoxworth and General MacDougall. Most of the stuff I wrote is based on the general's calendar entries. In case someone watches over your shoulder, it'll look authentic. I also dumped the general's Huntsmen files on the diskette, just in case you need them."

"Thanks," Evans said. He took a leather briefcase from the locker, opened it, and placed the diskette inside. He began removing SFU folders and putting them on the top shelf. "I'll have a look at it when I get to Bolling. I'm not sure how things are going to go up there, but this is going to help me wing it."

"What do you hope *will* happen at the meeting?"

"I'm really not sure," Evans admitted. "Part of me hopes that nothing happens. We meet with the President, this man Hickock presents his fictious findings, we leave at eight-thirty, and I try to talk to Hickock. Find out what his relationship was with Graff, who else he works with, where he relaxes, eats, who he hangs out with. If Hickock's got something to hide, and he's smart, he may let me in a little and try to find out who I am. Then it becomes a chess game."

"Is that what you used to do overseas?" she asked.

"Occasionally," he said. "People tend to be much more relaxed on their home turf. If you aren't fluent in their language—which most of the time I wasn't—they tend to get a little superior on you. People let down their guard when they're confident."

"I don't understand. What was the point of being there if you couldn't speak the language?"

"I had a microchip transmitter in a very expensive watch I wore, and I'd either sell it to my target or it'd be stolen—a lot of terrorists are bullies. The transmitter would end up on the guy's wrist and broadcast to a nearby listening post. Gave a whole new meaning to security watch."

She smiled. "And what does the other part of you hope about tonight's meeting?"

Evans put his laptop on the bag and closed it. "Since this

is coming close on the heels of two murders, I hope that Hickock has a very specific agenda that tells us something else about the Huntsmen. Names he drops, questions he asks, what remarks seem to perk up his ears—"

"Formaldehyde he tries to slip into the President's coffee?"

"*That* would surprise me," Evans said. "So far the Huntsmen have proven very adept at keeping things off balance."

"What do you mean?"

"Formaldehyde poisoning of the senator, bloody murder of the general, a bold attack on our facility. The lack of a pattern, of predictability, is lethal. Then, there's also the danger that my being at the meeting may change things."

"Hmmm—good point," Victoria said. "It's like when physicists study an electron."

"Sorry?"

"In order for an electron to be a *functioning* electron it has to be in motion—in which form it's an electrically charged cloud. Effectively invisible. If you immobilize it to observe it, turn it into a visible particle, you remove the charge—"

"And it ceases to be a real electron."

"Right."

Evans nodded. "Good assassins are like that. If there's a chance they may be compromised, they'll usually abort whatever they were planning and wait for another shot."

"What if they know this is a one-time-only opportunity?"

"Most of them roll the dice, even if it costs them their lives. Without their reputations, they're dead anyway." His briefcase in one hand, hat in the other, Evans walked toward Victoria.

"I wish there were some way we could monitor you while you're down there," Victoria said.

"Nothing gets out of those White House sublevels that

isn't hardwired," Evans said. "Bugs, cell phones—because of the electronic jammers built into the walls they're useless as communications devices."

"What about e-mail?"

"I believe it goes through a main computer system where it's encrypted. That's what they do at the Pentagon. You need an Omega-7 descrambler at the other end. Otherwise, all you get is garbage."

"Not a simple hack."

"Which is why they use it," Evans said. "Don't worry. I'll be fine."

"I'll stay on-line just the same. VICHUD@opcen.com. What about the risk of N-Gen being exposed?"

"How?"

"If the Huntsmen check up on you the way we checked up on them, follow you back here."

"By satellite?" Evans asked.

Victoria nodded.

"They can't do that because this area isn't covered by satellite," Evans explained. "And from what I understand, the air force has a satellite buster on the base—I believe it's a ruby laser—that would target the gyrostabilizers of any enemy satellite that tried to look down here."

"Clever."

"Anyway, I don't want you to worry about this now," Evans said. "I want you to rest. And don't go charging right into the ALDR disk when I leave."

She smiled at Evans. "Be careful."

He told her he would. But as he left the room he knew that what he had to be careful of wasn't just the danger represented by Hickock and the Huntsmen.

He carried out the justice of the Lord.

The words of Deuteronomy flashed through his mind, and the Rowbuck burned in his belly—burned with the desire to turn the hunters into the hunted. Like all those who sought to satisfy their needs at the expense of others, Evans knew that what he had to be careful of was the danger from within.

That danger that he could become like the Huntsmen.

Twenty-eight

Tuesday, 5:59 P.M.
Langley Air Force Base, Virginia

"So, Major—are you all in one piece?"

Colonel Lewis stepped into the doorway, and Major Taylor looked up. He was sitting on a metal chair between the room's two cots. Spread on the desk before him were the contents of a field medical kit that had been given to him by Captain McIver. It had been augmented by test tubes and several compounds he'd had the captain bring from the base infirmary. The kit had been designed by the United States Army Institute for Military Assistance. Three feet wide by three feet long and two-and-a-half feet deep, the sixty-four pound aluminum trunk contained a portable ventilator, a compact heart monitor and defibrillator, a battery pack, and instruments and drugs to identify and treat everything from combat injuries to NBC exposure—Nuclear, Biological, and Chemical. Taylor had just finished checking his blood pressure and was waiting to finish one more test before he attacked a large glass of water mixed with a saline solution to help him rehydrate.

"I'll be sore as hell tomorrow from carrying the extra weight of the suit," Taylor said, "and I'm a little more dehydrated than I'd like, which worries me. You don't want a soldier pinned down in the suit, passing out, and having an enemy trip over him. We'll have to figure out some kind of dietary supplement. Other than that, I'm doing fine, sir. How's everyone else?"

"Tired. Concerned. How did the commander seem?"

"Alert, undistracted, very cool," Taylor said. "Why?"

"Just curious," Lewis said. "Evans has been away from command for several years."

"Sir, I don't think that matters."

"Oh?"

"I think it's like tennis and sex," Taylor said. "It's one of those things you never forget how to do. Maybe it even makes you hungrier for it when you haven't had it for a while."

Lewis smiled. It was the first break in his nothing-fazes-me Delta Force–issue expression that Taylor had seen since they met.

"I had a look at your stealth suit." Lewis went on. "That seems to have held up pretty well."

"Apart from perspiration pooling in the microphone and shorting it out, the SFU performed pretty much the way Commander Evans expected," Taylor told him. "My only problem with it was the knee and elbow joints, and the instep. They're extremely stiff."

"Like new shoes?"

"No," Taylor said. "It's more like trying to fold layers of bubble wrap. I don't know how much breaking-in those layers of fabric are going to allow. We'll see tomorrow." The medic wrapped an elastic band around his right arm, above the elbow, and pulled it tight with his left hand and teeth. He removed a syringe and several test tubes from the case.

"Tell me something about your martial arts," Lewis said.

Taylor glanced up. "My health, my suit, now my martial arts. Am I being interviewed for something, sir?"

"In a way, yes."

"And what, if I can ask, would that be?"

"Round two, if there is one. I like to know my teammates, their qualifications, what they're thinking. I haven't watched you drill. If we're attacked and I see you facing three intruders, I may have to decide whether to help you or evacuate a wounded team member first."

"I'll save you the rest of the interview, sir," Taylor said. "Take the casualty out. Those three intruders are goin' down like bowling pins."

"I like your style," Lewis said. He sat on the cot to Taylor's right and watched as the medic dabbed a cotton swab with alcohol. "I'd still like to know more about your skills."

Taylor washed the inside of his elbow and set the swab aside. He picked up the syringe and poked it into his arm. "I've been training for a little over seventeen years. Until medicine and girls came along, it was all I cared about."

"What style do you practice?"

"Zujitsu. It was developed back in the 1970s by a marine, Master Chaka Zulu. It uses traditional punches, blocks, kicks, and locks like traditional jujitsu, but in conjunction with constant movement and redirecting your opponent's attack. It's great for multiple opponents. Medicine was actually an outgrowth of my interest in martial arts."

"You mean how it moves?"

"That and how it breaks, how it repairs. Also it's uniqueness."

"Uniqueness?"

"Sure. We're bipeds," Taylor said. He finished filling the first test tube and set it aside. He slipped a second into the plastic chamber. "Most hunters are quadrupeds. Even most simians move along on all fours."

"Never thought of that," Lewis admitted. "Over in Delta, we do mostly Krav Maga these days."

"I know it well." Taylor said. "The Israeli Defense Force style. I studied it for a while when I joined the air force. Anything goes in Krav Maga. Eyeball-gouging, elbow-in-the-teeth, testicle-grabbing, hair-pulling. Quick, nasty, effective." He finished filling the second test tube and inserted a third. "Would you mind releasing the elastic band, sir?"

Lewis obliged. "Will you be up to taking one of the watches?" the colonel asked.

"Wouldn't miss it."

"Good. I'll put you on the three-to-five shift. Commander Evans wants us all suited up at six. That'll give you time to get back in the saddle."

"Fine."

Taylor finished and put the last test tube aside. He pressed a dry cotton swab inside his elbow and folded his arm over. When he was finished here, he'd give the test tubes to Captain McIver to take to the Langley medical lab. He wanted to know how dehydration might have affected the size and efficiency of his red blood cells, the segmentation and number of white blood cells, and the iron stores in his hemoglobin. The major began sipping his water. He looked at the colonel. Lewis had grown thoughtful.

"Is there something else?" Taylor asked.

"Yes," Lewis said. "Like the commander, I'm bothered by what's going on. Not just what happened here today but with these Huntsmen. I know Captain McIver was able to get a delay, but once the official investigation into the deaths of this Bannon and Graff start, the Huntsmen'll scatter. They'll crawl under every rock they can find."

"I know that." Taylor said. "And if I knew where the sons of bitches were, I'd take them out now."

"Would you make a CODE PA?"

"Yes," Taylor said without hesitation.

A COmmand DEcision, Personal Authority, was an offensive strike ordered by a ranking member of a unit against an enemy. It was undertaken in the absence of a present or imminent threat or proof thereof, as well as a lack of explicit orders from central headquarters. In the case of the stealth team, a CODE PA would be an attack without the approval of either General Jackson or Gideon Gynt, the Under Secretary of Defense for Acquisition and Technology, to whom General MacDougall reported. In March of 1968, the destruction of the Vietnamese village My Lai was a CODE PA.

Lewis smiled again. "So would Holly and Diaz and so would I." He rose from the cot.

"And that's what you really wanted to know."

Lewis didn't answer. He didn't have to. "Get some rest," the colonel said. "If there's an emergency, the bells and whistles will go off. If you can't find me, take out anyone you don't know. Otherwise, Diaz will be waking you when he comes off watch."

Taylor said he would. After giving his blood samples to Captain McIver, he sat on his cot drinking his water and wondering whether Commander Evans would go CODE PA against the Huntsmen. It was one thing to talk about it when you weren't in command, quite another to actually have to make the decision.

Taylor was still sitting there, wondering about it, when he leaned his head against the wall beside the bed and fell asleep.

Twenty-nine

Tuesday, 8:04 P.M.
Washington, D.C.

The black air force sedan carrying Commander Evans pulled into the Ellipse, a permit parking zone south of the White House best known as the site of the National Christmas tree. He got out and walked to the Southeast Visitor Entrance. He walked as if he belonged there, but his stomach was gurgling as he waited for the armed guard to check his computer.

"What did you say your name was, sir?" asked the young officer.

"Commander Amos Evans." He spelled his last name.

"And you're here to see—?"

"The President, at eighty-thirty."

The tall, young guard's expression didn't change as he turned his back and picked up the telephone in the booth. Evans knew that he could be calling for confirmation or for security. A second guard in the booth was watching monitors from four surveillance cameras. Evens was on one of them, which seemed strangely redundant. His stomach continued to burble. He'd been on missions where his life was in danger. Yet somehow this was more nerve-wracking—the standing still and waiting. He resisted the urge to tap his foot or look away.

After a short conversation, the guard hung up the phone. He turned back toward Evans.

"I'm very sorry, sir," he said. "You were in the top clearance file and not on the general appointment list. Go straight ahead. Ms. Alice Doyle will meet you at the East Appointment Gate."

The guard passed Evans a clip-on photo ID. Now he understood why the video camera had been turned on him.

He thanked the young men and walked across Hamilton Place to spotlit East Executive. He wondered if Victoria had realized where she'd placed him—or if she even knew. He suspected that as the time of the appointment neared, names were shunted to different lists for easier handling and coordination. It was a good thing they struck as early as they did.

· The White House stood to his left, smaller than in the mind's eye and less majestic than it appeared on TV. Yet it was exquisite in its stately simplicity. Even from here he could see where wood was slightly warped and white paint was peeling along the south portico. It was a reminder that as much as this was a national symbol it was also a two-century-old house, exposed to the region's pounding winter rains and blistering summers.

He reached the door, passed through a concealed metal detector, and was met by a short, slender woman with blond hair. She shook his hand firmly, and he handed his bag to a waiting guard. The older man hand-searched it, flipping through the papers, booting the laptop, then plugging the diskette in to make sure that both were real. Then he passed the bag back and thanked the commander.

"Sorry about the confusion at the appointment gate," Ms.

Doyle said as they turned and walked toward the East Wing access elevator. "Procedures have changed in the three years since you were here last."

They checked that, too. He wasn't surprised.

Evans and Doyle walked down a carpeted corridor, she slightly ahead. They passed portraits of the Presidents and First Ladies as well as small offices, which the staff had long-ago outgrown. They stopped by a white, six-panel door. There was a keypad on the jamb to the left and a small, dark camera eye looking out from just above it. Ms. Doyle entered a five-number code. There was a click, and she turned the knob. They entered. Evans first. Inside, to the left, was a small mahogany desk with a computer and a black phone. A female guard sat behind it. To the right was a wall with three rows of three black-and-white TV monitors each. Ahead was a silver elevator door. It was extremely quiet with the door closed and the blue carpet with gold trim muffling their footsteps.

"Good evening, Ms. Doyle," the guard said.

"Good evening. Commander Amos Evans for sublevel three." Doyle spelled the name.

The armed guard remained seated as she typed in the name to let the guard downstairs know who was coming. She sat quite still, and Evans knew why; he'd asked DARPA's NSA liaison the first time he'd been here. Her foot was on a small pedal. If she removed her foot—or if she were shot and fell over—an alarm would sound and vents in the ceiling would quickly fill the small room with phosgene, a colorless choking gas that smells like freshly cut grass and disables an intruder. As the NSA liaison had put it, *"No one gets in without an invitation."* Evans asked what the guard did when the President entered the room. He was informed that the phosgene trigger was not activated and the guard stood.

A moment later, the elevator door opened soundlessly. Evans saw it happen live and also from inside the elevator on one of the monitors. He stepped in, followed by Ms. Doyle. The carriage was small, and the ride downstairs took less then five seconds. There were no buttons inside; everything was controlled from a station underground.

The elevator let them out in a part of the White House that was quite different from a building that was largely unchanged since the time of Abraham Lincoln. The colors were white, but they were antiseptic. The corridor they were in was lined with white tiles, which were fire and explosion-resistant. The fluorescent lights shone from behind milk-white plastic and bounced off sound-absorbant white tile. They were acknowledged with a nod by a guard who was sitting behind a desk and watching the same monitors as the female guard upstairs. Ms. Doyle smiled at him and turned to the left. They walked down the long, straight corridor. Known as "The East-West Passage," it ran from one end of the sublevel to the other. They passed several closed doors. All of them white, like the one in the corridor upstairs. Vents in the ceiling filled the hall with very cool air. Evans saw only a few people coming and going, most of them military personnel.

Evans looked at his watch. It was coming up on 8:28. "Has anyone else arrived?"

"Under Secretary of Defense Fitzpatrick is here, along with Assistant Attorney General Benson and her associate Deputy Assistant Attorney General Hickock. They had no idea you were coming until they saw the nameplates in the conference room. Do you know any of them?"

"No," he replied, "but then DARPA isn't exactly a high profile facility." His stomach grew tense again. This wasn't like going on a mission where he was watching, observing, participating only when he couldn't sink into a shadow or rest under a tree. He was the outsider, and for all he knew the other three were Huntsmen. "How is the President running?"

"Late, though not as late as usual," Ms. Doyle said. "The President and Vice President should be down in about fifteen minutes. Senator O'Hara is en route from the Capitol and will be here a little sooner."

They stopped by a large conference room that Evans knew from his last visit was the Situation Room—also known as the War Room. The large oval room was wood-paneled with a large desk in the middle and twenty-four chairs. There were two doors on the other side of the far wall; the one on the left was shut. Ms. Doyle led him through the door to the right.

The room was rectangular, brightly lit, with bare, ivory walls and a very low ceiling. It was slightly less than half the size of the War Room. There was a smaller rectangular table, made of dark oak, with eight chairs around it. There were computer monitors at the head and foot of the table and electrical and phone jacks built into the other stations.

Three people were standing in the far corner, near where the President would be sitting. They formed a tight ring, which broke up when the newcomers entered. Ms. Doyle introduced Evans according to seniority. First, he met Julius Benson, Assistant Attorney General of the Office of Legislative Affairs. Benson was in his middle sixties, a tall, distinguished-looking man in a three-piece charcoal gray suit. He had a mane of white hair and pale blue eyes that looked as though they'd never trusted a soul. The men shook hands in silence.

Next she introduced red-haired, barrel-chested Thomas Fitzpatrick, Under Secretary of Defense for Personnel and Readiness. The slightly more gregarious fifty-something

Fitzpatrick greeted Evans with a lively handshake and a few words of welcome.

Finally, Ms. Doyle introduced Deputy Assistant Attorney General Clark Hickock. Hickock had been standing in the corner, behind and between the other men, his arms folded rigidly across his chest. Compared to them he looked like a kid. He was in his late twenties and stood several inches under six feet. His black hair was collar-length and there was a dark five o'clock shadow on his square jaw. His eyes were deep-set, penetrating, and steady. Evans saw a powerful build beneath the tight blue suit, felt it in his strong handshake. He had the kind of confidence Evans usually saw in ROTC greenies who hadn't experienced combat.

Ms. Doyle pointed out the water pitchers and coffee on a corner table. Then she excused herself and left. Evans put his briefcase on the table.

"Commander Evans," Fitzpatrick said. "Ms. Doyle tells us that you're with DARPA."

"That's right."

"You weren't originally scheduled for this meeting."

"No, sir." Evans said. "I was reviewing General Mac-Dougall's files. When I found some things that appeared to be of interest, I had my assistant call over. She made the arrangements."

"What sort of things did you find?" Benson asked.

"Correspondence between General MacDougall and Senator Hoxworth. E-mail that demonstrates, I believe, the general had no reason to poison the senator."

"If that were true, why would he confess?" Fitzpatrick asked.

"The question is, did he really confess?" Evans said. "And did he really shoot himself?"

"Another Vince Foster case," Benson said dismissively. "Spare me."

There was a moment of silence. Fitzpatrick turned toward Benson, and the two men began discussing the status of the new DOD budget, especially with Hoxworth no longer present to oppose key spending elements. While they spoke, Hickock faced Evans.

"You've got the sun baked into your face," the young man said. "You didn't get that in the Dungeon."

There was nothing accusatory in Hickock's tone; it was simply an observation, cocky and a little smug.

"No," Evans replied. "I was with the SEALs for over seventeen years before joining DARPA."

"In what capacity?"

"Command."

"Field or HQ?"

Evans was being interrogated, but as a threat or a potential recruit, he wondered. The Huntsmen *had* lost two men today.

The idea offended him, and the notion of tracking this bastard and infiltrating the Huntsmen vanished in a hot blast of anger. Evans looked at the poised young man. And as he had often done in the field when the opportunity presented itself, he decided not to collect intel for a future attack but to seize the opportunity and strike then and there.

"I spent most of my career in the field," he replied, "though I'm not working in the Dungeon right now. I'm stationed at Langley."

Evans watched as, for the briefest moment, Clark Hickock's easy manner hardened. The young man recovered quickly except for the eyes. They seemed hot and restless.

"What's DARPA got going at Langley?" Fitzpatrick asked.

"I'm afraid that's classified, sir," Evans said, still looking at Hickock—the traitor. The murderer.

"Figured it might be," Fitzpatrick said. "Still, doesn't hurt to ask."

"No, sir." Evans decided to turn up the heat. "But I can tell you that they're not spending any of the taxpayers' money on amenities. They've got us working inside a series of spartan old bomb shelters."

This time Hickock didn't flinch. Evans suspected he'd been half-expecting that one. The young man's eyes continued to burn.

Another White House aide came in just then with Senate Majority Whip Mark O'Hara of California at his side. The huge former L.A. Raiders fullback entered the room slowly, like a bull easing into a stall, his massive shoulders rocking gracefully from side to side. Like Senator Hoxworth. O'Hara was a fiscal conservative. However, because of the large numbers of aerospace and electronics contractors based in California, O'Hara had been less aggressive on matters of military austerity than his colleague.

The aide introduced the Senator around just moments before President John Gordon and Vice President Lionel Catlin arrived. They came with one executive assistant each, both sharp middle-aged women. The White House aide left quickly, the President's assistant shut the door, and the men quickly shook hands, Evans saluting. The fifty-eight-year-old President was a short, wiry former New York police commissioner who had leap-frogged from two-term mayor of New York to two-term senator to President. He had a devilish smile and a sarcastic wit that had won him the votes of women and cynics in a tight race. The Vice President was a forty-nine-year-old former Michigan governor who stood nearly six-four and had the zeal and charisma of a televangelist.

The President's assistant went to the coffee cart across from the door and poured her boss black coffee in a Brooklyn Dodgers mug. Everyone else took their seats, the President at the head of the table, the Vice President at the foot, the other men where the cardboard nameplates had been placed. Hickock was directly across from Evans. Hickock and Fitzpatrick opened the laptops they'd brought and plugged them in. Evans did likewise. The executive assistants sat behind the President and Vice President. Each woman opened an electronic notebook which she placed on her lap. Both assistants were within easy reach of wall phones, which hung directly behind them to their right.

All the while, Clark Hickock looked like a man who was trying hard to act pleasant. He had gone to the coffee cart and poured himself coffee, his back to the group. He stirred in milk and some nonsugar sweetener and made small talk with his boss as everybody settled in, and he expressed his regrets to Senator O'Hara, who was sitting directly across the table, to the left of Evans, over the events that had brought them here. But his movements were stiff, unnatural, and he didn't look at Evans once after their exchange. Not once. He adjusted the position of his laptop as if he were a concert pianist fixing the position of his bench.

The President asked Senator O'Hara to chair the meeting. O'Hara thanked him and asked Assistant Attorney General of the Office of Legislative Affairs Benson to bring them up to speed on the DOD's investigation into the death of Brigadier General MacDougall. Benson said that he hadn't had a chance to review whatever data Commander Evans had in his possession, but he would tell them what the DOD had found.

And then something happened. Something Evans hadn't anticipated.

Thirty

Tuesday, 8:39 P.M.
Allegheny Mountains, West Virginia

"Who is that bastard *really*?" Axe snapped at the monitor. "Is he one of the hackers?"

The Huntsman leader and Mark McQueen were looking at a computer monitor in the communications shack. On the screen was a slightly pixilated image that was coming from a pin-thin camera built into the latch of Clark Hickock's laptop. It had been activated when he popped the lid and was being fed through the jack in the table to the computer of the guard stationed at the downstairs elevator. The guard was also one of Axe's men. He was the one who first noticed the addition of Evans's name to the list two hours before and alerted Hickock. They quickly checked the government databases and found out that he was with DARPA. They also found out everything he'd done since he entered kindergarten. What they couldn't find out was what he was doing now.

"His uniform's navy," McQueen said as he looked at the twenty-one inch screen. He lit a fresh cigarette with the one he was smoking. "He probably wouldn't have been at Langley. And he sure doesn't look like a hacker."

"Maybe he wasn't at Langley," Axe agreed. "But he wasn't supposed to be here either."

They listened as Julius Benson began to speak. The sound and video were coming through the jack in the desk, picked up by dedicated lines linked to the security guard's computer and modemed out. Axe was angry at himself. They'd arranged it so they could eavesdrop on meetings in this fashion, but they hadn't made it possible to communicate with their personnel on the inside. Anything that was typed into the keyboard was dumped into the central White House computer and saved—as "minutes" according to the White House. As a form of control, according to many who came here. To them, it wasn't much different from tape recording conversations in the Oval Office.

Commander Evans hadn't come to the White House from DARPA. They'd hacked the computer logs at the security desk. He hadn't been there for two days. He'd come from somewhere else, but they had no idea where. The log at the entrance gate said he'd walked to the checkpoint. The only navy vehicles in the parking lot belonged to known personnel.

"What will Hickock do?" McQueen asked.

"What he's supposed to do." Axe replied confidently. "He's been part of this from the start. He worked with the team writing the Fitzpatrick dossier. He matched the laptops. He *knows* the score. But something's not right."

Axe picked up the phone on the wall and punched in the number of the training area. Diablo answered.

Axe told him that he wanted the team ready to get under way by midnight. Granite was to notify the drivers and have them be prepared to make the adjustments. Axe said that if anything happened, he didn't want his personnel pinned down here.

Diablo asked him what he thought could happen.

"I don't know," he replied, "but I'm hoping that in a few minutes the question will no longer matter."

Axe hung up. He was also hoping that in a few minutes he could place the call he had been waiting to make to the man who was the cornerstone of the 415 operation.

The man who would do what others had tried to do and failed. Move the world forward under one hand, one vision.

Thirty-one

Hickock jumped back and swore as he spilled hot coffee in his lap. Julius Benson stopped his recitation.

"Damn!" Hickock said, rising quickly and furiously patting the front of his thigh. He looked at the President. "I'm so sorry, Mr. President."

"It's all right." Gordon replied. "Are you okay?"

"Yes," he replied. "More embarrassed than anything."

The Vice President's aide rose to get paper towels from the coffee cart. Evans watched Hickock.

"If you'll all just excuse me for just a moment," Hickock said.

"The men's room is down the hall to the right," the vice presidential aide said as she placed paper towels on the spilled coffee.

"Thank you." Hickock said as he started toward the door. "Again, I'm very sorry."

He opened the door and left. Evans was staring blankly at the back of Hickock's computer.

What was this about? Was Hickock trying to smoke him out, see whether Evans suspected anything? Did Hickock want to force Evans to make a move, warn the President about something when there was no danger at all? Make it seem as though he'd flipped out?

Or had Hickock actually put a plan into motion, gone ahead with whatever he may have been planning? *Just like any good assassin would do.* But who said that Hickock was an assassin?

Senator O'Hara got the meeting going again. Evans wasn't listening as Benson began talking again.

What would an assassin do if he only had one turn at bat? Or if there were a timetable that depended upon him striking at a certain time and place?

Evans looked at Hickock's station. What had he left behind? The spilled coffee. The water in the coffee could be a catalyst for something, a powdered chemical agent that he may have left on the table. Evans had done something like that once. It was in a restaurant in Antigua where Israeli arms dealers had come to sell their wares. He'd sneezed in order to bend, cup his nose in his hand, and slip filters into his nostrils while a packet of sugar—really powdered tear gas—was rehydrated in his tea. In the confusion that followed, he was able to collect utensils with the dealers's fingerprints.

But nothing was happening with the coffee.

There was no briefcase. Hickock had left nothing on the seat. What about the computer? Was there something inside, a bomb the security check might have missed?

Evans considered going after Hickock. But if the Huntsman had left something lethal behind, that wouldn't save the President. It would only keep Hickick from getting away. If he were expendable to the Huntsmen, that might not help to stop them.

Evans rose. "Mr. President, please evacuate this room at once!"

Benson stopped speaking and looked up. The President and the others appeared startled.

"Quickly!" Evans said urgently.

"What the hell's going on?" the President demanded.

Just then Evans heard a high, faint hum. He looked back at Hickock's computer. The CD-ROM drive was on. There was the hint of a tart, familiar odor. In a single motion, Evans leaned across the table and swept the computer aside with his right arm. The cable connecting it to the table snapped, and the laptop flew off the table.

"Move back!" Evans screamed as he stood and leaned to the left.

The Vice President was nearest to the door. He and his assistant got up and started toward it. As they did, Evans reached in front of Senator O'Hara and pulled the edge of the table toward him, moving it away from the President. Computers fell off, and O'Hara jumped back as the bottom of the table legs dragged across the carpet.

"Jesus, man!" O'Hara cried.

Sitting behind President Gordon, his assistant had already picked up the receiver of the wall telephone and was calling security when Evans suddenly grunted and flipped the table over. Even as it was falling, the room filled with a deafening roar and a white flash as Hickock's laptop exploded.

Thirty-two

Tuesday, 8:47 P.M.
Washington, D.C.

When he left the conference room, Clark Hickock did not go down the hall to the right in search of the rest room. He quickly walked the fifteen yards to the end of the corridor toward the security desk. His mouth was tight, and his hands were fists. His shoulders were straight and rigid.

The new millennium and the new America were ready to set out together, toward the same goal: the creation of a new and more glorious American century. The first of many.

This will not be stopped.

Hickock looked at his watch then looked back at the conference room as he walked. He wanted to fuck that SEAL bad but would settle for him being dead. He was looking forward to leaving here, going back to Axe, and telling him that the mission had been successful. That a new generation of make-nice politicians like the ones who had let his own father rot in a North Korean prison for seven goddamn years were dead.

That was something he had in common with the security

guard down here, navy Lieutenant Richard Thatcher.
Thatcher was a member of the navy's White House Communications Agency. The WHCA controlled security checkpoints of the sublevels under the supervision of the National
Security Agency. Apart from being a good man, one of
Graff's "gets" among the recent Huntsmen recruits.
Thatcher's father was a Vietnam vet who remained missing
in action. He had a lot of anger for peaceniks. As soon as the
laser in the CD-ROM drive heated the explosive in the disc
and the package went up, Thatcher would be the first one on
the scene. He'd move debris around in order to get to the
President and help him—as if anything could. The thermal
blast was designed to superheat the air to 195 degrees for a
radius of fifteen feet. It wouldn't fall below 110 degrees for
thirty seconds. If the shards of plastic from the computer
didn't kill them, the heat would destroy the windpipe and
lungs of anyone who breathed. In the process of trying to
reach the President, Thatcher would make sure that whatever was left of the laptop was located as near as possible to
Fitzpatrick. When he had arrived before the others, Hickock
had taken pains to move the name cards so that he was sitting in the seat which had been assigned to Fitzpatrick. The
records upstairs would show that the Under Secretary had
been sitting at ground zero.

At the same time, at exactly 8:50, data would be dumped
from Huntsmen computers into Fitzpatrick's computer at the
Department of Defense, and money would be placed in his
name in a South Korean bank account. The data would link
Fitzpatrick to General MacDougall—who was bitter about
his "demotion"—and a plot to rid the government of financial conservatives like Stuart Hoxworth, President Gordon,
and Vice President Catlin. The money would link them both
to Asian and European interests that were tired of American
financial terrorism—trade and loan sanctions, multibillion

dollar United Nations debt, undue influence over the World Bank and the International Monetary Fund, and the ability to finesse interest rates to keep the stock market soaring.

Or at least, that's what people would be led to believe thanks to careful leaks from Huntsmen sources in government. The story-hungry press would inhale the leaks, and the conspiracy-minded public would turn innuendo into fact. The faceless foreigners and discredited American officials would be presented as people determined to destabilize the government of the United States and send investors back to other markets.

The new President, Speaker of the House Wyler from New Mexico, would tell the nation that he had heard the rumors and would see that they are investigated thoroughly. In the meantime, fanned by the leaks, American sentiment would turn quickly against the anti-Americans abroad. Getting a new agenda, a new militarism through Congress would be easy. Especially with a Huntsman assassin threatening every decisionmaker who was inclined to vote against the new President. When faced with compromise or extinction, the decisionmakers would quickly become Wylerites, just like the doves who had opposed intervention in World War II until Pearl Harbor was bombed.

But that was not what preoccupied Hickock right now. He was responsible for the assassinations and at any cost they would happen. If for some reason the bomb failed, he had an alternate plan, one which he would have to take the fall for. But he was willing. The Huntsmen also had a file attaching him to MacDougall, just in case it was needed. He waited for the blast, all the while half-expecting Evans to come out before then under some pretense, checking to see where Hickock was. When he did, he would die. They'd worry about tying him to the plot later. The security guard had stood when he saw Hickock coming and had the elevator waiting—not just to get Hickock away but to keep other people from coming down for the nine o'clock session. But Hickock did not get in.

He stopped, turned to the desk, and leaned forward on his knuckles.

"There was a navy man in the conference room," Hickock said thickly, "a Commander Evans from DARPA."

"Yes, sir. He was a late addition."

"Approved by whom?"

Thatcher sat. He looked down at his computer and clicked on Evans's name. A short profile came up along with a photograph, thumbprint, and a code indicating which computer the name had come from.

"Commander Evans's attendance was authorized by the President's secretary," Thatcher told him.

"Bullshit. I'll bet she doesn't even know who he is."

Thatcher reached for his phone.

"No, don't call," Hickock said. He looked at his watch. "We don't have time for that. But something's definitely up. He was baiting me in there. Said he was from Langley."

Thatcher's face grew stony. "What did he know?"

"I'm not sure," Hickock replied. "Do you have a throw-away?"

Thatcher nodded. He bent and yanked up his right pants leg. There was a small, leather holder tied to his lower leg. He unsnapped the top flap and slipped out a sharpened object that looked like an ice pick. It was one piece made entirely of plastic. Evans could easily have walked the weapon right past the magnetometer at the gate. All Thatcher would have to do was clean his own fingerprints off and place it in Evans's dead hand.

"Good." Hickock said.

Thatcher replaced the stiletto, closed the flap, and smoothed out his pants leg.

"Does Robinson have C-4?" Hickock asked.

Thatcher nodded again. "Small stick. Do you want him to be ready for something?"

"I'll know in a minute. Meanwhile, call Sabal. Tell him to prepare a se-cam and telephone shutdown if we need it."

Thatcher picked up the phone. If it were necessary to go to the next level, Hickock wanted to be sure the security cameras were down. There mustn't be a record of anything that was being done down here. Computer logs recording the shutdowns would be erased by a virus that had been entered earlier in the week by Graff.

"Done," Thatcher said.

"And you're ready to cut the Internet line and erase the log?"

"Sabal's software is installed. All I need to do is press two buttons, and the records are gone."

"That should be all we need," Hickock said.

The software would cut their only link to Axe, a line that also carried the video feed from the conference room—the proof he'd need to show others that he had gotten to the President in his innermost sanctum and could get to them if they didn't cooperate. The program would also eliminate any record that the link had ever existed.

"As for that son-of-a-bitch Evans," Hickock went on, "if he comes out cut him down. Say he attacked me. We can always make him a part of the MacDougall-Fitzpatrick group."

Hickock looked at his watch again. There were just seconds left. He turned, walked to the elevator, and waited. Because of the ban on taping participants at any White House meetings—even for security reasons—the section of the hallway leading to and from the conference room was not covered by video surveillance. Hickock would tell investigators later that he was on his way to the rest room when the explosion happened. As Thatcher went to investigate, Hickock panicked. His only thought was to get to safety.

A moment later, ground-shaking thunder rolled from behind the closed door. Alarms howled almost at once.

"False alarm," he said with a grin. "I guess you won't be needing that throwaway."

"No, sir."

Hickock was still smiling as he stepped toward the elevator. What he really needed to do, arriving upstairs and feigning panic as he reported the explosion to the guard, was to get out of the building. Reach the cabins as soon as possible, not just to get himself away from the investigation but to inform Axe that someone at Langley had been onto him. That the NRO hackers may have found out more than Axe suspected.

The Huntsman turned and faced the buttons. He reached out to press main floor.

"Hickock!"

He looked out as Evans swung into the hall and ran toward him. The officer was dirty, and there were red flash-burns on his arms where his uniform had burned away. But he was obviously unharmed.

"Stop him!" Hickock hissed.

Thatcher was already on his feet. He stepped around the desk and reached for his side-holstered automatic.

"Wait!" Evans said. "The President's all right! It's Hickock who—"

The guard's automatic came free. Evans was about six feet from the Situation Room door. He stopped.

Hickock watched as Thatcher fired.

Thirty-three

A moment before the guard fired, Evans saw the gun being drawn.

During SEAL training, Evans learned that there are several ways to survive a gun attack. Typically, shooters don't expect their target to charge them. If the target is trained, he or she can do a forward somersault and come out of it standing to the front or to the side of the gunmen. Getting control of the gun in close proximity is relatively easy. If the shooter is too far to be reached in a single somersault, the target needs to drop, straighten the body with legs pressed together, toes pointing in a line with the legs, and hands across the chest, and go into a pencil roll—the quickest way to move from side to side, The pencil roll also presents a narrow moving target that is relatively difficult to hit.

Perhaps Hickock had managed to convince the guard that Evans was the one who'd engineered the explosion. Or maybe the navy guard was in league with the Huntsmen. In either case, once Evans saw the firearm, he knew he had to get back into the Situation Room. He wasn't close enough to reach the weapon and disarm the gunman before he could fire again. Removing himself from the line of fire was his only option.

Evans dropped backward onto his butt, slapping his hands on either side of him to break his fall. Then he pencil-rolled to the wall and somersaulted once to the door to his left, back into the main conference room. Through the cloud of dusty debris, Evans could see the President and Senator O'Hara emerging from the smaller room.

"Go back, sir!" Evans cried as he rose. He had to shout to be heard over the alarm.

"Commander, Benson and Fitzpatrick are hurt—"

"Go *back*!"

The President stopped just outside the conference room. O'Hara ran up behind him. His forehead was bleeding.

Evans placed himself between the President and the main door as he motioned the men back. "The guard tried to kill me," he said.

"Maybe he thought you planted the bomb," the President said. He started forward. "Let me go out and speak with him—"

"Sir, Hickock was with him. They may be working to-gether. Who'll be answering that alarm?"

"The fire squad."

"Coming from—?"

"Staff quarters, right below us. Seven men."

"If they're even on our side," Evans said.

"What are you saying?" O'Hara said. "That this is some kind of goddam conspiracy?"

"Yes sir, that's exactly what I'm saying. Is there any way we can call for backup?"

"The Secret Service will be coming down with the fire team," the President said.

Just then, Evans heard footsteps in the corridor. They were hard soles, not the soft-soled shoes Hickock had been wearing. It was the guard. Evans felt naked. He pushed the President back.

"Please, sir, stay inside."

The President backed up several steps, though he remained in view. He appeared calm and very alert. Evans hurried toward the outer door. He removed his belt as he ran.

The walls of the smaller conference room had sustained some damage, mostly dents and some buckling. While they might not be entirely bomb-proof they were probably bullet-proof, which meant that the would-be assassin would have to come through the door if he intended to do any shooting. Evans intended to make that extremely difficult. He held the belt by the tongue, buckle end out, and stopped just inside the jamb facing the hallway. If the bastard tried to poke gun or eye in, he'd get the whip.

The footsteps stopped just outside the door. Evans breathed silently through his nose. He heard a quick series five of high beeps, like a pager. From the inner doorway the President was listening, too. Could the guard be setting a timed explosive to toss into the room?

"The fire door!" the President shouted suddenly. "They're lowering it manually!"

Evans remembered seeing the small numeric panel on the wall beside the jamb. He swore as a chrome steel plate dropped from the top of the doorway. It came down so fast there wasn't time to try and slip something under it, give them a handhold to attempt to raise the door again by hand. Evans pounded it with the side of his fist as it closed.

"Is there a control panel in here?" he asked the President.

"On the wall to the right," the President told him. "See it there, near the phones?"

Evans looked to the right. "Got it!" he said, just as the power died.

"Jesus!" said O'Hara. "What now?"

A pair of bright emergency lights flashed on in the Situation Room. The small conference room remained dark. The lights in there must have been damaged by the blast.

Evans picked up one of the wall phones. It didn't work. The President walked over. With the fire door shut there was no longer any reason for him to stay in the back room.

"Anything?" the President asked.

Evans shook his head. "Mr. President, I think you've got some design flaws down here which need to be addressed."

"These sublevels were designed to survive a nuclear strike, not sabotage," the President said.

The President was still calm. Evans liked this man. He hung up the phone and tried another. It was dead.

"Who has access to the fuse box and phone system?" Evans asked. He was still trying to ascertain the extent of Huntsmen penetration.

"The sublevels have their own power supply and switchboard," Gordon said calmly. "The generators and the fuse panel are both located on the bottom floor under the Executive Wing."

"The guard probably couldn't have gotten to them this quickly."

"It's unlikely."

"So they probably have accomplices." Evans looked around. He saw the vents in the ceiling. They were too small to crawl through, but that wasn't what he was thinking. "Can they shut the air down?"

"If they kill the pumps, yes. That will stop the air from circulating everywhere down here—"

"But they can't reverse the fans."

"I don't believe so," the President said. "If nothing else happens, we can last for hours."

"Maybe," Evans said. "But I'm not counting on nothing happening."

"Why? What can they do?"

"They can open the door and come at us with something else. They can hold you hostage, slip in reinforcements for an attack, or pump in a toxic agent," Evans said.

"Do you really think they'd be *that* prepared?"

"I don't know. But I want to be prepared. These men obviously wanted to assassinate you and probably the Vice President. That's why they selected this time and place to strike. One or more of them are probably seasoned assassins, and I don't think this setback is going to stop them." Evans looked around. "Just how bomb-proof and fireproof are these rooms?"

"You know as much as I do," the President said, glancing back at the smaller room. "As I understand it, these sublevels were designed to survive an above-ground nuclear attack."

"That's percussive, not concussive."

O'Hara walked over. "What's the difference?"

"A nuclear weapon exploding several thousand feet in the air, as most do, or even on the ground would hit this place with shock waves. The earth would soak up a lot of that. We'd also be protected from fallout."

Just then they heard muted gunfire. The men looked at each other in the bright white light.

"What the *hell* is this all about?" Senator O'Hara asked of no one in particular.

"Mr. President, do you have any idea where those shots are coming from?" Evans asked.

"From underneath us, it sounds like."

"Agreed. From the staff quarters, would you say?"

The President nodded. "I guess not everyone has signed onto Mr. Hickock's agenda."

"What agenda are we talking about?" O'Hara demanded.

"A coup d'état would be my guess," Evans said.

O'Hara stared at him. "You've got to be kidding. By who? The Speaker of the House?"

"I wouldn't rule anyone out," Evans said. "Or the Speaker may be a target as well."

"Christ!" O'Hara said.

The senator's exclamation didn't usually bother Evans when it was said by men under fire in combat. There, it seemed like a tough little prayer said under pressure. Here it was an expletive, and Evans didn't like it. But this wasn't the time to let it get to him.

Evans also didn't like the idea of waiting to be rescued, especially when they had no way of knowing who was winning. He was trying hard to get a step ahead of the Huntsmen, figure out what they might try next. He looked at the computers on the desk of the Situation Room. They were useless, all of them run off the room's main power source.

"You're right about Hickock facing resistance, Mr. President," Evans said, "but the assassins obviously don't intend to run. The question is what will they do next? What else is down here that they can use?"

The President stood there shaking his head slowly. Then he stopped and looked at Evans. "The SAMs."

"You mean the White House security net?"

President Gordon nodded. "The controls are down there."

"How can they hurt us?" O'Hara asked.

"That depends," Evans said. "How are the missiles arrayed?"

The President hesitated.

"Sir, I have psi-level clearance at DARPA," Evans said.

"If I'd meant you any harm, I'd have left the room with Mr. Hickock."

"There are four missiles located on the roof, eighteen more in underground tubes," the President informed him.

"I thought this place is bomb-proof," O'Hara said.

"If they target this room with eighteen SAMs, we're going to feel it," Evans told him.

"But the password changes daily," the President said. "Even if Hickock's people can get to the controls, they may not have the password."

"Or they may. Do you have it?"

The President nodded.

"I wonder if we could put in a close-down order and make it stick," Evans said.

"Not from here," the President said. "The control room is a completely dedicated system for exactly that reason."

"What about the central computer?" Evans pressed. "Would that have gone down with the phones?"

"No," the President said. "There's a shut-out system down here, but it's a separate network."

"I'll bet they didn't shut that down," Evans said.

"Why?"

"Phone calls are logged and outgoing cellular calls would have been blocked by the electronic grid down here," Evans said. "A computer is the only way they could communicate with their group without being detected."

"Maybe they're still on-line," the President said.

"I was just thinking that," Evans said. "I'm also thinking that if the system's still on line we may be able to get a signal to someone on the outside. Would anyone be on station in your office, sir?"

"If there's a Code Red or Blue in effect, the Secret Service will be outside the Oval Office. But what good would that do? They know where we are. They just can't get to us."

"Maybe not," Evans said. "But there might be someone who can."

"Who?"

Evans started running toward the back room. "Mr. Vice President, did my laptop survive?"

"It looks pretty banged up."

The President was following Evans. "What are you thinking?"

"If it's working, I may be able to reach someone," he said.

"Who?"

"The only people who may have any kind of chance to get in here."

Thirty-four

Mind-sets change quickly.

Just a few minutes before, all that mattered to Clark Hickock was completing his mission clean and reporting back to the cabins and to Axe. Now, as he followed Richard Thatcher and Sublevel Chief Engineer Pete Robinson down the corridor for a rendezvous with Joe Sabal and a trip to the missile control room, nothing mattered more than completing the mission whatever the price. Hickock disliked failure. He disliked it more than Axe did. And even if it cost him his life, he had no intention of failing.

Robinson had already shut down the access elevators from the main control panel near his office, meaning that there was only one way to get into or out of the sublevels, which was via a staircase in the Executive Wing. While Thatcher shut the Situation Room fire door, Hickock had locked the staircase door. It would take security personnel over an hour to cut through the steel panel—about as long as it would take for them to cut through the Situation Room fire door or restore power. By then, it wouldn't matter.

The three men had come to the bottom level to meet the fourth man the Huntsmen had down here: Assistant Director of Data Security Joe Sabal. The plan was to get to the missile control section, crack the password, and detonate the East-Wing SAMs in their launch tubes. Thatcher calculated that the explosion would take out the second, third, and fourth sublevels on that side. If they timed it right, Hickock and the others could get to the West Wing and safety. The explosion would not only kill the President and Vice President, it would destroy all evidence of their activities down here.

The fire alarm on the third sublevel and the elevator shut down had set up a Blue Alert situation—the presumption of a state of siege. Secret Service operatives whose job it was to know where the President was at all times would quickly secure the upstairs, the grounds, and protect the First Family. But they weren't a threat to Hickock because they couldn't get down here. The only ones trained and willing to throw their bodies in front of a bullet to save the President, and they were completely helpless.

Off-duty navy guards and NSA personnel were being mustered in the corridors. The problem with 'the gathering of the clans,' as Axe had once disdainfully labeled it, was that the military no longer shoots first and asks questions later. Vietnam kicked the policy of what was now called "extreme preemptive force" into the shit can. Official military policy was to defend without yielding, but not to attack without a clear goal and identifiable enemy.

And that was what was wrong with America today, Hickock thought as the body count climbed.

Thatcher worked under no such limitations. He and the others walked confidently, purposefully, as though they belonged here. And they shot down all military personnel they encountered. The security cameras were out, and the dead men couldn't sound alarms or get on their radios and provide locations. That was what had enabled the four Huntsmen to get to the fourth sublevel uncontested before locking out that access elevator. Thatcher scored an Uzi from one of the dead guards, which made taking out resistance much quicker and easier.

Sabal's usual station was in the communications room on the bottom level. It was his computer program that had allowed Hickock's video to be fed through Thatcher's station on out to Axe's computer. Sabal assured Hickock that by using discarded passwords from the past few days he could quickly translate the launch code for today.

Hickock knew that as word of the killing-path spread, things would close up tight around the missile room. That was why they'd had to move quickly: the missile control room was a red-zone. Along with the communications center and power station, it was one of the first places that would be sealed off. If that had already happened, he'd use the C-4 that Robinson kept for emergencies. If Axe had stressed anything in the years Hickock had known him, preparedness had to be at the top of the list.

Sometimes things went wrong, and Commander Evans had been one of those surprises. Ultimately, however, it would mean only one thing: that at the end of the day, the Huntsmen would have one less enemy.

Thirty-five

Tuesday, 9:11 P.M.
Washington, D.C.

Evans's laptop had survived, more or less.

None of the computers had come through the blast intact, nor any of the monitors. All they had in the conference room was one working keyboard with some of the keys melted from the heat of the blast. Not that it mattered. There was nothing to plug it into. Without power, they couldn't boot and use any of the dedicated stations in the situation room.

Perspiring, Evans lifted his machine off the floor and blew off the powder that had once been part of the surface of a conference table. He looked at the computer. The screen was shattered and missing big chunks, but the insides seemed to have survived and the battery was still working. The cable on the side had popped from the unit, and the connector was broken, but that was all right. He could probably cannibalize a line from one of the machines in the other room.

"What do you want to do with it?" the President asked.

"I've got personnel based at Langley who may be able to get us out," Evans said.

"So you said. How?"

"I'm not at liberty to say," Evans replied.

The President made a face.

The number keys were melted along the top of the keyboard. So were some of the control keys along the right and left sides. With luck, though, he wouldn't need them.

"This may be doable," Evans said.

"What may be?" the President asked.

"I'll tell you in a moment, sir."

The President made another face. Evans wasn't trying to be evasive. He just didn't want to stop and explain.

Evans walked quickly into the situation room. He set the damaged machine on the large conference table, found a cable that would fit the jack on his computer, and plugged it into one of the outlets in the table. He looked at the keyboard under the white light.

"All right," Evans said. "Mr. President—how do I get up to the computer in your office?"

"Enter, all in caps, KISMET, backslash, PIPPIN, colon."

Evans did. "Theoretically now, I'm connected to the Internet."

"That's correct."

"Will anyone upstairs see this?"

"Perhaps. But they won't interfere. I've given you the emergency code, which only the Vice President and I have."

"Okay," Evans said. He looked at the keyboard and logged on—he hoped. He felt some of the sweat on his neck begin to cool when he heard the familiar welcome. He moved the cursor to where the mailbox should be. Again, he hoped that he'd got it right. There wouldn't be any more audio prompts.

His own stolid reflection in what remained of the shattered screen taunted him. Unadorned reality wasn't what he wanted right now. He needed cyberspace to contact invisible soldiers.

After giving the computer what he hoped was enough time to open his mailbox, Evans typed:

VICHUD@OPCEN.COM

Then he typed in a series of letters and symbols:

e_____w

_____

x_____

"Mr. President," said Evans. "I've just typed in a map of the three sublevels. I need the locations of the missiles."

"There are four missiles on the roof, two of them just north and south of center. There are three each located to the east and west of the first, second, and third sublevels."

"And the missile control room?"

"Directly underneath us."

Evans added the below-ground missiles and control room location to the rendering.

!!! e_____w!!!

!!!_____!!!

!!!x_____!!!

!Control=>_____

Then he typed—carefully, since he couldn't read what he was writing—"Our location is third sublevel 'x' along with location of SAMs and control. Missiles may be under enemy control for possible implosion aimed at President. SAM control computer is dedicated. Our monitor is down."

"What if the enemy monitors this communication?" O'Hara asked.

"Then they know that we know," Evans told him. "That isn't going to stop whatever they're planning."

"Hopefully, if the people upstairs see this, they'll evacuate the entire area," the President remarked.

Evans liked hearing that. In the middle of everything, the President was concerned about others. That was the way it should be.

The commander finished by typing his name. Then he moved the cursor to where the send command should be. Then he folded his hands in front of him and prayed to God to help him protect the President—and to make sure that Victoria had done what she promised.

Thirty-six

Tuesday, 9:22 P.M.
Langley Air Force Base, Virginia

Victoria couldn't sleep.

She was tired, and her eyes burned. But she huffed into her small pillow, turned, lay still for a minute, then exhaled again. Usually, it was her husband who made her feel like this—as though she'd forgotten to do something that he was going to find and use against her.

But this wasn't about Stephen. It was about Amos Evans. And it wasn't about what she may have forgotten but what she couldn't forget. That he was out there without a support system. She didn't know what kind of backup he'd had when he went into the field years before. Maybe faith in God and in his own abilities had always been enough. But it wasn't enough to let her sleep well.

And then she heard Captain McIver in the hallway, informing Colonel Lewis about "a situation" at the White House. Victoria threw off the cover and opened the door.

"What's happened?" she asked.

McIver looked at her. "We're not sure. General Jackson's received a report of gunfire in the White House."

"Where?"

"Sublevels three and four."

"Commander Evans is down there."

McIver nodded. "It hasn't broken in the media yet, and we have no other details."

"What's being done?" Lewis asked.

"General Jackson said it'll be SOP."

"Sorry?" Victoria said.

"Standard Operating Procedure," McIver said. "Everyone down there is trained to hit the deck running—"

"Which could also be their downfall," Lewis said.

"What do you mean?" McIver asked.

"They'll gather at assigned places for specific duties. If Commander Evans is correct and a mole has been working at the White House, the enemy will know their procedure."

"And avoid them," Victoria said.

"Not necessarily," Lewis replied. He didn't have to say more. He glanced back at the commander's room. "Dr. Hudson, do we know exactly where Commander Evan's was going?"

"No. But if he managed to jack in, perhaps he sent—"

There was a faint voice in the other room.

"You've got mail."

They looked at each other and ran into the room.

Thirty-seven

Tuesday, 9:23 P.M.
Washington, D.C.

Hickock entered the small, brightly lit room. He set his .38 beside the computer keyboard. He just now noticed spots of blood on the cuffs of his trousers. He checked his shins; it wasn't his.

"Your cherry's been popped," Thatcher said with a little smile. "You did good."

Hickock acknowledged the comment with a tight nod. He didn't want to bond with the man, do anything to invite closeness. Respect? Yes. Shared goals? Yes. But camaraderie, no. Not when it might be necessary to shoot him in the back if they were in danger of being caught.

Yet Thatcher was right. He had lost his innocence today. Though Hickock had poisoned Judge Howland with formaldehyde, what had happened down here was real killing. When a twitch of your finger sent a flash of pain through someone's gut or leg or head. When you could see a man's surprised or pained or disbelieving expression the moment the bullet struck. When your will, your choice, your timing ended his life.

The young man had never served in the military, but like all of the Huntsmen he had learned to shoot and kill at Axe's mountain training center. Shortly after he was recruited— while working for Judge Howland, two months before the judge's death—Hickock had learned to fire at targets. Later, he shot animals inside cages. It was Axe's belief that if you could kill a helpless, nonthreatening dog or cat or rabbit, you could exterminate without hesitation a man, woman, or even a child that was threatening your mission.

Axe was correct. Together, the four Huntsmen left over thirty bodies lying in the corridors behind them. Mostly men but some women. Pulling the trigger the first time hadn't been as difficult as Hickock had expected. Not with the mission at risk. Not with the prospect of letting the team down hanging over him. And after that—after that it was like sex. He knew what to expect and how to control it, and he had enjoyed it. Like sex, there was also a keen sense of clarity when it was over. When the four Huntsmen finally reached the missile control room, they shot the guard and the two launch officers who were inside, tossed their bodies into the corridor, and lowered the fire door. Now there was no one left to kill, and they could focus on the one thing they had left to do.

Short, bald Joe Sabal sat down at the master computer with Hickock behind him, while Thatcher and the tall, barrel-chested Schneider waited. Schnieder was another paid flunky, one of Graff's gets. But he was a cool, former military man who had pulled a gun from a fallen soldier and used it on several of the man's comrades. He was an unflappable man, and Hickock liked him.

They had left the power on in this section of the fourth floor; though the ventilator was shut down, everything else was working. Across from the door, the wall was lined with twenty-two black-and-white video monitors that showed the insides of the silos. There was a desk against the back wall with several telephones and a stack of magazines, everything from *Time* to *Mad*. One man on duty, one man backup—standard.

Sabal slipped his ID card into the side of the computer. That didn't give him access to launch-security level, but it got him into the system. He looked up the discarded passwords from the past few days.

Hickock read over his shoulder.

> *MONDAY:* DANGER-MAN
> *SUNDAY:* VALUED-XRAY
> *SATURDAY:* CAR-DECK
> *FRIDAY:* ICE-LOOKOUT

"Oh, this is a fucking gift," Sabal snickered. He began typing.

"You've got it?"

"I will."

"How?" Hickock said. "I don't see anything there."

"What *do* you see?"

Hickock studied the monitor. "I see days followed by two-word sequences that don't appear to be related. Is the clue hidden in the number of letters in each word?"

"No. And not in rearranging the letters or having to go up or down to other letters," Sabal added. "Look at the individual letters. Each of them. See if you notice anything."

Hickock broke out the vowels and consonants, searching for a pattern. He checked for acronyms—MDM, SVX, SCD. He assigned numbers to letters but that was too obvious.

Sabal had typed 500–1000, 5–10, 100–500, 1–50. Then

he accessed one of the D and A—decrypton and analysis—programs stored in his own computer. He asked the software to run a sequence analysis and try all combinations. Then he sat back and folded his arms.

"The big, bad United States government," Sabal sneered. "You still don't see it?"

Hickock kept looking. He didn't like feeling stupid.

"They're using the same system we used to use at NASA to encode computerized specs for new orbits," Sabal said. "The security geniuses have hidden Roman numerals in the codewords." He pointed. "DANGER-MAN. The only Roman numerals are 'D' and 'M'—five hundred and one thousand."

"Jesus. It's so obvious." Now.

"If the code were DANGER-MICE," Sabal continued, "it would be five hundred and one thousand-and-one. So all we have to do is drop the non-numeric letters, and you have numeric sequences. The launch system is keyed to work with ones, fives, and zeroes with that is probably a top numeral of three thousand and something."

"Why three thousand?"

"Because it's tough to do a word with more than three "M's. Where do you go after 'mummy'? As a security measure, they gave the guys down here the words but not the numbers. If the launch operators ever blabbed them to someone, the words themselves would be useless. When they type them in here, the computer does the interpolation. Since we don't know today's two-word code, we have to do it ass-backwards. I've asked the computer to go through previous combinations and look for any repetitions. If the sequences don't get recycled, then the computer has to eliminate previous combinations, then shoot through new ones until it finds today's code."

"How long will that take?" Hickock asked.

The computer signaled that there was no repetition and that there was no pattern to the numeric selection. Sabal told the machine to eliminate combinations that had been used before and to start trying new ones.

"How long will it take?" Sabal repeated. "Anywhere from right this second to maybe an hour."

"I need it faster than an hour," Hickock said.

"Why? If the President's still alive, he isn't going anywhere," Sabal assured him. "And no one is sure as hell getting down here."

"Yes, but Axe has a schedule to keep," Hickock said.

"I understand, but it's up to the computer," Sabal said. "I've done all I can. Given the speed and possible combinations, I'm guessing it'll take another forty minutes or so."

Hickock looked at the monitor. The screen was a light blue. In the center were large flashing white letters that said *Working*. The Huntsman hated having everything depend on this mercenary.

It was close and warm in the room. He could hear his heart beating in time with the flashing letters. He picked up the .38 and held it. There was something comforting about it.

"You thinking of using that on me?" Sabal snickered.

"No," Hickock replied. "You still have fifty-three minutes to get me the password."

Sabal's grin faded. He unfolded his arms, sat up, and moved his chair closer to the computer as though that would hurry things up.

Thirty-eight

Victoria sat at the computer and opened the e-mail message from Commander Evans. Captain McIver and Colonel
Lewis stood on either side of her, looking at the monitor.

As he stood there reading the mail, which was addressed
to Dr. Hudson, Colonel Lewis took a mental and emotional
rocket-sled ride to where he really wanted to be: in the field.
In the thick of it, instead of busting the stones of new recruits or making sure bad guys didn't slip in the back door
of an air base.

"I'll be damned," McIver said as she read the message.

"He sent us a diagram," Victoria said. "Very clever."

Lewis was impressed, but he was also deeply concerned
by Evans's sense of the enemy's plan: to blow up some or
all of the SAMs in their launch tubes. The fact that that
hadn't happened already suggested there were codes the
Huntsmen didn't have. No doubt they were in a heavily reinforced bunker trying to get those codes, perhaps by tortur-
ing launch personnel.

There wasn't a lot of time to think about this.

It had been nearly ten years since Lewis's last mission. Before the start of Desert Storm, British Gulf Commander Lieutenant General Sir Peter de la Billiere recommended sending small teams of commandos into western Iraq to chew away at Saddam Hussein's supply lines, hardware, and personnel. Lewis and Delta Force commandos were among the first groups to go in. Traveling in a heavily armed truck convoy, they were charged with finding the mobile Scuds and helping to target them for Air Force strikes. At the start of hostilities, the US/Coalition Tactical Air Control Center in Riyadh, Saudi Arabia, reassigned Lewis and his team. Already behind enemy lines, they were instructed to find Iraqi troops and attack, using mortars and antitank missiles. Lewis and his people were recalled after six weeks, by which time the Iraqis had retreated to the north.

During that time Lewis felt as he did when he was a young boy sitting on his bed with one of his adventure novels—only more so. As a child, he couldn't turn the pages fast enough, get to the next battle scene or confrontation or revelation. In the field, he couldn't move fast enough to the next target. There was danger, and there were casualties, and he had lost one very good friend in a mortar exchange near Al Q'aim.

He had also lost friends and relatives in car accidents, in a brawl in a pool hall, and in the crash of a small plane. When they died, those people weren't living to the extreme. That wasn't a judgment, it was a fact. They weren't in the big game, the one where the ante is your life. There's an excitement that comes with tossing that chip in the kitty, a sense that time has suddenly slowed down and you're packing high-resolution living into every second. Smelling every smell, seeing every bug, hearing every sound, looking down at the back of your hand and noticing every hair and not taking one of them for granted. Not one.

Colonel Lewis could feel himself racing to that point right now. Most military personnel who were about to go into combat took the ride: that was how they got up the energy and determination to put their lives on the firing line. And it was tough if the acceleration either stopped suddenly or burned for too long without finding an outlet.

"Colonel, can the Huntsmen really do what Commander Evans says?" Victoria asked.

"Looks like they're well on the way," Lewis said. "Each of those missiles has a warhead packed with two-plus pounds of high-explosives launched at near-supersonic speed. If the blasts have nowhere to go, they'll probably take out most of the East Wing above the below ground." As he spoke, he had ducked into the hallway. "Captain Holly!"

The pilot stuck his head from the supply room where he was helping to re-seal the door. "Colonel?"

"Come here, please."

"Yes, sir," Holly said. He jogged over.

"Captain, what've they got on this base that you can fly?" Lewis asked him.

"There are a number of—"

"Something small with some firepower."

"The LHX-2B's here," he said.

"The stealth chopper."

"Right."

"How many seats?"

"Two with a cargo bay."

"What's the DSR?"

The DSR was the "dip-stick reserve," the amount of fuel an aircraft was required to have left in the tank when it landed. The DSR was typically enough fuel so the aircraft could reach another base in the event that the primary landing area was fogged-in, under attack, or otherwise inaccessible.

"It's around twenty percent," Holly said. "Maybe less if Ronnie was on the stick, since he's heavy on—"

"Enough to get us to the White House?"

"More than enough."

"What about prep time?"

"Minimal," Holly told him. "They have her on loan from Holloman, so they'll be workin' it and keeping it flight-ready."

"Ten minutes?"

"Maybe not even. If it's already armed, less than that."

Colonel Lewis turned to McIver. "Captain, I'd like you to try and get us the LHX-2B."

She looked at him. "Sir, that won't happen. We won't even get a Huey from squadron command. They don't know who we are and the mission itself, with the White House as your target, is going to get a deep scrub—"

"I understand," Lewis said. "I also don't have time for this," he said. "Forget squadron command. Go directly to General Jackson. Delete Commander Evans's name to keep it secret from Jackson's staff and forward the e-mail to him. Tell the general that the hostiles who are apparently holding the President are the same people who hit us. Ask him to verify the situation at the White House and request permission to make a fast surgical strike back. Does the general know about Captain Holly?"

"No—"

Lewis turned to Victoria. "Will you forward his service record but without his name or other personal details?"

Victoria nodded.

McIver shook her head. "I'm telling you, the general won't like that. He won't like any of this."

"He doesn't have to," Lewis said. "All he has to do is help us save the President's life. What's in the SOK?"

"The field backpack?" McIver said. "First aid kit, emergency rations, two extra clips, fifty feet of nylon rope, plastique, and two detonators."

"Excellent. Make the call, then get the backpack and help Taylor put it on."

McIver turned to the wall phone. Victoria had already looked up General Jackson's e-mail address and attached Holly's file to it.

Lewis turned back to the door. "Taylor! Diaz!"

The men came running. They entered the room and swapped looks with Holly and Victoria. The pilot's pinched little smile told them something was up. Victoria's concerned expression confirmed it.

"Get into your SFUs," Lewis told them.

"Sir?" Taylor said.

"Now!" Lewis ordered. "I'll join you in a second."

"Me too?" Holly asked.

"Do you think you'd be able to pilot in it?"

"The seat'll be snug with the SFU on, but I think so, sir."

"I'll let you know," Lewis said. "Go help the others suit up."

"Will do, sir," Holly said and left.

McIver covered the mouthpiece. "Colonel? General Jackson would like to speak with you."

Lewis took the phone. "Sir?"

"Colonel, there is indeed a situation at the White House. Have you verified this e-mail for source and content?"

"No, sir. I was hoping we could get under way while our computer scientist does that from—"

"Colonel, you're not going anywhere that isn't expressly covered in my orders pertaining to your group," Jackson said. "I've had to accept the secrecy of your mission and your personnel, but I have no intention of authorizing an attack on the White House."

Lewis's jaw tightened. He looked at Captain McIver. She didn't have to hear to know what was being said. She left to get the backpack.

"I'm going to turn your e-mail over to the Presidential Protection director of the Secret Service," Jackson continued. "He'll handle whatever needs to be done. I gave Captain McIver some leeway this morning because of what happened. But that is as far as it goes. Any questions?"

"None, sir."

Jackson hung up. Lewis slowly replaced the receiver.

The acceleration had hit a wall. Lewis could feel it revving there. He looked at Victoria who was watching him. He wasn't going to let this sit. He couldn't.

"Can you get into the Secret Service computer?" Lewis asked.

"If General Jackson forwards the e-mail, I can probably attach a spider and ride it in."

"Do it, please."

Victoria turned to the computer and began typing.

"When you're in there," Lewis said, "try and get me a detailed layout of the sublevels. Especially in the depth and dimensions of the floor the President is being held on and the control room beneath it. I've got your e-mail address. I'll contact you."

She nodded as she typed.

McIver returned. "The backpack's ready. Taylor's got it."

"Thanks." Lewis turned toward the corridor. "Captain Holly!"

"Coming!" Holly said as he ran from down the corridor.

"What are you going to do?" McIver asked.

Lewis turned toward her. "Do you know where the LHX-2B is?"

"I do—"

"Good."

Holly arrived. "Sir?"

"I want you suited up as well," the colonel told him. "If there's gunfire, the suit may protect you. Be ready to leave in five minutes. Everyone wears a weapon and I want the suit's stealth option engaged before we depart this complex."

"Yes *sir*!"

Lewis looked at the monitor and made a mental note of Victoria's e-mail address. Then he turned back to McIver. "Captain, our commander-in-chief is being held by an enemy force. The Secret Service may not be able to help him. We can. Will you help us take the LHX-2B?"

She hesitated. "Sir, if we meet with resistance will the handguns be used against our airmen?"

"Never. The guns are for the Huntsmen."

The hesitation was gone. "Then I'm with you."

"Thank you," Lewis said. After telling McIver they'd meet her in the rec room, Lewis hurried to join the other stealth team members.

Thirty-nine

Tuesday, 9:49 P.M.
Langley Air Force Base, Virginia

The LHX-2B is nicknamed "the slug" by those who designed her.

The stealth helicopter is low and black, with smooth contours and LOLs—low-observable lines—around the wedge-shaped cockpit and a flat underbelly. The airframe is constructed of radar-absorbent and transparent materials, and the five-blade main rotor is constructed of slender, swept-tip blades. The LHX-2B is powered by two flush engine air intakes and a conformal exhaust nozzle, which features extremely low infrared and acoustic signatures. The shrouded tail rotor sports two nearly vertical fins. In order to achieve stealth operation, the missile mounts—adaptable to either Hellfire or Stinger missiles—are internal, built on swing-out launchers, which are activated when the chopper reaches its target. There's also a heavy-caliber chin-mounted gun that is aimed by the pilot's helmet sights. These are linked to the helmet's day and night-vision capacity. The LHX-2B isn't the fastest helicopter in the air—its maximum flight speed is 196 mph—and it can only carry 3,500 pounds of cargo, which includes the two-person flight crew. But it can come and go in places no other aircraft can get to.

The LHX-2B was housed in an open hangar that was part of the three-hangar complex of which the Morgan was a part. The structures were side by side with the Morgan hangar, the westernmost of the three. The LHX-2B was housed in the center hangar; it was the only one of the three hangars in active service. The others were used mostly for storage.

Captain McIver lit a cigarette when she left the bomb shelters. She needed one. And in case anyone was watching the spot—either friend or enemy—it gave her an excuse to stand there while Lewis and the others emerged behind her. Before the men pulled up their faceplates, Taylor suggested that they bend their knees slightly as they walked. That would lower their center of gravity and make their step quieter. Then they put up the faceplates, activated the stealth capacity, and phased away from the outside in, like the picture on an old TV set. Commander Evans had told her that it didn't feel any different from the inside when the stealth option was engaged, *"Unless you happen to be looking at your hands or feet."* He said it was also a little disorienting to walk, especially on steps, without being able to see your feet. She could just imagine.

It was damned eerie to hear them without being able to see them. As she walked briskly across the open field and onto the tarmac, her mind started going in a weird and paranoid direction. What if time travel were perfected in the future? What if time travelers wore even higher-efficiency SFUs? They could watch any time period, influence any event, snatch any person without being seen. As advanced as the suits were, she suddenly felt as though they were novices here. As if the future she imagined were already a reality.

Or maybe she'd just been a DARPA liaison way too long. She was starting to think like one of the long-range planners who worked for the DOD—the "sci-fi guys" they called them. It was their job to assess the potential impact of new technologies and spinoffs on future society, then make recommendations about whether the science was to remain a secret or be fed to the private sector. She wondered if they'd thought of time travelers. Probably, she decided. She'd met some of those people, and they were out there.

Whether it was weird or not, thinking about time travel was better than contemplating her own future if the team failed to rescue the President. There had been no way to plan this operation. They didn't know exactly where the LHX-2B would be or who would be with it or whether they'd have to go for a back-up vehicle, which would be Captain Holly's call if things got dicey. Regardless, McIver would be staying behind after helping the team steal the chopper. Her arrest was not only a certainty, and only an executive pardon would save her from a court-martial and twenty years to life in prison for her part in helping to steal the LHX-2B. Even then, General Jackson would have her transferred. Not that she's miss him, but she didn't particularly want to serve in Alaska. The code name for Eielson Air Force Base up in Fairbanks was Icebox—and with good reason, she'd been told.

McIver was on her second cigarette when they reached the big black and white signpost that said to extinguish all cigarettes before passing the sign—as if the strong smell of fuel here wasn't tip-off enough. Then again, everything in the aircrafts was labeled, including the door handles and which way to pull them. The tie-down cables, which held the choppers to huge eye hooks in the concrete fields, had

big black and white tags that read *Remove before takeoff.*
With lives and billion-dollar aircraft at risk, it was probably
a worthwhile precaution.

She dropped the half-finished cigarette and crushed it.
She didn't want one of the stealth soldiers stepping on it and
putting a hole in the sole of his boot.

The chopper had not been wheeled into the hangar.
Though the LHX-2B was technically still a top secret aircraft, it was going to be unveiled to the press over the weekend. This, in an effort to dazzle the public and pressure
lawmakers into restoring budget cuts. So while the wraps
were not yet off, security was not as tight as it would have
been back at Holloman.

It was an impressive-looking aircraft. Nearly forty feet
long and thirteen feet high, resting on three low wheels,
the matte-black chopper looked as though it had been
vacuformed. There were no angles, no rivets, no sign of as-
sembly. The rotor blades were extremely thin and fragile-
looking. They reminded her of snake tongues without the
forks.

McIver was coming at the chopper head-on. There were
four men standing by the tail rotor. She could tell from their
uniforms that two were pilots and two were senior officers.
The ground crew had finished working on the chopper and
were removing their equipment from the site. Except for fu-
eling, most of the checks were done electronically. It was
still bizarre to see technicians leaving a site with laptops instead of toolboxes. McIver wondered if they were getting
ready to bed the LHX down or take her up.

"Captain, can you hear me?"

Though the voice was muffled through the thick mask,
she could tell it was Lewis.

"Yes, sir. I hear you."

"Holly just gave me a subvocal," Lewis said. "It looks to

him like they're getting ready for a night flight. The chopper will be fueled and possibly armed. Taylor and Diaz have gone ahead to create a distraction in the hangar. If anyone stays behind you've got to get them away from the rotors so they aren't hurt. I'll be right behind you."

"I understand."

The backs of the two officers were toward her. They turned as she approached. One of them started walking toward her. In the dark, she couldn't see who it was or what his rank was.

Suddenly, the man saluted.

Thank God, she thought. He was a lieutenant. She returned the salute.

"She ready for her night flight, Lieutenant?" McIver asked.

"Yes, ma'am." He was a rugged looking man in his late twenties. He seemed slightly perplexed. "Was something going on out in the field, ma'am?"

"Why do you ask?"

"We checked the perimeter before rolling the 2B out, and we've still got men out at the fence," the lieutenant said. "We thought today's action might have been directed against her."

"No. We're out in the shelters."

" 'We,' ma'am?"

"I am." *Did I slip up?* she thought quickly. No. "I'm there with my research team—"

There was a roar as a dark orange fire brightened the dark sky behind the lieutenant. He turned, silhouetted, as a tall metal can filled with greasy rags caught fire beside a shelf of parts. Almost at once, the plastic containers began to soften, melt, and fall to the hangar floor.

The officer who had been standing with the pilots ran toward the fire. So did several mechanics who had been working in the back, behind a Huey. A moment later, a fire alarm began to wail.

"Excuse me, ma'am," the lieutenant said to Captain McIver.

The lieutenant spun around and ran back to the stealth chopper. McIver jogged after him. Captain Wilson was shouting something to the other pilot, and a moment later both men swung toward the low, sharply back-angled doors.

"They're going to get her out of here," Lewis said to McIver. He was running alongside her.

"I know."

"As soon as Wilson gets her fired up, Holly and I will take him," he said. "You'll have to get the copilot out of there."

"What do I do?"

"He's a second lieutenant. Order him away. If he doesn't listen, pull him out. I'll come around as soon as I can."

"Roger," she said.

McIver neared the low-slung cockpit. The main rotor began to turn with a fast, high, feathery *whuh-whuh-whuh*. The tail rotor was nearly silent. She walked faster as the copilot opened the slender black door on the starboard side of the aircraft. She had never been in combat and her training had been just the basics. Yet she knew she had to do this and make it stick. There wasn't time to reason with the fliers and officers, and that wouldn't work anyway. But she hated this. And the poor guys were making it easier for them.

"Lieutenant!" she yelled.

The copilot didn't hear her. He stepped inside the cockpit.

"Lieutenant!"

The young man stepped and looked back.

"Hold a minute!" McIver said.

"Captain, we're just going to move the chopper to a safe—"

The lieutenant stared across the cockpit as the port door popped open, and Wilson followed it out. He was pulled along by his left arm, yanked clear of the main rotor. Then, suddenly, he stopped, tripped backward, and landed on his butt. A moment later, his arms and legs shot up as though something had been dropped on his belly.

Like a knee.

"Captain Wilson!" the copilot cried.

He jumped from the cockpit, ducked low, and ran around the front of the helicopter. McIver ran after him. She grabbed him around the waist, from behind, and kept running forward.

"What the fuck are you doing?" the copilot yelled.

She didn't answer.

The copilot stopped and tried to turn, but she ducked her head down and hung on. He called for help, but the cry died in his mouth as his head suddenly twisted to the left.

"I've got him," Lewis said.

McIver let go and staggered back. The pilot stood there for a moment, struggling to try and reach whatever was holding his head to the left. An instant later, his head straightened. McIver heard him utter a low *oof*, and his body bowed quickly toward the hangar. Then his legs moved in the same direction, out from under him, and he landed hard on his backside. There was a muffled *thud*, the copilot's head snapped toward McIver, and then he flopped back onto the landing field, his arms splayed at his side.

Lewis had obviously bent when he struck the copilot. For a moment, as he straightened, she could see objects distorted in a narrow line along the contours of his body. The objects were slightly curved as though they were being viewed through the edges of a magnifying glass but without being magnified. And it only happened around the sides and top of his head, along the tops of his shoulders, and beside his hips. She already imagined a second-generation series of suits with microchips to compensate for the warping.

"Would you please open the cargo door?" Lewis said to McIver. "That's where Diaz and Taylor will be coming."

"Yes, sir."

McIver could see him move toward the port side of the helicopter. Then she blinked and lost him.

She ran around the front of the helicopter. She felt as though she was blindfolded, and half-expected to collide with the other two stealth team members as they hurried to get aboard. But they were already there, and the hatch was opened, gull-wing style. The hinge mechanism was mounted entirely on the inside; otherwise, rivets would present a radar image.

"Are you in?" she asked.

"Diaz is—now I am," Taylor said. "You can shut her."

She did, pulling up her sleeves so they covered her palms as she pushed down. She didn't want to leave a grease stain on the exterior.

"Sorry you have to take the heat for this," Taylor said as the door lowered. "We'll fix it with the President when we get back."

"Good luck," she said.

The slender, curved panel shut without a sound.

McIver ducked, turned, and ran from the chopper. She stopped when she cleared the main rotor and turned to watch the 2B rise. It was a breathtaking sight. The helicopter seemed to float straight up about twenty feet, the *whush, whush, whush* becoming almost inaudible. Then it banked toward her and rose swiftly and silently as though it were weightless. It reminded her of a Frisbee being flung skyward, though without a hand guiding it.

Then the flying lights snapped off, and it was gone.

McIver lowered her eyes to the field. The sense of wonder inspired by the takeoff passed quickly as she saw the two men lying prone on the concrete. Wilson had raised one knee and was beginning to move. The copilot was still out. So was the fire, and the mechanics were running toward her. What was probably an MP jeep—she could only see the bright headlights—was just swinging around the hangar. The localized fire alarm had been shut off, but now McIver heard a screaming sound she'd only heard in twice-yearly drills: the more strident base-wide klaxon, which was wailing to warn all aircraft to stay on or clear of the airfields because of an unauthorized fly over.

McIver had no idea whether the wing commander would scramble a pursuit team. She wondered if they even had a simulation for this eventuality yet, the theft of a chopper that was designed to be undetectable. It was probably still in a think tank somewhere and not yet in the system.

The captain decided to tell the military police that she had no idea who had taken the chopper or why. She'd come out of the shelter complex to have a smoke, saw the 2B, and wandered over. As for the intruders, they were dressed in black and came out of the night. She would say that she'd grabbed the copilot from behind to keep him from running into one of the attackers. The fliers themselves would probably buy that. They'd buy it before they bought the idea that they'd been hit by invisible soldiers.

She'd have to come up with something else to explain why she went to the hatch. To try and stop the men from stealing the chopper? If no one saw her shut the door, that might stick.

And then it hit her hard that while she was worrying about her cover story, the lives of the President, Vice President, and possibly the nation itself were at stake. She began walking toward the two fallen fliers. Her own problems faded to insignificance as the headlights closed in and the mechanics arrived and two of the four MPs came over with guns and attitude bared.

Forty

Tuesday, 10:01 P.M.
Washington, D.C.

"We've got a pair of live Hellfire air-to-ground missiles on board," Holly said to Colonel Lewis.

The pilot had stripped off the cowl and faceplate so that he could put on the black helmet. A warning had come in from the control tower at Langley to turn the chopper around. Instead, he'd turned off the radio. Even if they could see him, they wouldn't shoot him down over the city. Holly settled into the armored crew seat, and, while climbing to his cruising height of 900 feet, he awkwardly slipped on the shoulder harness and leg restraint system—belts that wrapped around each leg and came up through the crotch. The stick was located between his legs, and as he guided the ship with his right hand, he used his left to activate the visor gunsight. If he needed to use the 20 mm gun as a deterrent, he wanted to be ready. If the captain or his helmet sight were not in use or disabled, the copilot had command of the guns, operated through an optical relay tube that was attached to the control panel just below the windshield. It looked like a pair of large binoculars. From both seats, the guns were operated by small handgrips on the left side.

Colonel Lewis was still in his SFU, the faceplate lowered, and there was a transparent blast-shield between the pilot and copilot seats to protect against shell fragments. But the cockpit was quiet, and normal conversation could be heard clearly.

"Why would the air force have been running the 2B with armed missiles?" the colonel asked.

"Because you fly her differently when she's armed," Holly said. "When you train your men, do they react the same to a rubber knife as they do to a real one?"

"Point taken," Lewis said. "Now what about the information Dr. Hudson was going to get us?"

With the lights of Washington shining darkly through the polarized window—which was treated with didymium to cut down on reflectivity, since glints of sunlight or moonlight might give the chopper away to search craft—Holly pointed his gloved finger toward a fifteen-inch video display unit. It was located below the control panel and just forward of the seats, between the pilot and copilot. There was a keyboard beneath it, almost on the floor of the cockpit, and three buttons on the top of the black plastic casing of the monitor. From the pilot's side, the buttons were red, white, and blue.

"Press the red button, sir," Holly said.

Lewis did. The keyboard shot up on a slender, pneumatic swivel stand. It was facing the copilot, though the keyboard could be rotated if the pilot needed to access it.

"Now press the white button."

Lewis pushed it in. The monitor winked on, and a map pf Washington was displayed on the screen.

Since 1992, all on-board computers in newly built air force planes and choppers were preprogrammed by mission

specialists with maps and tactical information for a given
flight. The 2B computer would be able to give them Wilson's flight path and schedule, but Holly didn't need that.
Because the chopper had been armed, he was probably
going to stay mostly in base air space. Besides, Washington
was one of those cities where there were enough landmarks,
brightly illuminated, so that he could eyeball his way
around.

"Now input my code HOLYHOL, Dr. Hudson's e-mail
address, and send her the following return address: 2BOR-
NOT2B@AFSEC.com."

Lewis began typing. "You've got to be kidding about that
address. I didn't think you air force guys knew from *Ham-
let*."

"Of course we do, sir," Holly said. "I rented the Mel Gib-
son movie."

As he piloted the chopper just beneath a low cloud cover
and passed inside the Beltway, Holly picked up the cowl
from his shoulder and slipped it on so that the microphone
was at his mouth. "How're you guys doing back there?"

"I'm fine," Taylor told him, "but Mr. Diaz is awfully
quiet. I think he's asleep.

"He tends to do that when he's airborne. He's probably
dreaming about Diogenes in his tub."

"Who?"

"Have him tell you all about it when we're back at the
base," Holly said as they passed over the Washington Mon-
ument. "It's highly interesting."

"Done, Captain," Lewis said. "What's next?"

"You send it?"

"Yes."

"Hit the 'clear' button to get rid of the map—it's under
the enter button."

"Got it."

"Then press the button on the top right that says 'OC' to open a channel to receive."

"Done."

"Now," Holly said, "we wait."

As they flew toward the White House, Holly kept a close watch on the skies. Flight within the Beltway was restricted for fear of terrorist attacks, but he didn't want to collide with a stray traffic or police chopper because the 2B wasn't registering on their radar.

Even through the tinted windshield, the White House was so bright that it was nearly washed out. There were spotlights on the building itself, front, back, and sides, and also the grounds adjoining the Executive Mansion. Someone either intercepted Commander Evans's message or figured out that the missiles represented a threat. It looked as though they were being dismantled on top of the White House. Crews appeared to be working with computer equipment along the sides of the mansion, possibly trying to jam the missiles remotely. The guidance systems could be screwed with, Holly knew, though he didn't think the missiles could be disarmed like that.

A *transmitting* banner flashed briefly on the VDU.

"She's coming through," Lewis said.

Then a typed message appeared on the screen:

Information not available. All lines to White House
shut down. Trying DOD.

"They probably did that to keep the terrorists from communicating with anyone on the outside," Holly said.

"Yeah," Lewis said. "But we don't have time for her to go searching other files."

There was an aerial perimeter determined by four air force choppers hovering at around two hundred feet above and around the White House. All were equipped with what looked like Sidewinder air-to-air missiles. Holly slowed. Not only hadn't the 2B been picked up on radar, no one had seen or heard the chopper.

Lewis thought for a moment. Then he typed:

We'll try to get to the President. Cdr's PC may be voice-enabled. Send message: Hellfire from southeast. Duck.

Forty-one

Tuesday, 10:11 P.M.
Washington, D.C.

"I've got it!" Sabal said. "LUCKY-MOMS—50-2000."

Hickock had been standing behind him, staring at nothing in particular as he listened to the sound of the computer *chick-chick-chicking* as it tried to find the code.

He looked at Sabal's eager, slightly panicked eyes.

Hickock wanted to say it was about fucking time. What he said was, "Fire."

Forty-two

"They're lighting 'em up on the east side!" Holly shouted to Lewis. "Five in a row!"

The stealth chopper was still hovering unseen above and outside the cordon of Secret Service helicopters. There had been military personnel working in groups along the east side of the White House; they were scattering now. Either they'd picked up the ignition sequence of the underground missiles or someone had intercepted and passed along Commander Evans's message or both. At least that left the area clear for the 2B to act. His only concern was with the Sidewinders. No doubt the air force choppers were in place to try and shoot down any missiles that might be launched from the tubes. But as soon as Lewis made a move, those birds could also turn around and fire at the 2B.

Holly was looking at the remote thermal sensor, a small horizontal gauge located on the control panel, just left of the VDU. It was lawn-green with red circles indicating "hot-spots," chamber temperatures in excess of 2000 degrees

Fahrenheit. Two fish-eye sensors, one on the nose and one on the tail, were providing the readings.

The pilot had already opened the missile bay and was rolling out the twin Hellfires.

Lewis had to make a quick decision about what to do. He remembered the May 1987 fire onboard the naval ship USS *Stark* in which two Exocet missiles burned in their compartments. One missile exploded, the other did not. There was considerable debate later in the military think tanks about the "big match" aspects of sabotage, whether the temperature and heat release rate of burning propellant was a good or bad igniter. The finding was that in some cases, the infusion of fire byproducts into the compartment reduced the combustibility of the air and that much of the time burning missiles did not explode.

In some cases, Lewis told himself. *Much of the time.* He didn't like those odds. Not with the security of the republic at stake. And then there was the chance that the missiles might actually be launched in the closed tubes. That would guarantee an explosion.

"Take them out *now*!" Lewis said.

"Yes, sir."

Lewis was aware that the Hellfire alone could destroy the East Wing of the White House. It could also take out the upper levels of the underground facility. But in addition to the explosion of the underground SAMs, there was also the chance that smoke from the fire could kill the President. All things considered—in the few seconds that he'd had to consider all things—Lewis preferred to attack.

There were two buttons above the remote thermal sensor: *Target* and *Disengage.* The screen was usually set at *Disengage.* He punched on *Target* and hit it five times; one for each missile. The on-board computer automatically selected the optimal strike point to do the most damage against the missiles.

He flipped up the safety cover on the missile button, located in his right armrest.

He pressed the red button once to activate, then a second time to fire. The stealth helicopter seemed to dip very slightly and kick backwards at the same time, toward the port side, as the Hellfire there took off. The orange-white contrail washed across the tinted windshield but only for a moment as the Hellfire's reduced-smoke rocket sent it straight away from the chopper, then sent it dipping sharply toward its target.

Guided by a Cassegrain telescope in its hemispherical glass nose, which kept the target clearly in sight, the five-foot, four-inch long, one-hundred-pound Hellfire has a range of over sixteen thousand feet and lock-on accuracy. When in pursuit of a moving target, the missile is capable of making 13-G turns at supersonic speeds. It didn't have to use that capacity on its way to the missile silos. The trip took a little over one second. The Hellfire struck before the air force choppers even picked it up on their radar.

The explosion was like nothing Lewis had ever seen. The Hellfire hit at computer-calculated sixty-seven degree angle some forty feet from the East Room wall. The explosion was a fat white flash, which shot skyward like a reverse waterfall, pushing a rolling cloud of ivory-gray smoke up at incredible speeds, nearly to the roof of the White House. It was followed, moments later, by a cockpit-rattling clap. Beneath the Hellfire blast, five small red holes appeared in the grounds: these were the SAM silos, the six pizza-slice doors of each having been torn away by the explosion. The openings were diffuse for an instant beneath the massive white column, and then the SAMs exploded with raw, red fury, detonated by the heat of the Hellfire strike.

Three of the SAMs on the north side exploded and burned in their silos. The roaring pops reached the cockpit a moment later. Two SAMs on the south managed to rise slightly before the explosion of the others caused the warheads to blow up. The two open-air blasts were black-red fireballs that punched the East Wing and ground-floor visitors' corridor with two devastating hammerfists. The blows shattered the old wood, plaster, and large windows and blew away the third-floor terrace and roof. Shards of all sizes were thrown into the night, then came raining down on the West Wing, the Rose Garden, and on the security forces gathered there. Several searchlights winked out, smashed by falling debris. At the clouds cleared, Lewis could see a section of the third floor and the rood above it sag and then fall in, pulling along priceless furniture and paintings. They were swallowed up by the string of holes in the ground, adding small, pathetic puffs to the thinning cloud of smoke that covered the east side grounds. Fires burning in the three northern holes quickly consumed the old wood and canvases. Lewis felt heartsick.

Within moments of the Hellfire blast, the two air force choppers on the north side of the White House had swung around to meet another attack. They moved closer to center to cover the main entrance. The other two choppers held their positions facing south. But the target was gone.

Captain Holly had taken the 2B up to seven hundred feet immediately after the Hellfire was launched. The ascent was almost like riding a soap bubble. Choppers were notoriously noisy, and they shook; Lewis found it odd being in one so silent and smooth. At the colonel's instructions, Holly flew over the White House toward the wide lawn on the southern grounds. While they headed there, Lewis used his suit radio to order Diaz and Taylor to engage the SFUs and get ready to disembark.

"Where should I take the chopper once you're off loaded?" Holly asked.

"Nowhere. I want you to land and come with us," Lewis said. "The security people have to figure we're with the terrorists. I don't want them chasing you around D.C., firing at phantoms. If we need to get out of here, is there anything you can do to cripple this bird so they can't move it?"

"No," Holly told him. "But they won't move it without an experienced 2B pilot, sir—not over the city—and I don't think Ronnie will be seein' clearly for a while."

Holly settled the chopper onto the lawn. Even as it descended, the other air force helicopters were closing in above it and security forces from the navy and Secret Service were moving in.

Lewis switched on his stealth option. He dematerialized from the outside in, as though twin squeegees had wiped him from view. As soon as he shut down the rotors, Holly pulled on his cowl and engaged the stealth.

"Taylor? Diaz?" Lewis said.

"Sir?"

"Get out fast, and shut the door. We'll meet you there and then move toward ground zero, double time. I'll take point followed by Taylor, Holly, and Diaz."

"Sir," Holly said, "we've got to watch out for that dust cloud—"

"I know, blowing to the east. You hear that back there? We head to the west or the particles will stick to the suits."

The other men acknowledged.

Lewis lifted the door handle. "We go in fast and get the President, Vice President, and Commander Evans. If they're dead, we leave on my command with SFUs engaged. No one draws a weapon unless ordered. They'll be visible, and we're on the same team as most of these guys. You got that?"

The cargo door and both cockpit doors of the stealth chopper opened and shut quickly. Lewis looked out at his team. The men appeared as flat, translucent, brownish-gray shapes through the polarized visor. They were almost like walking shadows. They were standing still, waiting for Lewis to take point. The colonel moved to the front of the line and led the unseen soldiers in a wide, southwesterly arc toward the White House. As they did, both naval and Secret Service security forces moved in, along with a team of firefighters.

The security forces hung back to watch for attacks on the firefighters, Lewis presumed. The firefighters arrived moments before Lewis and the stealth warriors did. There were over a dozen of them, their shoulder patches identifying them as members of the Federal Emergency Management Agency, which was called in for crisis situations rather than day-to-day firefighting at the White House. Dressed in orange fireproof suits and white helmets, and wearing full-face masks and air tanks, six teams of two firefighters each used high-pressure hoses attached to large tanks on dollies to coat the flames with a fluoroiodocarbon-based foam. The heavy, tannish foam smothered the flame and dissolved almost on contact, leaving no residue.

Lewis stepped carefully around the debris of the exploded missiles so as to make as little noise as possible. Then he moved in and around the fire brigade, being careful to keep his distance so no one bumped into him. The silos were about six feet across with two feet of metal separating them. Sod had been thoroughly blasted away for hundreds of feet in all directions, exposing the concrete bunkers in which the silos were housed. Lewis looked inside the southernmost silo.

Smoke from the fast-dying blazes was black and churning. If it weren't for the one working spotlight on the White

House roof, Lewis would have had a difficult time seeing anything through the faceplate. It was also brutally hot in the suit, and sweat was trickling into his eyes. He'd have to remember to wear a headband next time.

Because the Patriot missile had gotten out of the tube, there was less debris here than in the other silos. It had also been where the Hellfire struck, so the debris was smaller and scattered more widely. The silo went down about fifty feet, but the explosion had torn a hole in the bottom. Lewis had no idea how far down that went. He leaned in further. Inside the silo, there was a ladder, which was twisted, with a few rungs missing, but it still looked navigable.

The stealth team was standing in a tight line behind Lewis. He looked back at them.

"Taylor," he said into the subvocal mouthpiece. "You follow me down. Diaz, Holly—I need distractions. Diaz, fuck with the generators powering the spotlights. Holly, you hit the com tent. Keep them busy and away from the silos. I'll be in touch."

"We're on it," Holly said.

While Diaz and Holly moved to the northeast, moving around what was left of the smoke, Lewis turned and swung down the ladder. There were no fires left in this hole and no reason for anyone to hose any more foam along the walls. Lewis descended quickly, but he held the rungs tightly, since the suit was heavy and changed his balance. Where the rungs were missing, he had to drop, using the rails as "slide-guides," as Delta called them when they slid down ladders into basements. Taylor was keeping up with him, despite the fact that the backpack he was wearing had to weigh an extra forty or fifty pounds.

Lewis wished he could take the chance of contacting White House security. It would be easier working with them than around them. But not knowing where the Hunstmen moles were made that impossible.

As they came to within fifteen feet of the bottom, Colonel Lewis tried to see what was down there. But the tube was dark, and the faceplate of the SFU made it even darker.

He stopped. "Hold a second, Taylor," he said. Then he raised his visor and looked down.

At the base of the silo, on the White House side, was a large blast hole in the metal. The edges were charred and jagged. Something, probably a large portion of the Patriot missile, had been driven clean through the wall when either it or the Hellfire blew up. The rent was about five feet high and three feet wide. The blast had also taken out part of the floor, like a small bite from a cookie.

Lewis flipped his faceplate back down. "I think we can fit through the hole down there. When no one's looking down, break out the rope."

Lewis started back down the ladder. He had no idea what was beyond the hole, but it didn't matter. It was the only way in, and it was inviting. As they taught the tyros in Delta, *"If it looks like a door, don't go through it. Go in the one that doesn't: no one'll be expecting you."*

Forty-three

Hickock found that killing empowers the body. He was still pumped, still excited. But for the soul, there's nothing more invigorating than an improvisation that works. As he had so many times, he used his tongue to feel the false tooth in the back of his mouth. All operatives who had knowledge of the Huntsmen hideout or Restoration had one. But Hickock had known he'd never need his. He was too bulldogged. Once he set his mind to something, it *was*.

The young Huntsman had smiled when the five missiles exploded above and to the east of the control room. The blasts were more powerful than he'd expected, running together in an echoing roll that shook the floor and crawled up Hickock's legs into his belly. Poisoning Judge Howland had proved to Axe—and to himself—that he could carry out deadly orders. But the success of this operation demonstrated that he was a professional, that he could think in a crisis, that he wasn't just a mole, a specialist. It proved that he had what he wanted most: the right to a code name and second-in-command spot along with Badger and the others.

"I told you I could do it," Sabal said.

The assistant director of data security was looking up expectantly at Hickock. The Huntsman's moment of self-satisfaction slipped away as he looked down with contempt. Why was Sabal just sitting there, waiting for a pat on the shoulder instead of asking for instructions? Why didn't he try to earn their respect instead of just his pay?

"For your six fucking figures, I expected no less," Hickock said.

"You paid for a shutdown, Mr. Hickock," Sabal said. "This wasn't part of the deal."

Hickock turned to the chief engineer. "Mr. Schneider, can you get us back to the third floor?"

"Yes, sir. No extra charge."

Mercenary or not, Hickock did like this guy. "No one else will have access to the elevator?"

"No more than they've had till now."

"Fine. I don't want to restore power. Mr. Thatcher, will your C-4 open the fire door?"

"Absolutely."

Hickock nodded. He took a large flashlight from the wall. "Mr. Sabal, Mr. Schneider, you'll come with us to the third floor. Then you'll both hide somewhere."

"Hide?" Sabal asked.

"That's right," Hickock said. "From all the shooting that took place. You've been in a closet or under a desk since this thing began. You have no idea what happened or why. You're very grateful when someone finds you and escorts you to safety."

"Of course," Schneider said.

Thatcher had set his Uzi against the door. He picked it up. "Where are we going?"

Hickock was still holding the .38. "We're going back to make sure that the President is dead."

Forty-four

Tuesday, 10:22 P.M.
Washington, D.C.

For several minutes, Evans couldn't hear much more than the ringing in his head.

When he was a kid he used to toss cherry bombs into metal trash cans. The blasts were what it might have been like if his head had been in one of those cans. It was also difficult for Evans to open his eyes and virtually impossible for him to see when he did. The room was filled with ash and opaque clouds. The emergency lights had gone out, and the fires burning in the smaller conference room provided the only illumination. The back room had apparently taken the hammer-fist heart of the explosion. The wooden door had been blown from the hinges and was burning somewhere in front of him.

The clouds rolling from the smaller room were thick and choking, with a sour, sulfurous smell. Evans had managed to pull his handkerchief from his pocket and was holding it in front of his mouth. He sucked in air slowly, afraid that poison or pollutants might cause him to pass out. Fierce heat from the superheated air made it painful to move, the perspiration on his forehead and cheeks becoming hot as match heads. Each time he dabbed at the sweat, the beads returned, cool for just a moment and then quickly heating up.

But they were alive. Against some kind of odds, they'd survived the in-hole detonation of five SAMs.

Evans had received Victoria's e-mail voice message a few minutes before the explosion. They were already in the process of moving the large conference table, hoping that it would provide them with some protection against the blast. They had set it close to the far wall, on the west side, and then "ducked and covered" beneath it. Too close to the blast, and Evans was afraid the table would be incinerated or blown apart. He'd been relieved when he felt that first, room-shaking punch of the Hellfire explosion. The roof had started to buckle, and heat had begun to roll in from the pressure of the unvented exhaust of the five SAMs. If those missiles had blown up with nowhere to go but the sublevels, the conference table would have been torn to splinters and them with it.

Not that they were in a significantly better position right now. He wanted to try and get to the walls, feel his way along, and look for any place where they might have buckled. A hole they could squeeze through or enlarge. He knew he wouldn't necessarily feel fresh air coming from the outside. Not if the rents were in the missile tubes or in the smaller room and there were fires burning.

Evans didn't yet know how the others were. Though the President and Vice President had been directly behind him, against the wall, the explosions had knocked everyone down. Then, through the ringing in his ears, Evans thought he heard coughing.

"Mr. President!" he rasped.

"Here!"

Evans turned to his left. The heat was awful, scalding the streams of perspiration into his face and the backs of his hands as he reached for the President. He bent close. There were bloodstains on the President's jacket but he didn't appear to be hurt.

"Sir, we have to try and find a way out of here!" Evans said through the handkerchief.

"No. The Secret Service will come—"

"So will Hickock and whoever might've been helping him. They'll want to make sure they succeeded." Evans leaned across the President. "Mr. Vice President, are you all right?"

"Pretty good. Others aren't moving—"

"All right," Evans said. "I'm going to leave you here, to try and find a break somewhere. Maybe get out to shout for help."

Evans started out, still holding the handkerchief to his mouth and shaking his head regularly to get rid of the burning perspiration.

He also prayed. Not for himself but for the President and the nation.

The commander made his way toward the back room, crawling around the burning door that had been blasted in half widthwise. If he could get through the flames in the back room, that was where he stood the best chance of finding a way out.

There was a loud pop in the back room. It sounded like a lightbulb or one of the computer monitors exploding. The underlying metal walls had to be intensifying the heat. And if it were that hot in there, then getting in—let alone getting through—was going to be damn near impossible.

I ask nothing for myself, Evans thought.

He squinted. The moisture in his eyes was heating painfully, and each inch forward was agony. The arms and legs of his uniform were soaked with sweat and savagely hot.

I only want to save the others. Help me.

Suddenly, there was a loud bang directly behind him. Evans turned as cool, fresh air rushed in from the corridor. The smoke was rolling out through a jagged hole blown in the center of the door. He saw a man in a uniform and his first thought was that the Secret Service had gotten through. He heard the President call to whoever was out there.

The smoke had risen to form a thick tester beneath the ceiling. Then a flashlight shined in the dark. Someone else was there, someone Evans couldn't make out at first.

Something popped in the small conference room behind Evans. It sounded like a pocket of fuel igniting. The burst threw a flash into the main room, lighting the doorway and illuminating the elevator guard—and then lighting Hickock, who stepped into the room gun-first, looked to his right, aimed at the President, and fired twice.

Forty-five

Tuesday, 10:27 P.M.
Washington, D.C.

The President flinched as the .38 flashed. But he never felt the impact nor the anticipated pain.

Something stirred the layer of smoke overhead just as the gun coughed. Evans had started to crawl toward the President when he thought he saw a shadow move through the room, into the line of fire. The next moment Hickock was thrown back against the wall. Something caused his arms to fly out, like a squeeze doll, and then he *oofed* out all the breath he had in him. His jaw fell open and stayed open. He tried to swing the gun around but could not. The guard followed him a moment later. While Hickock stayed upright against the metal wall, the guard remained standing for only a moment. Immediately after being driven back, he doubled over at the waist and then dropped forward as though he'd been knocked down from above. He tried to get up and was knocked down again, face first, his arms splaying. This time, he stayed down.

And then a black-suited figure materialized standing over the guard. He turned to the President.

"Mr. President, are you all right?"

The President stared at him. "I'm fine." He crept from under the table and stood. "You are?"

"Colonel Matthew Lewis, 1st Special Forces O.D. I'll explain later, sir."

Lewis ran over to Hickock. He twisted his fingers low, in front of Hickock, and another figure materialized. He was holding Hickock against the wall. Lewis raised the man's faceplate. It was Major Taylor.

Evans was on his feet and moving toward him.

"Get something into his mouth, sir," Taylor gasped. "Don't let him bite down."

Lewis reached across Taylor's back, wrenched the .38 from Hickock's hand, and shoved the barrel into the prisoner's mouth. He put his other hand against the man's throat and held him to the wall.

"I've got him, Major," Lewis said.

Taylor staggered back. Evans caught him. There were two bloody holes in the left side of Taylor's SFU. Evans held the officer around the waist and helped him back toward the conference table.

"Hold on, Major," Evans said.

"I'm not going anywhere, sir."

"I'm going to lay you down," Evans said. "Do you want us to get you out of the suit?"

"No, sir. It's helping to hold me together," Taylor said through his teeth. "The bullets feel like they went through the external oblique muscle. No vital organs, but there's gonna be some nasty bleeding."

Working in near-total darkness, the President helped Evans ease Major Taylor onto the conference table as the Vice President checked on the other three men who had been on the floor. As soon as Taylor was settled on the table, the President took his gloved hand.

"Those bullets were meant for me, Major."

"I—I believe you're correct, sir," Taylor said, wincing.

"After we get this taken care of, I want to thank you properly," the President said. "I also want you to tell me if I saw what I *think* I saw. Or didn't see."

"Yes, sir," Taylor said, managing a pained smile.

The Vice President climbed from under the table.

"Are you all right?" the President asked.

Catlin nodded.

"And the others?"

"Mr. O'Hara is dead," the Vice President told him. "The others are bleeding and unconscious."

The President turned to Lewis. "Colonel, can we get the wounded out of here?"

"We can, sir, once we let the security people know how to get in."

"Can I get out the way you came in?" Evans asked.

"Yes, sir. There's a rope. We climbed through a break in the concrete wall and C-4ed our way in here."

That was the pop and flash Evans had seen and heard.

Evans told the President he was going out to get help and then ran toward the small conference room.

When Evans was gone, Lewis whipped Hickock around. Still pushing the gun barrel deep into his mouth he raised his right foot behind Hickock's legs and pressed the side of his foot behind Hickock's knees. Then he swung his own leg forward. Hickock's legs bent from under him, and he fell backward onto the floor. Lewis stayed with the man, throwing a leg over his shoulder and sitting on his chest. Hickock struggled for a moment, until Lewis used his left hand to pound a hammer-fist into the bridge of the man's nose. The second blow drew blood and got the man's cooperation.

"Okay, asshole," Lewis sneered. "You don't want to die. You know how I can tell? Because you're listening to me instead of fighting. If you tell me who sent you and where I can find him, I won't kill you." Lewis withdrew the gun slightly.

Hickock closed his eyes. He tried to swallow. *"Pl-please—"*

"Please?" Lewis pounded him again on the bridge of the nose. The young man's eyes shot open, his mouth went wide, and a wild cry of pain opened his throat even more. The gun barrel slid deeper, and Hickock began to gag. The colonel held the gun where it was, and Hickock struggled hard to suck air around the gun barrel. "You don't have the right to beg! Your choices are talk or die. Now *talk,* sonofabitch! Because if you don't, your friend *will* when he sees your fucking brains on his uniform."

Hickock stared up at him.

Lewis pulled back the hammer. "Last chance."

"Ahhhk!" Hickock shouted around the gun.

Lewis pulled the gun out a bit. "Say again?"

"Axe!" Hickock said. "He's the leader."

"Where do I find him?"

"The Allegheny Mountains. There are cabins."

"There're a lot of mountains and cabins. Where, exactly?"

"Lake Miasalaro."

"Are they planning anything else?"

"Yes," Hickock said. "An operation abroad. Assassinations. I don't know the details."

He might be lying. There was one way to know for sure. "One more question, asshole. What's the name of your group?"

"The Huntsmen," Hickock said. "They're called the Huntsmen."

Lewis withdrew the gun. He backed away. "Okay. You can bite your poison pill now if you want."

Hickock was breathing hard. He began to cry.

"Can't do that, can you? But you could shoot at the President," Lewis said. "Guns always make assholes like you strong. Except when they're pointed at you."

Colonel Lewis grabbed Hickock's right hand with his own left hand and twisted hard to the outside, inflicting intense pain on the wrist. Lewis rose, forcing Hickock to rise with him. Then he walked the young Huntsman to the back wall and shoved him against it hard.

"Put your hands on the wall, over your head," he said.

Hickock did as he was told. As Colonel Lewis pulled the dazed White House guard to his feet, Evans returned with several units of navy security forces. The soldiers were all dressed in black, wearing spandex ski masks and carrying Uzis and flashlights. A rope ladder had been lowered through the break in the concrete, and a medic was rushed in. The doctor went directly to the President, who told her to take care of Major Taylor.

She reached into her kit.

"Don't cut away the uniform," Taylor told her.

"Why, is it rented?" She turned toward him with the scissors. She leaned toward the bullet hole while her assistant used the rest of the table to set up for sterile procedures.

Taylor grabbed her hand. "Please don't," he said. He told her where the zippers were.

Grudgingly, the medic put the scissors aside and opened the zippers to expose the major's side.

The navy men took charge of the prisoners and also moved a team out from the conference room to secure the hallways. One of them, a captain, briefed the President on the damage to the White House. His second in command organized a team to restore electricity and communications to the sublevels and to keep everyone down here until the security team could ascertain whether there were other accomplices.

While order was quickly established, Evans walked over to Lewis. "This was a pretty brilliant piece of soldiering, Colonel."

"Thank you," Lewis said. He turned to Evans. The colonel's expression was Rh-positive—Rock Hard, Pissed-off. "Sir, Hickock just told me where the Hunstmen are."

Evans shot him a look. "Where?"

"They're based in the mountains about a half-hour's flight from here. And they've got another part of this operation ready to go."

"You believe him?"

"I do. The guy hasn't got ball one. Anyway, he needs us to take the Hunstmen down. He wants to live."

Evans had always believed in justice, not in revenge. Even in Miami, Father John had said that boxing ears should be done with the realization that only God can exact the ultimate punishment. *"Because the Philistines have acted revengefully, therefore thus says the Lord God: See! I am stretching out my hand against the Philistines."*

But who was to say that Evans and his stealth team were not the tools of God? *"In Him everything in heaven and on earth was created, things visible and invisible."*

Things invisible, Evans thought. Including His angels. If God did not want it to be so, then he would stop them.

"Where are Holly and Diaz?" Evans asked.

"Out on the lawn in their SFUs," Lewis said. "We borrowed the stealth chopper from Langley to get here. We still don't know who else is in on this, but the President trusts you. I say we use that trust, Commander. We get back in the chopper and take the Hunstmen out before their boss learns what happened here and everyone scatters."

"They're going to know as soon as the President sets foot out of here," Evans said. "But he's got to do that for the sake of the nation."

"Sounds like we'd better get moving."

"I agree," Evans said. "I'll talk to the President."

Lewis walked to Taylor's side, as Evans went over to the President. Some of the navy security forces had moved into the blasted corridor door to make sure the conference room was secure.

"Mr. President, we need to talk," Evans said.

"Yes, we do."

"Not just about the stealth uniforms," he said quietly.

"Is that what they are? Why didn't I know about it?"

"That was a DARPA call, Mr. President," Evans said.

"That's who you're with?"

"Yes, sir."

One of the navy security people told the President that they wanted to get him up the ladder as soon as possible and to a place of safety. The President thanked him. Evans asked for just another moment.

"Sir," Evans said quietly, "we know who was behind this operation and where he is. We also know he's planning another attack somewhere. What we don't know is who we can trust outside of my small group. My men came over in a borrowed stealth chopper. We'd like permission to take her up again and finish the job."

"Where was the chopper borrowed from?"

"Langley, sir."

"You're asking for my permission to take it back, then?"

Evans looked at him. "No—"

"Very well. Let's get upstairs. I'll inform the officer in charge that you're bringing it back on my authority."

Evans was a little slow, but he finally caught on. "Yes, Mr. President. Thank you, sir."

The President looked at Evans. "Commander, I'll expect a full report tomorrow morning."

"You'll have it, sir," Evans said.

Lewis gave Taylor a reassuring pat on the shoulder and told him that he'd check on him later. Then Evans and Lewis followed the President and his navy escort through the small conference room and up the rope ladder. When they reached the top of the silo, the President waved to reporters who were a safe distance away on East Executive in front of the Treasury Department.

Then he called over General Sam Crockett and told him to move his men away from the stealth helicopter.

The general did not question the order.

Less than two minutes later, the rotors had been fired up by one man who had opened the cargo door, looked into the bay, and then climbed into the copilot seat. Two minutes after that, the chopper was moving swiftly to the east.

Forty-six

Axe hadn't needed any special equipment to learn that President Gordon was alive. As soon as Mack McQueen had picked up radio communications about the explosions at the White House, he turned to CNN for live coverage. Then he called Axe.

Axe had come in from the seaplane where he had given the assassins some final instructions before their departure. They were all aboard, waiting only for his go-ahead, word that the President and Vice President were dead. Axe had watched the TV report with a mixture of relief, sadness, and confusion. The explosion couldn't have been powerful enough to do all of the damage he saw on TV. And he was disturbed by the images he saw. Though recent occupants of the Oval Office had been a disappointment, it was still the home of Lincoln, of Woodrow Wilson. He wondered if the bomb had been powerful enough to set off the missiles that lined the West and East Wings of the Executive Mansion.

Then he saw the President and, shortly after that, a quick

glimpse of Hickock and Thatcher being led out. Rage replaced all other emotions. He didn't believe what he was seeing. The computer bomb had gone off. He'd seen it on the fiber-optic camera. Even if the President had left the conference room, the guard was supposed to have shot him. The videotape and the death of the President and Vice President were what mattered. The men were expendable.

And Hickock hadn't taken the suicide option. He'd yellowed. Thatcher didn't know about the mountain base, but Hitchcock did. He might have told his captors.

Axe wanted to put a bullet in the coward's head, not just for being caught but for failing. One day he would. Four of the assassins were due to fly from the compound to Cuba, where Axe still had friends. From there, they were supposed to take flights to various countries. But there was no point in that now. A videotape showing the near death of the President and Vice President would make the Huntsmen seem like amateurs. No one would care how good the team had been just to get in that close.

This was the reason that the original Huntsmen had remained small. All of the field personnel under Uncle Jack were former spies, saboteurs, and assassins who were as ready to die as they were to kill. They didn't make mistakes. Their courage didn't evaporate when the weapon they'd been pointing at someone else was suddenly pointed at them.

The worst kind of courage, he reminded himself. But Axe had wanted to cap his decades of leadership with something big, a permanent change in America. And to do that he'd had to recruit from outside the professional ranks. He always knew that there was a risk. *This* risk.

Axe turned away from McQueen and from the TV monitor. He walked slowly to the other side of the cabin. Standing in the shadows, away from the TV, he was furious, though not just at Hickock or that self-righteous, smirking, ivory-tower lawman President Gordon. He was burning with a fire that flared whenever his mind had nowhere good to go.

The failure of the Bay of Pigs invasion.

It filled him with a rage that was utterly alive, even after forty years. He could still see clearly the dead patriots, smell the burning fuel of the landing craft, feel the helpless, miserable desire to be with them in death instead of racing away in a CIA helicopter. Flying home and carrying the burden of failure. He hated John Fitzgerald Kennedy as much today as he had when the Huntsmen had organized his assassination.

God, why *did it have to go that way? So many lives, so much honor, and for what?*

And as he often did when he relived the failure, Axe screamed. He screamed until his voice was weak, and then he stopped screaming. But the pain and the fury were still there and the desire to channel them was even greater. He looked around him. Where were his targets? Where could he strike?

McQueen had been watching the monitor and listening to transmissions the entire time, in case Axe needed information. Smoking a cigarette, he was outwardly unfazed by the leader's outburst.

Suddenly, McQueen turned. "Badger is calling from the lake," he said. "He reports—I don't understand this."

Axe turned. "What do you mean?"

"He reports incoming," McQueen said.

"Incoming what?"

"He doesn't say. But it's slow—looks like about 150 miles an hour. Chopper speed."

Axe felt himself calming as his anger turned toward possible danger. "What does the radar show?"

"Nothing. Nothing at all."

"But the screen's functioning?"

"Perfectly."

Axe walked over to McQueen. He glanced at the round, bright green radar screen on the shelf above McQueen's head. Save for the outlines of the mountains, it was empty.

"Tell Badger I'm coming back," Axe said. He turned and walked quickly toward the door.

The compound had weapons and people who knew how to use them, from handguns to rocket launchers. If Hickock had given out their location, no one who came in was getting out.

And suddenly he had a target, a purpose.

Forty-seven

The Huntsmen communications cabin was located just below Axe's cabin on the top of the hill. Leaving it, Axe ran down the sloping, dirt path to the lakeshore. His eyes were on the distant hills across the lake. The stars reflected brightly off the quiet waters.

Badger was standing on the pebbled, horseshoe-shaped shore. He was dressed in khaki shorts, sandals, and a polo shirt. There was a hunting knife in a sheath attached to his left ankle. The Silent Killer, he called it. He held a radio in his left hand and binoculars in his right. He was peering through the binoculars at the mountains.

Axe stopped beside him. Badger handed him the binoculars.

"Check out the treeline on Wayneford Peak," Badger said. "About four hundred feet up."

Axe looked up and to the west. He saw a shape. It was indistinct but moving toward them.

"I was coming back from the plane, and I saw the stars start to black out," Badger said. "What's radar say?"

"Nothing."

"That's impossible."

"No," Axe said. "The President survived the bombing, and Hickock is in custody. And this, ironically, is what we've been fighting for. The next generation of weapons."

Badger looked at him.

"This is starting to make sense. There were rumors that the LHX-2B stealth helicopter was going to be final-tested at Langley. We struck at Langley. Hickock talked, and now they're striking back."

"I swear, I'm going to hunt, find, and kill that bastard," Badger said as he started running back along the shore. He was headed toward the cave where the seaplane was moored.

"What are you doing?" Axe called after him.

"Right now I'm going to relocate the team from the seaplane to the bunkers. We don't want them to catch us in the cave."

"We don't have time for that," Axe said. "I want you to get on board and prepare for takeoff. I'll explain when you're there."

Badger stopped and glared at Axe. "Run?"

"No!" Axe yelled. "*Bait!* There's only one ship coming in. Start the plane and wait in the cave. Hydra and I will get a MAW from the arsenal. I'll notify you as soon as we're ready. Then you'll fly over the bunker—fast, with your lights off so they'll have trouble targeting you. They'll turn and follow, and we'll take them out."

Badger apologized for questioning Axe. Turning and putting the radio to his mouth, he told the pilot to start the engine and began running the four hundred yards to the cave.

Forty-eight

Tuesday, 11:16 P.M.
Lake Miasalaro, West Virginia

"A super-advanced billions-of-dollars helicopter and no IRV," Holly complained.

Infrared vision—familiarly, night vision—would have been a big help as the 2B swung in through the mountains. The terrain had been programmed into the onboard computer for Ron Wilson's test flights, just in case he strayed off course. But Holly was flying without lights. Neither the map nor the window would have been much good down among the trees. They were just too close together. So he had to stay well above the tree line. Though the 2B was radar-proof it wasn't eyeball-proof. And at this height, they might be spotted.

It had taken them over a half-hour to fly here at top speed. Commander Evans was in the starboard copilot's seat, and Holly was wearing the SFU cowl in case he had to relay orders from Commander Evans to the men in back. Holly had pushed the 2B to the maximum because Evans wanted him to make time. Even though they were traveling light, Holly expressed doubt that they'd have enough fuel to make it back to Langley. Evans said he would worry about that later.

Holly had just cleared the mountains and was heading toward the fifty-acre lake when there was a high distinctive beep from the cockpit's audio monitor. That meant the ODS—the on-board digital scanner—had picked up something different in the real world from what had been programmed into the computer. It could be anything from a new structure to a thermal reading that was outside the expected ranges—typically the heat of an incoming missile.

Holly looked at the video display. As the map changed in tandem with what was dark outside his window, a white banner with red letters appeared on the top of the small screen:

$$85 \text{ dB@SU-FP}$$

Holly looked to the left.

"Commander," he said, "we've got approximately 85 decibels at a source unknown, forward port."

Evans followed Holly's gaze. The men were silent for a moment, and then they heard the sound coming faintly from ahead.

"Sounds like an engine," Evans said.

"If I was back in Texas, I'd've rolled down the window of my 'Vette and listened."

There was a knock on the small door that separated the cargo bay from the cockpit. "Commander?"

It was Diaz. Evans turned and slid the small, oblong door to his right. He felt like he was in a confessional. He craned around. Lewis was sitting directly behind Evans in a folddown seat. Diaz was behind Holly. The coast guard SHARC leaned forward.

"Sir, you're hearing something out on the lake?" Diaz asked.

"We think so."

"Are there any lights reflecting off the water?"

"No. Just stars."

"Get lower and watch them," Diaz said.

"The stars on the water?"

"Yes, sir. Engines vibrate. You'll see a ripple pattern, be able to follow them back to the source."

Evans told Holly to drop the helicopter lower and turn toward the west, toward the sound. They were flying less than thirty feet above the water. It was still and quiet, no lights on the shore. If there were a base of any kind here, they were having a blackout. Evans began to wonder if Hickock hadn't been a little smarter and a little less scared than Colonel Lewis had thought—

"There!" Evans said.

The commander was pointing to the ten o'clock position. On the far side of the lake, about four hundred feet away, stars were jiggling fitfully on the water. Beyond them was a wall of barren rock.

Holly slowed and peered ahead. The ripples seemed to be coming from just below a dark spot in the face of the cliff. It could have been a cave. He maneuvered closer.

"I see something," Evans said. "I definitely see something. Movement coming from what appears to be a cave about two hundred feet ahead."

"There's probably someone idling in there. Hiding," Diaz said.

"If they're trying to hide from us, then why not just shut the engine?" Lewis asked.

"Maybe we caught them as they were just about to go," Holly said. "Or if it's a seaplane, maybe we're just in the way."

Evans was looking ahead. "They have to have spotted us by now."

"Unless they're blind, sir," Holly agreed.

"Or maybe they're waiting for us to come in after them," Evans said. "Whatever is in there, a boat or a plane, they could just be the bait. They may have heavy artillery there or someplace else. A Dragon or some other shoulder-fired Medium Assault Weapon."

"Just waiting until they know they've got a target that's staying put," Holly said.

"Exactly."

"The bad news is, depending on where they fired it from, I might not see something like that coming in time," Holly said. He shifted the chopper to a slightly southerly direction, away from the horseshoe shore. After a moment, he turned toward the northwest, just to keep moving. He also rose and descended in a gentle arc.

"Captain, if it is a plane, and they do get airborne can they outrun us?" Evans asked.

"They certainly can, sir," Holly said. "They've got at least twice the speed we have. And if they fly without lights, we're screwed. No night vision. Even if we give the air force a heads up, they stay over populated areas, there ain't no one going to shoot them down."

"Commander, I have an idea," Diaz said. "Let me out."

"What?"

"Drop me in the lake. I can swim to the cave and have a look around."

"Swim wearing the SFU?" Holly said.

"Why not? I once jumped off the dock wearing my rain-coat and galoshes, pretending I was a deep-sea diver."

"You were young and stupid."

"Okay, so I'm not young anymore. But I want to do it. Besides, I worked with NASA on spacesuit tests," Diaz went on. "They were as heavy as this thing. And I've got good arms. Unless the SFU isn't waterproof—"

"It was in the lab," Evans said. He looked at Lewis. "What do you think, Colonel?"

"Hickock said there was another part to the Huntsmen operation," he said. "If this is it, we've got to stop it."

Evans looked back at Diaz. "What do you plan to do when you get inside the cave?"

"If you move the chopper off they might turn on a cabin light or running light. Maybe I'll see something—guns, ski masks, rockets, anything that'll give us a reason to stop them. Maybe I can even find a way to stop them. Put a hole in the fuel tank or something."

"All right," Evans said. "But we won't move away until you say so."

Holly said, "Do you want to be lowered down or jump out frogman-style?"

"I want you to lower me down in case the suit leaks," Diaz said. "I don't want to plunge down fifteen feet and start filling up fast."

"Understood."

Diaz closed and fastened his faceplate. As Holly dropped lower and sailed closer to the cave, he turned the helicopter so that the cargo door was facing away from the cave. At his signal, Lewis opened the hatch. Meanwhile, Diaz had unlocked a small winch and swung it out. It was fastened to the wall on the port side, just above the remaining Hellfire. There was about twenty-five feet of metal cable ending in a small hook.

"Captain, I just had a thought," Diaz said. "Can you eject the cable once I'm down?"

"Sure," Holly said. "There's an emergency jettison function to keep us from being pulled down by overheavy cargo."

"Good. Do it."

"Why?"

"Did you ever see those movies where they string a line in front of guys on motorcycles—?"

"I copy," Holly smiled.

"I don't," Evans said.

"I'll get in, see what I can see, then tie the cable across the mouth of the cave on my way out," Diaz said. "May keep them from going anywhere."

"But that cable is fifty-five feet long. You'll have to tread water while it plays out completely. Otherwise the end will whip down when we pop it."

Diaz said he understood.

With the winch locked into place, Diaz fit his boot into the hook as best he could. The helicopter was five feet above the water and less than fifty feet from the cave.

"You ready?" Holly asked.

"Ready," Diaz replied.

Holly pushed a round white button directly in front of him on the control panel, just above the VDU. That sent power to the winch; he could hear the motor purr through the open panel. Then he pressed the button again, and the cable began to lower.

"Colonel Lewis," Holly said, "do you see that silver handle on top of the winch?"

Lewis looked. It was a small lever with a red button on top. "Got it."

"When the cable stops, push the button and pull the level back. That'll release the cable."

Colonel Lewis repeated the instruction to make sure he had it. Diaz was in the prop-whipped water and dog-paddling with his left hand while holding the cable with his right.

When the cable stopped, Lewis released it. It slid silently from the spool below the winch and plopped into the lake.

A moment later, Diaz ducked beneath the choppy water, and Lewis shut the door.

Forty-nine

Tuesday, 11:25 P.M.
Lake Miasalaro, West Virginia

Diaz was glad when Holly swung forward. Without the prop wash, the waters became calm. Holly stayed in front of the cave to buy Diaz time, in case whatever boat or aircraft was in there tried to get out. But he remained slightly to the north, to the side of where Diaz was swimming.

"You okay?" Holly asked.

"Yeah. At least it's cool here," Diaz said in short gasps as he swam for the cave. "And so far the suit's holding up."

"How about your arms, Diogenes?" Holly asked.

"Them, too," he said. Which wasn't quite true: it took a lot of strength to bend the suit at the elbows, and his arms tired quickly.

"Hey, you find any treasure down there, we split it," Holly said.

"Any old pop bottles are yours."

As he neared the cave, Diaz headed for the north side. He pulled himself ashore, dragging the cable behind him. The swim had been exhausting, and his arms felt as though they had sandbags strapped to them. He slowed literally to a crawl and engaged the stealth option as he neared. The cave was about fifty feet across, and there was a narrow ledge along the water. Diaz pulled himself up, then coiled the cable around his arm; in the dark, he wasn't worried about being seen. He began walking along the wall, feeling his way. There was deep, straight, horizontal scoring in the rock. This was not a naturally occurring cave.

In the dark, the idling craft up ahead and the softly humming helicopter behind made Diaz feel as though he were between two big, slumbering animals.

"Still holdin' up?" Holly asked.

"Yeah."

"What's it look like in there?"

"Dark. I've got to get closer or else get them to turn on some lights. I think you should give me another minute or so to get closer, then go away. I've got a feeling these guys are just going to sit still then."

"You stealthed up?"

"Yeah."

The master chief petty officer continued moving ahead. The ledge was about a foot-and-a-half wide and went straight back.

"It's tough to tell how far ahead the engine is," Diaz reported. "Sounds are muffled in the suit, and there's an echo in the cave. Lots of distortion. But it sounds bigger than an outboard."

Suddenly, the wall sloped away, and Diaz found himself in an alcove. He felt around. There were drums—of fuel?— what felt like a large generator, and, tied to a large outcropping of rock on shore, a motorboat.

"Talk to me," Holly said. "What've you got there?"

"Captain, there are drums and equipment here," Diaz replied. The SHARC felt the outcropping. It was a column about three feet high, still wedded to the rock of the cave floor. "Hold on. I'm going back in the water."

Diaz put the slender cable down by the outcropping, slid into the kale, and swam ahead. He heard something sloshing directly ahead. He slowed. Kicking underwater and paddling with his left hand, he felt ahead with his right. And touched a pontoon.

"It's a seaplane," he said into his microphone.

"Can you see inside?"

"No, but I've got an idea," he said. "Something that may force them out of the plane. Keep 'em penned in a minute more, okay?"

"You've got it," Holly said.

Swimming back to shore, Diaz tied the hook end of the cable around the outcropping of rock. Then he swam back to the plane holding the other end. He had a little more than forty feet of cable left.

There were two struts on each pontoon, one forward, one aft. Working quickly, Diaz looped the free end around the thin forward pontoon strut and knotted it tightly. He had a flashback to when he had used to knot towropes for his father, the trouble the braided three-quarter-inch lines gave him when he tried to tie a clove hitch or overhand knot—

"Okay, Captain," Diaz said. "You can move away!"

He slid from the pontoon back into the water. Swam to shore, and climbed into the alcove. He crouched behind the generator. Though Diaz was invisible, the dripping lake water wasn't.

He heard the faint swooshing of the 2B rotor as it faded. He was looking ahead and up, where the seaplane's cockpit should be. Just then a small, shielded light came on. He could see the pilot and copilot through the door window. The pilot was wearing a headset and night-vision goggles.

"Captain?" Holly said.

"Here. I've set down about three hundred yards away."

"These guys were obviously waiting for you to leave, but I'm not looking at anything threatening. Got 'em tied up, though. They try to take off, they're gonna cripple themselves."

"Good work," Holly said. "The commander says to get yourself out of there now."

"I'm okay. I want to give it another few seconds."

Infiltration wasn't Diaz's line of work. Neither was spying or combat. But he was the one who was in here, and he wanted to pick up any intel he could. When the plane started to taxi, he'd go back in the water and swim out.

The pilot's mouth was moving. The engine started revving up. The 2B wasn't visible from the cave; someone on the outside must have told him the chopper was off the lake.

"Diogenes, the commander wants you out now!" Holly said.

"All right. He's starting up," Diaz said. "But you're obviously being eyeballed from some other point."

"There are some dark cabins along the shore," Holly told him. "Probably spotters there."

Suddenly the plane bolted forward, not taxiing but racing.

"Holy shit!" Diaz screamed.

"What is it?"

"Captain, we've got trouble—"

That was the last thing Diaz said before the pontoon strut snapped. The speeding plane nosed down sharply and to the port side. The propeller hit the water, and it flew off, cartwheeling backward and sheared through the wing. The loss of the propeller and wing turned the aircraft from the cave opening toward the west side of the cavern. The Cessna smashed into it hard, crumbling to the cockpit then scraping along the stone to its tail. The collision ripped open the fuel tank, sparks from the crash igniting the gas. A low carpet of blue-orange flame rolled back toward the alcove as the cabin door of the Cessna flew open. Four men jumped into the water, three with fire on their arms and clothing, the fourth covered with flame. A fifth man was still inside the aircraft, trying to extricate the pilot and copilot from the crushed cockpit.

Moments later, the small plane exploded. The cavern lit up, and the loud blast sent pieces of plastic, metal, and glass sizzling into the water and flying through the cave. There were smaller pops as shells exploded inside clips that had been on board.

The light and echo died quickly. As fiery pieces of fabric and paper fluttered down around him, MCPO Diaz rose. He'd been crouched behind the outcropping of rock, stunned and sickened by what had happened. He hadn't intended to hurt anyone, just stop them. These men may have been terrorists, killers, but they hadn't been tried or judged. And he had executed them.

"Diaz!"

It was Holly.

"Diaz!"

"Here," Diaz said.

"Are you all right?"

"Yeah," he said, "fine."

"Can you get out of the cave?"

Diaz raised his faceplate and looked out at the water. The flames were thinning quickly as the gas burned off. His back felt warm, and he turned and looked behind him. Debris was burning everywhere in the small alcove, most of it in the midst of over a dozen drums. If those drums were filled with gasoline, he really didn't have time to reflect on what he'd done. Not now.

"I can get out," he said.

"There's no way I can scoop you out," Holly said. "But the shore's about twenty yards to your north."

"I'll make it," Diaz said. Numb, he began walking back toward the ledge. His legs, like his arms, like his heart, were extremely heavy. He'd have to back-float to shore.

Suddenly, something shot up from the water. Diaz stopped as a gray-haired, powerfully-built man sucked down air and pulled himself ashore. His shirt was in shreds; and there were burn marks on his shoulders and arms. Behind him, the other man appeared on the black lake. One was floating facedown, the other faceup. None of them was moving.

Diaz backed into the alcove. He didn't know whether to help the man or knock him back in and swim past him. He waited.

In the dying light, the man suddenly noticed the outcropping of rock and the cable tied around it. The broken strut was bobbing on the water, still attached to the line.

"Diogenes, are you on your way out?"

Diaz froze. His visor was raised. The sound was audible.

The man from the lake looked over. He squinted ahead. It seemed to take him a second to convince himself that someone was there. "What the fuck? Who the hell are you?"

The lake water on the SFU hadn't entirely dried. Diaz glanced down. His outline was clearly visible and his face was right there beneath the faceplate he'd stupidly opened.

The coast guard SHARC watched as the man dragged his hand across his eyes, squinted again, and then squatted. The man drew a knife from a sheath around his ankle and then rose. He held the knife waist-high as he walked forward, limping slightly. Just then, Diaz noticed the small animal tatooed on the man's chest. It looked like a small ferret. Or a badger.

"I asked who you fucking *are*?" the man shouted. He was about six feet away.

Diaz said nothing.

"Who *sent* you? The Feds? The fucking marines?"

Diaz backed into the alcove. He didn't speak. He didn't even look at the man. He was staring at the water. He wondered if he had enough time to reach his gun and fire. And if he did, Diaz wondered whether he would even hit him. The last thing he'd fired was a spear gun at a tuna off the shore of Vavau, Tonga. That handled a lot differently.

"Talk!" the man screamed.

Diaz looked at him. What the hell was he doing on land anyway, facing a man with a knife? He looked past the man at the water.

"Sorry," Diaz said. "Silent running's more my speed."

Hunching his shoulders, Diaz ran into the man and pushed him backward. They both fell into the lake, Diaz on top. Because his faceplate was up, the SHARC straightened himself quickly and made sure that his shoulders didn't sink below the waterline.

Diaz kicked hard to stay afloat, leaving both hands free to grapple with the knife. His opponent was having trouble remaining above water, especially with the weight of the SFU against him. Though it was pulling him down, he refused to drop the knife and swim. The men were face-to-face, spitting anger, snatched breaths, and water as they struggled.

The blade was close below Diaz's chin, the man pushing up hard and Diaz fighting to push him down. Even if Diaz's arms weren't tired, the man was strong and determined. The knife came closer.

This was not the way Diaz wanted to die. Not how, not when, and not with whom. With a cry, he dropped backward, still holding the knife, and pulled the man with him. They both went under, Diaz quickly turning so that he was on top of his assailant.

Water dribbled into the tight cowl. Diaz could feel it slipping down his neck, back, and chest. A few moments more, and the suit would start to pull him under. Pushing down on the man but not releasing him, Diaz raised his own head and broke the water and breathed through his teeth. Keeping his cowl above the surface, Diaz held his assailant's knife hand with both of his own, knelt on his chest, and refused to get off. The man kicked and flailed beneath him but Diaz easily maintained his balance.

The man didn't release the knife. Not when his kicks and struggles began to weaken and not when he finally stopped moving. Not even when the bubbles stopped rising from his open mouth and there was only stillness beneath the waters.

Silent running.

Diaz waited a few moments longer before sliding from his body and swimming to the alcove. Now he had killed a man with his bare hands. Yet it didn't bother him as much as what he'd done to the others. This man had been warned.

He didn't pull himself up when he reached the ledge. The fires were still burning, and there wasn't time to get out of the SFU and empty the water. Lowering the faceplate and locking it up, he turned toward the mouth of the cave and began swimming as quickly as his sluggish arms and legs could manage. What was left of the plane was still on fire, but most of that was above the water to the north. He'd be able to swim around it.

Diaz had gone about twenty-five feet with some thirty feet left to go when he suddenly felt as though someone had clapped him hard on the ears, shoved him between the shoulders, and set the clock to noon with the sun directly overhead.

Fifty

Tuesday, 11:49 P.M.
Lake Miasalaro, West Virginia

When Captain Holly heard someone else's voice coming through Diaz's microphone, he realized the SHARC's faceplate was raised and shut up at once. He hoped the seaman could handle whatever it was. Besides, they had problems of their own.

After Diaz reported that they'd been spotted from somewhere outside the cave, Evans had watched the shore. There were cabins about two hundred yards from where they'd set down and there appeared to be activity in front of one of them. Evans told Lewis that they were going to get out and have a closer look, then ordered Holly to get the ship airborne and out of range. Holly would remain in contact with Lewis through the SFU headset. The pilot gave Evans his weapon before the commander got out.

Lewis had mixed feelings about Evans being there without his SFU. There was jealousy because the man had no shielding except his reflexes and skill. Lewis didn't like to be the guy with the advantage. But there was also an incredible sense of freedom. The bastards had tried to kill his commander in chief. He wanted to hurt them as much as he could. The edge he didn't want, invisibility, made that goal more attainable.

As long as you don't get sloppy, he reminded himself.

When they left the helicopter, Evans had told Lewis to go ahead as far and as fast as he could. Evans planned to hang back slightly, let whoever was there think he was alone. He wanted to try and draw them past Lewis, so that he could find out what they were planning. Before leaving, Lewis gave the commander his handgun as well. He said he'd take one from the enemy.

While Evans stayed among the rocks and foliage in the low foothills, Lewis ran along the shore. He crouched low, dropping his center of gravity and making as little noise as possible.

He was about ten yards from the first two men. They were outside the nearest of four cabins. One man was wearing night-vision goggles and carrying a launcher for a shoulder-fired guided missile. He was looking out at the lake as he got down on one knee. The other man was yelling back at the cabin. He seemed extremely agitated, especially after the cave exploded a second time, blowing a huge fist of fire and what was left of the seaplane out across the lake

Lewis hoped to hell that Diaz had been able to get out of the cave and out of the water before that hit. But he couldn't think of that now. He turned his attention to the MAW man.

"Holly, they're aiming six pounds of warhead at you," Lewis said. "It's got at least three thousand feet of range—"

"I'm 55 feet up about 400 back, and I'm pushin' it."

Lewis swore. He wished he hadn't given his gun to Evans; so much for having an edge. There wasn't even a way he could signal the commander to take a shot at the bas-

tard. The colonel started running forward, but he wasn't
going to reach the MAW man in time.

"Holly, you see their position. First cabin?"

"Yeah."

"You're gonna have to come in at him. When you do,
lighten him up, try and blind him."

"I'm there," Holly said.

Lewis stopped running as the chopper suddenly reversed
climb and retreated. Silent as it was, Lewis could hear as
Holly bore down on the shore. It was a billion-dollar-plus
game of chicken, and in spite of the risks—also because of
them—Lewis was as revved as the 2B.

Four other men were running from the cabin with guns.

"Stay back!" the leader yelled at them. He was standing
beside the man with the missile. "Fire, damn you!"

Before the man could site the MAW, Holly turned on the
nose lights of the 2B. The white glare shone down, literally
knocking the missile man over. He screamed and clawed at
the night-vision goggles, losing the rocket launcher in the
process. The leader shouted to one of the other men to retrieve it just as Holly's chin mount began to fire. He was obviously not wearing the helmet targeting unit because he
was wide. But he caused the men to run back to the cabin.

Except for the leader. He stared up at the helicopter and
then looked around as though he knew someone was near.

Former special ops, Lewis thought. Had to be. The man
could smell a penetration.

Suddenly, the leader turned, shouted instructions for an
evacuation, then disappeared up the foothills and into the
night.

"Good work!" Lewis said to Holly.

Holly swooped overhead and circled back over the lake.
"Bad news is I shot the wad," he said. "They only had a
small load in the gun."

Just then, two lines of Huntsmen came running from the nearest cabin. All of them were armed. None of them wearing infrareds. The man who'd been holding the MAW was obviously in command here.

"Cactus, you take seven men up the hill," he said. "Solomon, Bud, Magic, and me will spread out on the shore and watch for traffic from the lake or around the cave. Radio when you're ready to leave and we'll join you."

Lewis stood still and silent as Hydra and his three men ran by along the rocky shore. One of them passed less than a foot from him. When they were gone, Lewis got back on the suit mike. He didn't want to go after them until the others were far enough away. Divide and conquer.

"We'll be there in ten," Cactus said and started up the hill.

"Sir," Holly said. "I'd like to go over to the cave and look for Diaz—"

"Negative," Lewis said. "The Huntsmen are the target, and they're getting ready to leave. Go up the hill and keep your light on the leader, point him out to the commander. I'll track the line coming up to meet him and pick off the guys in back."

"Sir, the chicken-charge burned me down to about seven or eight minutes of flying time," Holly said. "And the 2B's fussy. If any of those guys puts a hole in me, I'm screwed. But I'm thinkin' if I radio for backup from Langley, they may get here in time to pick up the Huntsmen—"

"And they may not. Or the Huntsmen may monitor your communication and hunker down and give us Waco II. We don't know what kind of firepower they have up there or whether they're leaving by land, chopper, or—"

Suddenly, they heard static followed by a series of coughs crackling over the earphones.

Lewis and Holly were silent for a moment. Then Holly said, "Diogenes—is that you?"

"Yeah," he hacked.

"Shit, man, why didn't you say anything?" Holly yelled.

"I was holdin' my breath," he gasped. "Had to dive when the cave blew. Air vents took on water—everything shorting."

"Where are you?" Lewis asked.

"Ashore, about fifty feet from the cave."

Lewis looked back. That was where the MAW man and his team were deploying. "Are you visible?" he asked.

"I'm phasing in and out—"

"Diaz, they're going to see you. Can you move?"

"Not well. Arms and legs are dead, and I'm water-logged."

"Do you have a weapon?"

"A wet one," Diaz said. "It may not fire."

"Sir, I'm flyin' down to cover him," Holly said.

"No!" Lewis barked. "I'll deal with them. Stay with the leader as long as you can, let me know what they're up to." He started running after Hydra and his three men.

"Let me try something else," Holly said.

Lewis was unaccustomed to having his orders questioned, and Holly had already blasted past that line. On the other hand, Lewis wasn't accustomed to dealing with air force either, and he owed it to the mission to listen.

"Talk fast," he said.

"I'm out of ammo except for the Hellfire," Holly said.

Lewis perked.

"Let me try and mess 'em up a little," Holly said.

"Is the commander clear?"

"He's goin' through a pass, and the leader's over the hill," Holly said. "Looks like the commander's on to him, trying to catch up."

"Then do it," Lewis said without hesitation.

Holly flew ahead and over the hill, then turned around so he was facing the lake. The Huntsmen were about halfway up the peak. He opened the hatch, and the two-rail launch platform slid out. As he ran toward Diaz, Lewis turned to watch. Holly fired.

The missile spit a column of white fire, hissed, and whistled toward the hilltop. The thickly treed peak exploded in a dirty red ball. Trees and rocks tossed up and out in every direction. But most of it fell toward the lake. The man-made avalanche picked up speed and force as blasted boulders landed on the hill, bounded, and smashed into trees and dislodged other boulders. Clouds of dirt thirty feet high poured down like a tsunami, thick and blinding.

The Huntsmen on the shore had paused to watch. That was a mistake. Lewis had closed the distance before they started running again. He caught the nearest one with a "clothesline" strike, his arm held straight from the shoulder, to the side. It connected with the back of the man's neck and knocked him flat, face-forward. Lewis stopped to retrieve the man's handgun. When the Huntsman tried to push up, Lewis stomped on his extended left elbow and broke it. The man went down and stayed down.

The 2B was on its way toward the shore, its light off. The other men saw it and continued running. Lewis figured that they were headed toward huge, jagged chunks of boulder which were arrayed in a row to the right. The rock was probably excavated from inside the cave. They made good barricades from which to watch the shore.

The helicopter leveled off some thirty feet up and passed over Lewis's head. Holly was probably looking for Diaz. One of the Huntsmen looked back at the helicopter just in time to collect a fist in the face. He cried out and went down on his back. The other two men heard him yell and stopped running. One of the remaining men was the commander. He fired up at the chopper, forcing Holly to veer off sharply, back up the hill.

The other man was looking back at his fallen comrades. "No one's there!" he said.

The commander lowered his gaze. "Someone took them down!" He pointed the automatic ahead, arm's length. There was a series of pops and flashes.

The Huntsman leader watched as his companion twisted and fell. Then Hydra took two shuffling steps forward and dropped. A moment later, Diaz dragged himself from under a large, sloping boulder several yards behind the men. His faceplate was raised.

"I guess . . . the powder . . . was drier than I thought," he said before falling forward a few feet behind the dead men.

Lewis ran forward. Holly circled wide, landed behind Diaz, and ran ahead. He had engaged his stealth option but disengaged it when he saw that no one was moving. He raised his own visor. The two stealth soldiers reached their fallen comrade at the same time.

Holly knelt beside him while Lewis checked the two men he'd knocked down and then the two Diaz had shot. The pilot pulled off his gloves and felt under Diaz's nose for breath. Then he lightly slapped the seaman's cheeks. Diaz's face was wet and flushed, his eyes shut.

"Hey, tubman," Holly said. "Talk to me."

"Diaz smiled faintly, his eyes still closed. "About what?"

"About anything you want," Holly smiled back. "But first let me check for damage."

Holly straddled the SHARC and rolled him gently onto his side.

"I feel like . . . I'm in a tube of jelly," Diaz said.

"I'll get you zipped outta there in a sec," Holly said.

"What about—those men?"

"They're dead," Lewis said. He'd picked up the Huntsmen's guns and walked over. "How's he doing, Captain?"

"I don't see any wounds."

"Dead," Diaz said. "That's three . . . I've killed today."

"That's three less to worry about later," Lewis said. "We won't have to listen to their shit each day of a fuckin' trial."

"I ended three lives," Diaz said.

"It comes with the uniform and the pension," Lewis said. "You two gonna be okay here? I want to go after the commander."

"We'll be fine," Holly said. "I'm going to move him into the chopper. Give us some cover if we need it."

"Good. I'd tie up those other two first though," Lewis said. "I didn't hit 'em hard enough to kill 'em." He started up the hill. "And Captain?"

"Sir?"

"Thanks for the Hellfire. That was pretty."

Lewis hurried up the hill. Though he was tired and hot, he was anxious to get to the top. He didn't know if the landslide had stopped all the other Huntsmen, and he hated the idea of any man going in without backup, especially a man who hadn't been in the field for years.

Lewis also hated something else, and he wanted to be certain it didn't happen, either because of error or the religious convictions of his commander. He wanted to make sure that the leader of the Huntsmen would leave here in anything but a body bag.

Fifty-one

Tuesday, 11:57 P.M.
Lake Miasalaro, West Virginia

Evans had been following the black-clad man from the moment he spotted him under Captain Holly's spotlight. Lewis had no way of communicating with him; if he had Holly hovering, there was a reason.

The man had a considerable lead, and Evans decided to try and cut him off by picking his way through a very narrow, zigzagging pass. He was nearly through it when the Hellfire exploded. The ground literally hopped under him, knocking him against the rock wall and throwing up a shower of dirt—nearly as much as rained in. The wall was less then two feet taller than he was, and, still holding the guns, Evans crouched and hid his face in the crook of his elbow for several long seconds. When the falling dirt no longer bit his neck and the echo of falling rocks came from far down the hill, the commander stood and ran ahead, spitting out soil. The ground still trembled from the sliding land, and the sound had silenced everything else—the birds, the insects, and the predators that had been creeping in the brush. Evans hoped that his quarry hadn't been hurt. If the man he was chasing were a Huntsmen leader, Evans wanted answers.

The 2B sped overhead, toward the lake, as Evans emerged from the pass. He saw two cabins ahead, one lighted, one dark. The lighted one, which was closer, didn't seem to have been seriously damaged by the blast. He couldn't tell about the other, higher one. He made his way to the nearer cabin and circled it low and cautiously. From atop the summit, towns glittered in the distance, and the air was cool. A leader—or a demigod—would want to be up here.

The wood structure looked old. It was surrounded by lumpy hills and boulders half-buried by earth, weeds, and wildflowers. There were windows front and back and a door that was ajar. There was a dull orange glow coming from inside. Evans was evidently being invited in.

Evans's palms were sweating around the two guns as he moved forward. Otherwise, he was calm, loose. He and the team had seriously damaged these people, and the pressure that usually accompanied a mission—succeeding first, surviving second—was diminished.

He turned his back as he approached the door, then leaned that way so he could look in. The man in black was inside. He was facing a desk, his arms straight at his sides. There was a portable computer, a picture frame, and a secure TAC-SAT phone on the desk, and a fire dying to his left. Evans nudged open the door with his right foot.

"Tell me something," the man said. His voice was quiet, gravelly. He didn't turn. "There are rogue nations that have the capacity to strike our country with nuclear missiles. If they hit us, would we strike back with more than words? Or more importantly, if we knew who they were, would we strike first?"

Evans edged in. "I don't know."

"Don't you find that sad?"

Evans was inside now. He looked around. There was no one else here. He stood several yards from the man, both guns aimed at him from the hip.

"I do," Evans said.

Axe turned his head and shoulders as he spoke. His expression darkened when he saw Evans. "You."

Evans was surprised. He looked at the man more carefully. "Have we met?"

"I've seen you, Commander Evans," Axe replied. "It isn't important where, but I admired you, even as I wished— God, how I wished it—that I could shoot you where you sat."

Evans's vigilance had begun to wane. He brought it back up.

Axe turned completely around. "Do you know what I was within hours of accomplishing?"

"Save it for your trial," Evans said. "Turn yourself back around, spread your legs, and put your hands on the desk."

"There will be no trial," Axe replied. "Either you're going to help me, or you're going to kill me here."

"Sorry. I'm not a judge, and I'm certainly not a traitor."

Axe glared at him. "Is that what you think of me?"

He turned and popped a diskette from the computer on his desk. Evans moved toward him, thinking of the laptop in the White House Situation Room. He froze when the man turned back holding a diskette.

"Read what I've written!" he shouted. "My journal. I've kept it for over thirty years. I made the first entry on the back of a map as I flew from my dead comrades in the Bay of Pigs. That's here, and every entry since."

"I've lost comrades, too," Evans said. "To you, in fact."

"I'm sorry if they were on the wrong side of the barricade," Axe said.

"Your side."

"*America's* side! The side that was always out on a limb. Inventing, pushing, discovering, liberating! All the while towing the deadweight of doubters and critics and *pacifists*!"

This man was gone. Well-gone.

"I'm no traitor," the man went on. "The President who betrayed us, the nation that had immortalized him, the people who have followed his example of compromise and cowardice—*they* are the traitors. You're a soldier, Commander Amos Evans. I can tell by the way you move that you've been there, behind the lines. You should understand!"

Evans wanted to know how the man knew his name, but he had already broken the first rule of engagement, which was not to engage in conversation. Talk personalizes the enemy. It makes the opponent sympathetic or else so monstrous that you feel justified pulling the trigger and putting a hole in him. That was not Evans's decision to make.

"Turn and let's go" was all Evans said.

"I told you I won't be taken prisoner," Axe said. He dropped the diskette on the desk and walked slowly toward the fireplace. "My father had a vision of the American future. So did I. It was born in the past, in a time of nobility, courage, and honor."

"You tried to kill the President. You killed other men. There's nothing honorable in that." There were rules of engagement and then there were higher laws, commandments that this man had destroyed. Evans had to end this soon. He was losing self-control.

"You've killed, I'm sure," Axe said.

"In self-defense. In defense of my country."

"So have I," Axe said. He removed an old axe from above the fireplace. He held it diagonally across his chest and turned toward Evans.

The commander kept both guns pointed at the man's chest.

"The Vikings believed that they couldn't go to Valhalla, the hall of slain heroes, unless they died with a weapon in their hand."

"You don't have to die."

"I'm already dead. Whoever your people are, they've destroyed the last effort time and health will allow. My part in the master plan. I only hope is that someone with courage— maybe you, if you take the time to understand—will read my journal and continue where I've failed."

"You didn't fail. You were stopped," Evans pointed out. To hell with the rules. He had no patience for anyone with a god complex.

"Only for now," Axe replied. "There are others. I've downloaded my journals and data to them. They will continue the work."

Evans suspected that the only way to discourage those "others" was to bring this man in, not make him an Internet poster child to extremists everywhere. He put his guns on the floor and stepped over them. His right arm was extended. "Give me the axe."

"It was my father's. He protected my mother's honor with it. You'll not have it while I'm alive. Better go back for your weapons."

Evans continued to walk forward. He'd never have made a good hostage negotiator. In the end, maybe proselytizers never did.

"You've killed a lot of people," Evans said. "Will you kill me?"

"Easily."

"Do you believe in damnation and repentance?"

"Yes," Axe said. "One is life without honor. The other is reclaiming it with blood."

"No. That's vengeance. Hate."

"Good words," Axe said. "They keep a man going. Now pick up your gun or die."

Evans was nearly within reach of the axe. He wanted it, and he wanted this man. If he could get in close enough and hug the man, he could wrestle him down. An axe was useless at close range.

The other man obviously knew that, too. Suddenly, Axe cried out, stepped back, and swung his weapon down. Evans raised his right arm to meet the attack, forearm cocked across his forehead, meaty part out.

A single shot punched through the room, and the struggle stopped suddenly. Axe stumbled backward. He tripped over the screen in front of the glowing fireplace and fell in. Evans ran over to pull him out. Lewis rushed from the doorway, deactivating his stealth capacity as he ran. He was still holding the gun he'd fired.

Blood dripped from a single bullet wound in the back of Axe's head. It sizzled on the embers as they lifted him from the fire. Evans felt sick as they lay him on the bare floor in front of the desk. He felt for a pulse. There wasn't any.

"Are you all right, sir?" Lewis asked.

"Yes." He didn't ask why the colonel shot to kill. Training, he hoped. Anger, revenge, or a special-ops TOTAL hit—Take Out To Avoid Legalities—were not explanations he cared to consider.

Evans said as he rose, "There's another cabin beside this one—"

"I saw it," Lewis said. "I'll make sure it's secure."

"Prisoners," Evans said. "If anyone's in there, you try to take him."

"Of course," Lewis said.

When the colonel had gone, Evans knelt on one knee and said a short prayer over the dead man. There was nothing he could use to cover the body, so he left it where it was. He rose and turned to the desk. The fireplace had been stirred when the man fell, and the figures carved in the wood seemed strangely animated. Evans walked over and retrieved the diskette.

The history of a patriot, he thought, unhappy with his own cynicism. He used to feel good when he won. Maybe Evans was just too old to harbor any of the innocence that used to keep him going from mission to mission. Or maybe he knew that this time there was no winning. The man had probably deleted the names of anyone who had received his journal. The Huntsmen would be back—maybe tomorrow, maybe in a year, maybe with the same name, maybe with a new one. But they would be back.

Evans slipped the diskette into his shirt pocket, closed and unplugged the laptop, and walked from the cabin.

Fifty-two

McIver found it odd.

When they'd gathered here in the rec room three days before, and no one knew each other, they didn't shut up. Now they'd shared combat together, knew each other as only fellow soldiers could, and they were dead silent. The only chat came from Taylor, who was tightly bandaged and still pissed that he'd missed the action in the mountains.

The others were pissed too, but for different reasons. Chief among them was that Commander Evans was gone.

Catching up on sleep, the rest of the group gathered here late in the morning for breakfast. Lewis made it clear by the set of his mouth and eyes that he had no interest in talking, but Victoria, Taylor, and Captain McIver had been able to pull a few things out of Holly and Diaz.

The men told them a little about the attack itself, and then about the aftermath. After the Huntsmen's hideaway had been secured and the few remaining men rounded up—including a cowering communications officer—Holly had used the 2B radio to call for air force rescue. A squadron of choppers came in with medics, SHOUTs—Secure/Hold Operations, Utility Team—fuel, and questions, which Evans had instructed his men not to answer. The stealth team and the prisoners were returned to Langley. The soldiers were placed in the bomb shelters with armed guards at the field exit, and their phone and computer lines were shut down. Until the DOD gave him some answers or told him otherwise. General Jackson was keeping the team that stole the 2B under station arrest.

Late on Wednesday morning, a naval officer and four men came for Evans. He was told nothing about where he was going or when—or even if—he'd be returning. The only thing Evans took with him was the laptop and diskette he'd brought from the mountain hideout.

A little over a day later, the door at the front of the rec room opened. One of the Langley guards stepped in and held it for Evans. The guard saluted. Evans saluted back, and then the sentry was dismissed.

Evans turned and faced the group. Taylor's bare chest was heavily bandaged from the flesh wounds and shattered ribs he'd suffered, injuries that were relatively superficial thanks to the SFU. He was stretched on a cot beside a wheelchair. The other team members were packed around the table. Lewis, followed by McIver, Holly, and Diaz all rose and saluted. Taylor saluted from the cot. Victoria smiled. They looked at Evans with a combination of surprise, expectation, and hope.

Evans saluted the troops and smiled at Victoria. "It's getting to be a habit," he said to the group. "Me showing up in this room and surprising you."

Now the others smiled. Even Lewis.

"Sit down," Evans said. "Is there any coffee left?"

Diaz rose and poured some for the commander. He was

slightly hunched, and the bandages around his legs and arms had to pinch. But McIver was glad that Evans asked. As low man on the military totem, coffee was Diaz's unofficial job. The seaman was still weak, bruised, and he'd been scalded in spots by his own superheated sweat. But it wasn't good to coddle "the mobile wounded," as they were called. It eroded self-respect and the confidence of the others.

Evans thanked him. He took a sip then sat on the edge of the desk. "It's good," he said. "Much better than White House coffee."

The others waited as he took a second sip.

"I think the rapport here is better, too," Evans said. "Which is good, since we may be seeing quite a lot of each other."

The others waited as he took a third sip. Captain McIver was glad to see him enjoying this—whatever "this" was, though she had a good idea. From everyone's expectant looks, they all did. But they all had the smarts not to step on the commander's moment.

"The President sends his thanks and congratulations for the work you did," Evans went on. "He's deeply appreciative and very proud of all of you."

"Maybe I can get a photo of the President for me and for my mom's wall," Taylor chuckled.

"How is the President?" Lewis asked. He was the only one who did not appear to have entirely signed onto the roomwide optimism.

"He's very well," Evans said. "The Oval Office was slightly damaged, and he's moved to other offices in the West Wing. Reconstruction of the East Wing and the sublevels are going to present noise and security problems so it'll be months before he can return. A lot of priceless art and furnishings were damaged, some destroyed, but things weren't as bad as they could have been."

"Except that we didn't go far enough," Lewis said. "We should have exterminated those bastards in their hive. Like Saddam during the Gulf War, we stopped too short."

"We went as far as we needed to go with *this* operation," Evans responded. "And one good thing came from all of this. The President is determined to do whatever he can to see that nothing ever threatens our elected government or our Constitution again. That includes the Huntsmen. The FBI have the radio operator you rounded up and several other members in custody, including Hickock and the White House guard. And Dr. Moses Cole has agreed to testify about his activities in exchange for immunity."

"He was General MacDougall's friend, wasn't he?" Victoria said.

"Yes," Evans replied sadly. "Cole also treated the Huntsmen leader Bernard Schiller for years, most recently for pancreatic cancer, without knowing who he was. By the time Cole found out, it was too late. The Huntsmen got him to cooperate by threatening his family. But we don't imagine that breaking this particular group has ended the threat. Before Schiller died, he downloaded his computerized journals to we don't know how many other people and then erased those names from memory. They or someone like them will be back."

"Like cockroaches," Taylor said.

"Right, which is where we come in. Before I arrived at the White House, President Gordon met with the Joint Chiefs of Staff. Officially, they've turned back the clock. None of us had anything to do with the White House infiltration, the theft of the 2B, or the attack on the Huntsmen base. Those were all navy, air force, and Secret Service operations."

"So we're all in the clear," Diaz said.

"Right."

"Sir," Holly said, "there's only two of us can fly the 2B and one of 'em was lyin' facedown on the tarmac."

"That's right," Evans said. "But he doesn't remember a thing. Doesn't even remember going out there."

There was silence. Then Holly said, "Oh. I understand."

"That means I was never at the White House," Taylor said. "There goes my photo op."

"To the contrary," Evans said. "You'll *have* that, though not right away. The President will come to see us when we're settled in at Camp MacDougall."

The silence was back, deeper than it had been a moment before.

"As soon as the paperwork is finished under the Terrorist Property Reclamation Act, we'll be moving to old cabins on Lake Miasalaro in West Virginia, refitted for our use," Evans continued. "We will operate clandestinely, have special access to NRO, CIA, and other intelligence services data, on a need-to-know basis, and will answer to just one man. The President."

McIver looked around the room. There were slow smiles, even from Lewis. She wanted to remember this time, this moment.

"That is, if you're interested," Evans added.

Taylor smiled.

"I get my very own lake," Diaz said. "Sweet."

"And in time, I hope you'll get a next-generation wetsuit SFU to try in it," Evans said.

"Does the move include all of us?" Victoria asked.

Evans looked at her. "That's up to you. The President has said I should do whatever it takes to keep the team intact and functioning. I told him I wanted you to stay with us and that I wanted to add one member, Dr. Fraser from N-Gen. Have you worked with him?"

She said she had.

"Did you get along well?"

"Pretty well," Victoria said. "He's a nutcase."

"He is. But he's also a brilliant scientist, and he has no family. And as Mr. Diaz proved with his initiative, we need someone who has the skills to repair and upgrade the suits."

"So those would stay with us," Taylor said. "We would truly be a stealth operation."

"That's right."

"What about transportation? For missions, I mean." Holly asked.

"Your chopper went down in the lake," Evans said.

"Went down?" And then Holly said, "Oh. I understand."

"We'll be using the 2B as well as ground transportation for routine comings and goings."

Lewis shook his head. "I don't want to piss on everyone's parade, but I've got a lot of questions about our commission and logistics. I'm also concerned about security. Who else will know of the team's existence?"

"Just the President," Evans replied.

"Like the Untouchables," Taylor said.

"It worked once," McIver pointed out.

"Do you really believe the government can keep a secret like that?" Lewis asked. "The military?"

"They've done it before, from D-Day to Desert Shield. How we'll communicate with the President and exactly what we may be asked to do are things I can't tell you yet. For the present, our only mandate will be to continue with what we started. Testing the SFUs, albeit under more controlled conditions."

Diaz shook his head. "I'm a sailor with the coast guard, sir. I'm not in the same class as the rest of you."

"Horseshit," Lewis said. "You entered that cave and collected intel and fought like you'd been doing that your whole life."

"You're the man," Holly said.

"Ask if I liked it," Diaz said.

"Did you?" Holly asked.

"Not the killing," he said. "Not that."

"I don't either," Evans said. "Which is why, in the end, you have to believe that it isn't your doing but God working through you."

"St. War," McIver muttered.

"Pardon?" Evans said.

"God working through someone to engage in combat. Stealth warrior—St. War. Almost like it was destined."

"A discussion for another time," Evans said. "This is the kind of assignment the President doesn't want to order anyone to take. I'd like you all to take some time and think about this—but not too much time. The President would like an answer by this evening. Now that he knows about the SFUs, he feels strongly that the commander-in-chief needs an elite personal unit that can deal with threats anywhere at any time, swiftly and efficiently."

"I don't know about anyone else," Holly said, "but I don't need time to think. I'm in. I am definitely, totally in."

"Same here," Diaz said.

"Do we get leave to see our friends and families?" Taylor asked.

"Same as before," Evans replied.

"Which means I'll get pulled away before breakfast," Taylor laughed.

"Sometimes."

"I can live with that. Where do I sign?" Taylor asked.

"Unfortunately, I don't have anyone to go home to," Victoria said. "I'm with you, Dr. Fraser notwithstanding."

Evans held her eyes for a moment before looking at McIver.

"There're probably more places I can smoke in the great outdoors without getting kicked in the ass," she said.

"Not while I'm around," Taylor grumbled.

"Right, mummy-man." She turned back to Evans. "Count me in."

The commander looked at Lewis.

The colonel looked back. "Would we be going there to win, sir?"

"We'd be going there to serve the President, Colonel."

"I understand that, sir," Lewis said. "I also understand that these people we're supposed to be fighting—the Huntsmen, the backwoods lunatics who want to blow up federal buildings, the religious fanatics who have it in for people of another faith—these people need to be taught a lesson."

"They will be."

"I don't believe in hell—"

"This isn't about damnation," Evans said. "It's about justice. Our job will be to apprehend the enemy. Justice will follow. That's all I can promise."

"The only person who can promise justice is the person who serves it up then and there, fresh," Lewis said. "But you don't want to hear my views, sir. You want an answer. And my answer is that this group has pulled it together under some very extreme circumstances. It will be my privilege to work with them and contribute whatever I can."

Taylor and Holly each pounded a fist lightly on the table.

"Thank you," Evans said. "Thank you all."

The commander finished his coffee, told the group to shake it out in their quarters, that he'd be meeting with them at 1400 hours to get their input about things they would need to best use their individual skills.

The group stood up. Lewis and Holly helped Taylor into his wheelchair. As they filed out the door, Evans asked

Holly to stay behind for a minute. When everyone else was gone, the commander closed the door.

"Sit down," Evans said.

Holly took his seat at the table. Evans was dying inside as he sat across from the flier. Holly seemed eager, happy, qualities that the young man might never again experience as pure as now.

"Forgive me for being forward, sir, but I want to thank you again for everything," Holly said. "All of this."

Evans looked at him for a long moment. "Whatever you've got you earned. You know that."

"Thank you, sir," Holly said. "But I always was lucky enough to have people lookin' out for me, too."

Evans continued to look at Holly, into his eyes. "When I was in the cabin of the Huntsmen leader, Bernard Schiller, I picked up a computer diskette. It was a journal, one that he'd kept since 1961. Did you ever hear that name—Schiller?"

"No, sir."

"Former CIA. He helped plan the Bay of Pigs invasion in 1961. But that wasn't all he helped to plan. Two years later, he and the Huntsmen executed the President of the United States for failing to lead the country in a direction that satisfied their needs."

"The Huntsmen killed President Kennedy?"

"That's right. He was one of at least a dozen assassinations they ordered in this century."

The unfallen state of Captain Peter Holly seemed to change a little. The Texas boy who'd wanted to fly and did and had a bit of the angel about him.

"I've told you this for a reason," Evans said.

"Because we're not finished, sir? We're goin' after more of 'em?"

"No, Captain. The President was concerned about something in Schiller's journal."

"What was that, sir?"

"Your father's name was Timothy Holly—"

"Yes, sir."

"And he took his life."

"Yes, sir."

Evans said softly, compassionately, "His name was in Schiller's journal."

"Sir?"

"He was a member of the Huntsmen."

"My father? My father was one of those killers?"

Holly glanced away, then down, then away again. He looked like he wanted to cry. "That's why he did it. That's why my dad killed himself. He was ashamed. And the President—he wanted to know if you were absolutely sure I could be trusted. Is that right, sir?"

"More or less. Though he knows what you did to save him and the rest of the team."

"Oh, Jesus. Jesus. Well I guess I can't blame him," Holly said. "They blew up the White House, tried to kill him."

"I told him that you had my complete confidence, and that was the end of it," Evans said. "But I wanted to tell you this because a man has a right to know what goes on behind closed doors if the conversation is about him. Also, Captain, I never wanted you to hear this from anyone else."

"I understand completely and I appreciate it, sir. I—I truly do."

"Then that'll be all for now," Evans said. "We'll meet again later, as scheduled."

"Yes, sir," Holly replied. He rose slowly and saluted. "I want to thank you, sir."

Evans stood and returned the salute. "No. You've earned my trust, and you've earned your place on the team—"

"Not for that, sir," he said. "What I wanted to thank you for is—" he hesitated, still at attention. "Actually, I don't know. I don't know what I want to thank you for. But I feel like you just did the right thing. Somehow, I feel that. Now I need to go think about this."

"I understand," Evans replied. "Go have your think in my room, Captain. It'll give you some privacy."

Holding back tears, Holly thanked him and left.

Fifty-three

Thursday, 12:32 P.M.
Langley Air Force Base, Virginia

"May I come in?"

Evans stood in the open door of Victoria's quarters. She was sitting on the cot, looking at her datebook. Captain McIver had gone to see General Jackson—swaggering out the front door of the shelters with a big smile—leaving the scientist alone.

"Of course," she said. She'd wanted to say *"Any time"* but chickened out.

He stepped down. He moved with assurance, the kind that came from life experience and real confidence. Not the bullshit pomposity that Stephen had. He also seemed unusually peppy, though she wasn't surprised. He'd just led the team that saved the United States of America from a coup d'état.

"I wanted to make sure you were really okay with all this," Evans said. "Leaving New York, your job, coming to work for the federal government."

"In exchange for fresh mountain air and work I love? I

think I can live with that," she said. "This is something I've wanted for a long time. Besides, I'll bet the health coverage is pretty good."

"Considering the work we do, it'd better be more than pretty good."

She smiled. So did Evans.

Damn, she thought.

"I also wanted to tell you that when you have to go back to New York we'll arrange that," Evans said.

"Back?"

"For the divorce," he said. "It came up in court papers during your last security check. And I'm sure there are things you have to take care of at work."

"Like quitting," she said. She closed the book. "Yes, I was thinking about that. At some point, I'll have to go back for both of those. Or you know what? Maybe you can send the Stealth Warriors back to take Stephen out. Save me a couple of trips. That'd work for me."

He smiled.

"I'm not sure the President would okay that mission, but you can certainly take whatever time you need. It's going to take at least four weeks for the government to officially reclaim the Schiller property, and I don't expect we'll be moving over there for another two or three weeks after that. So when you want to go back—"

"I'll let you know," she said.

"Also Dr. Fraser will probably want to meet with you at some point, if you're interested in a trip to the Pentagon."

"You let *me* know," she said.

"Will do," he said. He hesitated, grinned, slapped the doorjamb, and turned to go.

"St. War!" she said.

Evans stopped. He looked back.

"It's going to be a busy few weeks, but don't be invisible," she said, smiling.

He smiled back before turning away.